Praise for *Once Upon a*

With her signature action-packed, page-turning tension, as well as sweet second-chance romance, Michelle Griep has written a tale that pays homage to Charles Dickens and will delight fans of Elizabeth Gaskell's *North and South*. A Christmas gift readers will love!
> —Julie Klassen, bestselling author of the series Tales from Ivy Hill

A truly heartwarming Christmas story that reminds me of the great Dickens classics. A story of second chances that will have you holding your breath, laughing, worrying, and crying right along with the characters. This is one of those books you curl up with by a warm fire and don't stop reading until you turn the last page. Highly recommended.
> —MaryLu Tyndall, author of the award-winning series
> Legacy of the King's Pirates

Fans of Victorian Era romance will swoon over *12 Days at Bleakly Manor: Book 1 in Once Upon a Dickens Christmas* by Michelle Griep. Her characters are mesmerizing, her writing flawless—a winning combination!
> —Elizabeth Ludwig, author of *A Tempting Taste of Mystery*

A Tale of Two Hearts invites your heart to go on a wild roller-coaster ride. Trapped in a lie, can they find their way out before irreparable damage is done? Add to the plot sweet Uncle Barlow, adorable Miss Whymsy, and a pair of deplorable cousins, and you've got a story your heart won't forget.
> —Ane Mulligan, award-winning author of the Chapel Springs series

A Dickensian delight! Victorian London and the characters within come alive within these pages. I thoroughly enjoyed riding the characters coattails through bustling streets between the Golden Egg Inn, Purcell's Tea Room, and more as they wove a tangled web of their own design—and then desperately tried to unravel it before falling through the strands. A refreshing tale perfectly paired with a cup of Christmas tea.
> —Jocelyn Green, award-winning author of *A Refuge Assured*

Delightful Christmas fare perfect for fans of English historicals, brimful with Dickensian details and the beautiful Christian truth of second chances.
> —Carolyn Miller, author of Regency Brides: Legacy of Grace and Regency
> Brides: A Promise of Hope series

When a seemingly harmless deception escalates to alarming proportions, the characters in *A Tale of Two Hearts* are forced to question their values and decide if sacrificing their integrity justifies the altruistic outcome. This delightful story combines a host of interesting characters, fresh writing, and a heartwarming ending that will leave the reader smiling.

—Susan Anne Mason, award-winning author of
Irish Meadows and *A Most Noble Heir*

In *A Tale of Two Hearts*, Michelle Griep tells a skillfully woven tale both elegant and heartwarming. Charles Dickens would be delighted with the way she tucked into this story's pockets truths and observations he penned long ago. Highly recommended reading, no matter the season.

—Cynthia Ruchti, author of *An Endless Christmas*, *Restoring Christmas*, and more than twenty other novels and nonfiction

I have found another favorite author and it's Michelle Griep. With an incredible ability to spin a beautiful tale, Griep sucked me into the story from the very first paragraph. From the historical detail to the English setting to the unforgettable and enjoyable characters, I didn't want to put this book down. William and Mina will stick with me for a long time. This will be a story to read again and again. And now I'm off to find every Michelle Griep book I can get my hands on.

—Kimberley Woodhouse, bestselling author

Just when you think you're about to embark on a cheeky, fun Christmas lark, you realize what a multifaceted, complex story Griep has crafted. With characterizations Dickens would envy, and bright, fresh writing that pulls you in, *A Tale of Two Hearts* will have you cheering on Mina and William and appreciating the skill with which they have been wrought.

—Erica Vetsch, author of *A Perfect Christmas* in *The Victorian Christmas Brides Collection*

A heartwarming tale of second chances coming from the least expected places. I loved the many nods to Dickens and the inventive twists on a few other classics. In *A Tale of Two Hearts*, romance isn't only for the young, and fresh starts aren't only for the faultless. An uplifting and charming holiday story!

—Jennifer Delamere, author of *The Captain's Daughter*

3 Charming Christmas Tales Set in Victorian England

UPON A DICKENS

MICHELLE
GRIEP

SHILOH RUN PRESS

An Imprint of Barbour Publishing, Inc.

12 Days at Bleakly Manor © 2017 by Michelle Griep
A Tale of Two Hearts © 2018 by Michelle Griep
The Old Lace Shop © 2019 by Michelle Griep

Print ISBN 978-1-68322-260-6

eBook Editions:
Adobe Digital Edition (.epub) 978-1-64352-373-6
Kindle and MobiPocket Edition (.prc) 978-1-64352-374-3

Cover Image: Ildiko Neer / Trevillion Images

Published by Shiloh Run Press, an imprint of Barbour Publishing, Inc., 1810 Barbour Drive, Uhrichsville, Ohio 44683, www.shilohrunpress.com

Our mission is to inspire the world with the life-changing message of the Bible.

ecpa Member of the
Evangelical Christian
Publishers Association

Printed in Canada.

Dear Reader,

What do you think of when you hear the name Charles Dickens? Most people are instantly whisked back to merry ol' England. A light snow is falling on the narrow lanes of old London town. Gas lamps glow. Children dart about with red cheeks and redder noses. And standing in the doorway, watching all the hubbub with a scowl and a humbug, stands Scrooge, lamenting the coming of Christmas.

All that with the mention of one name. How can it be?

Charles Dickens was a master storyteller. He had a way of drawing in the reader, presenting life unvarnished, yet always leaving an ember of hope burning bright at the end of a tale. And that, my friends, is what Christmas is all about. Hope. The hope of reconciliation between Creator and created, the complete and eternal forgiveness of our foulest thoughts, our ugliest words, our blackest sins. And all that with the mention of one name, as well.

Jesus.

It has been my joy to pen these tales in the spirit of the great storyteller Charles Dickens, and by the spirit of the kindest soul this world will ever know. . .Jesus.

Blessings to you, dear reader.

~ Michelle

CONTENTS

On a stormy night 2,000 years ago,
a babe was born,
and in a land far from that rugged stable
a coin was forged ~
both the bearers of a second chance.

The God-man returned to heaven,
but the coin yet roams the earth,
passing from hand to hand,
hope to hope. . .

12 Days at
Bleakly Manor

The First Day

DECEMBER 24, 1850

CHAPTER ONE

London, 1850

Christmas or not, there was nothing merry about the twisted alleys of Holy-well. Clara Chapman forced one foot in front of the other, sidestepping pools of. . .well, a lady ought not think on such things, not on the morn of Christmas Eve—or any other morn, for that matter.

Damp air seeped through her woolen cape, and she tugged her collar tighter. Fog wrapped around her shoulders, cold as an embrace from the grim reaper. Though morning had broken several hours ago, daylight tarried, seeming reluctant to make an appearance in this part of London—and likely wishing to avoid it altogether. Ancient buildings with rheumy windows leaned toward one another for support, blocking a good portion of the sky.

She quickened her pace. If she didn't deliver Effie's gift soon, the poor woman would be off to her twelve-hour shift at the hatbox factory.

Rounding a corner, Clara rapped on the very next door, then fought the urge to wipe her glove. The filthy boards, hung together more by memory than nails, rattled like bones. Her lips pursed into a wry twist. A clean snow might hide the sin of soot and grime in this neighborhood, but no. Even should a fresh coating of white bless all, the stain of so much humanity would not be erased. Not here. For the thousandth time, she breathed out the only prayer she had left.

Why, God? Why?

The door swung open. Effie Gedge's smile beamed so bright and familiar, Clara's throat tightened. How she missed this woman, her friend, her confi-dant—her former maid.

"Miss Chapman? What a surprise!" Effie glanced over her shoulder, her smile faltering as she looked back at Clara. "I'd ask you in but. . ."

Clara shoved away the awkward moment by handing over a basket. "I've brought you something for your Christmas dinner tomorrow. It isn't much, but…" It was Clara's turn to falter. "Anyway, I cannot stay, for Aunt's developed a cough."

Effie's smile returned, more brilliant than ever. "That's kind of you, miss. Thank you. Truly."

The woman's gratitude, so pure and genuine, rubbed Clara's conscience raw. Would that she might learn to be as thankful for small things. And small it was. Her gaze slipped to the cloth-covered loaf of bread, an orange, and used tea leaves wrapped in a scrap of paper. Pressing her lips together, she faced Effie. "I wish it were more. I wish *I* could do more. If only we could go back to our old lives."

"Begging your pardon, miss." Effie rested her hand on Clara's arm, her fingers calloused from work no lady's maid should ever have to perform. "But you are not to blame. I shall always hold to that. There is no ill will between us."

Clara hid a grimace. Of course she knew in her head she wasn't to blame, but her heart? That fickle organ had since reverted to her old way of thinking, pulsing out *"you are unloved, you are unwanted"* with every subsequent beat.

"Miss?"

Clara forced a smile of her own and patted the woman's hand. "You are the kind one, Effie. You've lost everything because of my family, and yet you smile."

"The Lord gives, and the Lord takes away. I suppose you know that as well as I, hmm?" Her fingers squeezed before she released her hold. "I wish you merry, Miss Chapman, this Christmas and always."

"Thank you, Effie. And a very merry Christmas be yours, as well." She spun, eyes burning, and pushed her way back down the narrow alley before Effie saw her tears. This wasn't fair. None of it.

Her hired hansom waited where she'd left it. The cab was an expense she'd rather not think on, but altogether necessary, for she lived on the other side of town. She borrowed the driver's strong grip to ascend onto the step, then when inside, settled her skirts on the seat while he shut the door.

Only once did she glance out the window as the vehicle jostled along London's rutted roads—and immediately repented for having done so. Two lovers walked hand in hand, the man bending close and whispering into the woman's ear. A blush then, followed by a smile.

Clara yanked shut the window curtain, the loneliness in her heart rabid and biting.

That could have been her. That *should* have been her.

Why, God? Why?

She leaned her head back against the carriage. Was love to be forever denied her? First her father's rejection, then her fiancé's. She swallowed back a sob, wearier than twenty-five years ought to feel.

Eventually the cab jerked to a halt, and she descended to the street. She dug into her reticule and pulled out one of her last coins to pay the driver. At this rate, she wouldn't have to hire a cab to visit Effie next Christmas. She might very well be her neighbor.

"Merry Christmas, miss." The driver tipped his hat.

"To you, as well," she answered, then scurried toward Aunt's town house. A lacquered carriage, with a fine pair of matched horses at the front, stood near the curb. Curious. Perhaps the owner had taken a wrong turn, for Highgate, while shabbily respectable, was no Grosvenor Square.

Clara dashed up the few stairs and entered her home of the last nine months, taken in by the charitable heart of her Aunt Deborha Mitchell. The dear woman was increasingly infirm and housebound, but in her younger days she'd hobnobbed with people from many spheres.

Noontide chimes rang from the sitting-room clock, accompanied by a bark of a cough. Clara untied her hat and slipped from her cloak, hanging both on a hall tree, all the while wondering how best to urge Aunt back to her bed. The woman was as stubborn as. . . She bit her lower lip. Truth be told, tenacity ran just as strongly in her own veins.

Smoothing her skirts, she pulled her lips into a passable smile and crossed the sitting room's threshold. "I am home, Aunt, and I really must insist you retire—oh! Forgive me."

She stopped at the edge of the rug. A man stood near the mantel, dressed in deep blue livery. Her gaze flickered to her aunt. "I am sorry. I did not know you had company."

"Come in, child." Aunt waved her forward, the fabric of her sleeve dangling too loosely from the woman's arm. "This involves you."

The man advanced, offering a creamy envelope with gilt writing embellishing the front. "I am to deliver this to Miss Clara Chapman. That is you, is it not?"

She frowned. "It is."

He handed her the missive with a bow, then straightened. "I shall await you at the door, miss."

Her jaw dropped as he bypassed her, smelling of lavender of all things. She turned to Aunt. "I don't understand."

"I should think not." Aunt nodded toward the envelope. "Open it."

Clara's name alone graced the front. The penmanship was fine. Perfect, actually. And completely foreign. Turning it over, she broke the seal and withdrew an embossed sheet of paper, reading aloud the words for Aunt to hear.

The Twelve Days of Christmas
As never's been reveled
Your presence, Miss Chapman,
Is respectfully herald.
Bleakly Manor's the place
And after twelve nights
Five hundred pounds
Will be yours by rights.

She lowered the invitation and studied her aunt. Grey hair pulled back tightly into a chignon eased some of the wrinkles at the sides of her eyes, yet a peculiar light shone in the woman's faded gaze. Aunt Deborha always hid wisdom, but this time, Clara suspected she secreted something more.

"Who sent this?" Clara closed the distance between them and knelt in front of the old woman. "And why?"

Aunt shrugged, her thin shoulders coaxing a rumble in her chest. A good throat clearing staved off a coughing spell—for now. "One does not question an opportunity, my dear. One simply mounts it and rides."

"You can't be serious." She dissected the tiny lift of Aunt's brows and the set of her mouth, both unwavering. Incredible. Clara sucked in a breath. "You think I should go? To Bleakly Manor, wherever that is?"

"I think"—Aunt angled her chin—"you simply must."

CHAPTER TWO

Running an absent finger over the burnt scabs on his forearm, Benjamin Lane sagged against the cell's stone wall, welcoming the sharp sting of pain. It wouldn't last long. The crust would fall away, leaving a series of black numbers etched into his skin. A permanent mark, forever labeling him a convict to be feared, and driving a final stake through the heart of his efforts to be something in this world. Turning aside, he spit out the sour taste in his mouth, then his lips curled into a snarl. He was something, all right.

An outcast.

Anger rose in him like a mad dog, biting and completely impotent, for he had no idea who'd put him in this rat hole. The only thing he did know, he wished he didn't. Not now. Not ever. Growling roared in his ears. Was that him? *Oh, God.* Not again.

Betrayal from an enemy he could understand, but from the woman he loved? What man could fathom that? For nine months he'd turned that question over and over, examining every angle, each nuance, and still he could not reckon Clara's duplicity.

Why, God? Why?

A finger at a time, Ben opened his hand and stared fiercely at a small chunk of stone, barely discernable in the darkness. Worn smooth now by nearly a year of caressing. He flipped it over, just like his unanswered questions, the sleekness of the rock against his palm reminding him he was human, not beast. Outside his cell, a shriek crawled beneath the crack in his door, reaching for him, taunting him to believe otherwise. To join the howl and become one with the pack of hopeless men.

He flipped the rock again. The movement tethered him to sanity.

Cocking his head, he listened with his whole body. Something more than screams crept in. The scrape of boot leather. Growing louder. Metal on metal, key battling key. The low murmur of a coarse jest shared between two guards.

Sweat popped out on Ben's forehead. He pressed his back into the wall, an impossible wish to disappear digging into his gut. The footsteps stopped. Only a slab of scarred wood separated him from his tormentors. Some Christmas this would be.

The key jiggled in the lock, and his stomach twisted. It was safer to remain here. In the dark. At least in this womb of crumbling brick and blackness he still heard the cries of other prisoners, as regular as a mother's heartbeat. He yet felt the dampness of rot on his skin, tasted the rancid gruel served once a day. Still breathed. Still lived.

He flipped the rock again.

The door swung open. A lantern's glow silhouetted two ghouls.

One stepped forward, a club in his grasp. "Out with ye, Lane. Warden's got a little Christmas gift with yer name on it."

Ben wrapped his fingers tight around the stone. Should he make a run for it? Spring an attack and wrestle for the club? Go limp? He'd sigh, if he had any breath to spare, but even that seemed a precious commodity nowadays.

No, better to face this head-on and not relinquish the last morsel of his dignity. He shuffled forward, the chains on his feet rasping. Shackles bit a fresh wound into his ankles with each step.

Leaving behind the only haven he'd known the past nine months, he stumbled into the corridor, guards at his back, prodding, poking. He lurched along, passing other doors, other convicts, inhaling the stench and guilt of Millbank Prison. How many wretches as innocent as he perished behind those doors?

One foot. Then the other. Drag, step. Drag, step. Until the stairway. The weight of his chains pulled him back as he ascended. By the time he reached the top, blood trickled hot over his feet.

"Move it!"

The guard's club hit between his shoulder blades, knocking him forward and jarring loose his precious stone. It clacked onto the floor, as loud to him as the hammer pounding in Christ's nails, then bounced down the stairs, taking his soul along with it.

No!

He wheeled about, diving for his only remainder of hope.

But a boot caught him in the gut. A club cracked against his skull. Half-lugged, half-dead, he landed in the warden's office like an alley cat thrown against a curb. The warden's sigh barely registered.

"Don't know why I expected anything different. Thank you, gentlemen. You may wait outside. Up you go, Lane." Warden Hacksby extended a hand.

Ignoring the offer, Ben sucked in a breath and forced his body up, staggering until the room stopped spinning.

"If nothing else, you are consistent." Hacksby chuckled and seated himself behind a desk as angular as the man himself. "Do you know what day it is?"

Ben worked out the soreness in his jaw before words could escape. "Sorry. I'll have to check my calendar and get back to you. Or. . .wait a minute. Ahh, yes. Am I to sail for Australia today?" He narrowed his eyes. "But we both know I'll never reach the shore."

"Ever the cynic, eh? Really, Lane. After all the hospitality I've shown you." Hacksby tut-tutted, the curl of his lip exposing yellowed teeth. "But no. There's been a change of plans. You've received another offer, should you choose to take it."

Bitterness slipped from Ben's throat in a rusty laugh. "What, the gallows? A firing squad? Or has Queen Victoria invited me for Christmas tea?"

"Aha! So you do know what day it is. Always the sly one, are you not?" Hacksby rose from his seat and leaned across the desk, a creamy envelope with Ben's name in golden script on the front. "For you. Your freedom, possibly—providing you play by the rules. If not, you're to be shot on sight for any escape attempt."

Ben eyed the paper. What trick was this? He was supposed to be transported to a labour camp halfway across the world, not handed an engraved invitation. He stiffened. This was a trap. He knew it to the deepest marrow in his bones.

Nevertheless, he reached out, and for the smallest of moments, the warden held one edge, he the other. Liberty hanging in the balance.

Maybe.

CHAPTER THREE

Despite her cold fingers, Clara rubbed away the frost on the coach's window, then peered out into the December night. She ought be sore by now, riding such a distance over country roads, but truly, this carriage was magnificent—and so was the mansion that popped into view as they rounded a bend. She leaned closer, then reared back as her breath fogged the glass. With a furious swipe of her glove, she stared out the cleared circle, slack jawed.

This was Bleakly Manor?

A grand structure, torches ablaze, lit the night like the star of Bethlehem. The building stood proud at three stories tall, with candles winking behind row upon row of mullioned windows. Clearly whoever owned Bleakly didn't care a fig about window taxes. Clara held her breath and edged closer, careful not to muddle her view with rime. Garland swagged from the roofline the entire length of the building. How on earth had they managed that? Red bows with dangling ribbons hung from each wall sconce, and as the carriage drew nearer, a gust of wind lent them life, and they waved a greeting.

She sat back against the cushion, stunned. There was nothing bleak about this manor. Who had invited her—a lowly lady's companion—to such an estate? Who would even want to keep company with her? And more importantly, why?

The coach stopped, and the door opened. She gave up trying to solve such a puzzle as the footman helped her to the drive.

"I'll see to your bags, miss." A lad, no more than fourteen yet dressed in as fine a livery as the older man, tipped his head in deference.

The respectful gesture stung. She hadn't been so favored since that awful day, that nightmare day nine months previous, when she'd stood in front of an altar in a gown of white.

"Ready, miss?"

The footman's voice pulled her from the horrid memory. She lifted her skirts to follow him without tripping. "Yes."

She was ready, truly, to meet whoever had invited her. Perhaps if she explained the frail state of her aunt, she wouldn't be required to stay the full

Twelve Days of Christmas.

After ascending granite stairs, she and the footman passed through an arched doorway and entered a foyer the size of Aunt's dining and sitting rooms combined. A crystal chandelier dripped golden light over everything, from a cushioned bench against one wall to a medieval trestle table gracing the other. Fresh flowers filled a cut-glass vase atop the table. Marble tile gleamed beneath her feet, the echo of her steps reaching up to a mounted lion head on the wall in front of her, just above a closed set of doors. She couldn't help but stare up into the cold, lifeless eyes, wondering how many people before her had done the same.

"I should be happy to take your cloak and bonnet, miss." The footman held out his arm.

Her fingers shook as she unbuttoned her coat and untied her hat, though she was hard-pressed to decide if the jittery feeling was from cold air or nerves. Handing over her garments, she waited for further instruction from the tall fellow.

But without a word, he pivoted and disappeared down a darkened hallway to her left.

She stood, unsure, and clenched her hands for fortification, sickeningly aware of a gaze burning holes through her soul. Yet the only other pair of eyes in the foyer besides hers was the lion's.

She sucked in a breath. Nerves. That's what. Had to be.

To her right, another set of doors hid secrets, merry ones by the sound of it. Yellow light and conversation leached out through a crack between threshold and mahogany. Licking her lips, she squared her shoulders, resolved to meet the master of the house, then pushed open the door.

Across the Turkish carpet, perched upon a chair and balancing a small box on her lap, a white-haired lady held up a quizzing glass to one eye and peered at Clara. "Oh, lovely! Such a beautiful creature. Don't you think, Mr. Minnow?"

"Why yes!" A lean man, more bones than flesh, jumped up from a settee and dashed toward Clara so quickly she retreated a step.

He bowed, deep enough that his joints cracked, and held the pose longer than necessary. The scent of ginger wafted about him. When he straightened, he smiled at her with lips that were far too elastic. "Mr. Minnow at your service, mum. William Minnow, esquire. Well, not quite yet, but soon, I am certain. And you are?"

Clara blinked. Was this the master of Bleakly Manor? A lanky eel in a suit?

Instant remorse squeezed her chest. Who was she, a woman fallen from the graces of society, to judge the appearance of a man of substance? She dipped her head. "I am Clara Chapman."

"Clara Chapman! Oh, but I like the sound of that." The elder on the chair waved a handkerchief at her. "Step nearer, dearest, and let's look at you up close, shall we?"

Familiar with the idiosyncrasies of the elderly, she complied, but froze several paces in front of the woman. A pink nose with whiskers poked out of the box on the lady's lap, where a hole had been cut jaggedly into the side. Red eyes emerged, followed by a furry body and a naked tail, flesh-coloured and long. A second mouse emerged after it. The two scampered to the edge of the old lady's knee and rose up on hind legs, testing the air with quivering noses.

Clara stiffened. Hopefully the creatures would turn right around and disappear back into the box.

The lady merely scrutinized her as if nothing more than a teacup and saucer rested on her lap. "Such a marvelous creature, Miss Chapman."

Was she speaking of her or the mice? "Th–thank you," she stuttered. "I am sorry, but I didn't catch your name, ma'am?"

"No, you did not." The lady beamed at her. "I am Miss Scurry, and now we shall all be the jolliest of companions, shall we not?"

"We shall, and more." Mr. Minnow's heels brushed against the carpet, then he reached for her hand and placed it on his arm. "Come, sit and warm yourself, my pet."

Pet? She barely had time to turn the word over before he escorted her to a settee near the hearth and pushed her into it.

"I'm wondering, Miss Chapman"—Mr. Minnow smiled down at her—"not that Miss Scurry and I aren't exceedingly grateful, for we are, but why exactly have you invited us here to share the Twelve Days with you?"

"Me?" She shook her head, yet the movement did nothing to make sense of his question. "But you are mistaken, for I received an invitation myself."

"Bosh! This is a pickled herring." Flipping out the tails of his suit coat, he joined her on the settee, much too close for propriety. "I thought you, being a lady of such grace and beauty, surely belonged to this house."

"I'm afraid not." She edged away from him.

"Sh-sh-sh." Miss Scurry, evidently just discovering the two escapees had scampered to the top of the box, shooed both mice into the hole on the side and plugged it up with her handkerchief. "Rest, my dears." Then she gazed over at Mr. Minnow. "Don't fret so, my fine fellow. The day of reckoning will come soon enough, and all will be made clear."

Mr. Minnow clapped his hands and rubbed them together. "I suppose there's nothing to be done for it but to wait for the host to appear." His head swiveled, and he narrowed his eyes at Clara. "You're sure that's not you?"

"I am, Mr. Minnow. Very sure."

She bit her lip. Clearly neither of these two eccentrics was the host. So, who was?

CHAPTER FOUR

The prison cart juddered over a hump in the road, rattling Ben's bones. He'd curled into a ball in one corner, tucking his knees to his chest and wrapping his arms about them. Even so, after hours on end and with the chill of night bearing down, there was no stopping the chattering of his teeth. He snorted. Between teeth and bones he was quite the percussionist.

A low "whoa now" slowed the wheels, and finally the cart stopped. Ben jerked upright, crouched and ready, the sudden hammering of his heart forgetting the cold. The long ride here had given him plenty of time to consider his situation, and he'd come to one conclusion—these were his last hours on earth.

So be it. He'd go out fighting against such a wicked injustice and find some measure of worth in the fray.

The scrape of a key shoved into the metal lock, then a click, a creak, and the door swung open. "Yer ride ends here, Lane. Out ye go."

The dark shape of the guard disappeared and light poured in. Ben's eyes watered. Light? Was it day, then? How far had he travelled?

He edged forward, cautious, scanning, as more and more of the world expanded into his view. Black darkened the sky, so it was still night, but torches ablaze changed the immediate area to morning.

"Move along! I've still got a drive back to London." The guard spat out a foul curse. "Ye'd think I'd signed up to be a bleedin' jarvey. They don't pay me enough, I tell ye. Not near enough."

Ben dropped out of the door and immediately wheeled about, fists up, stance wide, prepared for battle.

The guard merely shoved the door shut and relocked it, ignoring him—and there was no one else around.

Truly? No one? Ben stared hard into the darkness beyond the light. The expansive grounds were rimmed with trees along the perimeter, black against black. Nothing moved except the wind through barren branches. Apparently he'd been taken some distance into the countryside. He turned to face the manor. Impressive, really. Tall. Well masoned. Crenellated at the top. Perhaps used as a stronghold centuries ago.

"Hyah!"

He spun. The cart lumbered down the curved drive, the guard urging the horses onward—without him. He was left standing alone. Unfettered. A brilliant mansion at his back and acres of freedom in front. He could run, here, now. Tear off and flee like the wind. Should he? He scrubbed a hand through his hair, recalling Hacksby's threat.

"You're to be shot on sight for any escape attempt."

The prison cart disappeared into the night. But slowly, emerging out of that same darkness, another shape loomed larger. A carriage, and a fine one at that. Should he wait and meet head-on whomever it carried?

Cold ached in his bare feet and up his legs, yet the pain of the unknown throbbing in his temples hurt worse. He'd have a better chance of putting up a fight if he could actually move his frozen body. Pivoting, he climbed the stairs to the main entrance and rapped the brass knocker.

The door opened immediately, as if the butler had stood behind it waiting for him.

"Welcome, Mr. Lane." The man's upper lip curled to nearly touch his nose.

Ben smirked. He ought be ashamed of his stench, but his time at Millbank had dulled that emotion, especially when it came to issues of hygiene. Even so, he took out his manners and dusted them off. "Thank you. I see you were expecting me."

"Yes, sir. We have a room prepared for you after such a journey. If you would follow me." Turning on his heel, the butler strode the length of the grand foyer toward a door with a stuffed lion head mounted above it.

Ben studied the man as he went. He could pose a threat, for his shoulders were broad as a ceiling beam and those stout legs might pack a wallop of a kick. But the silver streaks in his hair labeled the fellow past his prime. Even so, better to keep his distance.

He followed, leaving plenty of space between them, then paused and stared up at the lion head. Light from the chandelier reflected back brightly from those eyes, transparent, lifelike and—

"Mr. Lane?"

He jumped at the butler's voice. What was wrong with him? There were bigger mysteries afoot than a dead lion. "Of course. Sorry."

He caught up to the man, who'd opened double doors, revealing an even bigger lobby. A wide, carpeted staircase, lit by intermittent wall sconces, led up to a first-floor gallery, where more lamps burned. Interesting that pains had been taken to decorate the outside of the manor, yet not one sprig of holly or mistletoe hung inside.

Behind them, the front door knocker banged. Two stairs ahead of him, the butler stopped and pulled out a gold chain from his waistcoat, then flipped open the lid of a watch tethered to the end of it. His eyebrows pulled into a solid line, and a low rumble in his throat gruffed out. "Pardon me, Mr. Lane. If you'd wait here, please."

Here? On the stairs? A duck at rest to be shot from behind? He waited for the butler to pass, then tracked him on silent feet and slipped into the shadow cast by a massive floor clock.

A man in a sealskin riding cloak entered, frost on his breath and hat pulled low. He stomped his boots on the tiles, irreverent of the peace.

The butler dipped his head. "Mr. Pocket, I presume?"

"I am." The new arrival pulled off his hat and ran a hand through his shorn hair, the top of his head quite the contradiction to his bushy muttonchops. A rumpled dress coat peeked through the gap of his unbuttoned coat, and his trousers looked as if they'd never seen a hot iron. Clearly the man was not married, nor was he the master of the manor.

"You were not due to arrive for another half hour, sir." A scowl tugged down the corners of the butler's mouth.

Mr. Pocket twisted his lips, his great muttonchops going along for the ride. "Yet the invitation did not specify an arrival time, unless. . .ahh! I see. The deliveries were spaced out to ensure a regulated arrival schedule. Am I correct?"

"Very clever, Inspector."

"Part of the job."

So the fellow was a lawman. Ben flattened his back against the wall, sinking deeper into the shadow of the clock. Questions ticked in his mind with each swing of the pendulum. Was Pocket sent to make sure he didn't run or to finish him off? Or possibly set him up for something more sinister than embezzlement and fraud? But why the big charade? Why not just kill him in gaol or ship him off as planned?

"If you wouldn't mind stepping in here until dinner, sir." The butler opened a door in a side wall, but his back hindered Ben's view into the room. "You may meet some of the other guests while you wait."

"All right. Don't mind if I do." Mr. Pocket swept past the man and vanished.

Ben dashed back to the stairs, folded his arms, and leaned against the railing as if he'd never moved.

The butler hesitated on the bottom stair only long enough to say, "My apologies for the delay, Mr. Lane. Please, let us continue."

Ben trailed the man as he travelled up two flights, then noted every door they passed and any corridors intersecting the one they travelled. There were two, one lit, one dark. They stopped at the farthest chamber of what he guessed to be the east wing.

The butler opened the door but blocked him from entering. "You'll find a bath drawn in front of the hearth, grooming toiletries on a stand opposite, and a set of dinner clothes laid out on the bed. I shall send a footman up to retrieve you in"—he reclaimed his watch once more and held it up for inspection before tucking it away—"forty-five minutes. Is that sufficient?"

"Very generous," he replied.

"Very good." The butler stepped aside, allowing him to pass, then pulled the door shut.

Ben froze. The chamber gleamed in lamplight and gilt-striped wallpaper, so large and glorious it might overwhelm a duke. At center, a four-poster bed commanded attention, mattresses high enough to require a step stool. Against one wall stood an oversized roll-top desk and matching chair, decked out with full stationery needs. Several padded chairs and three different settees formed two distinct sitting areas. A screen offered privacy for necessary functions, and thick brocaded drapery covered what must be an enormous bank of windows.

He changed his mind. This would overwhelm a king.

Shaking off his stupor, he stalked to the copper basin in front of the fire. Steam rose like a mist on autumn water, smelling of sage and mint. Nine months. Nine never-ending months of filth and sweat and blood.

He stripped off his prison garb, heedless of ripping the threadbare fabric, and kicked the soiled lump from him, uncaring that it lodged beneath the bed. Good riddance.

Water splashed over the rim as he sank into the water, warmth washing over him like a lover's embrace. A sob rose in his throat. This time last year, he'd bathed before dinner just like this. Dressed in fine clothes similar to those laid on the counterpane. Dined by candlelight with the woman he loved fiercely. Kissed Clara's sweet lips until neither of them could breathe.

What a fool.

He snatched the bar of soap off the tray hooked to the tub's side, then scrubbed harder than necessary. Of course this wasn't like last Christmas Eve. It could never be.

For he wouldn't see Clara ever again.

CHAPTER FIVE

Enough was quite enough. Clara rose from the chair and crossed to Miss Scurry's side. Her step faltered only once as she drew near, her distaste of rodents almost getting the better of her, but surely the scrap of handkerchief would keep the mice snug inside the woman's box. Hopefully.

Tears glistened in Miss Scurry's eyes, her quizzing glass dangling forgotten on its ribbon. Clara laid a hand on her shoulder, squeezing a light encouragement. Then she faced Mr. Pocket, who'd stationed himself at the hearth, questioning them all as if they stood before the great white throne.

"Mr. Pocket, I fear your questions are a bit much for Miss Scurry."

"Oh?" The man sniffed, his large nostrils flaring. "Well, perhaps just one more then. Miss Scurry, you say that if you remain the duration of the Twelve Day holiday, your invitation guaranteed the lost would be found, which seems a small thing, depending of course on that which was lost. So tell me, please, what was lost and why is it of such importance? Why weren't you promised money, as in Miss Chapman's case, for then you could replace what was lost? Or if the missing item is not of monetary value, then why not the hope of companionship, a friend, so to speak, which is Mr. Minnow's lure?" Mr. Pocket swept out his hand to where Mr. Minnow primped his cravat in front of a mirror on the other side of the sitting room.

"I…I…," Miss Scurry stuttered, her words tied on the thread of a whimper. "All will be clear on the day of reckoning."

Clara patted the lady's shoulder. Were all inspectors so bullish? "Mr. Pocket, I believe it is time for you to tell us exactly what *your* invitation stated. It's only fair, and I should think that to a man who upholds justice, fairness is one of your utmost concerns. Is it not?"

A grin stretched the man's lips, from one edge of his long sideburns to the other. "Delightful, Miss Chapman. Were you a man, you'd make a fine inspector." Leaving his post, he strode to a chair adjacent them and sat. "I have nothing to hide, and so I shall state my case plainly. My invitation pledged me a new position. A higher rank. One with more importance."

"And that is?" Clara pressed.

"Magistrate, Miss Chapman. No more slogging through alleys to collar a criminal. No interrogating doxies or cullies or cutthroats. Just a seat on a tall bench with an even taller wig, a blazing hearth fire at my back, and the felons brought to me. Ahh." He closed his eyes, serenity erasing the lines on his brow.

From this angle, lamplight lit some of the shorn hairs on his head with silver. Looking closer, Clara spied the same threads of white sprinkled throughout his sideburns. Her heart softened, imagining the rugged life he'd led roaming the dangerous streets of London. No wonder he wanted to trade professions.

The door opened, interrupting her thoughts and pulling Mr. Pocket to his feet.

"Dinner is served." The butler, resplendent in a black dress coat, matching trousers, and starched white collar, held out his gloved hand in invitation. "If you would all follow me, please."

Mr. Minnow shot to Clara's side, nearly toppling Mr. Pocket as he darted past him. His gingery scent assaulted her nose.

"Allow me to escort you, my pet." He grabbed her hand and placed it on his arm without waiting for an answer.

She gritted her teeth. It was going to be a very long Twelve Days.

They filed out and had just entered the foyer, when the front door burst open and a grey whirlwind blew in, lugging an overstuffed carpetbag and muttering all the way.

"*Les idiots! Le monde est rempli des idiots!*"

The woman stormed up to the butler and shouted in his face. "Why no one help me carry my bag, eh? Help me from the carriage? Open the door? I will speak to the master of *la maison*. Now!"

Clara blinked. Miss Scurry clutched her box to her chest. Mr. Pocket took a step closer, scrutinizing the interaction.

Yet the butler merely lifted his hand and snapped his fingers. "Mademoiselle Pretents, I presume?"

"*Oui!*" The short lady stamped her foot.

A footman appeared and, without a word, managed to remove the woman's woolen cape and sweep the bonnet from her head, then collected her bag. The quick movements were so unexpected, even Mademoiselle Pretents stood gaping. Her dark little eyes, which were far too close together, narrowed, following his retreat with her possessions. For half an instant, Clara wondered if she would chase after him like a hound to the kill.

"Let us continue then, shall we?" The butler passed beneath the lion head, the doors now open to reveal a great lobby and a grand stairway.

Mademoiselle Pretents flew across the room, yanking Clara's hand from Mr. Minnow's arm and placing her fingers on his sleeve. "Oui, let us continue."

Clara hid a smile. The woman could have no idea the service she'd just rendered.

The group filed after the butler, Mr. Minnow and Mademoiselle Pretents in the lead, followed by Miss Scurry, then Clara, and finally Mr. Pocket. They passed from elegance to splendor, with gilt-framed portraits decorating the corridor walls and thick Persian runners beneath their feet. The sitting room was a bleak den in comparison. Suddenly it made sense that the master who'd invited them would greet his guests in the dining room, for surely such a great man would want to be seen housed in the finest glory.

"Très magnifique," Mademoiselle Pretents breathed out as she passed through cherrywood doors into the dining room.

"Indeed," Mr. Minnow murmured beside her.

Miss Scurry entered next, then paused and looked over her shoulder at Clara. "Oh, my beauty, it is glorious in here. Come and see."

Crossing the threshold, Clara sucked in a breath. She'd attended some of the finest dinners in London. Danced in many a grand ballroom. Visited and taken tea in posh surroundings. All were slums in comparison.

She entered on cat's feet, padding carefully, unwilling to break the spell of enchantment created by hundreds of crystals raining from chandeliers, lit by candles that must have taken the staff at least a half hour to ignite. Wine-coloured wallpaper, embellished with golden threads, soaked in the light, then reflected it back ever brighter. Silver utensils and fine china adorned the table. Truly, only Buckingham Palace could compare.

At the head of the table, a man stood with his back to them. Tall. Broad of shoulder. Hair the colour of burnt cream, slicked back yet curiously ragged at the ends. Power clung to his frame as finely as his well-tailored dress coat. He belonged here, surrounded by wealth, intimidating any and all who trod weak-kneed into his domain. No one spoke a word. Not even Mademoiselle Pretents.

Clara trembled. Why would such a powerful man invite her here, especially now that she'd sunk so low in society? She was no one.

Slowly, the man turned, gaze passing from person to person. And when those hazel eyes landed on her, she gasped.

A nightmare stared back at her, a ghost from the past who never—*ever*—should have risen from the grave. The audacity! The gall!

For a moment she froze, gaping, then she shouldered past the other guests and slapped him open-palmed across the face.

CHAPTER SIX

Ben's head jerked aside, the slap echoing in his skull, the crack of flesh upon flesh reverberating in the room. Unbelievable. This whole day had been one big snarl of impossibility. Even more stunning, Clara raised her hand for another strike. The nerve of the little vixen! He grabbed her wrist, unsure who shook more, her or him.

"How dare you invite me here?" Crimson patches of murder stained her cheeks. "And how foolish of me to have walked into your trap. Was my humiliation not enough?"

"*Your* humiliation?" He ground his teeth until his jaw cracked. This was not to be borne. He'd rotted in a gaol cell, been beaten, left cold, hopeless, while this pampered princess suffered what? Dinner parties and suitors in his absence?

She yanked from his grasp, rubbing away his touch. "You are a beast."

A short woman draped in grey and as blustery as a November breeze nudged Clara aside. "I am your servant, monsieur, Mademoiselle Pretents. Shall I dismiss this rabble for you, hmm?" She fluttered her fingertips at Clara.

He frowned. "Surely you're not under the impression that I. . ." He looked past her to the three others inhabiting the dining room. Expectation gleamed in an elderly lady's eyes. Next to her, a thin man's gaze burned with eagerness, and even the muttonchopped inspector, Mr. Pocket, leaned back on his heels in anticipation.

Clara turned and strode to the far side of the table, her body so rigid a carpenter could lay beams across her shoulders.

"Monsieur." The grey lady stepped closer, head bowed. If she were a dog, no doubt her tail would be tucked. "I am so greatly honoured to be in your presence."

He stifled a snort—barely. He'd laugh her off, if the situation weren't so brutally ironic. All his life he'd worked hard to achieve status such as this, and now that he was a condemned felon, apparently he had it. A perfectly beautiful paradox, really.

Yet a complete lie. He shook his head. "I am not the master of Bleakly Manor, if that's what you think."

The grey lady's mouth puckered and she spit out a "Pah!" Grabbing handfuls of her skirts, she whirled away.

The inspector edged toward him. "Then who are you, sir?"

"Not that it signifies"—he glanced down the table to where Clara stood, back toward him—"but I am Benjamin Lane."

She did not turn at the name that should've been hers by now, but he did detect a flinch.

"*Lane?* Lane, you say? Hmm." Mr. Pocket stopped in front of him. This close, his magnificent nose took on a whole new proportion, eclipsing the inspector's face. The fellow was nothing but one great beak with side-whiskers. "What were you promised if you stay the duration, Mr. Lane?"

Ben studied him. If the lawman had been sent here to keep an eye on him, then the fellow already knew the answer. But that didn't mean he had to make things easy for the inspector.

"Are you a card player, sir?" Ben asked.

The man's eyes narrowed. "Been known to indulge now and then. Why?"

"Then you will appreciate it when I hold my cards close to my chest."

Mr. Pocket's lips parted to reply, but the butler announced from across the room, "Dinner is served. Please, be seated."

Savory scents entered the room, along with servants bearing all manner of platters and tureens. They lined up their offerings on sideboards against the wall.

Ben waited to see where the odd assortment of guests might land, hoping to distance himself from all and especially from Clara. The betrayer. Unbidden, his gaze slipped to where she sat, near the end of the table. Her beauty goaded. Her raven hair done up in a chignon, loose curls falling to her shoulder, taunted him with memories of when she'd let him nuzzle its silkiness with his cheek—the same cheek that yet stung from her slap.

The thin man sat next to her, far closer than decorum allowed. A footman marched over and bent, whispering into the man's ear. The bony fellow shot up from his chair, upsetting it onto two legs for a moment, then darted to the other side of the table and sank like a kicked puppy onto a different seat.

Only two open seats remained, both next to Clara, one of which was at the head of the table. That gave him only one option, really.

He strode to the seat next to her, the one the bony little man had tried to take, then grimaced to see Benjamin Lane written in gold on the place card. Whoever arranged this meeting was clearly toying with him—with all of them. But to what end?

He grabbed the chair and scooted it as far from her as possible. She inched hers away, as well. Had ever a Christmas Eve been so awkward?

A servant placed bowls of steaming green soup in front of each of them, leastwise what he assumed had been served to all. Hard to tell what went on opposite him now that they were seated. A huge centerpiece, filled with green fronds and peacock feathers, ran the length of the table and blocked his view. But he could hear them. Mademoiselle Pretents's voice berated the server for a perceived slight. The elderly lady cooed about something or maybe to someone. The thin man and the inspector didn't say a word.

Neither did Clara. Nor did she eat. She sat as a Grecian statue, cold, marble, staring into her bowl. Did she even breathe? Not that he cared.

Liar.

He grabbed his spoon and started shoveling in soup. He *did* care, and that's what irked him most. He cared that she'd so easily thrown away everything they'd shared, every laugh, every whisper. Every kiss.

He slammed down the spoon and shoved the bowl away, speaking for her ears alone. "Whatever you may think, I didn't do it."

"I cannot believe you deny what you did." Only her lips moved, for she refused to look at him. Her voice sharpened to a razor edge, one he'd never heard her use before. "You are a thief of the highest order."

Rage coloured the room red. He'd flattened men for lesser insults. His tone lowered to a growl. "Nor can I believe you so easily accepted such a lie. Tell me, did you lose faith in me immediately after you first heard the accusation, or did you give it a full five minutes?"

She jerked her face to his, blue eyes blazing to violet, the dark kind of purple before a storm. "You are insufferable!"

"I?" Her boldness stole his breath. "Did you even try to find out the truth?"

"What truth? That you put Blythe Shipping out of business? That you ran off with my family's investment? That you've been living like a king God-knows-where while I have been reduced to nothing?" Her chest heaved, and her nostrils flared. A wild mare couldn't have been any more inflamed. "Or are you speaking of the truth wherein you left me standing alone and unwanted at the altar?"

He clenched his hands to keep from throttling her. What nonsense was this? "It's a little hard to attend a wedding—even my own—when locked in a cell at Millbank."

The angry stain on her cheeks bled to white. "Millbank?" she whispered.

Was this a ploy? Some kind of feminine manipulation? He narrowed his eyes. If so, her mistake. He knew her too well, and if her right eye twitched, even the smallest possible tic, her lie would be exposed. "You didn't know?"

"All I know is that you walked out of my life in the worst possible way." A fine sheen of tears shimmered in her gaze, begging for release.

But nothing else. No twitch. No tic. For the first time in nine months, his heart started beating. Perhaps—just maybe—she truly hadn't known he'd been imprisoned. The thought lodged in his mind like a stone, all he'd believed of her swirling around it like water in a river.

By all that was holy, was he falling under her spell yet again? He hardened his resolve and his tone. "On the way to church the morning of our wedding, I was accosted and charged with the embezzlement of Blythe Shipping and your family fortune. I have been at Millbank ever since. Had you the slightest bit of faith in me, you'd have done a little digging and unearthed that nugget of truth."

"This is hardly the garb of an inmate." She swept out her hand. "That suit alone must've cost fifty pounds. Why should I believe you?"

So many emotions waged war; he tugged at his collar, unable to breathe. Whoever had indicted him had not only stolen his freedom, but the good opinion of the only woman he'd ever cared about. Blowing out a sigh, he edged his chair nearer to her. "Look closer, Clara. Look beyond what you think you know to what really is."

Her gaze travelled over his face, pausing on leftover bruises, widening at recent scars, and finally landing on the bump on his nose caused by one too many breaks. For a moment, the tears in her eyes threatened to spill, and then a hard glaze turned them to glass. "For all I know, you've been brawling over some gambling debt. Tell me, have you lost everything you've taken so soon?"

"I did not do it!" He growled like the beast she'd claimed him to be.

At the opposite end of the table, the inspector stood. "Everything all right down there, Miss Chapman?"

"Don't concern yourself on my behalf, Mr. Pocket." She glared at Ben and lowered her voice. "No one else has."

He gaped. He'd taken a punch in the lungs before, but never something as breath stealing as this. He shoved back his chair and stood, done with dinner before the main course and definitely done with Clara Chapman.

"Oh, flap! Oy me rumpus! Who's the wiggity scupper what called me here? Watch yer driving, Jilly." A wheeled chair barreled through the dining-room doors, pushed by a slip of a girl. She shoved the chair to the head of the table, jiggling a large toad of a man seated atop, until both came to a stop. Everyone's wineglasses quivered from the impact.

The fellow grumbled as if he were the one being inconvenienced. "Now that I'm here, whyn't we just pay me debt straight off and drink away the rest o' the days? Which one of you guppers holds the money bags, eh?"

Murmurs circled the table.

The butler once again entered from a far door. "Ahh, Mr. Tallgrass. A bit tardy, but we are pleased you have joined us."

"Oh, flap! Oy me rumpus! Jilly, lend a hand."

The girl, face drawn into a perpetual sulk, left her post at the back of his chair and grabbed ahold of the front of his shirt, yanking him upward. Then just like that, she let go, so that he flopped backward, now straightened, with a huge sigh.

His head swiveled to Clara. "Well, here's a fine tablemate. I likes the look o' you, I do."

Ignoring them all, Ben stalked away from the macabre gathering and took the stairs two at a time. Australia would've been better than this.

The Second Day

DECEMBER 25, 1850

Chapter Seven

Clara startled awake, heart pounding. Bedsheets tangled around her legs, and she clutched the counterpane to her neck. Grey light slipped in through the drawn draperies where they didn't quite meet. Not fully morning, but it would do. She'd tossed and turned enough to call it a night, waking from every dream, each one a variation of Ben's face. Of the hurt in his eyes. The wildness. The pain creasing his brow. If she listened hard enough, she might yet hear the haunting echo of the anguish in his voice.

"I did not do it!"

She knotted the sheet in her hands. What if he spoke true? His pale skin had lacked his usual healthy luster. A fresh scrape had marred the temple near his left eye, a new crescent scar cut across his jaw, and his once straight nose was now aquiline. Not to mention the stark bones defining his cheeks, testifying to a lack of nutrition. All lent credence to his claim of being locked in Millbank. It wasn't a huge leap of faith to change her belief that indeed he'd not run off to Europe with embezzled funds—but that merely meant he'd been caught beforehand. Didn't it?

So why would her brother, George, allow her to believe otherwise?

She shoved the counterpane aside and sat up. Why indeed. She lifted her face to the ceiling, breathing out the prayer that was now as much a part of her as flesh and bone.

Why, God? Why?

Snatching her wrap from the end of the mattress, she shivered into it. The fire in the hearth had long since died out. Good thing she'd kept her stockings on. Hopefully Aunt would not venture from her bed on this chill of a Christmas morn.

Clara dressed in the semilight, unwilling to lose any warmth to the windows until fully clothed, then she pulled the draperies wide and gasped. La! Such a view. A walled garden coated with a light dusting of snow lay just beneath her wing of the building. Beyond that, rolling hills and, farther on, a wood with towering trees. How lovely this would be when spring blew green upon it.

But for now, wind rattled the panes. Cold air snaked in through a gap in the caulk, and she retreated a step, feeling the chill beneath the grandeur. Both the manor and the grounds were beautiful, yet she could not shake the morbid feeling the place was somewhat of a sham.

Turning away from the scene, she settled in front of a small dressing table and set about pinning up her hair. Winter or not, Ben or not, she would celebrate this Christmas morn, leastwise in spirit, in memory of the Babe sent to atone for all.

She shoved in the last pin just as a small envelope was thrust beneath her chamber door. What on earth? Rising from the chair, she crossed the rug to retrieve it. The thick envelope weighed heavy in her palm, definitely denser than the invitation of yesterday. Would each day bring a new set of instructions, then?

Breaking the seal, she opened the flap, then shook out a single gold coin. Nothing else. No note. No directions. She held the coin up, catching the light from the window. Jagged edges detracted from what used to be a perfect circle. On one side, letters too worn to be read ringed around a raised X. No, wait. Maybe it was a cross. Hard to tell. She flipped it over. An ornate twining of embellishment encircled two words:

Secundus Casus

"*Secundus casus,*" she whispered, but even voicing the words aloud didn't make any sense of them. Absently, she rubbed her thumb over the engraving, a sinking feeling settling low in her stomach. If her assumption was right, the message was in Latin—a language Ben had studied as a boy. Did she care enough about this mystery to ask him for his help in translation?

She tapped a finger to her lips. Did it matter what the thing said? Perhaps the coin was a simple gift, given to everyone by the master of the house, a master they'd meet at breakfast. Surely that must be it. Tucking the coin into her pocket, she smoothed her skirts, then opened the door, prepared to meet the host who had called them here. Indeed, this would be a day of answers and—

A scream violated the sanctity of Christmas morning. She froze, hand still on the knob, and debated if she ought turn back and lock herself in.

Farther down the hall, another door opened, and Miss Scurry, toting her box, darted out. Her frantic steps swirled the hem of her skirt around her ankles. "Oh! Dear me!" She jerked her face toward Clara, the quizzing glass pinned to her bodice swinging with the movement. "Dear you! Are you quite all right, Miss Chapman?"

"It wasn't me." She sped to the old lady's side, offering an arm in case she swooned.

Footsteps pounded down the stairs, and three men bolted toward them,

Ben in the lead, followed by Mr. Pocket, and finally Mr. Minnow.

Breathless, cravat yet untied, Ben stopped in front of them. "What's happened?"

Biting her lip, Clara shook her head, unsure how to answer.

He slid his gaze to Miss Scurry. "Are you ill, madam?"

"Such a dear. Such a gentleman." Miss Scurry beamed up at him. "I am well, sir."

But the next scream indicated someone else was not.

Chapter Eight

Ben wheeled about and sprinted down the hall, the inspector at his side. Retracing their route past the staircase, they bolted into a different corridor. Halfway down, a door stood ajar. Heated words raged within, a woman's voice calling down brimstone upon some unfortunate soul.

Slowing, Ben glanced at the inspector, who had his gun drawn. Unarmed, Ben wouldn't be much help to the man. Their gazes met for an instant, and Pocket gave a single nod of understanding, then took the lead.

The inspector shoved the door open and barreled into the chamber. "Halt! Whatever's afoot, be done with it!"

Ben stationed himself at the threshold, prepared to collar a fleeing rogue if necessary. But the room was empty, save for the grey lady, Mademoiselle Pretents.

The woman spun, brows pinched low enough to hood her eyes. "Oui, monsieur! Such villainy must be stopped."

The inspector swiveled his head, scanning the room, then loosened the hammer on his pistol and tucked it away. "What has you in such a state, mademoiselle? Are you unwell?"

"No! I am not well." Her fists popped onto her hips. A ruffled peahen couldn't have puffed up nearly as much. "There is a thief at loose. My jewels have been stolen. All of them!"

Ben advanced and studied the room. The windows were shut tight. There were no adjoining doors to this chamber. All was tidy, even the bed, as if the woman had slept atop the counterpane, for surely such a firebrand would not deign to make up the bedclothes herself.

"Now, now, miss." The inspector pulled out a chair from a nearby dressing table. "Why don't you sit yourself down and tell me all about it?"

"No! I will not sit. I will not rest. Not until my jewels are returned." She stamped her foot, and the inspector retreated a step.

Ben sighed. Some Christmas morning this was turning out to be. "Mr. Pocket can't help you if you don't tell him exactly what happened, madam."

Were he a superstitious man, he'd motion the sign of the cross to ward off the evil eye she shot him. Yet she lifted her skirts and settled on the chair.

Pocket dragged over a cushioned stool and sat in front of her. "All right, then, let's have it."

"Before I went to bed last night, I hid my pouch—a velvet one, black—inside my chamber pot, for who would think to look there, no? I rose early, before any maid could come take it away, and voila." Her arm shot out, and she pointed to a porcelain urn next to the bed. "Empty!"

Rising, both he and the inspector crossed to the pot and peered in. Only a hairline crack at the bottom stared up at them.

Pocket turned back to the woman, his chest expanding with a deep breath. Ben hid a smile. The woman likely had no idea the interrogation that was about to rain down upon her head.

"What was in the pouch?" the inspector asked.

"My jewels."

"Yes, you've said that. What kind, exactly?"

"Valuable ones."

"Details, mademoiselle." The inspector cocked his head. "Details, please."

"A necklace, a bracelet, and a ring. All gold."

"The stones?"

"Diamonds, so glittery."

"The chain?"

"As I have said, gold."

"Single? Twisted? Any kind of pattern?"

The woman glowered.

The inspector leaned toward her. "Family heirloom?"

"Of course!"

"Whose?"

Clearly rattled, the woman sank against the chair. Ben smirked. The inspector had fired out his questions so quickly, she'd not had time to speak anything but the truth. Yet it wasn't so much what she said, but what she didn't say, a trick he'd learned after suffering one too many examinations himself.

A curious transformation took place. Instead of tears or even a whimper, the grey lady shot to her feet and clenched her hands. Red crept up her neck and bloomed on her cheeks. "Why you question me when it is my jewels that have been stolen, eh?"

Interesting. Anger combined with a lack of minute description of her goods? And no grief whatsoever about the family connection to the jewels? Ben studied her set jaw and glittering black eyes. Perhaps the woman wasn't the original owner of the trinkets but had stolen them herself.

"Oh, dear. Oh, my!" The words cooed from behind.

Ben glanced back to the door. The thin man, the elderly lady, and Clara all stood, eyes wide.

"Out! Out! All of you." The grey woman threw out her hands, and Ben had no doubt she'd shoo them off like a murder of crows. "Go! I will manage this on my own."

"Then you shouldn't have screamed in the first place, madam," the inspector grumbled as he passed by Ben. "Nevertheless, I will see what can be done to find your jewels."

Before Clara turned to tread down the hallway, Ben caught a glimpse of her face. Skin pale. Curved shadows beneath each eye. Her shoulders drooped and her step lagged. Apparently she'd not slept. A yawn overtook him as he followed the group to the top of the stairs. Neither had he, despite the comfort of a feather mattress instead of a cold stone floor. This should have been the first Christmas shared with his wife—as one flesh. Whoever stole that from him and poisoned Clara's mind against him would pay. He clenched the handrail so tightly, his fingers ached.

The inspector led the pack, followed by the thin man, Mr. Minnow, who pelted Pocket's back with questions. Miss Scurry clutched her box with one hand and the railing with the other. Clara hovered behind her. Ben brought up the rear, mulling over the quirky behaviour of all the guests, Mademoiselle Pretents foremost. Whether the jewels were hers or not, the fact remained that a thief roamed this manor, one bold enough to enter a woman's chamber in the middle of the night and steal. And if this one had no qualms at such flagrant behaviour, what other devious acts might the villain stoop to?

At the bottom of the stairs, Ben sprang ahead. No matter what Clara thought of him—or he of her—he would not allow her safety to be compromised. "Clara," he whispered, reluctant to draw the attention of the others.

She glanced at him but did not stop.

"Please, a word."

Her mouth flattened into a line, but she complied, stopping near the clock where he'd hidden in the shadow the night before.

He drew near, abhorring how her rosewater scent made his pulse quicken. A stranger stared back at him. He hated that love and hope and a life together had been ripped out from beneath them both. But most of all, he hated who-ever had been responsible for the confusion and hurt wounding Clara's gaze. Of all the things he wanted to say, wanted to know, he simply said, "Be sure to keep your door locked whenever you're in your chamber."

CHAPTER NINE

Clara slipped past Ben, escaping as much from his concern as her confusion. Oh, for the days when everything made sense and the world ran in perfect order. A groan lodged in her throat. Convict or not, Ben made it impossible for her to think straight when he was standing but a breath away. His direct gaze unnerved her with an untamed light she'd never before seen. Surely he hadn't been the one to steal the woman's jewels. Had he? She hurried along the hallway, swiping a loosened strand of hair from her eyes along with the question.

Mr. Minnow pounced the moment her toe crossed the dining-room threshold. "Over here, Miss Chapman." His fingers wrapped around her upper arm, and he tugged her to an empty chair next to his. "I shall plate you the tastiest morsels, my pet. Don't trouble yourself to move an inch."

She covered a grimace with what she hoped came off as a small smile. As much as she'd disliked the arranged seating of last night's dinner, was this truly any better? "Perhaps we ought wait, Mr. Minnow, until the master of the house arrives."

But her words were too late to stop him. He already stood at the sideboard.

Next to her, a dish landed on the table and Mr. Pocket sank onto the chair with a huff. "Curious choice of fare, I'd say."

An odd aroma—a mixture of jasmine and headcheese—wrinkled her nose. She peeked at the man's meal. His fork prodded a mound of brownish gelatin, each poke bleeding out colourless liquid. Lemon slices added stripes of yellow to the lump. This was breakfast?

"A curious morning, to be sure." She pulled her gaze from his plate. "Do you know who's taken Mademoiselle Pretents's jewels, Inspector?"

"That I do not, miss, but don't fret. I shall figure it out, sooner or later. Guilt has a way of coming to light no matter what dark corner it tries to hide in. All the same, be sure to lock your door at night." He shoveled in a big bite, and she turned from the sight, unwilling to watch it travel down his throat.

She reached for the tea urn as Ben entered the room and Mr. Minnow graced her with a plate of the quivering aspic. "Thank you, sir."

Mr. Minnow drew himself up a full six inches at her gratitude.

"Oh, flap! Oy me rumpus!" Mr. Tallgrass rolled in, his wheeled chair crashing into the table with such force it bounced him backward. "Jilly, lend a hand," he rumbled.

The dark-haired waif—how could one so thin push about such a great toad?—dashed to his side and yanked him upward, then let go. The wind punched from his lungs in a cough, but then a churlish grin rippled across his lips.

Ben took a seat at the far end of the table, which for some reason irked Clara, but before she could think to dissect such a feeling, the butler filled the doorway and rang a bell, drawing all their eyes—except for Mr. Tallgrass.

"Turn me about, Jilly!" He snaked out his hand and cuffed the girl on the head. "Poxy rag-a-ma-tag."

Setting down the small bell, the butler struck such a pose that Clara couldn't help but wonder if he'd served in the military. "Excuse me, ladies and gentlemen, but your gracious host—"

"And who would that be?" Mr. Minnow leaned forward in his seat.

The butler rocked on his heels. "I am instructed to inform you all that while your invitations stand as is, there is a recent addendum. Only one of you will receive a reward for staying the duration of the twelve nights."

"Who, dear? Which one?" Miss Scurry's voice squeaked. Or was that one of her mice?

"The one who remains."

Mr. Pocket angled his head at Clara. "Rather cryptic, eh miss?"

"Indeed," she whispered.

The butler cleared his throat. "Christmas dinner shall be served promptly at 7:00 p.m." His dark eyes shot to Mr. Tallgrass for a moment. "Charades will follow in the drawing room, with a basket of prepared scenarios that will be atop the pianoforte."

"Rather explicit instructions for so early in the day. I take it you will not be in attendance?" asked Mr. Pocket.

"Another astute observation, Inspector. You are correct. I shall be leaving the premises after breakfast."

Miss Scurry murmured an "oh, dear," but the butler went right on with his last words. "As you all may have noticed, the outside of Bleakly Manor has been properly decorated for the Twelfth Night festivities. The inside, however, requires Christmas decor. I've been given a list of assignments you are expected to accomplish before dinner tonight."

He pulled out a small slip of paper from an inside pocket. "Mr. Minnow, you are paired with Mademoiselle Pretents, as soon as she makes an appearance."

Mr. Minnow's lower lip quivered, and he spoke so only Clara might hear. "I'd so hoped to be with you, my pet."

The butler narrowed his eyes at him. "The two of you will hang the mistletoe and drape the ivy." His gaze returned to the instructions. "Mr. Pocket will aid Miss Scurry—"

"Oh!" Miss Scurry fluttered her free hand to her chest. "But I'd hoped to be with Mr. Minnow. Such a kind man."

Once again, the butler continued as if nothing had been said. "You are to decorate the Christmas tree, which is placed on a table in the drawing room. Mr. Tallgrass and his assistant, Miss Jilly, shall—"

"Oh, flap! Yer not sticking me with grunt work what ought be done by some kiddly-wugget of a slackin' servant." Mr. Tallgrass's cheeks puffed out, his skin mottling to a deep red. " 'Tain't right! 'Tain't fair! 'Tain't—"

"Mr. Tallgrass!" The butler's voice thundered. "Pay attention, if you please."

"No, I don't very well please," he shot back. "This is a load o' horse droppings!"

The butler's brow creased, and he bent at eye level with the man. "Then you may leave now, if you wish."

Mr. Tallgrass's stubbly whiskers stuck out like white porcupine quills, so tightly did his face squinch up.

The butler straightened as he explained their task, but Clara's thoughts snarled. That only left—

"Mr. Lane, you shall escort Miss Chapman on an outing to retrieve the Yule log for the holiday. You'll find all you should need in the carriage house."

The butler droned on, but his words faded to gibberish. She was to spend the whole of the morning outside with Ben? The man who may—or in his words may not have—caused her and her family so much grief. This was too much to be borne!

Pressing two fingers to her temple, she rubbed little circles to ward off the birth of a headache. She should leave. Now. Just pack up and go home to Aunt.

Spending Christmas, or any other day, with Ben—alone—was the last thing she wanted to do.

CHAPTER TEN

Frigid air slapped Clara on the cheek, and she tucked her chin to her chest, warding off further assault. On the far side of the wagon seat, Ben snapped the reins, urging the horses onward. Once they reached the shelter of the woods, the wind wouldn't attack with such a wicked sting. But here, on the expanse of rolling hills between manor and forest, the cold was relentless.

So were the warring emotions battling inside her. Anger. Confusion. Doubt and indignation. It was a wicked jest to have been paired up with Ben, and when the master of Bleakly Manor finally showed his face, she'd have a word or two—no, three or more—to share with the man.

"Move closer." Ben glanced at her sideways, face unreadable. "I vow I won't pick your pockets."

"I'm f–fine." Brilliant. Her chattering teeth branded her a fraud. Not that it should matter, for one fraud ought abide with another, should he not?

"Whoa." Ben eased the horses to a halt.

She wrapped her arms tighter and lifted her face. They were hardly near the woods or the house. "What are you doing?"

Shrugging out of his coat, he reached for her with one arm and pulled her toward him. He tucked the wool around her shoulders, then settled her at his side. Leftover heat from his body penetrated her cloak, warming her in ways that went beyond such a generous deed. He grasped the reins and started the horses moving again, the weight of his coat hugging her like an intimate embrace—one that irked and soothed at the same time.

The wagon rambled on, his big arm jostling next to her, his thigh bumping against hers. Hard to tell what made him shudder. The uneven ground? Guilt? Or the thinness of his dress coat against the bitter air?

"Please, take back your coat." She started to peel it off. "You'll catch your death."

His hand caught hers, gently forcing it to her lap. "Isn't that what you want?"

She frowned up at him. "No, I do not wish you ill."

She wished him to be gone.

A tense silence followed, and her heart ached for the way things had been, when she'd believed in his integrity and was for once in her life sure of love. This Ben, this stranger with the clenched jaw and stiff shoulders, was a shocking replacement.

"I am sorry. My manners are not as pretty as they once were." Pulling his attention from the horses, he gazed down at her. "Are you feeling warmer?"

"Yes, though I insist you take back your coat as soon as we stop."

"Trust me. I've suffered worse than cold." A half smile lifted his lips.

He pulled the wagon to a stop at the edge of the woods, then hopped down and circled to offer her a hand. As soon as her feet hit the ground, she removed his coat and held it out.

He shook his head. "Stubborn as ever, I see."

"I insist. Besides, I am much warmer now that we are more sheltered."

While he shoved his arms back into his coat and buttoned up, she studied the unending maze of tree trunks. Better that than dwell on all the what-might-have-beens that Ben's presence unearthed.

"So, now what?" she asked.

Ben stared into the woods, the sullen sky as clouded as his expression. "Try to spy a large piece of downed wood. Then I'll loosen a horse and retrieve it. We may end up doing this again, for I doubt we'll be able to load a log large enough to last the entire Yuletide."

He stalked ahead, his long legs eating up the ground. She did double time behind him in a vain attempt to keep up—until he glanced over his shoulder and saw her predicament.

A sheepish smile quirked his mouth, and he stopped. "Forgive me. I've not had the pleasure to hike free in so long that I've gotten carried away. This pace is far too fast for you."

He waited while she caught up, and she offered him a wry smile in return. "I'd like to see you try tromping through the frozen woods in petticoats."

He grunted. "No doubt."

Side by side, they advanced, scouring the ground for a fallen tree weathered enough to burn well. Other than the whoosh of wind rattling the branches up high, they walked in companionable silence. Too companionable. How could a thief walk so carefree next to the one he supposedly robbed? The incongruity of it all shivered across her shoulders.

Her step faltered, and Ben grabbed her elbow, righting her. Would that the grief and sorrow of the past nine months could be as easily righted.

"Oh, very well!" She spoke as much to herself as to him, frustrated with the whole situation. She stopped and peered up at him. "I am ready to hear what happened to you and how you came to Bleakly Manor."

"Are you?" His amber gaze held her for a moment. So many emotions shone in those depths. It would take years to sort them all by name. Time froze, the space between them brittle and sharp as the cold air.

Then he wheeled about and strode ahead, pausing only long enough to hold back a low-lying branch for her to pass beneath. Stubborn man!

She grabbed his sleeve before he could pass her again. "Please, Ben."

He blew out a puff of frozen mist, a slight shake to his head. "It is nothing different than what I told you last night. I was on my way to the church, speeding, actually, for such was my eagerness to make you mine, when a gaol cart pulled in front of me, blocking my path. So focused was I on the impediment, I did not notice the men behind me." His voice lowered, yet gained in strength. "I was bagged without seeing who attacked. I awoke two days later in Millbank, where I've been rotting ever since, until I received an invitation to Bleakly Manor, promising me freedom. Freedom." A bitter chuckle rent the cold air. "I no longer believe in such."

He stomped ahead, apparently finished with the conversation.

But she wasn't. Gathering her skirts, she darted after him. "Are you saying you were held without representation? Without bail?"

He snorted. "Often without food or water."

The fine hairs at the back of her neck prickled. If what he said was true. . .

She hugged herself tightly, as an image of him deprived of nourishment, robbed of dignity, quaked through her, more unsettling than the cold.

She hastened her steps to catch up to him. "I find it hard to believe the justice system could fail on such a grand level. Did you have no trial whatsoever?"

"Oh, I had a trial. At least in word. But my accuser never appeared, sending a proxy instead. The documents remained sealed and unread. As was the evidence. I have no idea who indicted me of the embezzlement of Blythe Shipping or your family fortune." His hands curled into fists at his side. "I was sentenced to transportation before year's end."

Her jaw dropped. Banishment without due process? Unheard of. Wasn't it? "How can that be? Surely that is not how our courts function."

His feet hit the ground harder than necessary, grinding sticks and frozen brush beneath his step. "Enough money can make anything happen. Anything."

His words swirled over her head, as ominous as the darkening clouds pregnant with a winter storm. How was she to understand that? "Are you saying someone bribed the judge to convict you for a crime of which you were innocent?"

He wheeled about before she finished the question. In two strides, he gripped her arms and pulled her close, his voice deadly quiet. "Look me in the eyes, Clara, and tell me you believe I am guilty."

Desperation roughened his tone, harsh and dreadful, compelling her to obey. Never had he used such severity with her.

Swallowing the tightness in her throat, she slowly met his gaze, fearful yet strangely eager to discover the truth. Would she find healing or damnation?

She stared deeply, beyond the golden flecks in his hazel eyes. The purity she saw there flattened the house of cards she'd carefully constructed over the past months. Oh, how much easier it would be to cling to the belief that he was a vile cullion. But God help her, she could not.

"No—" Her voice broke, and she sucked in a shaky breath. "I do not believe you are guilty."

A groan rumbled in his chest, and he closed his eyes. "Thank God."

"But. . ." Who had done this? Stolen his freedom? Robbed them of happiness? The world turned watery, and hot tears burned down her face. "I don't understand."

He pulled her into his arms, wrapping her tight against him, and she wept into his shirt. Oh, how she'd missed this. His heart beat hard against her cheek, and she clutched his back, burrowing closer. How good, how right it felt to be in his arms again, share his warmth, lose herself in his comfort. For one glorious moment, she dared surrender to the feeling of being wanted and cherished.

Too soon he broke the embrace. He stepped back and tilted her chin up with the crook of his knuckle. "I should like to hear why you suspected me of such a heinous crime."

A familiar ache throbbed in the thin space between heart and soul—the empty hollow where she stored all her hurt, carved out long ago by her father and his rejection. To speak it aloud would only breathe life into that pain. Love, once poured out, could never go back into the same bottle.

But how could she refuse the earnest expectation on Ben's face? He looked like a lost little boy, abandoned and forlorn. She didn't think it possible, but one more piece of her heart broke off, leaving a jagged edge in her chest.

He reached for her hand. "Perhaps it will be easier if we carry on with our search, hmm?"

Side by side, they pressed on, and he was right. Without facing him the words came easier. "I stood alone that day. Waiting for you to come. The eyes of God and those gathered alternated between me and the front door. At first I suspected the worst had become of you. Some accident or illness, perhaps. I searched every hospital. Inquired with physicians and surgeons. I even sent a servant to visit the morgue. It wasn't until a week later that I learned the truth. Or thought I did."

She paused to step over a snow-dusted rock. "George was summoned to the solicitor's and told the bulk of our family investments—along with Blythe Shipping's—had been stolen. By you."

She studied him from the corner of her eye, expecting some kind of outburst. None came.

"From that day forward," she continued, "we lived just above poverty. Great Aunt Mitchell took me in as her companion, and George sailed for America, hoping to find a living large enough to pay for my fare. In the meantime, I've learned sewing skills beyond mere ornamentation. I intend to earn my keep by soliciting a mending and tailoring service once he sends for me."

For a long time, Ben said nothing, just kept stalking through the frozen woods until he stopped in front of a tree trunk long since fallen. Squatting, he rubbed his hands together, then brushed off the top coating of snow from the wood. "This will do."

He rose and faced her, blowing warmth into his hands. "Think carefully, Clara. Are you certain that meeting between George and the solicitor took place a full week *after* I had been arrested, and that your standard of living didn't alter until then?"

"That's right."

"Hmm." A muscle jumped on his jaw, a sure sign his mind raced.

"What?"

"I am wondering how I could have taken the money, yet it didn't disappear until long after I'd been gaoled?" The question hung between them, icy and bitter as the winter wind, and she trembled at the flatness in his voice.

For the first time, she began to fathom he'd been wronged every bit as much as she—or more. "Who would do such a thing?" she whispered.

"I don't know." His face hardened, the dark gleam in his eyes fearsome. "But I intend to find out."

CHAPTER ELEVEN

A monster rumbled inside Ben's gut, clawing and angry. A familiar feeling, this hunger. He shifted on the settee. Maybe the movement would stop the grumbling, for the odd Christmas dinner they'd eaten this evening certainly hadn't. There'd been no goose or chestnut stuffing. No pâtés or oysters or puddings. Just a plain bouillon, followed by a single roasted Cornish hen and mince pie for the eight of them. No doubt if he listened hard enough, he'd hear echoing growls from the stomachs of those gathered in the drawing room.

Rubbing his fingers together, he stared at the ink stains that would not disappear, though he'd scrubbed hard enough in the basin. After retrieving the Yule log with Clara, he'd spent the afternoon at the desk in his chamber. When he received the promised freedom by Twelfth Night—*if* he did—he'd still need his family wealth reinstated. Money once taken by the Crown was not easily gained back, but it could be done. Ten letters to various officials had left his fingers cramped. If even one of those missives made it into the hands of a sympathetic ear, he'd gladly endure the blackened skin. And with the hope of justice, he'd do the same on the morrow.

In the center of the room, Mr. Minnow flapped about, then fell and curled into a ball.

"Oh, dear! Such wonderful dramatics." Miss Scurry grasped her box of mice close to her chest. "Are you a goose, Mr. Minnow? Taken down by an arrow?"

The man uncurled long enough to touch his nose, then he smiled at Clara. Whether she ventured a guess or not, he always sought her out. The unwarranted attention annoyed Ben as much as his empty belly.

"So, the second word is *goose*, eh?" The inspector sniffed, his nose rubbed raw from having to touch it so many times for when he'd performed his charade, such was the length of "God Rest Ye Merry Gentlemen, Let Nothing You Dismay."

Next to him, Clara leaned near, speaking for Ben alone. "I daresay neither of us expected to be playing games with strangers this Christmas Day, though I fear Mr. Minnow thinks of himself as our bosom companion."

Ben hid a smirk. The man wanted to be her companion, not his.

Clara's gaze followed the game, his travelled the room. The great log burned in the hearth. It wouldn't last the whole of the twelve days, which had set off a superstitious flutter from Miss Scurry, but for now the flames were merry. Ivy swagged over the doors, a little crooked, but if he'd had to work with Mademoiselle Pretents, he'd have made haste in hanging the greenery, as well. For tonight, the Christmas tree on the table glowed with candles attached by clips to the branches. A single servant, an odd little woman, stood nearby with a bucket of water should a fire break out.

A round of applause ended his surveillance. Minnow flopped a bow, then retrieved a basket from the pianoforte and delivered it to Ben.

He shook his head. "I am content to watch. My playacting skills leave much to be desired."

"Oh, but you must." The tang of ginger travelled on the man's words. Minnow shoved the basket into Ben's hands. "There's one in here for each of us."

Scowling, he pulled out an envelope with his name penned on the front. How had Mr. Tallgrass managed to escape this fate? Truth be told, though, Ben's spirits had lightened when the toady fellow rolled off after dinner with a curse about the food and something about the queen.

Clara peered up at him. Lamplight sparkled in her eyes, and—dare he hope—a renewed spark of trust in him, as small as it may be. Even so, this was not the carefree woman he'd known before, not with that buried layer of hurt dulling her gaze. A familiar rage coursed through his veins, heating him from the inside out. He would discover who'd caused this pain, for him and for her, or die in the trying.

"You saw what a poor charade I rendered." She smiled. "You can do no worse."

He snorted. She had no idea.

"Oui. The woman speaks true." Mademoiselle Pretents left her perch on a chair near the hearth and sat nearer the door, face flushed.

Ben rose, and Minnow immediately took his spot, sinking next to Clara. No wonder the fellow had chosen him next.

Resigned to death by humiliation, he crossed to the middle of the room and opened the envelope, but the words made little sense. Thus far, all the charades were related by a holiday theme. Not this. Still, it should be easy enough to perform. He tucked the envelope into his pocket and pretended to pull out a gold piece, holding up the imaginary coin then pantomiming a test of it with his teeth.

"A farthing?" asked Mr. Minnow.

Miss Scurry held up her quizzing glass to one eye and strained forward in her seat. "A sovereign?"

"A gold sovereign?" Clara wondered.

Ben shook his head. This would be harder than he thought. How else to show a—

"Coin!" The inspector shouted.

Ben tapped his nose then held up three fingers.

The inspector nodded. "The third word is *coin*."

He tapped his nose again. Now, how to playact the first two? He froze, the weight of all eyes squashing the life out of his creativity. Or maybe it wasn't the guests' gazes at all. He spun, certain someone watched him from behind. Nothing but the eyes of the portraits on the walls stared back.

"A spinning top?" Mr. Minnow ventured.

"No, a whirligig, you stupid fellow." Mademoiselle Pretents's voice was venom.

Ben wheeled about, shaking his head. The sooner this was over with, the better, but should he act out the only idea Clara was sure to guess? Sucking in a breath, he crossed over to her and dropped to one knee, taking her hand in his.

Colour flamed on her cheeks, and her fingers trembled. Clearly she understood his meaning.

"Proposal!" Minnow aimed the word at him like a dagger to the heart.

Without pulling his gaze from Clara, he shook his head. Slowly, he rubbed his thumb over her third finger, just below the knuckle—the skin now naked where she'd once worn his ring. Dredging up all the memories of passion and whispers they'd shared, he lowered his carefully constructed mask and allowed a forgotten desire to soften the hard lines on his face.

"Oh, lovely!" Miss Scurry twittered.

Clara gasped.

But playacting a second chance of asking for her hand turned sour at the back of his throat. Why had he ever thought to do such a thing? He shot to his feet and stalked to the hearth, done with the whole charade.

"Love is a two-sided coin?" the inspector guessed. "Oh, I get it. Two-sided coin, eh?"

Ben yanked out the envelope and tossed it into the flames, watched for a moment until fire caught hold of the three words, then spun and touched his nose.

A lie, but so be it.

The Third Day

December 26, 1850

CHAPTER TWELVE

E arly morning light hung like a haze in Clara's chamber. Yawning, she rubbed her eyes, and a terrific growl rumbled in her belly. Hopefully today's breakfast would be more palatable than last evening's Christmas dinner.

She threw off the counterpane and snatched her dressing gown from the foot of the bed, heart sinking into her empty stomach. If the burnt smell on the air was any indication, there wasn't much hope of a hearty meal today, either.

Stretching a kink out of her neck, she silently thanked God for tea, for therein she might wake fully and fill her—

"Fire!"

A woman's cry came from below. Danger thudded a crazed beat in Clara's ears. No, were those footsteps? She shot to the door and darted into the hall. A foggy blur softened the edges of everything as she raced to the stairs. Ahead, Ben, Mr. Minnow, and Mr. Pocket surged down the steps, taking several at a time, nightshirts flapping untucked from their trousers. She followed.

At the landing, the men split. Mr. Minnow and Mr. Pocket veered right. Ben headed left. By the time she descended, Ben shouted, "Over here!"

They converged upon the drawing room, where Miss Scurry stood outside the door, wringing her hands. Her usual box of mice was absent. Inside the room, charcoal clouds billowed near the ceiling, pushed upward by flames on the Christmas tree burning at the far corner of the room.

Miss Scurry turned to Clara, fear leaking down her cheeks. "Oh, dear! Oh, my."

"The drapery, men! Haul to!" Ben no sooner issued his command than he faced Clara. "We'll try to smother it, but seek water just in case. Miss Scurry, check on Mademoiselle Pretents, if you please."

Ben tore into the room, leaving them in the hall with smoke and dread.

Next to her, Miss Scurry whimpered. "The reckoning. Oh! The reckoning is upon us."

Clara reached for the older lady's hand and gave it a squeeze. "All will be well. I am sure the men will smother the flames. We must do as Ben says."

A wavery smile rippled across the old lady's lips. "Such a dear." Then she whirled and fled down the hall, skirts flying behind.

Clara hurried the other way. Why had the old lady dressed so early? And why venture to the drawing room when surely her stomach was as empty as theirs? The dining room made more sense to seek out.

But there was no time to ponder such things. There must be a doorway nearby to a stair leading down to the kitchen, perhaps disguised as mere paneling, for only servants would use it. She studied the wall as she went, disliking the way all eyes on the portraits seemed to watch her struggle.

The farther she advanced, the more her throat burned. Odd. Was she not moving past the fire? She bent, coughing away the discomfort, then stopped, horrified.

Smoke billowed out from a crack between floorboards and wall, from a door blending in against the dark wood. She shoved her shoulder against the paneling, and it gave. Air thick with smoke hovered near the ceiling inside of a small antechamber. Clara dropped to a crouch. Eye to eye with the legs of furniture, it appeared to be a sitting room, but no time to speculate whose. Flames crawled up the draperies on the far window, as did muffled shrieks behind a farther wall. Despite the heat, Clara's blood turned to ice. Someone was trapped, and she'd never be able to do this alone. Was there enough time to get help?

There'd have to be. Whirling, she ran back to the drawing room. The stench of burnt fabric and sweat violated last evening's scent of pine and fresh holly.

"More fire!" she hacked out as she bolted across the threshold. "It's worse, and someone is trapped."

Ben and Mr. Pocket, soot blackened and chests heaving, paused in whaling their draperies against what remained of the flames. Mr. Minnow stood to the side, clutching his portion of ripped brocade to his chest, hair askew but otherwise untouched by labour of any kind.

Mr. Pocket exchanged a glance with Ben, then they both sprinted toward her. Ben hollered over his shoulder at Mr. Minnow, "Finish the job, man!"

Gaining her side, Ben dipped his head. "Lead the way."

By the time she returned with the men in tow, smoke belched from the door like an angry dragon. Ben and the inspector charged into the room. Fear barreled into her heart—and squeezed. Was she to lose him again now that they were just starting to make amends?

Her hands curled into fists. Not if she could help it.

She tore back to the drawing room and raced over to Mr. Minnow, who stood exactly as they'd left him. The last rogue embers smouldered not five paces from him.

What a wastrel! She snatched the draperies out of his hands. "Mr. Minnow! Either put the rest of those flames out now or we shall all perish."

He gaped, arms flapping at his sides. "But how am I to do so?"

"Remove your nightshirt and bat them out." She huffed, then flew back to the real danger.

And real it was, more so from the smoke now than the flames. Inhaling the better air of the corridor, she charged into the room—just as glass shattered. Like a flock of demons, the black cloud poured out the window Ben had broken. Slowly, the room cleared, leaving behind the hacking and coughing of Ben and Mr. Pocket, her own laboured breaths, and a dull thumping accompanied by a mewling cry.

Ben wheeled toward the sound. "There!"

The men dashed to the far wall, where a board had been nailed across a door. What on earth? What kind of villain barricaded helpless victims, then set fire to ensure their demise?

Grabbing a candlestick fallen to the floor, Ben wedged a corner of it behind the wood and pulled. The board crashed to the floor with a clatter. Mr. Pocket yanked on the knob, and Jilly flew out the door like a bat from an attic, screaming all the way. From the depths of the attached room, Mr. Tallgrass's curses swelled as black as the former smoke—but that was all. No real smoke or flames infected that room.

Ben dropped the candlestick. "Thank God."

"Indeed." Mr. Pocket rubbed a hand over his shorn head.

Clara shuddered, afraid to believe. Where might the next fire spring up? She picked her way past a tipped-over chair, edging to Ben's side. "Is it over? Truly?"

A muscle stood out on his neck like a steel rod, until he blew away the tension with a deep sigh. "Let us hope so." He cast her a sideways glance, and a shadow darkened his face. "You are trembling. Come, I'll see you to your room."

Offering his arm, he slipped his gaze to Mr. Pocket. "I believe you can handle Mr. Tallgrass, can you not, Inspector?"

Mr. Pocket leaned a hand against the doorframe and coughed, long and hard, then straightened as if he'd not just nearly hacked up a lung. "Righty-o. I've managed worse. See to the lady, Mr. Lane."

Wrapping her fingers around Ben's arm, she allowed him to lead her from the charred room and up to her chamber, grateful for his strength. The morning's peril and chaos had poked holes in her courage, draining her dry, so much so that she stumbled at the top of the stair.

Ben covered her hand with his strong fingers, steadying her. "Are you all right?"

The sleeve of his nightshirt moulded against hard muscle, and for the first time, she realized she wore naught but a robe over her chemise, a thin one at that. No, she was definitely not all right.

"I am fine," she answered.

God, forgive me.

Willing her feet to behave, she managed to make it to the door of her chamber without further misstep. A miracle, really, for the heat of the man at her side—the one her body remembered despite what her mind might say—sped her heartbeat until it was hard to breathe.

She wanted to ask him to hold her. To wrap his arms around her as he had yesterday out in the woods and pretend nothing had changed between them. But when he pulled away and his sleeve rode up his arm, a black number marred his skin. She stared, wanting to turn away from the awful sight yet completely helpless to do so. The mark of a felon stared back at her. He was not the same man. How could he be? The Ben she'd known—gentle and kind, compassionate almost to a fault—might never be the same again. Loss squeezed her chest, and a small cry escaped her lips.

Ben shoved down his sleeve and lifted her face to his. "Do I frighten you?"

She swallowed, throat burning as much from his question as from the remnants of acrid smoke. How was she to answer that? She feared the things he'd seen and had to do to survive, the sometime feral gleam in his eyes when he thought she wasn't looking. But him? Did she fear this man who was to have been her husband? Did not the same heart still beat inside his chest?

"No, you do not." She turned and fled into her chamber, closing the door between them. Leaning her back against the cool wood, she panted, fighting to catch her breath. It wasn't a lie, for in truth, she was even more afraid of the queer twinge deep inside her belly.

Hunger, yes, but for more than breakfast.

CHAPTER THIRTEEN

Ben strode to the door of the sitting room, tugging at his collar. Air. Just a draught of it. A moment on the front stoop to escape the leftover smoke permeating the manor. No one would miss him. At least no one had when he'd disappeared earlier to pen yet another batch of letters pleading for a fresh look into his case. Even should he gain his freedom by staying here the full twelve days, there was still the matter of recouping his estate funds from the Court of Chancery.

As he passed by, he smiled at Clara, who played cards with Miss Scurry. Near the hearth, Mr. Tallgrass pestered his brooding young attendant with instructions on properly roasting a chestnut. Mademoiselle Pretents looked out the window. Minnow hovered near Clara. And the inspector sorted through a box of ashes in hopes of finding a clue as to how the fire had started or a hint of who'd been wicked enough to intentionally trap Mr. Tallgrass and Jilly.

As Ben approached the threshold, a servant darted in, dropping a curtsy in front of him.

"Begging yer pardon, sir, but it's Boxing Day." The woman peeked up at him, then tucked her chin.

"And?" he asked.

She clutched and reclutched handfuls of her apron. Timid little thing, apparently. "There's a line o' tradesmen downstairs what are expecting their Christmas boxes, sir."

He ran a hand along his jaw. Why would she think it necessary to tell him such information? "Then I suppose you should give them their due, hmm?"

"That's just it, sir. There are none." She lifted her face, eyes shimmering. "I din't know what else to do, who else to go to."

So she came to him? He flattened his lips to avoid a glower, for surely such a look would push the woman into hysterics. "Has the butler not returned?"

"No, sir." She shook her head. "Mrs. Dram, the housekeeper, she's gone as well. Why, there's naught but a handful of us servants to manage, and most of those are still cleaning up from the fire."

Who invited guests without hiring proper staff? He grunted, for offering his true opinion would not be fit for mixed company. "Can you not simply send the tradesmen away?"

She wrung the life out of her apron. Were it a chicken, it would long since have died. "I tried, sir. I did." Her voice pitched to a whine. "They won't listen to the likes o' me. I fear I shall be overrun with the brutes."

The tone must've reached Clara's ears, for she rose and crossed the carpet, stopping alongside him. "What's wrong?" she whispered.

Mr. Minnow trailed her. "Is there a problem, Miss Chapman?"

Ben smothered a growl. Must the man track her like a dog on a scent? Ignoring Minnow, he spoke to Clara. "It seems some tradesmen are expecting their Christmas boxes, yet there are none to be given."

"Oh." Her brow crumpled. "That is dreadful."

"Miss Chapman." Miss Scurry, having been left alone at the card table, gathered her box and joined them. "Has the reckoning come?"

Clara smiled at her. "Don't fret, Miss Scurry. Just an issue of not having Christmas boxes for the tradesmen."

"Eh? What's that?" Mr. Tallgrass craned his neck their way. "Tradesmen expectin' boxes? Flappin' beggars!"

The little maid cringed and stepped behind Ben. Laughable, really, that she'd seek refuge behind a convict. If he rolled up his sleeve, revealing his brand, would she run away as Clara had?

Whirling from the window, Mademoiselle Pretents threw out her arms. "Shoo them away, *imbécile*. We are not their masters. We are the guests. They can have no claim against us."

Ben sighed. This was getting out of hand. "True, yet without the master in attendance, I suppose we are all the tradesmen have as his representative."

His proclamation lifted the inspector's head from his study of the ashes. A grey smudge smeared the tip of his big nose. "How do you know it's a *him*, Mr. Lane?"

"Mere speculation, Inspector. Nothing more." He slipped a glance at the little maid. "Go about your business, miss. I'll see to the tradesmen."

The woman darted out the door and down the hall.

Clara turned to him, admiration deepening the blue of her gaze. "How will you manage that?"

Indeed. How would he? But for the glimmer in Clara's eyes, the embers of respect, he must come up with something.

"Fie!" Mr. Tallgrass's voice rasped. "Grab some of the candlesticks and whatnot from around here, man, and shove it in a box. Give that to 'em. That's how I'd manage, and with a kick to their backsides to help 'em out the door besides."

"But these things are not ours to give." Clutching her box tighter, Miss Scurry whimpered, her mobcap flopping nearly to her eyes. "Oh! The reckoning of it all."

"Well." Clara bit her lip, a sure sign something brewed in that pretty head of hers. "I think I have an idea. I propose we each retrieve whatever trifles we can spare from our travel bags. An extra handkerchief. A hair comb. Perhaps a peppermint you've forgotten about and have tucked away in a pocket. I, for one, have brought along my sewing basket and may find an overlooked needle and thread to spare."

"Oh, lovely! Such a beautiful idea." The lines on Miss Scurry's face disappeared. "I may have just the thing." She shoved back her cap with her free hand as she disappeared out the door.

Ben watched her go. Hopefully she wasn't rushing off to wrap up her mice. Still, Clara's idea was worth a shot.

Mademoiselle Pretents flounced over to Clara, jabbing the air with a pointed finger. "My jewels have already been stolen, and now you want to take more? No! I will not have it."

The inspector set his box onto the side table nearest him, then rose. "Mademoiselle, unless you'd like me to rummage through your things, I suggest you find something to donate."

"Are you threatening me, monsieur?"

He halted in front of her and folded his arms. "Without doubt."

"Gah! I have no more to say to you." Her face pinched, nearly squeezing her dark eyes closed. "Any of you!" She stormed out of the room like a winter squall.

The inspector chuckled. "That's the best thing she's ever said." Then he tipped his head at Clara. "A generous proposal on your part, miss. The world could use more like you."

Pink bloomed on Clara's cheeks, quite the contrast to Mademoiselle Pretents's angry red. Ben tried not to stare, but the temptation was beyond a mere mortal such as himself. Ahh, he'd missed that innocent flush.

"I couldn't agree more, Inspector," he murmured, the words sounding huskier than he had intended—which only deepened her pink to the blush of a June rose.

"Well, I think it's a bunch o' flap." Mr. Tallgrass shifted on his wheeled chair, listing to the side. "Oy me rumpus. Jilly!"

"I'll leave him to you this time." The inspector grumbled under his breath as he passed by Ben and fled the room.

Carping and cussing spewed out Tallgrass's mouth the entire time Jilly propped him upward. "First my bones are rattled, then I'm fed fare what 'tain't fit for a street sweeper, and next someone tries to burn me in my own chamber. Now this? No! I ain't gonna give no one nothing. Tradesmen be hanged, I say."

Mr. Minnow puffed out his chest and blocked Clara's view of the man. If nothing else, he was a protective fellow. Then again, so was a rodent over a piece of Stilton.

"I'm certain I may find some trivialities that will suffice, Miss Chapman. Shall I see you to your room to retrieve some of yours?" His arm shot out.

Clara tucked her hands behind her back and stepped closer to Ben. "Thank you, but no, Mr. Minnow. I am sure I can manage on my own."

Minnow deflated, cast a withering look at Ben, then slunk away like a tot who'd been told no for the first time.

Clara watched him go and took another step toward Ben. Not that he minded, but such daring while Tallgrass eyed them?

"I was hoping to have a word with you," she said.

He looked past her, over at Tallgrass, who'd blessedly gone back to berating Jilly and her chestnut-roasting skills at the hearth. Still, one never knew when the man would lash out at them again. He guided Clara to the door with a nudge to the small of her back. "Out in the hall."

In the foyer, the lion head stared down at them. Ben smirked. Was this really any better?

Clara removed something from her pocket and held out her hand. A gold coin stared up at him.

He looked from the coin to her. "You're offering gold to a thief?"

She shoved her hand closer. "Go on. I should like your opinion of it."

Narrowing his eyes, he plucked the coin from her palm. Lightweight. Roughened edges. Perhaps over the centuries people had shaved bits off during times of dire need. One side was worn more than the other, a cross, or maybe an X, was at the center—impossible to read the letters ringing it. He flipped it over.

"Secundus casus." He tasted the words like a foreign fruit. At first he'd thought it an old Roman coin, but none ever read thus. "Interesting. Where did you get this?"

"Someone slipped it under my door yesterday. Can you tell me what it says?"

"Second chance," he drawled, but by the time the translation finished rolling off his tongue, he knew—and sucked in a sharp breath. "This was my charade last night, Clara."

"What does it mean?"

"I don't know." Behind him, the eyes of the lion burned into his back, and he stiffened. "The mysteries are starting to pile up in a great heap, are they not?"

"Sounds ominous." She tipped her face to his, searching his eyes for God knew what. "Should I be afraid?"

"No. As you told Miss Scurry, don't fret. Be watchful, yet don't worry. I would not willingly allow any harm to come to you." He reached for her hand and pressed her fingers around the coin, holding on longer than etiquette allowed. The warmth of her skin burned hotter than a summer day. How he'd missed this, a simple touch, hushed words shared by them alone. The way her blue gaze looked to him for strength. Desire stoked a fire in his gut.

He pulled away before he wrapped her in his arms and never let go. "Keep that coin. For whatever reason, someone wanted you to have it."

"But who? And why?"

"Sometimes all we have are questions." He shook his head. Lord knows he'd had his share of them while rotting in a gaol cell. "But there's really only one that matters."

She blinked, an endearing little wrinkle bunching her nose. "What's that?"

"Is God in control, or is He not?"

CHAPTER FOURTEEN

Second chance. Second chance. With each stab of Clara's needle through the fabric, she mulled over what the coin in her pocket could possibly mean. Though she'd had nearly an hour to herself in the sitting room to think on it, nothing came to mind.

Ben entered, breaking her concentration. He strolled across the carpet, hands behind his back. "How goes it? Am I the last one to donate to your worthy cause?"

"No, I'm still waiting for Miss Scurry and Mr. Minnow's contributions." After she nipped the thread with her teeth, she tucked away her needle and held up the finished project for Ben's inspection. "As for me, I've sewn six pouches from fabric scraps. Not brilliant, but serviceable. And far better than what the others have dropped off."

"And that would be. . . ?"

Gathering her sacks, large enough for a few coins or some pinches of snuff, she led Ben to a side table and set down her offering. Then she pointed at a twist of waxed paper. "Mr. Pocket dropped off a half-dozen comfits." She moved her finger onward to a string of cracked leather. "Mr. Tallgrass had Jilly deliver this old watch fob, though I doubt very much it will hold anything without breaking." Lastly, she swept her hand above a nearly empty glass vial. "And why on earth Mademoiselle Pretents thinks anyone would want a few specks of smelling salts is beyond me, but at least she gave something, so I didn't think it fair to chide her."

"Then hopefully my addition will be welcome." Ben's hands appeared from behind his back and he set down a pile of folded papers.

Fascinated at what he'd created, she retrieved one and held it to eye level. A miniature crane, creamy white, complete with long neck, wings, and an inked-in dot for an eye stared back at her. She looked from the crane to the man. "I didn't know you were a master at paper folding."

His gaze locked on to hers, one brow curving ever so slightly. "A man must have some secrets to keep a lady intrigued."

Warmth settled low in her tummy. La! She was more than intrigued with this man—and as confused about the sudden emotion he aroused in her as she was about the meaning of the coin in her pocket.

"Pardon me, miss, sir."

They both turned as the small maid entered and dipped a curtsy. "You asked, miss, and so I've counted. There are five tradesmen remaining downstairs. Two tired of waiting and have since left."

"Very good." Clara smiled at her. "We shall deliver the boxes shortly. Thank you, er. . . ?"

The short woman tucked her chin. "It's Betty, miss."

"Thank you, Betty."

Once again she curtsied, then darted out of the room—as the sound of laughter and conversation ambled in. Miss Scurry and Mr. Minnow crossed the threshold, the lady lifting her gaze to Mr. Minnow, a brilliant smile stealing years from her face. Mr. Minnow's elastic lips moved at a steady speed, engrossing the older lady with some sort of story. Regardless of the age difference, the two seemed to draw as much happiness in their companionship as a married couple might. Both carried an assortment of boxes.

Ben nudged Clara. "Looks like Minnow's found himself a lady friend. Feeling jealous?"

She ignored him, for any response would only fuel his teasing.

When Mr. Minnow paused for a breath, Clara cleared her throat, and the two new arrivals looked her way.

Immediately Mr. Minnow dashed over, bypassing her and Ben to set the boxes he'd been carrying on the table. Then with clipped steps, he stood at smart attention in front of Clara.

"I've brought you something." He clicked his heels twice, then pulled out a collection of small paper bags from his pocket. Balancing them in the crook of his arm, he held a single bag out to her. "This one is expressly for you."

"Why Mr. Minnow, very thoughtful of you."

Next to her, Ben did a poor job of concealing a disgusted sigh.

Once again she ignored him and reached for the offered gift, then unfolded the top of the bag. The scent of ginger wafted out. Inside were amber balls, the size of her pinkie fingertip. She smiled up at the fellow. "Ginger drops are a favorite of mine."

"Isn't that lovely!" Miss Scurry exclaimed.

Mr. Minnow grinned so widely, Clara feared his face might split. With a military pivot, he strode back to the table to add his donation to the rest.

Ben leaned close and whispered in her ear. "So that's why he always smells of Christmas cakes."

She tried to shoot him a scolding frown but failed, for in truth, he was right.

Miss Scurry turned from the table, where she'd set her boxes, as well—except for one she carried over to Clara. "I've brought something also, my dear. Would you like to see?"

The fine hairs at the back of Clara's neck lifted. Clearly the woman wanted her to take the box and open it. But if she did, would a mouse rise up and possibly escape? A shiver ran across her shoulders, feeling like a hundred little rodent feet.

Ben reached for the box. "May I?"

"Oh, yes! What an honour. What a delight." The old lady beamed at him.

Stepping aside from Clara, Ben removed the lid, then turned to her and tilted it so that she might see. Inside, nestled on a folded white kerchief, lay a penny.

Clara's eyes widened. "I hardly know what to say. This is more than generous, Miss Scurry."

"Tush! We can't send those fine tradesmen off with naught but trifles."

Mr. Minnow gained the lady's side and gathered her hand. "You are a true lady, madam." He bent and kissed her fingers.

Miss Scurry fluttered her free hand to her chest. "Oh! Such a gentleman."

Rolling his eyes at the two, Ben turned away from the dramatics and strode over to the table. "Let's get packing. Those men have waited long enough."

They joined him, and before all the boxes were opened, Clara said, "We need only five for the tradesmen, but I thought it might be nice to make Betty one for all her hard work."

Between the four of them, it didn't take long to pack up the treasures. Clara even retrieved some red thread from her sewing basket and tied a bow on each one. "There."

"Beautiful!" Though only one word, Miss Scurry's voice warbled it like a song.

Ben stacked the boxes in his arms, and the pile sat precariously up to his neck.

Clara removed the top two. "You'll never make it down the stairs without dropping one. I'll go with you."

Miss Scurry clapped her hands. "Lovely! Now, Mr. Minnow, about that story you were telling me..."

"Ahh, yes! A real thriller, is it not?" He fairly skipped over to the settee and patted the cushion beside him. "Should you like to hear the end?"

"Indeed, sir."

Clara exchanged a glance with Ben as they exited the room.

Out in the foyer, well out of earshot, Ben smiled down at her. "Quite a little friendship those two have struck up."

"I think it's good for both of them."

"And what do you think is good for us?"

"I. . ." Her mouth dried. How to answer that?

He winked. "No answer required."

Heat flooded her cheeks. Thankfully, he averted his all-knowing gaze and turned down a rather poorly lit corridor. She followed at his side, uncertain what else to say. So she said nothing—and neither did he, until they came to a plain stairway near the back of the house.

Ben paused on the first stair. "This seems the most logical route."

She followed. The lower they descended, the stronger the aroma of cabbage soup. Clara's stomach clenched—as did her heart—but not from the scent. Cabbage soup had been a favorite of her father's. A dish he cherished even more than he did her. During his last days, she'd tried to make it just to please him, refining the amount of salt, the addition of ham bits, the sprinkling of a fine grating of pepper. Nothing satisfied him, least of all her. Just one more example of her failing to gain his love before he died. Her step faltered, and the boxes jiggled.

Ben reached the landing and turned to her. "Are you all right?"

Shoving down the sour memory, she forced a smile. "Yes, just a slip."

She cleared the last three stairs without incident while he waited. Then they navigated the barren maze of the downstairs world side by side. Finally, they found the kitchen.

Inside, five men rose from the slab of a table at center. Each wore work-stained clothing and frowns. A few of them exchanged glances. Without a word, all lined up with their hands out.

Ben went to the far end while Clara handed one of her boxes to the first man. "Thank you for your service," she said.

He nodded his head and gruffed out, "Thank ye."

Stepping to the next man, she held out his gift. "Thank you for your service."

But he didn't take it. He just stared, his eyes sharp and black as basalt. He studied her with a curl to his upper lip, like a mongrel facing an unknown adversary. He smelled of dogs as well. "Wouldn't stay 'ere if I were you. A house without its master is like a body without its soul."

He snatched the box from her.

She recoiled a step, wobbling for a moment. Must everything about this place cause her to teeter? She sucked in a breath. Nine more days. Just nine.

But what would tomorrow bring?

The Fourth Day

DECEMBER 27, 1850

CHAPTER FIFTEEN

Clara rushed through her morning routine, shivering all the while. Not that she could blame the housemaid for having an unlit hearth when she awoke. Hopefully more servants would arrive today from the nearby village now that the staff's one-day-a-year holiday was over.

She rose and smoothed her skirts, then crossed to the door. On second thought, she returned to the dressing table and picked up the gold coin, secreting it in her pocket. Ben was right. Someone wanted her to have it—no sense finding the coin stolen when she returned. Mademoiselle Pretents had yet to find her missing jewels, despite her snooping about the great house and Mr. Pocket's detective skills.

Reaching for the knob, Clara swung the door open, then stopped. The hall was empty, save for a pair of ice skates blocking her exit from her chamber. She picked them up with a smirk. Too big to fit under her door, eh?

She hurried downstairs to the dining room, hoping she wasn't the only one to receive such a gift. Once she cleared the landing and wove her way from foyer to corridor, her hope turned into reality. Mr. Minnow strolled ahead of her, a pair of skates slung over one of his thin shoulders.

He turned, and a huge smile split his face. "Ahh, Miss Chapman. A hearty good morning to you, and so it shall be, for I see you carry a pair of skates yourself."

She gripped her skates with both hands before the man could offer his arm yet again. "Indeed I do, sir. Do you suppose our elusive host is responsible?"

"I would imagine so, my pet."

The intimate name rankled. She'd hoped he'd tire of using it by now. Clearly not. "Mr. Minnow," she began, "I would prefer it if you would not call me—"

"La!" Mademoiselle Pretents blustered up from behind. "I am given ice skates but not my jewels. What's this? You have them too?"

The three of them entered the dining room before Clara could answer, but truly, did the woman really need confirmation when she could see they each toted a pair?

Ahead, Miss Scurry turned in her chair, where she took breakfast at the head of the table. Her elfish chin twitched when she smiled. "So lovely!" Then she swiveled back to Ben and Mr. Pocket, seated on either side of her. "You were right, gentlemen. We have all been blessed with ice skates."

In the nearest corner, three other pairs leaned against the wall. Clara laid hers next to them, then headed for the sideboard.

Ben and Mr. Pocket rose from their seats, waiting until she and Mademoiselle Pretents filled their bowls with a thin, gruel-like substance and came to the table. Ben held out the chair next to him, and Clara rewarded him with a smile.

"Thank you," she said.

He leaned toward her. "You may not be too thankful when you taste that porridge."

After one bite, she shoved the bowl away. Even a swine would turn up his nose at this slop.

Ben reached for the teapot and filled her cup, adding an extra sugar drop and more milk than usual. He winked. "For your skating stamina."

As usual, he was right, for the tea filled her tummy and warmed her to her fingers and toes.

Mr. Pocket stood and addressed the table. "In honour of our absent host, I propose we accept the challenge and resign ourselves to the frozen pond out back."

"Pah!" Mademoiselle Pretents spat out. "Go ahead and run off, Inspector. You are worthless at finding my jewels, anyway. But I do not skate. Nor do I see *Monsieur Tallgrass* having to submit himself to the cold."

Mr. Pocket pursed his lips, sticking them out nearly as far as his nose. "Speaking of which, has anyone seen him this morning?"

Mumbles circled the table.

"Right. Well, I'll go check on the fellow, then meet up with you, eh?" He exited before anyone could refuse.

Everyone grabbed their skates, except for Mr. Minnow, who not only finished off his porridge but was currently scraping out the dregs of hers as well. After retrieving their coats, they gathered in the foyer. Then the group roamed a few hallways with Ben in the lead, until discovering a door at the back.

They all paused, waiting for Mr. Pocket to join them. They waited so long, warmth trickled between Clara's shoulder blades. "Perhaps we could begin without Mr. Pocket?"

Ben nodded. "He seems a capable-enough fellow to find his way to the pond."

Clara turned to Miss Scurry. "Are you sure you'll be able to manage this?"

"Such a dear!" the woman twittered. She set down her box of mice and tucked it aside in a corner, then peered up at Clara, a sparkle in her eye belying the wrinkles on her face. "But you see, I am quite capable."

The woman darted outside.

"I suspect there is more than meets the eye in that one," said Ben.

Clara exchanged a glance with him, then exited as he held the door for her. Outside, a draught of wind nipped her cheeks, but oh how lovely to be away from the manor's dark-paneled walls. A path had been shoveled, bare grass peeking up and crunching beneath her shoes as she walked. Thicker blankets of snow snuggled amongst tree roots and crested in piles against the north side of rocks. The sun shone with glorious brilliance, and when the next gust blew, glittering fairy dust sprinkled over their hats and coats. The group stopped at the pond's edge, a great swath of which had been cleared of snow.

Ben guided Clara to a downed log, likely set there for just such a purpose. "Shall I help you?" he asked.

"Do you really think you need to?" She gave him a knowing smile.

He returned it—then added a wink and crouched in front of her. The touch of his hand guiding her foot into the skate sent a charge up her leg. A shameful response, but completely delicious. His head bowed over his work, a small blessing, that. For if he glanced up now, she'd be undone.

He buckled on her skates in silence, but she had no doubt as to what memories played in his mind. Two winters ago at just such a skating party, he'd first pledged his love. Despite the cold, she loosened her scarf. Keeping warm was not going to be an issue, for heat burned a trail from tummy to heart.

Standing, Ben offered his hand. "Off you go."

Refusing to meet his gaze, she righted herself and sailed onto the ice. Miss Scurry already whirled and twirled near the edge, while Mr. Minnow yet struggled to shove his long feet into his skates. Mademoiselle Pretents didn't even try to accommodate. Skates forgotten on the ground at her feet, she stood with her back to them, arms folded, a dark grey smear on the lovely day. Why had she even bothered to join them?

Turning from the sight, Clara dug in her blades. Brisk air tingled on her face, driving her onward, faster and—a big hand reached for hers and spun her around.

Ben laughed, his voice low. "Think you can outskate me, madam?" His eyes sharpened with a glimmer of victory.

Her breath caught in her throat. This close, his words puffed out on little clouds of vapor, warming the skin of her forehead. La! Every part of her was warm, for if he tugged with just a bit more pressure, he'd pull her into his arms. She tried to force a scowl, a nearly impossible feat when all she really wanted to do was surrender to the grin that begged release. "I should've known you'd accost me on the ice, sir."

"Yes." He leaned closer, his brow nearly touching hers. "You should have."

He grabbed her other hand and they set off, gliding in rhythm, moving together, blades cutting a fresh pattern into the ice. Closing her eyes, she pretended they were younger, before sorrow had stolen their innocence. She could live here, in this moment, content with the strength of his gait and the way his fingers gripped hers, so firm yet gentle.

Thank You, God, she prayed, silent of voice yet loud of spirit. This was a holy time, this sacred oneness—and her heart broke afresh, for indeed they should have been one by now. Even so, she soaked in this reality, memorizing his strength and grace and—

Without warning, a loud cry defiled the moment.

CHAPTER SIXTEEN

Wait here!" Ben shoved off, leaving Clara safely behind—hopefully. Too much weight on the ice where Minnow had broken through could send them both into a frigid bath. On the far side of the pond, each time Minnow surfaced, he howled another cry for help.

Digging in his blades, Ben tucked his head and sped toward the fellow. Ten or so paces from the man, he scraped to a stop. With one hand, he unwound the long scarf from his neck, then dropped to a crawl, displacing his weight. Testing the ice with each advance, he edged forward, trying desperately to detect any cracking sounds above the racket of Mr. Minnow's splashing and thrashing.

"Grab the side of the ice where you first went in," Ben shouted.

Minnow flailed, too panicked to do anything but froth up muddy pond water.

Judging the distance, Ben halted and knotted one end of the scarf. He secured the other end to his hand and threw it. "Grab on!"

Two tries later, the man snagged the fabric. Ben crawled backward, tugging the wriggling fellow out of the hole like a fish. Minnow shrieked all the way, but Ben didn't stop until they were halfway to shore. Deeming it safe enough to stand, he rose and let go of the scarf, then raced to Minnow, who still lay flat on the ice. When he reached him, Ben sucked in a breath.

The man's left leg jutted sideways between kneecap and ankle, a place where no leg ought to bend. No wonder he'd bawled.

"Clara!" Ben called, and she sailed to his side. "Help me get Mr. Minnow up."

He grabbed one shoulder, the side with the broken leg, and Clara took the other. Together they hauled the man to solid ground, his drenched, muddy clothing soaking into each of their sides.

"Set him down," Ben instructed.

Removing their skates to Minnow's cries and repeated interjections of "Oh, my!" from Miss Scurry was harrowing enough, but Mademoiselle Pretents's running commentary as they did so pushed Ben over the edge.

He stood and towered over the grey demon. "Mademoiselle, call this man *stupidé* or an imbécile one more time, and I shall retrieve my scarf to stop up your mouth."

Her lips pinched shut, rippling like a clamshell, and she stalked to the manor. Her billowing skirts created a wider path to tow Minnow. Miss Scurry fluttered behind them all.

The path to the big house ran at a slight incline. Ben leaned forward to compensate, hopefully taking the bulk of the burden from Clara. Once inside, he paused, glancing past the moaning Minnow to Clara. "You holding up?"

She nodded. "Better than he, poor man."

"Let's press on, then."

A few grunts and many cries later, they managed to drape the fellow on the largest settee in the sitting room.

Chest heaving from the exertion, Clara leaned against the sofa's back and lifted her eyes to him. "Now what? Call for a physician or send him to one?"

Miss Scurry twittered in the doorway, once again clutching her box to her chest. "Yes, indeed! What do we do, Mr. Lane? Oh, the reckoning. I feared it for him, I did."

"No!" Minnow howled. "I cannot leave. I'll lose my prize. Please, Mr. Lane."

Ben kneaded a muscle at the back of his neck, unsure if he ought feel pleased or cursed that they all looked to him for answers. Scrubbing his jaw, he crossed to the hearth, stalling for time and debating what to do. He snagged the scuttle and hefted what coal remained onto the grate. One thing he knew for sure—it wouldn't do for any of them to take a chill.

The next yelp from Minnow made up his mind, and he wheeled about. "Prize or not, it's cruel to allow Mr. Minnow to suffer. I shall go for a carriage at once, and we'll send a servant along with him to the nearest physician."

Minnow started weeping.

Clara knelt at his side, taking one of his hands in hers. "Mr. Minnow, please. Do try to bear up."

"Oh, the pain," he wailed. "And the loss!"

"I understand, sir, but. . ." She paused, as did Minnow, who sucked in a shaky breath and held it as if his very life hinged on her next words.

"Your wish was for a companion, was it not?" Clara asked.

Ben stepped closer, intrigued by the tilt of her head. She was up to something, for she used such a pose whenever trying to persuade him.

Minnow nodded.

"I think, sir, that you have received it already." Clara glanced at the doorway. "Wouldn't you agree, Miss Scurry?"

The older woman pattered in, cheeks flushed from their outside excursion. "How's that, dear?"

"Are you not now one of Mr. Minnow's friends?"

"Why, yes! I suppose that I am. How lovely." The woman drew near, quickly at first, then with more tentative steps. Finally, she stopped and lifted the lid on her box. Eight white mice rose on hind legs, scratching the sides to get out.

"Ch-ch-ch," she clucked and poked one to knock it back, then she beamed down at Minnow. "My friends are yours as well. Would you like to meet them? Ahh, but I thought you would." Her finger rested like a benediction upon each mouse as she spoke. "Here is Love and Joy, Rest, Want, and Peril." Hesitating, she shook her head, and her face darkened as she nudged the final three in the rump. "And here is Distress, Disease, and Turnip."

Ben studied the woman. Had she lost her senses?

But then as suddenly, her eyes cleared and the dimples at the corners of her mouth reappeared. "I am delighted to share my companions with you, Mr. Minnow, being that you are now one of my dearest friends. My, but we shall have a time of it, will we not? Until the day of reckoning, of course." She pressed the lid back on top of her box and clutched it to her chest. "But now my dears are weary, and so we shall retire." Without another word, she whirled and scurried off.

"And there you have it, sir. Your time at Bleakly Manor has been profitable, indeed." Clara pulled her hand from Minnow's. "Shall we send you to get mended up, then?"

Minnow's lower lip quivered. "I. . .I had hoped that companion would've been you, my pet."

Even in pain the man didn't give up. Serious rival or not, Ben stepped closer to Clara. "A friend is a friend no matter the age or size."

"Indeed," Minnow conceded, until a shudder ran the length of his body and he groaned, his face draining of colour.

Ben snapped into action, calling out as he strode to the door. "Clara, would you retrieve a blanket to cover Mr. Minnow while I arrange things?"

"Of course." Her sweet voice faded as he entered the hall.

Mr. Pocket careened around a corner, nearly bumping into Ben. The inspector, dressed for the outdoors, jumped back a step. "What's this? I was just coming to join you outside and here you are, looking as if you've rolled in snow and dipped half your body in mucky water. What's afoot now, Mr. Lane?"

Ben hesitated, the same eerie feeling of being watched shivering across his shoulders. No, more likely he was simply chilled to the marrow. He shook off the strange sensation. "Mr. Minnow took an unfortunate spill into the pond, breaking his leg in the process. We need a carriage brought 'round for transport to the nearest doctor."

"I shall see to it." The inspector pivoted and dashed down the corridor before Ben could say anything.

Running his fingers through his hair, Ben set off toward the stairway leading down to the servants' quarters. All the while, he mulled over the odd behaviour of the inspector. Ben hadn't been asking or commanding the man to retrieve a carriage. Why such instant accommodation?

A gruff-looking maid, the antithesis of Betty, exited the stairwell before he could descend. She neither met his gaze nor acknowledged his presence.

He blocked her from hurrying past him. "Excuse me, but we need an attendant to travel with one of the guests to the nearest physician. Could you see about finding one?"

She whirled and marched back down the stairs.

He watched her go, unsure if the woman was mute or just rude. A stranger household could not be found in all of England. Hopefully she'd carry out his instructions. Time would tell, no doubt.

And time he ought to retrieve his scarf. Retracing his steps to the back door, he pulled it open and stalked down to the pond. Once on the ice, he half slid and half walked to where his scarf lay in a heap. He picked it up, then wheeled about and dissected the path that Minnow had skated.

Off to one side, part of the man's skate lay forgotten. Could the silly fellow not even buckle on his skates properly? Bending, he scooped it up and squinted at the broken bit. File marks scratched the metal at the edges where the blade had snapped. He peered closer. Someone weakened that metal, in hopes that after not too many glides, the skate would break and Minnow would take a vicious tumble, especially if he were going fast.

Moving on, he scrutinized the pond near where Minnow had cracked through the ice. The area had been shoveled, just like the rest.

Or had it?

Dropping to one knee, he brushed the ice with his fingertips. Ridges marred the surface. So, this hadn't been merely shoveled. It had been shaved, thinned, so that a jab with a broken skate would snap it like a broken bone. He rose slowly, then turned and strode back to the manor. Minnow had been targeted. But why?

And by whom?

The Fifth Day

DECEMBER 28, 1850

CHAPTER SEVENTEEN

Oh, for the blazing sun of an August day. La! Truth be told, Clara would settle for the weak warmth of an April afternoon. Lifting her skirts in one hand and gripping her sewing basket in the other, she dashed down the staircase faster than decorum dictated, in hopes of creating some kind of heat. Since she'd arrived five nights ago, the manor had grown chillier with each passing day.

Hopefully the turn of weather was not making Aunt Mitchell's cough any worse. With effort, she shoved that thought aside. Of course she'd receive word should her aunt's health take a dangerous turn. Wouldn't she?

Upping her pace, she hurried to the sitting room. As she neared the door, Mr. Pocket's voice heated the air inside.

"Stuff and poppycock, I say."

Clara tiptoed to the doorway.

"Pah!" Mademoiselle Pretents swooped over to the man like a falcon on the kill.

Mr. Pocket kept his big nose in his book, refusing to look up.

"I tell you it is a bad omen. Dimwit!" The French tempest stamped her foot. "Everyone knows if a Yule log burns out before Twelfth Night, a year of bad luck follows."

Clara bit her lip, unsure if she ought to enter such a fray.

Spying her from across the room, Ben gave her a wink. A familiar gesture, yet her heart never failed to skip a beat, even if she hadn't figured out where their relationship yet stood.

"Mademoiselle." Ben tapped the fire poker against the hearth bricks, and Clara couldn't help but wonder if he had the urge to use it on Mademoiselle Pretents. "There was no possible way Miss Chapman and I could have hauled back a log large enough to last the entire holiday. Today is well spent, but I assure you, I shall retrieve more wood on the morrow. So you see, it is not a matter of bad luck whatsoever, but merely poor planning on the part of our host."

"What a bunch of flap. Jilly! Turn me around." The girl wheeled Mr. Tallgrass about from where he peered out the window. Facing them, he sneered. "The lot of us ain't had nothing but black luck since we arrived. Were Minnow here, he'd agree. But oh. . .he's nursing a broken leg now, ain't he?" Gruff laughter shook his bones, and he canted to one side. "Oy me rumpus. Jilly!"

The girl sprang into action, and Clara took the opportunity to scoot to Ben's side, clutching her basket handle with both hands. "Sounds like the natives are getting restless."

"Worse. They've taken to blowing poison darts at one another." He smiled down at her, then angled his head toward a leather-bound book on the mantel, a single red ribbon peeking out from the pages. "Thankfully, I discovered a library in the east wing and have taken refuge in the pages of a book, escaping any direct hits myself."

Across the room, Miss Scurry sat alone on a chair, bent over her box and trembling so that the fabric of her skirt shook. Clearly, she had not been so fortunate as Ben.

The sight broke Clara's heart, for it struck too close to home. Was Aunt even now suffering shakes and tremors all alone? Swallowing down the image, Clara lifted up a prayer for Aunt Deborha and strode over to Miss Scurry. "Are you well, ma'am?"

"It is wrong," she murmured without looking up. "Entirely wrong. But then, perhaps, the world was never meant to go right."

Had the woman even heard her? She tried again. "Miss Scurry?"

Slowly, the older lady lifted a blank face. Her eyes narrowed, little creases etching lines into her skin. How many years had this woman seen? How much tribulation?

Then just as suddenly, a smile flashed. "Such a dear, you are. Do you suppose Mr. Minnow has received his reckoning?"

"I am sure he is on the mend and feeling much better already. Furthermore, I have no doubt you will be able to visit him by the time we are finished here."

"Oh, but his parting foreshadows the final one, I fear. Something is about to happen. Ch-ch-ch." She wrapped her hands tighter around her box, the lace of her collar quivering, the black ribbon of her quizzing glass quaking as well.

What kind of grim prediction was that? Did the woman have gypsy blood running in her veins to foretell such an awful fortune? Clara opened her mouth to respond, but the old lady once again bowed her head over her precious mice, ending the conversation by murmuring endearments to her furry companions.

Clara returned to the hearth, where Ben poked at the few remaining coals.

He slipped her a glance, which despite the lack of flames, shot warmth through her heart.

She spoke in a low tone, unwilling for vulturelike ears to hear and peck her words to death. "I fear Miss Scurry is overwhelmed with what's been happening. If only—"

A deep thudding on the front door interrupted, and she jumped, skittish as the filly she'd once owned. She glanced toward the door, as did everyone else.

"Be at peace, Clara." Ben rose and squeezed her shoulder. "A servant will see to it."

More bangs followed.

And again.

"You sure about that, Lane?" Mr. Pocket set down his book and rose from the settee, then strode to the door.

The way they were slowly dwindling in number, was it safe for the man to go off on his own? She peered up at Ben. "Perhaps you ought to go with him."

"The inspector is a capable man." He released his hold of her. "But if you wish it."

With the exit of the only two able-bodied men, tension pulled the silence of the room into an almost unbearable tautness. Whom would Mr. Pocket and Ben usher in once the front door was opened?

Quietly, a low chant crept in from the foyer, slowly gaining in strength. Beautiful voices grew louder, raised in song.

"Fie!" A curse ripped past Mr. Tallgrass's lips. "What rubbish."

A lovely rendition of "Coventry Carol" held Clara in place like a sweet embrace, drawing her and the others toward it—save for Mr. Tallgrass. Jilly left him behind, following as far as the sitting-room door.

Clara crossed to Ben, huddling close for whatever warmth he might share. The open door allowed in not only the chorus of five carolers, but a wicked icy draught as well. Cold air coiled beneath her skirt hem and skimmed up her legs. Fighting a shiver—for surely Ben would force her to return to the sitting room if he suspected she were chilled—she focused instead on the chorus.

Harmony heightened and dipped in perfect rhythm as the five singers crooned, all bright eyed and merry despite the minor key of their tune. The women, two of them, wore matching cloaks of deep green, and the men contrasted in caramel-coloured overcoats. Smart bonnets and top hats tipped back as they lifted their faces for a crescendo.

Clara's spirit couldn't help but be lifted along with the swell. Giving in to the magic of the moment, she thanked God for small gifts such as this.

Mademoiselle Pretents and Mr. Tallgrass were entirely wrong. Silly naysayers. With music so melodious, ill luck didn't stand a chance this day.

But then a tremble crept down her spine as she remembered exactly what day it was and why the carolers had chosen this song above all others. December 28. Childermas. The day commemorating the massacre of innocents in the attempt to kill the infant Jesus.

The lovely spell shattered into shards of despair.

"You all right?" Ben whispered into her ear.

"I. . ." How to answer? That all she could imagine now were broken little bodies of wee babes and tots? Bloodied and ruined. Her stomach turned. *Pull yourself together, Clara.*

She peered up at Ben, hoping her skewed thoughts didn't show on her face. "I believe I shall go get my shawl."

He gazed at her, his stare dissecting truth from bone, yet he said nothing, just gave her a nod.

Whirling, the haunting music pushed her onward—until the horrid gaze of the lion she must pass under slowed her steps. Throbbing started in her temples, and her blood drained to her feet. Surely the thing didn't see her, didn't mark her as prey to be devoured. So why did she suddenly feel like one of those innocent babes in the carol?

The Sixth Day

CHAPTER EIGHTEEN

The wagon bumped over the same route to the woods Ben had taken four days earlier with Clara. This time, however, he wouldn't offer his coat to his companion, even though the inspector's big nose was reddened by the wind. With a "Walk on!" and a snap of the reins, Ben urged the horses forward. The best he would do for Mr. Pocket was get them to the break of the trees more quickly.

Hunching into his coat, the inspector pulled down his hat brim. "I've noticed you and Miss Chapman are well acquainted."

The next gust of wind hit him as sideways as the question, and he turned his face from it. Not an indictment from the man, just an innocent observation—laced with innuendo. But why? Of all the topics the inspector could've brought up, he'd chosen Clara?

Ben shifted on the seat. "You could say that."

"I believe I just did." Pocket sniffed, his nose growing redder by the minute. "She's been promised quite a sum if she remains the duration. Is her situation dire without those funds?"

Ben measured his words and his tone. No sense offering the man more than should be his. "Perhaps you should ask the lady yourself."

"I would, if I could ever get a word with her alone. You always seem to be nearby. Which makes me wonder. . ." Pocket turned to him, his head peeking out from his greatcoat like a turtle from its shell. "What do you stand to gain?"

A direct question, but still a covert attack—one that he wasn't quite sure how to parry. "Sorry?" he asked.

"Were you to marry the lady, why then, whatever is hers rightfully becomes yours. Don't tell me the thought hasn't crossed your mind."

Marry? The word bounced as pell-mell through his skull as the wheels juddering on the frozen ground. It had been simple once, straightforward, but now all the *ifs* of marriage tangled into a big snarl. *If* all his correspondence was answered, *if* he regained his freedom as promised, and *if* his family estate was restored, would Clara still have him? A branded convict?

He snapped the reins again, driving the horses much too fast toward the wood's edge. Pocket's head jerked up and down from the pace, and Ben set his jaw, staring straight ahead, refusing to make eye contact with the inspector. The rage burning up his neck and spreading like wildfire over his face would clearly be seen. Whoever had done this to him and Clara would pay dearly.

Shaving minutes off his last trek to the woods, he yanked the horses to a stop and set the brake. He hopped down and turned into the wind, brisk air stinging his skin. He drank it in like sweet, sweet nectar.

Rummaging at the back of the wagon, Pocket retrieved two axes, then walked to Ben's side and handed one over. "Here you go, Lane."

He grabbed the handle by the throat and hefted the blade over his shoulder, smirking at the irony. Only a week ago he'd have given anything for an ax or sledgehammer to break out of Millbank, with a few extra blows rained down upon the heads of his captors along the way. And now? Here he was, tromping into the woods with a sharp blade in his hands and a lawman at his side. Despite what anyone said, God surely did have a sense of humour.

Scanning the area for any dead trees, he wondered aloud, "Any luck figuring out who stole the jewels or started the fire, Inspector?"

Pocket shook his head. "Nothing solid, but I have my suspicions."

Ben glanced at him sideways. "Such as?"

Pocket snuffled, a great drop of moisture having gathered on the end of his nose. "I never accuse without solid evidence."

"Would that all law keepers shared your convictions."

Pocket's brows disappeared beneath his hat brim.

"Come now, sir." Ben smirked. "No need to continue the charade. I know you're here to keep an eye on me. I just haven't figured out why."

The inspector grunted, neither confirming nor denying the accusation.

Their trek continued in silence. Pausing at the crest of a ravine, Ben pointed down the slope at a snapped-off tree, the top half of the trunk lying downward, with the splintered ends still attached. A wind must have knocked it over last season.

"Looks like you've found our next Yule log," said the inspector.

The footing was tricky, but they set about taking turns swinging at the part of the trunk still clinging to the base. Once that was freed, and any frozen bits broken loose where the rest of it lay in the snow, they could haul it back to the wagon.

"The way I see it, Inspector," Ben said between swipes, "Tallgrass isn't physically able to steal, and Miss Scurry hasn't the mental capacity. That leaves you."

Pocket's ax stopped.

Chest heaving, Ben paused his next swing, as well. "Or the more obvious Mademoiselle Pretents."

"Interesting observation." Arching his back, Pocket removed his hat and swiped his brow. Then he straightened and faced Ben. "Yet you've conveniently left off naming yourself or Miss Chapman."

A slow smile curved his mouth. "Do you really think I'd incriminate her or myself?"

"Touché, Mr. Lane." Pocket inhaled so deeply, his chest puffed out. "I've got the rest of this part, I think. Why don't you go down to the end and pry the wood from the frozen ground?"

Wheeling about, Ben took his smile with him, convinced the inspector truly had no knowledge yet of the mischief maker's identification. The man's pride simply would not allow him to admit it.

Leaning his weight into his heels, Ben slid-walked deeper into the ravine. Maybe it would be better to assess the trunk midway before reaching the bottom. He turned partway—and a loud crack exploded.

He flew sideways. Snow, sticks, rocks mashed into his face as he hit the ground. Flailing, he tumbled headlong into the gorge, then slammed to a stop. He lay, breathing hard. Maybe. Hard to tell. Sound receded. Only a buzzing noise remained, irritating and high-pitched. Heat leaked down his cheek, from temple to chin. Each beat of his heart pumping out more thick warmth from his body to the cold ground.

But at least the thing was still beating.

"Lane?"

His name was far off. Like he'd heard in a nightmare once. No, at Millbank, from the guard outside his door, catcalling through the metal. Was he back there again? Had he never left? He clawed the ground, and his skull seemed to bust in half.

"You all right, Lane?" The words were closer now. Heavy breaths attached to them.

He groaned and pressed the heel of his hand to his head. Sticky fluid suctioned the two together.

A strong arm hauled him to his feet, and he stood on shaky legs, watching the world spin in a white haze. When he pulled his hand from his head, it came away bloody.

"What. . ." He staggered. "What happened?"

"My blade flew off, grazing you. Lucky you turned when you did, or you'd have taken the full brunt of it at the back of your skull." Pocket held up his ax shaft, pointing to the end of it where the sharp hunk of iron should've been. "Someone tampered with my ax."

CHAPTER NINETEEN

Pulling the last stitch through a stocking scarred by previous mending, Clara used the slack to tie a knot, then nipped the thread with her teeth. The chill in the sitting-room air nipped her right back. She tucked the stocking into her basket of sewing, trying hard to pretend she was sitting in Aunt's home instead of a cold manor.

Adjacent to her, Mademoiselle Pretents huddled on a chair, hands clutching a cup of tea near her face, seeking what warmth might be found. "What is taking so long, eh? I'll tell you. Those stupid men are probably lost in the woods. La! But all this cold is not good for my complexion."

Near the empty hearth, Mr. Tallgrass sneered. "Listen to you carping about yer skin. Such a little dainty, are we? A precious, tiny flower? Well, I'm freezing me rumpus off!"

Mademoiselle Pretents glared at him over the rim of her cup. "Unfortunately, your lips are still attached and working."

"So are yours, you shrewish bag o'—"

"Mr. Tallgrass!" Clara cut him off before he fired any more volleys. "I am sure Mr. Lane and Mr. Pocket will return shortly with a new Yule log. Let us wait in peace."

"He does not know the meaning of the word." Mademoiselle Pretents slammed down her cup, rattling the saucer beneath. "He barely grasps *ze* English language."

Clara clenched her teeth. This was going to be a very long day.

A rustle of skirts flurried into the room. Miss Scurry entered, scampering as quickly as one of her mice. "Such devastation. Such loss." The old lady's voice tightened into a shrill cry. "I have lost Love!"

"Oh, flap." Dragging the back of his hand across his mouth, Mr. Tallgrass wiped off a fleck of spittle, then flicked it onto the floor. "I should think at yer age love would be the last thing on yer mind, you crazy old titmouse."

"But Love is gone!" Turning to Clara, Miss Scurry held out her box. "Do say you shall help. She's only just gone missing. She can't have gotten far."

A prickle ran across the nape of Clara's neck. The woman wanted her to look for a mouse? She'd spent her twenty-five years avoiding the things. And if she did find the rodent, she'd surely scare it away with a scream.

"Miss Scurry." She spoke slowly, praying for wisdom. How to dissuade the woman from searching, yet comfort her obvious grief? "I am sorry for your loss, but your mouse could be anywhere in such a great manor."

The lady shook her head, her ruffled cap flopping to one side. "Not any-where, exactly. I had my pets upstairs. Do say you'll come along."

"Oui, go." Mademoiselle Pretents shooed them off with a sweep of her hand before she collected her teacup. "And good riddance."

Some choice. Remain in a room of vipers or search for a rodent. Sighing, Clara tucked her sewing basket against the side of the settee and stood. Miss Scurry led her to the grand staircase, but curiously enough, the old woman didn't stop on the first floor, where their chambers were located. She continued on, exiting on the second-floor landing—where the men resided.

Clara stayed the woman with a touch to her sleeve. "Why were you up here?"

"The reckoning, of course." Miss Scurry blinked up at her, as if she'd just explained the workings of the universe in layman's terms.

Clara's brow pinched. Though she tried, no sense could be made of the woman's strange words. "I'm afraid you'll have to give me more information than that if I am to help you."

Miss Scurry held up her box, and Clara prayed all the while that the ker-chief crammed into the hole on the side would not slip loose.

"My pets must romp, Miss Chapman. No good being shut in a box all the time." She whirled and scampered to the opening of a long corridor, the mirror image of the one that held the women's chambers one flight below. "With the men out collecting wood, I thought to let my companions run the length of this carpet and back. No one to step on them, you see."

It made sense, somewhat. Clara studied the hall. Two doors, one closer and one farther. Same paneled wood. Same carpet runner. But clearly no white mouse scuttled about. She turned to the old lady. "What happened?"

"Oh, such a frolic!" Miss Scurry's whole face lit. "Many happy paws, racing about. All came when I called, except for Love. I fear she darted beneath one of the doors."

Advancing, Clara stopped in front of the first door and squatted. There was a small gap, much like the one beneath hers. Perhaps a mouse had dashed inside, but clearly neither she nor Miss Scurry had any right to enter. She straightened and faced the woman. "These chambers are not ours. Let us wait until Mr. Lane and Mr. Pocket return. Surely they will help us."

Tears sprouted at the corners of the old woman's eyes. The first rolled down her parchment cheeks, then more, until wet trails dripped from her chin. Her lips quivered, and her face folded into grief. "Oh," she wailed. "I fear it will be too late for Love by then."

The old lady's sorrow hit Clara hard in the heart, and her chest tightened. What sufferings in this woman's life had driven her to embrace a sorry-looking box filled with small rodents? True, neither of them had permission to enter a chamber not their own, but did that license her to crush this woman's spirit? Both options seemed wrong.

"Please, Miss Chapman." The woman lifted watery eyes to stare into Clara's soul.

Clara fought to keep from flinching. She hated to give in, yet hated to refuse the old lady even more. "Very well, but I should like to go on record as being against this."

The woman's tears vanished, and she darted around Clara. "I'll take this room." She dashed inside and slammed the door.

Clara stared. Had this been some kind of ploy? She turned the question over, examining all sides of it as she wandered down the hall to the next door. Lifting her hand, she rapped on the wood. With any luck, either Ben or Mr. Pocket would answer, freeing her from having to violate whoever's sanctity this room was—yet no one answered. She tried the knob, and the door gave way easily.

Inside, she paused. On a washstand beside the bowl lay a man's shaving mug and brush, along with a straight razor. Next to the bed on a nightstand rested a book, small and leather-bound, with a single red ribbon hanging out, the one Ben had retrieved from the manor's library.

Tingles crawled down her arms, and she rubbed them. This was Ben's room. How indecent of her to have barged in here. What would he think if he found her thus?

She whirled to leave, but remnants of Miss Scurry's cries yet played in her head.

Fine. Better to get this over with while he was still out gathering wood. A cursory look and she could wash her hands of the whole affair. She strode to the center of the room, then dropped to all fours, for surely a mouse would be on such a level.

She searched from wall to wall, floorboard to floorboard. Nothing scampered except the erratic beat of her heart. A fruitless search, but an honest one nonetheless. She could shamelessly tell Miss Scurry she'd given it a good try.

But before giving up and standing, she saw the bedskirt ripple. Could be a draught from the open door or could be the wayward mouse. But which? She swallowed, unsure if she really wanted to find out the truth.

Slowly, she crawled toward the ruffle, then yanked it up, hoping to scare the fellow before it scared her. Nothing but a heap of stained fabric lay there. She sat back on her knees. No mouse. But wait a minute.

She bent again and pulled out the garment, then held it up.

Her heart broke when she realized what she held. A prison uniform. Torn. Bloodied. Reeking of sweat and despair. And no doubt belonging to Ben. Heaviness clung to her as if she'd put the garment on her own skin. She could only imagine the indignities he'd suffered. The desire to hold it to her breast and weep warred with the impulse to shove it away.

"Victory!" Miss Scurry's voice rang down the hall.

Clara thrust the horrid garment back beneath the ruffle and fled from the chamber.

The old lady grinned at the other end of the corridor. "Love has returned!"

How on earth had the old lady found the thing? Had she truly lost the mouse in the first place, or had this been some ruse to riffle through rooms she ought not be in? Clara puzzled as she closed the distance between them. Whatever the reason, the sooner they returned downstairs, the better.

"I am happy to hear it." Clara patted the old lady's arm, at the same time guiding her toward the stairs.

"The reckoning is complete, for me at any rate. Oh!" Miss Scurry stopped at the top stair and turned to her, lower lip quivering. "Don't fret, dear. Yours will come as well."

Clara hooked her arm through the old lady's, hopefully urging her onward. She'd not rest until they were at least down on their own bedchambers' floor. "I don't mean to pry, Miss Scurry, but I fear I am not very good at riddles. What is it exactly that you'd hoped to gain by coming here to Bleakly Manor? What was it you were promised?"

"That the lost would be found, dear." Thankfully, the lady grabbed the handrail and worked her way down beside Clara.

"Surely you don't mean your mouse?"

"Oh no, dear." The old lady chuckled. "Though I own I am relieved to have found Love. You see, most people mock me for my special insights, such as Mr. Tallgrass or Mademoiselle Pretents. Others simply ignore me, like Mr. Pocket.

But Mr. Minnow was such a gentle soul to me, and then there's you."

They cleared the landing to the second floor, and Miss Scurry turned to her. "Since the moment you arrived, Miss Chapman, you have been the dearest of creatures to me. Why, I'd forgotten how delightful it is to be seen and heard."

Clara licked her lips, still not following the scampering logic of the old woman. "I thank you, but I still don't understand."

"What I lost was my hope in humanity, dear." The old lady patted her arm. "But because of you, I have found it again."

The Seventh Day

DECEMBER 30, 1850

CHAPTER TWENTY

Setting down her plate of cold toast, Clara glanced at the sitting-room door, willing Ben to cross the threshold. A highly irregular chamber in which to eat breakfast, but it was the only room that held any warmth. Despite the blaze in the hearth, she shivered and tugged her shawl tighter at the neck. This manor, these people, were getting to her in a way that crawled under her skin and shimmied across her shoulders. Why had Ben not appeared last night for dinner or for breakfast this morning? Surely by now he'd sent out a letter to every magistrate, barrister, and perhaps every law clerk in the whole of England. It wouldn't do for her to visit his chamber, but she determined then and there that next time the maid Betty entered the room, she'd send her to ask after him.

"Looking at that door will not make your lover arrive any faster." Mademoiselle Pretents's dark eyes needled her from across the room.

A hot trail burned up her neck. Must the woman be so hateful? "Mr. Lane is not my lover."

The woman's lips pulled into a feline smile. "Ahh, but you want him to be, no?"

Near the hearth, Mr. Tallgrass ripped out a crude laugh.

Mr. Pocket rose from his seat and faced the woman, skewering her with a dark look. "Mademoiselle, your coarse innuendos are inappropriate. Besides, how do you know Miss Chapman is not looking for Miss Scurry? That lady has yet to join us this morning as well."

"Pah! Stupidé man. What do you know of ladies? Nothing, I tell you." She turned in her seat, murmuring more epithets beneath her breath and ending with a foul assessment at his failure to find her missing jewels.

Picking at a bit of something in his teeth, Mr. Pocket retreated and sat beside Clara on the settee. "I am sorry you must endure such language."

She turned to him, a sheepish smile quirking her lips. "Thank you, Inspector. But I confess I have been watching for Mr. Lane."

Leaning back against the cushions, Mr. Pocket folded his arms. "I wouldn't worry if I were you, miss. Perhaps he's just having a good lie-in this cold morning." The inspector's eyes widened. "Well, well. Speak of the devil and he doth appear."

Heedless of what Mademoiselle Pretents might think or say, Clara's gaze shot to the door—and she gasped. A scabby gouge ran from Ben's brow to his temple. Deep purple spread out in splotches to his eye. An awful, ugly injury. One that might've taken his sight. Or his life.

She flew to his side. "Are you all right?"

"A little mishap, but don't fret." He smirked. "I've seen worse."

No doubt he had, and the thought stung her eyes with tears. Gently, she pushed back his hair for a better look. Sweet mercy. There was nothing little about this. "What happened?"

Ben pulled her hand away and whispered, "All eyes are upon us."

Indeed. She could feel the sharp stab of Mademoiselle Pretents's gaze in her back. Of course Ben wouldn't give her any details. There was no way to have an unmolested conversation in here.

She retreated a step. "I am happy you are accounted for, but I wonder about Miss Scurry. She's usually the first one to breakfast. You didn't happen to see her on your way down?"

"I did not, but that determined look in your eye tells me I shall not rest until I have checked on her for you." He wheeled about and left as quietly as he'd arrived.

"Not without me." Clara followed.

So did Mademoiselle Pretents's voice. "That's right, chase him like the little puppy dog you are."

She tried to ignore the woman and then the lion in the foyer, but both managed to slip beneath her guard, prickling and uncomfortable. Hurrying on, she caught up to Ben on the stairs. "What really happened to you?"

He shrugged. "Yesterday, chopping wood, the inspector's blade flew off and caught me in the head. Had I not turned when I did, well, I have God alone to thank for that."

Lifting her gaze to the heavens as they climbed the stairs, she breathed out, "Amen to that." Then she peered up at Ben. "I was concerned when you didn't appear for dinner and said as much to Mr. Pocket, but he told me you'd said something about attending to business. I assumed that meant writing more letters. I had no idea you'd been injured. Why would he keep that to himself?"

"I don't know." At the top of the stairs he paused and kneaded a muscle at the back of his neck. "And I don't like it."

She caught up to him. "Oh, Ben, are you all right? Truly?"

"A bit of head banger, but I'll live. When I returned yesterday afternoon, I lay down for only a moment, or so I thought. Next thing I knew, the sun was up." He smiled down at her. "Forgive me?"

"Of course."

"Then let us check on Miss Scurry." He pivoted and strode to the old lady's chamber. Lifting a fist, he rapped on the wood. "Miss Scurry? Are you in there?"

No answer.

Stepping aside, he allowed Clara to advance and knock.

"Miss Scurry, are you well?"

Nothing.

Reaching past her, Ben tried the knob, and the door opened. "After you. We don't want to frighten the lady if she's abed."

Holding her breath, Clara padded in, afraid of what she might find. What if the old lady had passed during the night and was cold and grey beneath her counterpane? She forced her gaze to land on the bed.

But the covers were untouched, with nary a wrinkle.

"Over here." Ben stood at a curio near the window, holding out a small, sealed envelope. "For you."

Her? She retrieved the missive, and sure enough, *Miss Chapman* was written in shaky cursive. Breaking the seal, she withdrew a small note.

"What does it say?" Ben's voice rumbled behind her.

As she read, warmth spread in her chest, as much from the closeness of the man behind her as from Miss Scurry's sweet words.

"She got what she came for," she murmured as she read. "And she feels no need to remain any longer. She left early this morning."

"But that makes no sense."

"Surprisingly, it does." She folded the note and turned, face-to-face with Ben. "Miss Scurry told me yesterday that I had restored her hope in humanity, all because of my kindness. And that was what she'd lost. Her hope."

Ben stared deep into her eyes, never once varying his gaze. Slowly, he raised his hand and brushed his fingers along her cheek.

Her heart took off, the beat so deafening, surely he could hear it.

"You bring light and air where there is none." His throat bobbed, and a small groan rumbled low. Some kind of war waged behind his stormy gaze, frightful yet alluring, as if he wrestled with—

His mouth came down on hers.

And a thousand suns exploded. He tasted of a summer day, all warmth and promise, and she melted against him. Fire licked along every nerve, birthing a hunger for more. Running her hands up his back, she pressed closer. They'd kissed before, proper and polite, but not like this. Never like this.

Closing her eyes, she surrendered, giving in to a need she never knew existed. His mouth travelled along her jaw and down her neck, until her legs trembled and she could hardly stand. A tremor shook through him as well.

Then he pulled away, chest heaving.

And for some odd reason, her world fell apart. Loss cut sharp. Such passion, once savored, was impossible to walk away from so easily. Lifting a shaky hand to her mouth, she pressed her fingers against lips that felt full and hot.

"Clara, I—" There was an edge to his voice. Primal and raw. He raked his fingers through his hair, breathing hard.

Then he wheeled about and stalked from the room.

How long she stood there, staring at the empty door, she couldn't say. There was only one thing she was sure of. This new Ben was different from the former.

And she wasn't entirely sure what to think about that.

The Eighth Day
December 31, 1850

CHAPTER TWENTY-ONE

Sidestepping Mademoiselle Pretents, who stood with hands outstretched to the hearth, Ben wound his way across the sitting room. How she'd managed to oust Tallgrass from the spot was anybody's guess, though Ben suspected her forked tongue could prod a lame oxen to move along. But besides her continual grousing, events of the day had stretched into an uneventful New Year's Eve. A blessing, that, for his head still ached from the strafing by the ax.

And he wasn't sure he'd ever forget that kiss.

Shoving the thought away, he closed in on the sideboard and dipped the ladle into the punch bowl. This late into the evening, the wassail had chilled, but even so, the spicy scent of cinnamon and cloves wafted up. Outside, wind rattled against the panes, begging for entrance.

"It is a rather dreary New Year's Eve." Behind him, Clara's sweet voice tempered the clattering windows. "Shall we play a game?"

"What's it to be, then?" Mr. Tallgrass snorted. "Blind Man's Buff? Sardines? No, I've got it. How about a relay? A real sweat breaker of a mad dash. Give Jilly the race of her life."

"I—I didn't mean. . .I mean, I didn't think. . ." Clara faltered, her words dying a slow death.

Glass in hand, Ben turned from the table and impaled Tallgrass to his wheeled chair with a glower. "I am certain Miss Chapman meant no insult to you, sir. There are other games besides those requiring physical ability."

"Charades didn't turn out so well." The inspector set a figurine back onto a shelf, either satisfied he'd memorized the details of it or as bored as they all were. Mademoiselle Pretents whirled from the hearth and billowed over to the game table. She yanked out a drawer, then held up a deck of cards. "Come over here. All of you. Let us play Five Card Loo. Everyone has money, no? It is New Year's Eve, after all. Maybe I can earn back the value of my stolen jewels."

Gripping the glass so tightly it might shatter, Ben delivered the wassail to Clara. He was unwilling to admit no money weighted his pockets, though surely everyone suspected as much.

Clara smiled up at him. "Thank you."

He studied her as she took a sip. Her raven hair shone blue-black in the glow of lamplight. Her dress, while nothing as grand as she once wore, fit against her curves in a way that bewitched. He stifled a smirk. No, it wasn't bad luck at all that he didn't have any money, for he was here, with her, a far better lot than rotting in a ship's hold on the way to Australia.

Mr. Tallgrass rumbled in his chair. "Listen, you French witch, if I had any capital, then I wouldn't be here, now would I?"

Setting down her glass of punch, Clara searched in her pocket and pulled out a small silk pouch. Coins tinkled as she poured them into her palm and fingered through them.

Ben narrowed his eyes. What was she up to?

She crossed over to Mr. Tallgrass and held out a half farthing.

The man sneered, his gaze bouncing between the coin and Clara. "What's this?"

"A gift, sir." Her smile shamed them all. "To ward off poverty and misfortune this coming year."

Tallgrass snaked out a hand and snatched it from her, testing the metal of the coin with his teeth. Satisfied, he tucked it away with a grunt. "Fine. Right fine."

Whirling, she padded back to Ben, and his breath hitched. Did ever a purer soul walk the earth? He reached for her hand and gave it a squeeze. "He's right, you know."

Her nose scrunched, the little creases adding to her charm.

"That was a *right fine* thing you did," he explained.

She pulled away, then pressed a coin into his palm, shaking her head to ward off his refusal. "May you have a blessed new year, as well."

He swallowed against the tightness in his throat. "May we both," he whispered.

The first chime of midnight bonged low and resonant. Lacing his fingers with hers, he thanked God with each successive strike of the hour. Not the New Year's he'd expected, but expectations were a realm one ought not dwell in for long.

"A very merry new year to all." Mr. Pocket's voice was a benediction on the echo of the last chime. "A toast is in order, I think."

Smiling, Clara let go of Ben's hand and bent to retrieve her glass. He snagged one of his own, and the unlikely group all lifted their wassail.

"To the master of the manor and the winner of the prize, whomever that may be." The inspector's gaze slid from one person to the next, settling on Ben, then narrowed, his eyes nearly disappearing behind his big nose.

Mademoiselle Pretents tossed back her drink. Spinning, she threw her glass into the hearth, shattering the strange moment. "So, are we going to play some cards or not?"

Tallgrass sucked air in through his teeth. "A half farthing ain't gonna go far, but I never could pass up a good game o' Loo. Shove me over there, girl."

The inspector turned to Clara. "This may be a bit beneath your standards, miss. No shame in retiring now." Then he elbowed Ben as he passed by on his way to the table. "Come on, Lane. We can take the pair of them down."

Clara's gaze followed the man. Then she peered up at Ben. "Indeed. It has been a long day. Stay, if you like, for I bid you good night."

She turned and exited before he could argue the point, which perhaps was a good thing. Had he seen her to her room, the beast inside him might not have stayed leashed after another kiss.

"Will you stand like a lovesick steer, or shall I deal you in, eh?" Mademoiselle Pretents's voice pelted him in the back like grapeshot.

Such coarseness didn't deserve a response, but a retort perched on his tongue nonetheless. He opened his mouth—then as quickly shut it and squatted. There, on the carpet, lay a coin where Clara had stood. Gold. Ancient. He snatched it up and chased after her. She was halfway up the stairs by the time he gained the first step. "Clara, you dropped your special coin."

She smiled over her shoulder. "La! Silly me. I should take better care—"

Her foot shot out. Her arms flailed. She plummeted backward. If her head cracked the wood—

No!

He bolted ahead, taking the stairs two at a time. *Oh, God, help me reach her.*

Arms outstretched, he lunged upward and caught her. Barely. Widening his stance, he hefted them both upright, then leaned her back against the railing for support. Other than being wide-eyed and making little strangling sounds, she appeared to be whole.

He peered closer. "You all right?"

She gulped, then nodded slowly. "Yes, thanks to you. But if you hadn't been here—" All colour drained from her face.

"Thank God I was." Indeed. *Thank You, God.* He tucked back a loosened wisp of her hair, and she trembled beneath his touch—or more likely from the horror of nearly breaking her neck. He held out his arm. "Come on, let's get you to your room."

Her fingers dug into his sleeve, grasping for dear life, and no wonder, for so close had she come to losing hers. Blast those long skirts and feminine frivolities such as lace hems and—what on earth?

He transferred her grasp from his arm to the railing. "Wait here."

Three steps beyond where they stood, the carpet runner bled over onto the lower tread. Crouching, he dissected the step. No wonder Clara had lost her balance.

Someone had removed the brass rod holding the carpet in place.

The Ninth Day

JANUARY 1, 1851

CHAPTER TWENTY-TWO

The next day, Clara stood at the sitting-room window, peering out at a landscape smothered by a fresh coating of snow. Clouds, gravid with possibility, threatened to unleash more of the same. A frozen world wrapped tight in ice and cold—or death, should one venture outside unprepared. The thought prickled gooseflesh along her arms, and she rubbed them absently, praying all the while that Aunt was keeping warm.

"You hardly touched your breakfast this morning. Not that I blame you. I ate better at Millbank."

Ben's deep voice warmed her from behind, and she turned from the glass, letting the sheer fall back into place. He stood so close that she breathed in his scent of pine soap, tangy as a woodland forest. His gaze, hinting at unchecked emotion, made her forget about the wintry world outside. Ahh, but she could get used to spending all her days with this man.

He held out his hand. "I've brought you something." A small golden scone rested atop his palm.

"Where did you find that?" Regardless of his answer, she took the morsel from him, lips already moistened in anticipation.

He cocked a brow while she devoured the treat. "Surely you don't expect me to reveal all my secrets, hmm?"

Outside the closed doors of the sitting room, men's voices grew louder. A few good-natured shouts. Some laughter. Had the master of the manor finally arrived now, on New Year's Day? She peered up at Ben.

He swept out his hand. "After you."

Mademoiselle Pretents beat them to the threshold, sliding the doors open wide, with Mr. Pocket at her heels. Mr. Tallgrass merely grumbled in his wheeled chair, requesting Jilly to once more straighten him.

"What is this?" Mademoiselle Pretents marched into the foyer. By the time Clara and Ben caught up, crimson crept in ever-widening patches on the lady's cheeks.

"It is not fair to add more to our number with only four days remaining.

Non!" She stamped her foot, the clack of it resounding on the marble tile. "I will not have it. You hear me?"

"Mademoiselle"—Mr. Pocket leaned toward her—"I do not think it is up to you."

"Pah!" She whirled and stalked back into the sitting room, her grey skirt as puffed up as she was.

Near the front door, Betty, the petite maid who'd fretted over the Boxing Day incident, held out her arms, collecting all manner of brightly coloured hats and scarves and coats. Three men, lithe and lean, continued to add to her pile so that soon it grew to her chin. Any more and she'd go down.

The tallest man of the trio turned to them. "Greetings to you, fine residents of Bleakly Manor. We are the Brothers Penfold." He lifted to his toes and flourished his arm out to his side.

The two others, identically blue eyed and freckled of face, pranced forward with precise steps, lining up in a neat row.

"Dawson at your service." The first one dipped a bow.

"Lawson at your service." The second folded as well.

Mr. Pocket held out his hand, stopping them, and faced the tallest of the men. "Let me guess. You're Clawson."

The man laughed, his shaggy red hair sweeping his collar with the movement. "A valiant effort, but no. Charles, at your service." He bowed so low, his head nearly hit the floor.

Then the three of them snapped into action, tumbling and balancing and leaping into more gymnastics than were feasible in the foyer. All the while, they chanted:

"We come to bring you cheer,

for a very merry new year,

with song, and dance, and rhyme,

for a splendidly wonderful time.

We are the Brothers Penfold!"

The twin men clasped hands and raised them high, while the taller man, Charles, dove beneath the arc and somersaulted to a stop in front of Clara. He captured her hand and brought it to his mouth, pressing his lips against her skin.

She gasped.

Ben stepped closer to her side. She couldn't see, but if she dared a peek, no doubt his hands were fisted.

Charles winked up at her, then jumped to his toes. "My good people, your entertainment begins in an hour. Don't be late."

He pivoted and joined his brothers. As one, the three of them snatched up their bags and turned to the overburdened servant. "Lead on, my fair maiden," Charles said. "For we shall need time to prepare."

Mr. Pocket's gaze followed the retreating performers. "Interesting turn of events, I'd say."

Ben said nothing. He merely ushered Clara into the sitting room with a light touch to the small of her back.

For the next hour, each tick of the clock seemed to go slower, especially with Mademoiselle Pretents working herself into a frenzy. Despite Clara's best efforts at calming her, the lady bristled about the addition of three more people to compete for the prize.

After an eternity, Betty appeared in the doorway. "The Brothers Penfold request your audience in the drawing room."

"Flap and rubbish! I'll freeze me rumpus off in there." Mr. Tallgrass's lips twisted into a sour pout. "Why can't the blasted fellows come in here?"

Betty clasped her hands in front of her, and Clara knew the frustration she must be feeling. They all wanted to strangle the words from Mr. Tallgrass by now.

"Please," Betty continued. "If you would follow me."

Tugging her shawl tight at the neck, Clara huddled close to Ben on their way out. As much as she hated to admit it, Mr. Tallgrass's sentiments were correct. It would be cold away from the sitting-room hearth.

The hallway portraits stared like living creatures. She could feel them measuring and judging each one of them. Clara shivered. What a horrid thought. But the quiver melted as Ben escorted her into the drawing room.

No new draperies had yet been hung since the Christmas tree incident, but even without thick fabric on the windows, the chamber was as warm as a late spring day. A huge fire burned on the grate and appeared to have been lit for quite some time. Why had Betty not suggested they move their party into this room sooner?

"Have a seat, gentlefolk, and let the merriment begin." Charles waggled his fingers at four chairs lined up in front of a cleared area on the carpet. Then he disappeared behind a curtain hung from a frame.

Clara stared, wide-eyed. When had they time to construct that?

"Roll me over, Jilly," Mr. Tallgrass commanded.

The girl put all her weight into shoving the big toady toward the row of chairs.

Mademoiselle Pretents jumped back as Jilly careened too close to the woman's skirts. "Stupidé girl!"

Ben shook his head and led Clara to the seats on the farthest side, placing himself between her and Mr. Pocket.

Lawson, or maybe it was Dawson, strutted out first. Dressed in all black, the only coloured things about him were his shock of red hair, painted white face, and white gloves. The other twin followed, and they bent low, making way for Charles, who entered bearing a sign that read NEWS OF THE REALM ~ A SILENT REVIEW OF 1850.

Clara smiled up at Ben. He smiled back with an arch to his brow, and her heart warmed. So, he'd remembered. Pantomimes were her favorite sort of entertainment.

Without a word, the actors parodied an important event for each month from the past year, from the creation of the first public library last January, all the way up to December and the death of some banker.

A banker? Clara cocked her head. Not that a man's death wasn't important, but who was the fellow?

Mr. Tallgrass startled. "What's that? Who's the money-snatchin' banker what died? Act that out, ye blimey stooges."

Lawson and Dawson dramatized the man's name, but by the time they made it to the last syllable of the last name, Mr. Tallgrass pitched forward in his chair, practically spilling onto the floor.

"Flap! Bayham Bagstock is dead you say? Oh, that's rich. That's more 'n rich." Mr. Tallgrass laughed so hard, his breath wheezed and moisture ran from his nose and eyes. He tilted dangerously to one side. "Oy me rumpus! Jilly, lend a hand."

Clara exchanged a glance with Ben, who shrugged, as much at a loss as her.

"Mr. Tallgrass, are you quite all right?" she asked. "Did you know this Mr. Bagstock?"

"More 'n right, I'd say. Turn me around, girl." Jilly shoved him so that his chair faced them instead of the players, who now stood watching the show put on by the guests.

Mr. Tallgrass grinned. A rare occurrence—in fact, it was the only time Clara could remember ever seeing his teeth exposed in a truly pleasurable fashion. "Mr. Bayham Bagstock is the bugger what's been squashing me beneath his greedy thumb. Now that he's kicked off, there's no more Bagstocks to hound me, not a one. That's what's what and what's right. I'm free!" His shoulders shook with another peal of laugher. "Jilly! Get me rumpus out of here. We're done with this madhouse."

Scowling, the girl leaned her weight into the chair, wheeling him across the carpet and out the door.

"Good riddance." Mademoiselle Pretents shifted in her seat and looked down her nose at them. "That imbécile was getting on my nerves."

Clara pressed her lips tight, trapping a retort behind her teeth.

Mr. Pocket sniffed, his enormous nose bobbing with the force of it. "It seems our number is dwindling, by design or by accident."

Accident? Next to her, Ben snorted, and she would too were she not a lady. There was nothing accidental about anything related to Bleakly Manor.

The Tenth Day

JANUARY 2, 1851

CHAPTER TWENTY-THREE

The tallest Penfold wrapped his multicoloured scarf around his neck with a flourish, and Ben widened his stance on the foyer tiles, resisting the urge to help the brothers out the door more quickly.

Next to him, Clara squeezed his arm and whispered, "Patience is a virtue."

He quirked a half smile down at her. "Whatever gave you the impression I was virtuous?"

Despite their thick wraps, the three Penfolds backflipped, then lowered to one knee, aligned in a row in front of the door. "Adieu, good gentles," they said in unison.

"Pah!" Mademoiselle Pretents whirled toward the sitting room. "Goodbye, silly men."

Lawson and Dawson rose to their toes and pirouetted. Charles somersaulted to a stop in front of Clara.

Oh, no. Not again. Ben sidestepped between the man and Clara. "Godspeed on your journey, Mr. Penfold."

A rogue grin spread across Charles's face, and he rose to join his brothers. "A blessed new year to one and all."

The three dipped a bow, then slipped out into the waiting arms of a January morning. By the time the door closed, a blast of air embraced Ben and Clara as well.

She huddled a step closer to him. "They were merry fellows, were they not?"

His mouth twisted. "Perhaps a little too merry."

"I am sorry to see them leave. At least they were a diversion." She sighed, as if the weight of so many days inside the bleak walls could no longer be contained. "My mending basket is nearly empty, and I confess I shall scream if I must spend another day listening to the mademoiselle badger the inspector for a lead on her missing jewels."

Ben rubbed out a kink at the back of his neck. Just thinking of the harping woman tightened his muscles. "Nor do I wish to write any more letters.

By now I've canvassed every lawgiver in all of England." He blew out a sigh and smiled at Clara. "What say we go for a stroll? I've a new appreciation for fresh air."

She hugged herself. "It's rather cold outside."

He glanced at the front door, wishing for a good leg stretcher, but indeed, hoarfrost crept around the edges of the frame. He turned to Clara and offered his arm. "All right. We shall have an adventure indoors."

She gaped. "Do you think we should? I mean, what if the master of the manor finally arrives, only to find us nosing about his home?"

The shrill voice of Mademoiselle Pretents pestering Mr. Pocket couldn't have been timed better. Ben nodded toward the sitting room.

Clara grabbed his arm. "Adventure, here we come."

Before passing beneath the lion head, Ben veered left, taking them down a corridor he'd seen only the servants use. Before long, shadows closed in, and he retraced their steps back to the foyer.

Clara arched a brow at him. "That was a quick adventure."

Opening a drawer in the trestle table, he retrieved a vigil candle in a glass, lit the wick, and set off again.

Clara matched her steps to his, and that simple action caused an ache deep in his chest. Despite all the wretched treachery of the past year, and yes, even her betrayal at losing faith in him, his heart still yearned to make her his own.

But what did he have to offer her other than the status of a convict? He clenched his jaw to keep from grinding his teeth, determination to find who did this to him—to her—pumping a fresh rage through his veins with each step.

"Have you heard from any of the solicitors or barristers yet?" Clara's sweet voice pulled him back from such abysmal thoughts.

"No. I'm beginning to think my attempts to contact the outside world are being thwarted. That the desk set up in my chamber is nothing but a ruse and the stable boy isn't delivering any of the letters."

"To what end?"

He paused in front of a narrow door and shook his head. "Perhaps I'm being too cynical."

Trying the knob, he shoved the door open, expecting it would lead to a servants' stair. Daylight flooded into the corridor, blinding him for a moment. Blinking, he strode into the room.

"I don't blame you." Clara trailed him. "This is a curious situation."

Inside the chamber, Ben's shoes sank into plush carpeting. A hearth fire burned warm and inviting. A bed, rumpled bedclothes atop it, was to his left, and a small library lined the opposite wall. Writing pens, nibs, parchments, and bottles of ink inhabited every possible horizontal surface. He inhaled, dissecting the air. The smoky scent of Bright Leaf tobacco mixed with the spicy aroma of fine wine, possibly an aged Bordeaux, if he wasn't mistaken. Did the master himself reside in this small chamber?

Clara grasped his sleeve. "We don't belong here. Please, let's leave."

He patted her hand and led them out, taking care to close the door exactly as it had been. In the murk of the corridor, he winked at her, hoping to soothe her fears. "I promised you adventure, did I not?"

She swatted his arm.

Turning, he led them down the rest of the hall, Clara's fingers digging into his arm all the while. If he didn't put her mind at ease, his exploring would be put to an end before he could discover exactly who dwelt in this wing.

"Any news of your aunt?" he asked.

"No, but I suppose no news is good news. Perhaps she is on the mend."

He smiled down at her. "One would hope."

The corridor ended at another door. This time he rapped on it first, just in case it wasn't a stair—and if it wasn't, if a gentleman answered, what ought he say?

Clara grasped his arm with two hands, jostling the candle so that the light guttered. "I think I should prefer Mademoiselle Pretents's badgering to this. Let's go back."

He tried the knob. Locked.

"Ben!"

Ignoring Clara's protests, he pressed his ear against the wood and listened. Only Clara's quickened breaths filled the small space. He'd have to investigate the possibility another time.

Turning his back to the mystery, he offered her a half smile and led her the other way. "So, I take it you've not heard from your brother, either?"

"No, not since he sailed."

Strange, that. Why would a brother, so close to his family, not send word of a safe arrival after travelling the expanse of an ocean? He held the candle higher and glanced at Clara. "Then how do you know that's truly where he went?"

Her brow dipped. "What do you mean?"

"Just that your faith in him is unrivaled." He forced the words out smoothly, struggling to keep the bitterness raging inside from rushing out. Would that she'd have had that much confidence in him.

"I should think as his partner those many years at Blythe, working together for the good of the company, you'd have faith in him as well. Mr. Blythe certainly did, or he'd not have considered George for partnership. But you know this. So why question my brother's whereabouts? George lost his livelihood the very same day you lost yours."

"No, he didn't." He stopped and turned to her. This close to where the corridor opened up to the front foyer, light poured in so that he could read her face. "You said yourself that a week passed before he was summoned by the solicitor."

"Oh, Ben." She rested her palm on his cheek, the touch so intimate, so familiar, it almost drove him to his knees. "I know you want to find out who did this to you, to us, but my brother cannot be to blame. Lay such logic to rest, if for no other reason than for me."

He averted his gaze, looking at anything but the violet pleading in her eyes. Of course he didn't want to blame his friend, his colleague, but the timing of everything was off. And if—hold on. What the devil?

Candlelight caught on a gap in the paneling just beyond Clara. Sidestepping her, he ran his fingers along the edge.

"What are you doing?" she asked.

A nudge, followed by a shoulder shove, opened a small door, just wide enough for him to edge through sideways.

Clara grabbed his coat hem. "Do you think that's safe?"

"Wait here. I'll find out." Narrow stairs forced him to cross foot over foot. A dark ascent, impossible without the candle.

"What is it?" Clara's voice called from below. "What's up there?"

"Looks like. . ."The stairs ended, and he held the candle out in front of him. A remnant of Bright Leaf tobacco wafted like a ghost in the darkness.

"Ben?"

"It's a crawl space," he called down.

Crouch-walking, he worked his way along a thick timber, the walls barely wide enough for his shoulders. Ahead, a beam of light pulled him forward, not brilliant, but enough to indicate it leaked in from somewhere. He pressed on and stopped where a large circle had been cut into the plaster. Beyond the circle was a shadowy depression with two smaller holes at center and a larger one below. Cautiously, he leaned forward, putting his head into the tiny cave, and peered out the two gaps.

Below him was the foyer. The front door straight ahead. The sitting room to the left. A view that could only be seen from one angle.

The lion's head.

The Eleventh & Twelfth Days
JANUARY 3–4, 1851

CHAPTER TWENTY-FOUR

Tucking her needle case back into her sewing basket, Clara glanced at the mantel clock as it chimed. Then frowned. Both Mademoiselle Pretents and Ben had disappeared after breakfast—five hours ago. Now that she'd caught up with her mending, she'd have to invent something else to bide her time.

Across the room, Mr. Pocket gazed at her over the top of the book he'd been reading. "Looking at the clock will not make Mr. Lane appear any faster, you know."

Her face heated from his assessment, yet how could she not help but fret? Ever since discovering that locked door yesterday, Ben had been dead set on revisiting the area. She'd held him off, but apparently not for good—none of which was Mr. Pocket's business.

She straightened her skirts, smoothing her palms along her thighs. "I could just as easily be waiting for Mademoiselle Pretents."

"Could be." He rubbed a hand over his shorn head, the peppery bristles shushing with his touch, then ended by working a muscle in his neck. "But that pretty blush on your cheeks says otherwise."

She averted her gaze, suddenly preferring the burning embers in the hearth to the questions igniting the inspector's brown eyes. How to turn this around? She bit her lip and—that was it. Turn it around, back onto him.

She flashed him a smile. "Have you never been in love, Inspector?"

"As a matter of fact." He set down his book and leaned forward, hands dangling between his knees. "There's a certain woman I intend on courting very soon. Tell me, Miss Chapman, have you any advice on the matter?"

Leaving her sewing basket behind, she crossed the rug to take a seat adjacent to his. "Does the lady return your affections, sir?"

"She does." Mr. Pocket scratched at his side-whiskers before continuing. "Her father, however, is another matter altogether."

"I am sorry to hear that. You seem a fine-enough fellow."

"Thank you, miss. I like to think so."

The melancholy twist of the man's mouth tugged at her heart. He wasn't a dashing figure, to be sure, but neither were his garments threadbare. She looked closer. A ruddy complexion, but no pockmarks. Teeth somewhat stained, yet all present. Clearly he was a capable man, as evidenced by his keen mind and hale body. She tapped a finger on her skirt as she further evaluated him but came up empty-handed. "What is the problem, sir, if I may be so bold?"

"I wish I could say it wasn't money." Furrows creased his brow. "But it always seems to boil down to that, does it not?"

"Indeed." A bitter taste soured the back of her throat. She'd personally experienced all too well how lack of funding and social status turned away those she'd thought were friends. She swallowed and focused instead on the man in front of her. "But surely you make a sustainable living as an officer of the law?"

He nodded. "I'm comfortable enough, but it's not so much the jingle in my pocket. It's more than that. All the trimmings and show of society concern her father the most. He'll see her live nowhere but in a fine London town house." A shadow darkened his face, sinister and almost demonic. "As if Clapham wasn't good enough."

Clara edged back in her seat.

Then just as suddenly, his eyes cleared, and he smiled at her. "Not to worry, though. In three days' time, all will be remedied. I've put a deposit on just such a town house already."

Alarm tightened her tummy, and she pressed her hand to it. How did he know he'd be the one to receive the prize?

"Was that not a bit premature?" she asked.

His dark eyes pinned her in place. "Not if I can pay it off before mid-January."

"But what if you cannot?"

"Then I lose everything."

Her jaw dropped. "Mr. Pocket, do you think that was a very wise act?"

"Sometimes one must act boldly to bring about a bold hope."

"Or a bold failure," she whispered under her breath.

He leaned forward. "What's that?"

"Nothing." She forced a smile and glanced once more at the clock, longing for the sanctuary of Ben's presence. "I wish you the best with your lady, Mr. Pocket."

"Thank you. I believe you mean that, and as such, I am almost sorry my gain will mean your loss."

She shot her gaze back to his. "What do you mean?"

"Thief!" A grey storm cloud blew through the sitting-room door. Mademoiselle Pretents marched over and planted her feet in front of the Inspector—a gun in her hand. "You are *ze* one who stole my jewels. No wonder you could not tell me who took them."

Sucking in a breath, Clara shrank into the chair, putting as much space as possible between her and the crazed woman.

Mr. Pocket merely chuckled. "You are confused, mademoiselle. I operate on the right side of the law."

"Liar!" The woman's voice shook. So did the gun. "Give them to me."

All mirth faded from Mr. Pocket's face, replaced by the same disturbing shadow of moments before. "Put the gun down. Now."

"I will not! I will have my jewels or shoot you like the dog you are." Her voice rose to a screech. "You think I won't use this? Give me the jewel pouch."

With each quiver of the gun's muzzle, Clara's heart beat harder, seeking escape, as did she. She crept to the edge of her seat, debating if the woman would allow her to leave unharmed.

Mr. Pocket reached inside his dress coat.

And whipped out a gun of his own.

Two shots exploded. So did Mr. Pocket's chest. His pistol dropped from his hand, and he flew back against the cushions with a curse. Blood oozed out the torn fabric of his waistcoat. His hand slammed to his chest as he tried to staunch the flow. Red oozed between his fingers.

Clara stared, unable to stop a scream.

The gun barrel swung her way.

"Shut up, *lay-dee*, or you are next."

Chapter Twenty-Five

Two shots rang out, violating the solemn January afternoon. Ben jerked away from exploring the drawing room and ran to the door, listening with his whole body. The gunshot was nearby. Definitely on this floor. Down the hall. Likely the sitting room.

A scream next. Clara's.

His heart skipped a beat—then he bolted down the corridor. *Oh, God, please.*

Just before the door, he forced his feet to a standstill. Every muscle quivered to race in and sweep Clara away from danger, but he'd be no use to her with a bullet through his own head.

Holding his breath, he peered around the doorframe.

And his heart stopped.

Across the room, Mademoiselle Pretents aimed a gun at Clara. Nearby, the inspector slumped against the settee cushion, bleeding.

If that French hothead pulled the trigger again—

Shoving the consequences out of his mind, Ben yanked off his shoe and threw it at the window behind the woman.

Glass shattered.

Mademoiselle Pretents whirled toward the sound.

He strode through the door.

The woman jerked her face toward him, gun barrel trained on his chest. Excellent. Better at him than at Clara.

"*Homme fou!*" The grey menace spit out a host of curses. "Why you do that?"

He held up his hands, appearing to surrender, but continued walking. Smooth steps. Slow. If he could keep her talking long enough to draw close, he stood a greater chance of disarming her.

Unless she shot him first.

"I merely wanted to get your attention." He spoke as to a wee child on the verge of a tantrum. "What's going on in here?"

Across the room, Clara whimpered. Mr. Pocket eked out a painful grunt.

Ben kept walking. Five more paces, and he'd be in range to snatch the gun.

Mademoiselle Pretents's dark eyes rooted on him, murder glinting. "This is none of your concern."

He nodded toward the revolver. "Looks like you just made it mine."

Three more steps.

She straightened her arm like a ramrod, the muzzle jutting closer to him. "Stop! Or I will shoot."

He took another step.

A strangled cry garbled from Clara's throat.

"I told you to shut up, *lay-dee!*" Mademoiselle Pretents yelled.

One pace more. So close.

"She means you no harm, mademoiselle, nor do I." He raised his hands higher, shoulder level, and dared a final step. "Do you have a quarrel with me?"

She opened her mouth—

He shot out his left hand, grabbing the top of the barrel. His right hand snapped into the tender flesh of her inner wrist. The momentum directed the muzzle toward her belly, and she let go.

Transferring the revolver to his right hand, he aimed it at her. "Not so nice to be on the other end, is it?"

Wine-coloured blotches darkened her cheeks. French indictments thickened the air, along with vile names directed at him and Mr. Pocket.

"Clara"—he spoke without varying his gaze—"fetch me a stocking from your mending basket."

Keeping a wide berth from the Frenchwoman, Clara stole over to her basket and retrieved a long silken legging. Perfect.

He tipped his head toward the seat Clara had recently vacated. "Sit in that chair, mademoiselle."

"You are a devil!" She grumbled all the way to her seat, then plopped down, her skirts ballooning like a rain cloud. "I am not the criminal here. He is!" Her evil eye speared Pocket through the heart. "He stole my jewels, I tell you."

Before tying up the woman, Ben glanced at the inspector. A little pale, but not deathly. The heel of his hand kept pressure on the wound, upper right chest, near the shoulder. Blood soaked through his shirt and waistcoat, but not in a pulsing stream. It wasn't a killing shot, unless infection set in. He'd need attention soon, though.

First to secure the French firebrand. Turning his back to the inspector, Ben traded the gun for the stocking in Clara's hand. Worried eyes peered deeply into his. She'd likely never held a revolver in her life.

Mademoiselle Pretents started to rise.

Ben pushed her back. He tied each of her hands tightly to the chair arms. While he worked, the woman called down all manner of fiery oaths upon his head, his mother, and any future children he might sire. Finally, he fumbled with the knot of his cravat and freed his tie, then shoved the fabric into her mouth. The woman's eyes widened an instant before tapering to angry slashes.

For the first time in an eternity, he breathed deeply, pulse finally slowing.

Clara huddled next to him, face drained of colour. "Thank you. If you'd not arrived when you did—"

"Then there would've been one less person for me to deal with." Mr. Pocket's words snarled behind them, followed by the cock of a pistol hammer. "But no matter. I've drawn this out long enough."

Bile seared upward from Ben's gut. The Christmas tree fire. The thinned ice. The flying ax head and the loosened stair carpeting. It all made sense now. Fury quaked through him. Pocket hadn't been sent here to watch him—the man was here to make sure none of them remained.

"Put the gun on the floor, miss. Then turn around and push it to me with your toe. Slowly." Pocket's voice was kicked gravel. From intimidation or pain?

Ben angled his head, listening harder.

"Move one more twitch, Lane, and you're a dead man," Pocket warned.

"Don't worry, Inspector. I've got him covered." The steel in Clara's voice stabbed him through the heart.

He'd taken kidney punches before, sharp enough to stop his breathing, but this time, he doubted he'd ever breathe again. He slid his gaze to the left, where Clara backed away from him.

The gun in her hand aimed at his head.

CHAPTER TWENTY-SIX

The revolver shook in Clara's hands, but not from the cold bleeding in from the broken window or from inexperience with firearms. Her brother had seen to that, instructing her in the pursuit of marksmanship when his friends were scarce.

So while the weight and grip moulded in her palm was entirely familiar, it was the act of aiming the thing at Ben that caused the muscles in her arms to quiver. Calculating the probability of success for such a wild scheme was impossible. She wrapped her fingers tighter around the grip, heart racing. This *had* to work. It must. Or they'd both be dead.

And Ben would go to his grave thinking the worst of her.

"Hold it right there, missy." Mr. Pocket's pistol, smaller than the revolver in her own hand, wavered ever so slightly between her and Ben. "What are you about?"

She dared one more step back, gaining as much distance from Ben as possible. "I should like to parley, Mr. Pocket."

Mademoiselle Pretents whinnied some kind of comment behind the gag in her mouth.

Ben stiffened, the fabric of his dress coat stretching taut across his shoulders.

God, please, may Ben forgive me. Her stomach twisted. Had she not just minutes before portended Mr. Pocket's bold actions might be a bold failure?

"Parley for what?" Mr. Pocket snorted. "I hold the advantage. You shoot Mr. Lane, and I put a shot through you. There's nothing to negotiate."

"Ahh, but there is." The slight smile curving her lips tasted like rancid fat. But showing fear of any kind would attract a bullet. She lifted her chin. "Allow me to reach into my pocket, sir, for I have something of value to offer you."

Mr. Pocket narrowed his eyes. "In exchange for what?"

"My life."

A curse, foul as any Mademoiselle Pretents had uttered, flew past his lips. "I could just shoot you now and take whatever it is from you."

True, except as she studied the pallor of his skin, the red soaking through not only his waistcoat but his dress coat, she doubted he had much stamina remaining. She lifted her chin higher, looking down her nose at him. "You could, but in so doing Mr. Lane would no doubt attack you. You saw how quickly he moves. Do you really think in your state you'd stand a chance of reloading before he disarmed you? Oh, don't look so surprised, Mr. Pocket. I may be a lady, but I can tell the difference between a pistol and a revolver."

She flashed a glance at Ben. It wasn't much, but would he take the hint?

The smell of blood and curiosity tainted the chill air. Mr. Pocket's mouth twisted while he considered her words, as if he sucked upon a lemon sour.

"All right. What will you trade for your life, Miss Chapman?" he asked.

"A coin, sir. One of great value." She dared tiny steps backward as she spoke, inches really, but every bit of gained ground felt like a small triumph. "And in your current financial state, I believe if you add the coin's worth to the prize offered you as the last remaining guest at Bleakly Manor, your money woes shall be at an end. I give you the coin, and you let me leave the manor unharmed. Now."

Mr. Pocket sniffed, not nearly with as much gusto as usual, though. In fact, his nose barely bobbed at all. "All right. Let's have a look at it before I go making any promises. But so help me, miss, if you pull out anything other than a coin, I shall shoot you just for the pleasure of it."

Without moving his body, Ben arched a brow at her.

She prayed with each heartbeat that the poison of her movements and words would not taint what he knew of her trustworthiness from the past. Withdrawing the second-chance coin, she pinched it between thumb and forefinger and held it up so the weak afternoon sunlight would cause it to gleam.

"Very nice." The inspector narrowed his eyes, his tone lowering to a rumble. "But how do I know that's real?"

For the space of a breath, she glanced at Ben, pleading for understanding with her eyes.

Then she snapped her gaze back to the inspector. "Here. Catch."

She tossed the coin to him.

And Ben wheeled about, diving for the man.

Grunts, curses, and the crack of gunshot.

Then nothing but the crash of a picture frame across the room, smashed to the floor by a bullet gone wild.

Pocket moaned on the settee. For once Mademoiselle Pretents was completely silent.

Ben turned, chest heaving—with naught but a mark on his cheek to show for the scuffle.

Clara lowered her gun. "Thank God."

Ben's eyes burned like blackened embers, searching her from head to hem. "Are you hurt?"

"I am not." Her voice shook, as did her whole body, but other than that she remained whole.

With a nod, Ben turned back to the inspector. Heedless of the man's injury, he yanked open Mr. Pocket's dress coat and rummaged inside.

Mr. Pocket cried out like an animal.

Clara winced, the tender part of her heart competing with the vengeful side.

Ben retrieved a small black velvet pouch. "Like you, Inspector, I never accuse without solid evidence."

Mademoiselle Pretents rocked on her chair, throaty roars fighting to escape the gag in her mouth.

Ben turned on her. "Yet neither do I believe these are your jewels, mademoiselle. The courts will decide on the matter. Clara, ring for the maid, if you please. A constable and a physician are in order, I think."

Crossing to the bell pull near the door, she yanked on the golden rope. Cold air blasted in from the window, and she trembled. What an eventful day. A smirk tugged at her mouth. No, what an eventful holiday. With a sigh, she laid the revolver on the sideboard.

"I cannot believe what you just did." Ben's voice accused her from behind.

She froze, fearful to face him. Would he scold? Rebuke? Be angry that she'd pointed a gun at him? Oh, sweet mercy! One wrong move and she could've accidentally shot him. What had she been thinking?

"Clara."

His husky voice turned her around, and his smile weakened her already shaky knees.

"Well done."

The softness in his gaze tightened her throat, and with the last of her strength, she offered him a frail smile. "Thank you."

He stepped closer, smelling of battle and promise. "With those two out of the picture"—he nodded his head toward the subdued pair across the room— "that leaves just you and me. I'd say we are a brilliant team, are we not?"

"Yes." For a moment, she reveled in the unity, the embrace of his unfettered admiration shining in his eyes.

But then reality slapped her as stinging a blow as the next waft of frigid air. Her smile faded.

Ben reached for her but, inches from contact, pulled back. "What troubles you?"

"A team may not receive the promised prize." She bit her lip, working the fleshy part between her teeth. With Mr. Pocket and Mademoiselle Pretents out of the picture, only she and he were left.

She swallowed. Ought she give up the funds she desperately needed so that he might receive his freedom?

CHAPTER TWENTY-SEVEN

The front door closed on a writhing Mademoiselle Pretents, arm grasped tightly in a constable's grip, and the lagging Mr. Pocket, shored up by the strong hold of a physician. The thud of wood against wood faded in the foyer like the last beat of a heart. Clara rubbed her arms, chilled by the night air creeping across the tiled floor. She ought to be grateful there'd been no need to call an undertaker. And truly she was, but an uneasy pressure that'd been building since the day she arrived dwarfed her gratitude.

Fear. What would happen next? Nothing good, considering the way the lifeless lion eyes burned down from its perch on the wall.

Turning from the door, the maid faced her and Ben. "Will that be all, sir, miss?"

Ben nodded. "Yes, Betty. It's late, and tomorrow's a new day. It will do us all well to end this one, I think."

Betty dipped her head. "Yes, sir. Good night, sir. Good night, miss." She scurried past them, the scent of silver polish in her wake.

Clara watched her disappear down the corridor, wondering if the woman would catch a wink of sleep. Would she toil into the witching hours, shining silverware and soup tureens for a nearly nonexistent house party?

"Shall we?" Ben offered his arm. "I'll see you to your room."

She rested her fingers on his sleeve, and he tucked her hand into the crook of his arm. Secure. Warm. A queer tinge rippled in her tummy. Was it safe to hope again?

She peeked up at Ben as they mounted the staircase. "I do feel sorry that neither Mademoiselle nor Mr. Pocket received what they'd come for, and indeed left here with so much less."

"I suppose you could look at it that way."

She studied the strong cut of his jaw, looking for a humorous twitch, but he held it firm.

"What else is there to think?" she asked.

"Well. . ." Ben peered down at her. "Mademoiselle Pretents came here with the hope of a new position in a new household. I'd say she got both, though a cell wasn't likely what she had in mind for accommodations. She is, however, up to the challenge of teaching an entire prison population some new obscenities, in English and in French."

Clara bit her lip to keep from smiling—a nearly impossible task, for the twinkle in his eyes was almost her undoing. "You, sir, are wicked."

"Perhaps, but I am correct, am I not?" He turned to her at the second-floor landing, longing in his gaze—but longing for what? Approval?

Or for her?

Soft light flickered from the wall sconces, bathing half his face in brightness, the other in shadows. Fitting, really. Nine months ago his very life had been golden one moment, black the next. As had hers.

Ignoring his question, she let go of his arm and reached up, tracing a scar from his temple to cheek, one that narrowly missed his eye.

His skin burned against her touch, his gaze asking questions she wasn't sure she wanted to answer. If she leaned closer, raised to her toes, his mouth would be hers once again. She could be his. No one would know.

Except for God.

The thought sobered her, and she pulled back. "What, uh, what of Mr. Pocket?" She set off down the corridor leading to her chamber and called over her shoulder. "You cannot say he shall be rewarded with a magistrate position."

"True." Ben caught up to her in three long strides. "But he will be spending some very personal time with a magistrate, hmm?"

"That doesn't count, and you know it." She swatted his arm with a grin.

"No, but it did coax a pretty smile from you, which was my intent all along." He winked at her.

She matched her feet to her increased heartbeat, hastening down the hall. Passing Miss Scurry's door, she shivered. Now with Mademoiselle Pretents absent as well, she'd sleep alone on this floor.

"It's quite empty here without Miss Scurry," she murmured. "As quirky as she was, I do miss the old lady, but not her mice."

"Two more nights. That's all." Ben pulled ahead of her and reached for the knob on her door, opening it for her. "Just two, and I shall have my freedom and you your money."

"That would be breaking the rules."

"After all that's happened these past ten days, do you really think convention is a priority of Bleakly Manor's master?" He ushered her across the threshold with a sweep of his hand. "Now then, there's no need to worry about anything.

With Mr. Pocket gone, there will be no more mishaps."

She turned to him. "I hope so."

"I know so." Drawing near, he pressed a light kiss to her forehead, whispering "Sleep well" against her skin.

She stood, dazed, long after he pulled the door shut behind him. Sleeping was out of the question, though she did try eventually. She fought with twisted bedsheets the whole of the night, turning one way and another, until just before dawn when she finally surrendered the battle.

Faint light leached through the windowpanes by the time she opened her door, dressed for whatever the day might bring. But she stopped on the threshold, completely unprepared for the sight in front of her.

Across from her door, Ben slept, back against the wall, legs sprawled, head tipped back, wearing the same clothing as yesterday except for more wrinkles. Peace eased the lines on his face. Each rise and fall of his chest breathed life into the boyish good looks she remembered—so carefree, so handsome that the sight made her ache to the marrow of her bones.

A second later, he shot to his feet, knife drawn, scanning the hall.

Heart pounding, she grabbed the doorframe for support.

"You all right?" He peered past her shoulders, into her chamber.

"Fine, except for the year of life you just frightened from me." She drew in a long breath, slowing her pulse. "What are you doing here?"

He tucked away his knife—thankfully—then ran a hand through his hair. "I told you last night there'd be no more mishaps. I meant it."

Heat spread up from her tummy to her heart. He'd slept in front of her door all night, watching and protecting her?

Down the hall, a bobbing lamp drew near, the halo of light contrasting the maid's pale face with her ebony dress. Betty bobbed a curtsy despite her filled hands. "Glad to see you're both awake. There's a messenger downstairs for Miss Chapman. He said to give this to you directly."

Betty held out an envelope with Clara's name scratched on the front.

Clara's heart stopped. This could not be good. With shaking hands, she broke the seal. Each sentence, each word, stole strength from her legs, until she swayed.

Ben reached for her, his grip on her arm a steadying beam. "What is it?"

Betty retreated, taking the light with her. Light? La, as if any shone into this manor of despair.

"Clara?" Ben's voice sounded far away, somewhere overhead and fuzzy. "What's happened?"

She cleared her throat. How to make her voice work at a time such as this? "Aunt Mitchell is not doing well." The words came out jagged around the edges, but at least they came out. "The doctor says if I wish a goodbye, now is the time."

She stared, unseeing, into Ben's eyes.

He held her shoulders, firming her up on each side. "Then you must go."

Go? Were Aunt to die, then there was nothing for her anymore. Nowhere to go. No means to support herself. But if she stayed another day and a half at Bleakly, then she stood a good chance of being self-sufficient long enough to find another position.

Could Aunt hold on for that long?

Ben bent, peering closer. "What are you thinking?"

"If I leave now, I shall ruin my chances of five hundred pounds. I know that sounds callous and cold, but—" A sob welled in her throat. It sounded that way because it was. "Oh, Ben, what shall I do?"

"A last goodbye isn't worth any amount of money. It is priceless." Cupping her cheeks with his hands, he lifted her face. "I never got to say goodbye to you or my life before being cast away into Millbank."

The emotion in his gaze nearly choked her. "You're right, of course. Yes, I shall go. But I—"

She what? How to put into words the fear, the terror, of leaving him again? What kind of cruel joke was it to bring them together, then rip them apart for a second time? The dam burst, and hot tears scalded her cheeks.

Ben brushed them away with his thumbs. "What's this?"

"I—I shall miss you." Loss tasted as salty as the tears on her lips.

"As long as I draw breath, Clara, I vow I will go to you immediately after quitting this place. I swear it. Nothing, *nothing* will keep me from you." A muscle jumped on his jaw. Slowly he sank to one knee, pulling her hand to his lips. He kissed her so softly, she trembled. The hazel of his eyes burned up into hers. "Will you trust in me again? Will you allow me to show you how much I love you?"

Old memories of the pitiful stares, the whispered remarks as she stood alone on display in front of an altar, cut a fresh mark on her soul. How awful, how excruciating, to be burned twice over with the same fire. But was this time not completely different? *Oh, God, please let it be so.*

She reached into her pocket and wrapped her fingers around the second-chance coin. Hesitating for only a breath, she held it out. "Perhaps this coin was never meant for me, but for you."

His fingers entwined with hers, and his throat bobbed as he took it.

"I will trust you, Benjamin Lane. But please. . ." Each word cost in ways that she'd pay for eternity if he failed her in this. "Do not break my heart again."

CHAPTER TWENTY-EIGHT

Feeble afternoon sunlight faded into early evening shadows, darkening the library. At a table near the door, Ben retrieved a candle lantern and lit it, his breath puffing a little cloud in the frigid chamber. No stranger to the cold, he tugged the lapels of his dress coat closer and strode from the room. Once Clara had departed, he'd spent the bulk of the day re-exploring the empty manor from cellar to rafters, hoping to find the reclusive master. All he'd discovered was Betty debating with two kitchen staff about the freshness of the fish for dinner, a stable hand who'd come in for a mug of ale, and countless locked doors that hid secrets. Blast! But he was sick of secrets.

Quickening his pace, he stalked from corridor to corridor, finally stopping in the empty front foyer. He widened his stance and faced the lion head.

"Why not end the charade now? I am the last one remaining. Show yourself and be done with it."

Lifeless eyes stared down at him. Not that he expected an answer—nor the sudden rap of the knocker on the front door.

Wheeling about, he cast aside convention and opened the door himself.

A ruddy-cheeked fellow with frosted eyebrows and a red-tipped nose stood at attention. "Is there a Mr. Lane in residence?"

"I am he."

"Excellent. This delivery is for you, sir." He held out a canvas messenger bag.

Ben rolled his eyes. This was too convenient. Too coincidental. He glanced over his shoulder, back up at the lion head, feeling more than ever like a pawn.

Yet what else was there to do at this point but finish the game?

Stifling a growl, he took the bag with a forced "Thank you," then rummaged in his pocket for something to give the man. Nothing but Clara's second-chance coin met his touch. Ahh, but poverty was a cruel master, not only for him, but for the poor delivery man who'd have to trek back to God-knew-where with nothing but chapped skin to show for it.

Ben met the man's gaze. "I am sorry, but I'm afraid I have no tip."

"No need." The fellow swiped the moisture from the end of his nose with the edge of his sleeve. "I've been paid handsomely. Good night." He turned and jogged down the stairs, mounted a fine-looking bay, and trotted off into the twilight.

Closing the door on the cold, Ben tucked the bag under one arm and strode into the drawing room—the one chamber with a fire. He poured a glass of wine, then settled in the chair nearest the hearth as the mantel clock struck five. Untying the leather thong secured around two buttons, he opened the flap. Inside was a large packet, thick and weighty, and three smaller envelopes at the bottom. No, hold on. He fished his finger into one corner and pulled out a scrap of paper. Hasty penmanship scrawled across it, reading: *You don't have to be right. You just have to be.*

His brows pinched. What was that supposed to mean?

Setting it aside, he withdrew the envelopes and went first for the one that was unsealed. Dumping the contents onto his lap, he riffled through what appeared to be receipts. Many wrinkled. Some torn. All with large sums and different dates spanning the past nine months. A new top hat. A case of *Chateau Margaux*. Fees spent for villas and servants and travel arrangements to and from a spate of European countries. Ben shoved the papers back into the envelope. What had this to do with anything?

He paused to swallow a sip of his drink, then drew out the biggest packet and set the bag down on the floor. Perhaps by reading the rest he'd understand the cryptic scrap. Laying the folder on his lap, he flipped it open. Pages of parchment, lots of them, neatly penned. He picked up the first page, then gaped at the title written in black ink at the top: *Blythe vs Lane*.

A shock jolted through him as he read further. These were court documents. The papers he'd begged to see before, during, and after his trial. The key to discovering who'd brought embezzlement charges against him in the first place.

He riffled through the pile, scanning like a madman, revisiting the indictment, the verdict, discovering the names of the members of the jury, and finally the page naming the plaintiff. His hands shook. His whole body did. At last he'd know whom to seek out, whom to pay back all the horrors he'd had to live through the past nine months: *George Chapman*.

The paper slipped from his fingers. The name made no sense. Clara's brother, his friend and colleague, was his accuser?

He shoved the documents back into the bag and pulled out the other two envelopes. One felt heavier, so he opened that one first. A letter, folded into thirds, was addressed to High Court Justice Richard Combee.

Though his throat was parched, he ignored his glass of wine and shook out the missive, then skimmed the page. The first half was blotted in parts, the ink washed out where some sort of liquid had spilled onto the paper. It mostly looked like salutations anyway. But the words in the middle were clear enough:

> *. . .appreciate your handling with utmost confidentiality*
> *the matter of Benjamin Lane. As per our previous*
> *conversation, the sum of one thousand pounds shall*
> *be yours in exchange for his transportation.*
> *As always, your servant,*
> *George Chapman*

The paper crumpled in his hand as if his fingers squeezed about George's neck. It couldn't be helped. Such rage, when birthed, could not be shoved back inside any more than a babe could revisit a mother's womb. Of course he should have known—he just didn't want to. But it made perfect sense.

From the time they'd been lads, he and George had competed for everything, from trying to acquire the headmaster's praise before the other to rowing contests on the River Cam. Landing a partnership at the same shipping company, it was only natural they vied for the ultimate prize—the great Blythe warehouse industry. Had George somehow discovered he would not be the winner? The sweet aftertaste of wine soured at the back of his throat. Were that conjecture true, that meant *he* would have been the one to take over the prosperous business. Would George truly have been so heinous as to steal the money, cast the blame on him, and leave his own sister practically destitute?

Drawing in a deep breath to clear his head, he tucked the letter into the envelope and tossed back the rest of his drink. *Steady, steady.*

He opened the last envelope and pulled out a single half sheet. A block cut of a steamship adorned the left corner. At the right, written in red ink, the word *copy*. Across the top, the title of *Liverpool, London & Glasgow Packet Company* spread out in swirled letters. The line below that listed the destination—New York—and the departure date: January 5. Tomorrow, then. At ten in the morning. Berth No. 12. Balance due $0. Wapping Wharves. And the bearer's name—*George Chapman*.

Ben shot to his feet, the paper fluttering to the floor along with the messenger bag and the rest of the documents. Running both hands through his hair, he circled the room, heart racing. This was it. All he'd dreamed about for the past nine hellish months while rotting away in Millbank. Revenge in full. If he left now, he'd easily make it in time to London, to the docks, to the ship. He could drag George to a real court instead of the court of bogus justice Ben had endured—provided he could restrain himself from choking the life out of the scoundrel beforehand.

He stopped in front of the hearth and grabbed the mantel with both hands. If he stepped off Bleakly Manor property, he'd be shot for escape. Yet how else could he stop George? Once the rogue landed in America, there'd be no finding him. There'd be no justice. There'd be nothing but a grand life for George while he and Clara worked to scratch out a living.

Clara.

He hung his head and stared at the coals. He'd nearly forgotten his vow to her. Shoving his hand into his pocket, he pulled out the second-chance coin, then spun and glowered at the papers strewn on the floor.

If he walked out the door of Bleakly Manor, he'd face death—once again breaking his oath to Clara. The coin burned in his palm, and the need for righteousness in his gut.

There was freedom if he stayed. Revenge if he didn't.

Which one should he chance?

Twelfth Night Holiday

JANUARY 5, 1851

Chapter Twenty-Nine

Morning light cast oblong rectangles on the rug in Aunt's chamber. Clara watched them shorten, her head bobbing now and then, jerking her back to wakefulness. The wicked tick-tock of the clock tempted her to close her eyes. Just for a moment. To forget the pinch of her corset and ache of her bones. Ahh, but she was weary from travel, from worrying, life, and the eleven long days she'd spent at Bleakly Manor. Shifting on the chair she'd occupied since she'd arrived last night, she rested her cheek against the wingback and surrendered with a sigh.

"You sound as if you bear the world on your shoulders." A paper-thin voice rustled on the air.

Bolting upright, she dashed to Aunt Mitchell's bedside and dropped to her knees. Set in a face the colour of milk paint, watery eyes stared at her, open and alive. "Oh, Aunt, how are you?"

Aunt's lips curved into a frail smile. "A sight better than you, by the looks of it."

Pulling her loosened hair back over her shoulder, Clara leaned closer and studied the rise and fall of Aunt's chest. The counterpane barely moved. She bit back a cry. "I've been so worried."

"La, child." A raspy gurgle in Aunt's throat accompanied her words. "Worrying doesn't stop the bad from happening. It keeps you from enjoying the good."

"What would I do without your wisdom?" The world turned watery, and Clara blinked to keep her tears locked up. "What *will* I do without you?"

The old lady's fingers fluttered toward her, inching across the top of the coverlet. Clara reached for her hand, hopefully saving Aunt whatever strength she might have left.

Aunt's squeeze was light as a butterfly's wing. "Now, now, chin up. I'm not gone yet."

"No, you are not." She swallowed against the tightness in her throat. "And for that I am thankful."

"But I am ready to go, child. I have lived a full life. My only regret is I have nothing to leave you. Wicked entailments." Releasing her hand, Aunt's fingers trembled upward, landing on Clara's cheek. "How I'd wished you to be mistress of this house."

Clara leaned into her touch. "I am sure Mr. Barrett will make a fine master."

"Master, yes. Fine? Hardly." Aunt's hand dropped to the bed, and her pale eyes flashed a spark—albeit tiny—of spunk. "Be thankful you never crossed paths with that side of my husband's family."

Great coughs rumbled in Aunt's chest, draining her of an already thin colour.

Clara darted to a side table and retrieved a glass of watered wine. Most dribbled down Aunt's chin, staining her white nightgown like drops of blood, but enough moistened her mouth that the hacking fit abated.

"Rest now. I shall be right here with you." Clara stood.

But Aunt's fingers beckoned her back. "Soon this body will do nothing but rest. Please, humour me. I should like to hear of your adventures at Bleakly Manor."

Frowning, she studied the woman. Bird bones wrapped in white linen couldn't have looked more fragile, yet a thread of strength remained in Aunt's voice.

"Very well." Taking care not to jostle the mattress overmuch, she sat on the edge of the bed and took Aunt's hands between both of hers. Once again the ticking clock taunted her, counting down the final minutes of Aunt's life. How to explain the strange characters she'd spent the past eleven days with?

Aunt's gaze sought hers. "Just tell me what's on your heart, child."

"Ben was there." The words blurted out before she could stop them, and she sucked in a gasp.

"Was he now?" Despite the glassy shadow of death, Aunt's eyes twinkled.

Twinkled?

Clara frowned at the odd response, suspicion growing stronger with each beat of her heart. "Why, you *knew* he'd be there. That's why you encouraged me to go, is it not?"

"My body fails, but my mind does not." Aunt pulled her hand away and tapped her head. "There's still a little intrigue left up here."

The movement loosed the demon in Aunt's chest, unleashing a spate of coughing. This was too much, despite what Aunt Mitchell desired.

Clara rose. "Rest now, Aunt. I vow I shall be here when you next awaken and we will talk more."

"No!" The old lady's head flailed on the pillow, her voice as mewling as a newborn kitten's. "There's something you need to know. Bleakly Manor was no coincidence and in fact was my last hope for your future."

Stunned, Clara blinked, her own voice quivering. "What are you saying?"

"It started last fall, September. Charles, a dear old friend of mine, called on me. He told me he was struggling to create his next hero and heroine." Pausing, Aunt licked her lips, white foam collecting at the edges.

Clearly she would not be put off, so Clara propped up Aunt's head and helped her drink, then sat at her side.

"Mmm. So good. Now, where was I?" For a moment, Aunt closed her eyes, and Clara wondered if she'd doze off finally.

But her lids popped open. "Charles is a writer. He had a story in mind, and the plot pleased him, but his characters were. . . How did he put it? *All flattened and blowsy, like a handful of crushed chaff given to the wind.* Such a wordy fellow." A small chuckle gurgled in Aunt's throat.

Prepared for another coughing fit, Clara tensed, hating the awful smell of the mustard poultice on her aunt's chest, hating even more the thought that the next fit might be her last.

Yet the old lady rallied, drawing in a big breath. "So Charles concocted an experiment to help him create vibrant, believable characters by observation. He had several other people in mind, but none qualified as true leads. There are no two truer hearts I know than yours and Mr. Lane's, and so I suggested the two of you."

"But how could you? Did you know where Ben was all this time? That he was a convicted felon?"

"You and I both know he could never be capable of such a crime."

Clara shook her head, trying to make sense of the strange conversation. "Why did you not tell me of this sooner?"

"There were many logistics and legalities to arrange. And the timing had to be right—a friend of Charles owns Bleakly Manor and was about to sail for the continent on business. He offered Charles the use of his house. Some of his staff went with him. Others visited their own families during his absence. So Charles had to hire temporary replacements on limited funds. That left little in the budget for food, coal, or other necessities. He wasn't even certain until the last minute that his experiment would come together. I didn't want to get your hopes up only to see them dashed." Aunt's eyes leaked, dampening her cheek. "You've suffered enough."

Clara's jaw dropped. Understanding dawned as bright and clear as the late-morning sun leaching the last colour from Aunt's skin as it shone on her thin form. "I see. You hoped I'd receive the five hundred pounds as a means of support."

"No, child. I hoped that by reuniting with your Ben you'd receive love. Though you are brilliant at hiding your heart, I've long known you underestimate your own value. But that view of yourself is a lie. Each of God's creatures is inherently precious. And so you are." Aunt's head lifted, a flicker of passion in her gaze. "You have made this last year of my life a delight, easing my loneliness more than you'll ever know. And as my friend Charles says, '*No one is useless in this world who lightens the burden of it to anyone else.*'"

Deep down, in a place within her heart locked with chains, something clicked. A door opened. An awful monster rushed out at her, one that had resided in her soul since the day her father had come home drunk and blamed her for her mother's death in childbirth, saying he'd trade her in an instant if he could only have her mother back from the grave.

Clara covered her face and wept away the memory, the hurt, the lies. Wept it all away. And suddenly, the whys of life didn't matter anymore, for the love of her aunt, of Ben, of her Creator, flooded in and chased that fiend away.

"Child?"

Sucking in a shaky breath, she bent and embraced her aunt, then pulled back. "Thank you. I am grateful for your words and your friend's words."

Dabbing away a last tear, she wondered if Aunt's friend had been surprised by all the things that went awry in the manor and the near-death mishaps. A question that would have to remain unasked, for if Aunt knew what had truly gone on, it would burden her unduly. Instead, Clara curved her mouth into a small smile. "I should like to meet this wise Charles of yours someday."

"Indeed." Aunt's head sunk deep into her pillow, and she closed her eyes. "Mr. Dickens is a wise man."

Chapter Thirty

Ben paced circles in the drawing room, the spare light of a single candle his only source of illumination—save for the leftover glow of coals in the hearth and the thin line of grey on the outside horizon. Midnight had come and gone. His chance to stop George Chapman was gone as well.

Stopping in front of the window, he shoved his hand into his pocket and yanked out the second-chance coin, flipping it over and over in his hand. Regret choked him, leaving behind an acrid taste. He should've taken the risk yesterday. He should've raced down to that dock and never looked back. Three times he'd braved the cold and walked the vast length of the drive to the edge of Bleakly Manor property, debating the chance of a bullet for the sake of justice.

And three times he'd turned back.

What kind of coward did that?

Opening his hand, he stared fiercely at Clara's gift. How long would it take to wear it smooth like the stone he'd once kept at Millbank? Would he be sent back there, after all? Should he not take this last opportunity to run free? To escape?

He rolled the coin from knuckle to knuckle, the friction of the metal against his skin reminding him he was human, not some beast to be hunted. Not in Clara's eyes, at any rate. Not anymore. Wasn't her trust and love worth more than revenge? That's what he'd told himself yesterday. And yes, even now he knew it in his heart—but the blasted nagging doubts in his head would not be stilled.

Lifting his face to the sky, he studied the brilliant rays of sun painting streaks of pink against the grey, then closed his eyes.

"Hear me, God." His voice was as rugged as his emotions. "Though it kills me in every possible way, I surrender, here and now, any further thoughts of vengeance against George Chapman. Make things right. Make *me* right. I leave this matter in Your hands, where it's always been, despite my doubts and questions."

He shoved the coin back into his pocket and stalked from the room. Shadows crept out from corners, but weak light began to filter in. Taking the stairs two at a time, he dashed to his room, knowing exactly what must be done next. Regardless of a bullet in his back, he would go to Clara, for he'd promised he would. Or he would die in the trying.

He shrugged into his greatcoat, wrapped a scarf around his neck, then yanked down a hat atop his head, covering the tips of his ears. The walk to London would be long and cold.

If he made it past Bleakly lands.

Trotting down the stairs, he stopped in the great foyer and pivoted to the lion head. His hand snapped to his forehead in salute. "Thank you for your hospitality, such as it was."

Then he turned and strode to the door, ready to set foot on the next chapter of his life, be it a paragraph or a page.

But it was a sentence, and a short one at that.

"Mr. Lane, I presume?" A footman blocked his path—dressed in the same livery the servants had worn his first night here.

"Yes," he answered.

"Your carriage will arrive shortly, sir." The fellow's arm shot out, offering an envelope in his gloved hand. "Until then, this is for you."

Ben pulled the paper from the footman's fingers. The man immediately wheeled about, descended the stairs, and hopped up on the back step of a black-lacquered carriage, one clearly not meant for him.

No matter. His feet wouldn't move should he wish them to. The simple piece of parchment in his hand, folded and blotted with red wax at the center, weighted him in place. Perspiration dotted his brow as he ran his finger under the seal. Legal text filled the page, hard to read for the way the paper quivered in his hands, but three clear words stood out: *Writ of emancipation.*

The miracle in ink shook through him, and for a moment he leaned against the doorframe, closing his eyes. *Thank You, God.*

The jingle of harnesses pulled him from his thoughts. Blinking into the brilliant morning light, he saw a long-legged man entering the carriage. Just before the door shut, the fellow tipped his hat at Ben. Then the coach lurched into motion. Had that been his one and only glimpse of the master of Bleakly Manor? A nondescript, black-haired fellow in a houndstooth sack jacket and bowler hat?

Ben tore down the stairs, intent on thanking him, but the coachman laid into the horses, urging them into a run.

Ben stood in the drive, staring after the retreating coach, as alone as the night he'd arrived—but this time standing in the brilliance of sunshine and freedom.

Five Days Later

JANUARY 10, 1851

CHAPTER THIRTY-ONE

Aunt Mitchell's laboured breathing made Clara's chest hurt. But it was the chiming of the clock that really cut into her heart, carving out a hollow. Another day born in darkness. January 10. Days past the festive season.

Slumping in her chair near the door of Aunt's chamber, she debated leaving to go have a good cry into her pillow. Since her childhood, she'd always waxed melancholy after the flurry of Christmas. The walls stripped of decoration. The house empty of guests and laughter. It was the lonely time of year. The barren. With naught to look forward to but short grey days and frigid black nights. Yet none of that bothered her this time, not with Aunt's life balancing on the thin line tied from breath to breath.

And the fact that Ben had not come for her. Again.

Despair spread over her like a rash, hot, prickly, and entirely familiar. She knew it as well as the skin on her bones. At least this time the only eyes to witness her shame and grief were those closed nearly in death. Why had she been so foolish as to open her heart to the same man who'd crushed it once before? Was it any better to wonder if he'd been recaptured? Or killed? Would that make the pain any less?

Pressing the heels of her hands to her eyes, she stopped up the tears begging for release and whispered, "Why, God? Why?"

"If you knew all the answers, there'd be no need for trust, little one."

She jerked upright in the chair and swiveled her head toward Aunt—just as harsh words gathered out in the hall, growing louder the longer she listened. Dorothea Cruff, Aunt's housekeeper, howled like a baying beagle keen on the hunt. Clara bit her lip and shot up a quick plea of repentance. Truly it was wicked of her to compare the woman to a dog, but even Aunt referred to Mrs. Cruff's chambers as *the howlery*. What poor servant was the housekeeper gnawing on at such an hour? Clara turned up the wick in her oil lamp, intending on finding out, when the door opened.

Mrs. Cruff's mobcapped head peeked through the gap. "Begging your pardon, Miss Chapman. But there's a gentleman, leastwise he says he is, who will not—"

The door shoved wider and, sidestepping Mrs. Cruff, in strode a broad-shouldered shape, draped in a black riding cloak and dark trousers. Mud bespattered him from toe to neck, little flecks of it falling to the floor as he doffed his hat.

But before lamplight caught on the man's burnt cream–coloured hair, Clara jumped up and plowed into him. "You came!"

Faltering back a step, Ben chuckled and wrapped his arms around her. "So it appears."

Listening to his heart beat against her ear, she stayed there, nuzzling her cheek against his chest, breathing in deeply of his scent, all smoky and with a whiff of horseflesh. He'd come. He'd really come for her. All the anguish and doubt of the past several days melted as she nestled into the heat of him.

" 'Tain't right. 'Tain't proper." Behind them, Mrs. Cruff scolded as proficiently as Mr. Tallgrass might have.

Unwilling to forfeit such a hard-won embrace, Clara turned yet did not step out of Ben's hold.

Mrs. Cruff's face could kill an entire battalion of dragoons with one glance, so fiercely did she scowl.

Clara fired back her own evil eye. "Light the lamps and see to a fire in the sitting room, if you please, Mrs. Cruff."

"No, I don't very well please, and furthermore—"

Ben released her and held up a hand. "No need. Thank you, but this shan't take long. You are dismissed."

The woman's mouth opened, a magnificent howl about to issue, when Aunt Mitchell's voice floated across the room.

"Go to bed, Cruff. I would speak with Clara and her gentleman."

The housekeeper's lips snapped shut. Silence escorted her out of the room until she reached the corridor, where a low grumbling began—and no doubt would accompany her all the way to the howlery.

With a gentle yet firm hand on the small of Clara's back, Ben ushered her to Aunt's bedside. "Sorry for the hour, Mrs. Mitchell. I came as soon as I could. Between a lame horse, a broken axle, and a downed tree at Hounslow, the journey took longer than expected. I am happy you are still amongst us."

Aunt nodded, an almost imperceptible movement, so delicate her constitution. "Your expected arrival is what's been keeping me alive."

Clara exchanged a glance with Ben. Did he know what she was talking about?

The arch of his brow said not. He pulled her down to kneel alongside him at Aunt's bedside.

Ben reached for the old lady's hand and cradled it in his, the contrast between vitality and weakness stark in the shadowy light. "I am sorry to bear unwelcome news, but I've discovered the truth behind what really happened with the Chapman fortune and Blythe Shipping. Your nephew George stole all the funds, leaving me with the blame and you, Mrs. Mitchell, to care for Clara—for which I owe you my gratitude."

"No!" Clara sat back on her heels, the world tipping beneath her. "George would never. . .I mean. . .but he's gone to America. He's working even now to secure a place for me."

"No, my love." Amber eyes sought hers, and the compassion shining there nearly undid her. "In truth, your brother's been cutting a swath of decadent living across Europe. Only days ago did he sail for America."

"He did not." Aunt's frail voice pulled both their gazes back to her.

Ben leaned closer to the old woman, the lines on his face softening. "I am sorry to contradict you, madam, but—"

Aunt's fingers quivered upward, landing on his cheek. "If you are here, that means George did not sail for America but has been apprehended and will stand trial. You will be fully acquitted."

The words blew around Clara like a fine snow caught in an eddy of wind. In truth, she felt just as swirly. Was everything she'd believed for nearly the past year nothing but lies?

She huddled closer to Ben, hoping to draw strength from the sheer closeness of his broad shoulders. "Aunt, what are you saying?"

Air rattled in the old lady's lungs as she drew in a breath. "I long had my suspicions about your brother, but no evidence until recently."

Aunt's fingers dropped to the sheets. "George is not your full brother, my dear. He's but a half. His mother refused to marry your father, wild in all her ways. Despicable woman. I feared George would turn out like her, but one cannot accuse based on bad character alone. I needed proof."

Aunt's eyes closed, and her chest fluttered.

So did Clara's pulse. All she'd known, all she'd assumed, vanished, replaced with keen comprehension. She'd understood her father's coldness toward her because her mother had died in the birthing, but her father's detachment toward George had always been a puzzlement. Until now. No wonder she'd always felt the odd goose with her raven hair and olive skin, standing next to her brother, so fair in colour and handsome looks.

A chill crept across her shoulders, and she shivered.

Ben pulled her closer to his side and patted Aunt's hand. "We shall leave you to rest."

"Not yet." Aunt's eyelids flickered open. "You must know. My friend, Charles, rubs shoulders with powerful men. One, a barrister with a sharp sense of justice." She paused, her tongue working to moisten her lips.

Clara pulled away and retrieved a cloth she kept dipped in water, then patted it against her aunt's mouth.

A faint smile lifted one side of the old lady's lips. "That barrister laboured to trade Ben's transportation for house arrest at Bleakly, then worked the holiday season to gather all the evidence by Twelfth Night."

Her words stalled, and Ben leaned closer, bending his ear toward her mouth. "Are you saying I have been acquitted this whole time?"

"No. Had you tried to escape or gone after George, you would have been shot for evasion." Aunt's head shook like the last leaf in autumn. "Yet I vouched for your character, my son."

Ben reared back to his heels, nostrils flaring as he sucked in a breath. "But why?"

A flare of brightness lit Aunt Mitchell's eyes, for a moment driving colour into her whitewashed cheeks. "I never had children of my own, but I couldn't have loved them any more dearly than Clara and you. Promise me…promise…"

Rattles travelled from Aunt's chest to her throat, and both Clara and Ben leaned in close.

With a last rally, Aunt reached for Ben's hand and moved it to Clara's. "Take care of my Clara."

Ben's strong fingers encased both of theirs. "I vow it." He squeezed, gently. "This night and for always."

Aunt closed her eyes, her hand going limp in theirs. It wouldn't be long before she left the land of the living.

Grief welled in Clara's throat, and she pulled her hand free to press a knuckle against her mouth, trapping the noise.

Ben tucked the old lady's fingers beneath the bedsheet, then pulled Clara up along with him. "Come," he whispered, then led her, hand in hand, to the corridor and closed the door behind them.

Emotions assailed her, one after the other. Sorrow. Confusion. But above all a sense of duty to the man walking beside her. She stopped and turned to Ben. "You have been restored, and for that I am truly grateful, but please, despite what was said, do not feel obligated to keep such a promise to Aunt."

She tried to pull away from his grasp, but he merely captured her other hand and rubbed his thumbs along the inside curve of her palms. "Surely you know you are more than an obligation to me."

"But I am penniless! George saw to that by spending the money." Her voice caught, and she hung her head. "No one will welcome me back into their circles. I have fallen from grace."

"Yet it is grace alone that saves the worst of us." He released his hold and worked to shove up one of his sleeves. Blackened numbers, charred into his skin, stared up at her.

A single tear broke loose, landing on the hideous brand. She brushed it away, her finger travelling over the seared flesh. How could he love so much after having suffered because of her brother? Her throat nearly closed at the thought of such depth, such rock-solid devotion—to her.

He reached into his pocket and pulled out the coin, then pressed it into her hand. "And it was your grace that gave me a second chance."

Pulling her to him, he slid his strong hands upward to cup the back of her head. For a second, he hesitated, caressing her with a gaze that made her his own. Then his mouth came down, meeting hers, claiming her in deed. By the time he pulled away, breathing was out of the question.

"I am a free man now, Clara, and in time, the Court of Chancery will fully restore my family estate. All this gain, though, is empty without you. And so I must know"—his voice lowered, crackling with love and desire—"will you have a former convict as a husband?"

Tears would not be stopped, the taste of them salty on her lips. Oh, how she'd missed this man, this love, this part of her that had been torn and was now mended stronger than before. She smiled up at him, realizing that, indeed, she may never stop smiling for the rest of her years. "I would have none other than you, my love."

Two Weeks Later

January 24, 1851

CHAPTER THIRTY-TWO

A cold mist settled over London, dampening everyone's clothing to the same shade of dreary. It was the kind of late January day that crawled under the best of woolen capes and took up residence in the bones. In Cheapside, old men huddled at their hearths. On Aldred Street, mothers sheltered younglings beneath great black umbrellas.

But in Holywell, Clara stepped lively down the narrow lanes, ignoring the chill.

Stopping in front of Effie Gedge's door, she raised her hand and rapped, then smiled at the smudge left behind on her glove. It would be the last time this ragtag collection of boards marred her bleached kidskin.

The door swung open, and Effie's sweet face appeared—cheekbones prominent, skin sallow, yet her ever-present smile fixed in place. "Miss Chapman! What a grand surprise." The girl's brows drew together, and she dared a step closer despite the rain that would catch on her hair. "But what are you doing here? Is all well?"

"No. . .and yes. So much has happened in the past month, I hardly know where to begin." She'd never spoken truer words. Biting the inside of her cheek, she searched for some nicely packaged phrases, as she had during the entire ride over here, but still none came to mind. How to speak of passions and sorrows so great?

"My aunt Mitchell has died," she blurted.

"Oh! I am so sorry." Effie reached out and grabbed her arm, as if to impart strength—quite the absurdity from a woman worn to threads by circumstance. "She were a rare one, weren't she?"

"That she was." Clara fought back a fresh wave of tears, though should any slip, they could easily be blamed upon the mist.

"It's not much, miss, but I'm sure I can get you into the factory. It won't be easy, mind you. Hatbox work is hard on the hands, but it's a fair sight easier than being a silk piecer or a salt boiler, and far better than starving." Effie shoved the door wider, lips curving into a welcome. "You can share my room, though we'll have to snug up in the bed, for I've only space enough for that and a chair."

Though the January day did its worst to inflict a shiver, Clara pressed a hand to her chest, warmed through the heart at Effie's kindness. "Oh, Effie, you are the rare one. I did come here to ask you something, but not that." Loosening the drawstring on her reticule, she pulled out the second-chance coin and pressed it into Effie's reddened hands.

Effie looked from the gold piece to Clara. "What's this for?"

"It's a second-chance coin."

"A what?"

Clara smiled. How many times had she wondered the very same thing? "I am here to ask you for a second chance. Would you consider coming back as my maid? There is much to be done, and I could use your help."

"I don't understand." A tremor shook Effie's head, though hard to tell if the movement was from the cold or confusion. "I thought once your aunt was deceased, the house and all her means passed on to her stepson. Don't tell me you and him...?"

"No, nothing of the sort. That is not the household I am asking you to serve."

"Then whose?"

Her grin widened, for whenever she thought of Ben, a smile must be allowed. "Mr. Benjamin Lane's household, my soon-to-be husband. We have a wedding to prepare for. Are you up to it? It won't be easy, but it's a fair sight easier than hatbox making—and you won't have to share your bed." She winked. "What do you say?"

Effie beamed. "I say let our new lives begin!"

HISTORICAL NOTES

Victorian Christmas Traditions

The Twelve Day Celebration
Since medieval times, the Twelve Day celebration has been a recognized holiday. It traditionally begins on Christmas Day, December 25, and ends at midnight, January 5, immediately before Epiphany.

Boxing Day
This holiday is celebrated the day after Christmas Day. Tradesmen and servants receive gifts from their masters, employers, or customers. These gifts are boxed up, hence the name Boxing Day.

The Yule Log
A Yule log was dragged in on Christmas Day and kept burning for twelve days (until Epiphany). The leftover charcoal was kept until the following Christmas to kindle the next year's log. It was considered bad luck if the log went out during the Twelve Days.

Childermas
December 28 is known as Holy Innocents' Day or Childermas. It's a day commemorating when King Herod ordered the murder of children under two years of age in an attempt to kill the baby Jesus. The "Coventry Carol" recounts the massacre from the eyes of a mourning mother whose child was killed. The song was commonly sung by itinerant carolers.

New Year's Coin
No matter the age, it was a must that every person in Victorian England should have money in his or her pocket on New Year's Day, even something as small as a half farthing (worth an eighth of a penny). To be without a coin meant risking poverty in the coming year.

Travelling Entertainers
During the Christmas season, entertainers travelled from manor to manor. The most common form of their performances was pantomime, which is still a popular form of entertainment today during the holidays.

Wassail

Originally, wassail was a greeting or a toast. Revelers would hold up a mug of spiced cider and shout, "Waes hael!" which means *be hale* or *be well*. The drink was often offered to visitors in a large wooden bowl. Eventually, the greeting fell by the wayside and wassail came to mean the drink instead of the toast. Many great traditional wassail recipes can be found on the internet. Here is one of my favorites: http://www.curiouscuisiniere.com/wassail-recipe/.

DEDICATION

To the One and Only who gives mankind
a second chance—Jesus Christ.
And to Deborha Mitchell, the namesake of Clara's aunt.

ACKNOWLEDGMENTS

Writing is a solitary profession that cannot be done alone.
Thank you to Annie Tipton and the awesome staff at Shiloh Run who continually make my writing dreams come true. A shout-out to my long-suffering critique partners: Lisa Ludwig, Ane Mulligan, MaryLu Tyndall, Julie Klassen, Shannon McNear, and Chawna Schroeder. . .ALL talented authors in their own right. And as always, my gratitude to Mark, who endures many a frozen pizza and Chinese takeout when it's crunch time.

Plus a special thank-you to you, readers,
who make this writing gig all worthwhile!

A Tale of Two Hearts

CHAPTER ONE

London, 1853

Whether I shall turn out to be the hero of my own life,
or whether that station will be held by anybody else,
these pages must show.
David Copperfield

I n the tiny back courtyard of the Golden Egg Inn, Mina Scott lowered her copy of *David Copperfield* to her lap and lifted her face to the October sun. Closing her eyes, she savored the warmth and the first line to a new adventure, as was her wont whenever Miss Whymsy stopped by and lent her a book. Though she no longer stared at the page, the shapes of the words lingered, blazed in stark contrast to the brilliance against her lids. What a curious thought, to be one's own hero—for the only hero she wanted was William Barlow.

Ahh, William. Just thinking his name lit a fire in her belly.

"Mina!"

She shot to her feet, and the book plummeted to the ground. Her stomach dropped along with it—both for being caught idle and for the dirt smudges sure to mar the cover. With her toe, she slid the novel beneath her skirt hem, then patted her pocket to make sure the note Miss Whymsy had left behind hadn't fallen out as well. The small, folded paper crinkled beneath her touch, hidden and snug. Satisfied, she faced her father.

Jasper Scott, master of the inn and commander of her life, fisted hands the size of kidney pies at his hips. "What are ye doin' out in the yard, girl, when ye ought to be serving?"

She dipped her chin. "It's hardly teatime, Father. I thought to take a break before customers arrived." From the peak of the inn's rooftop, a swallow not yet flown to warmer climates chided the frail excuse. Not that she blamed the bird. It was a pitiful defense.

Her father fumbled his big fingers inside a small pocket on his waistcoat and pulled out a worn brass pocket watch. He flipped open the lid—and the whole thing fell to the ground. "Oh, bother!"

As he bent to pick it up, she stifled a smile. How large Father's grin would be on Christmas Eve when he opened the new watch fob she'd been saving all her pennies for.

Swiping up the dropped watch, Father first frowned at the time, then at her. "It's past tea." He snapped the timepiece shut and tucked it away. "I wager ye were reading again. Am I right?"

How did he know? How did he *always* know?

Slowly, she retrieved the book and held it out. "Maybe you ought to keep this until we close tonight."

"I thought as much when Miss Whymsy stopped by. Keep your head in the world, girl, not in the clouds. Ye'll never get a husband that way." He snatched the novel from her hand. "And besides that, this being the last day o' October, ye must turn yer sights away from make-believe tales and toward Christmas. Only a little over seven weeks remain to make this the best celebration the Golden Egg has ever seen, so ye must focus, girl. Now off with ye. There are patrons already clamouring for a whistle wetting."

"Yes, Father." She scurried past him. Since she'd been a little girl, the annual Christmas Eve celebration at the Golden Egg meant everything to Father. 'Twas a poor replacement for her departed mother, but a replacement, she supposed, nonetheless. She darted through the back door and nearly crashed into Martha, the inn's cook.

"Peas and porridge!" Martha stepped aside, the water in her pot sloshing over the rim and dampening the flagstones. "Watch yer step, missy."

"Sorry, Martha." Giving the woman a wider berth, she grabbed her apron from a peg and a cloth for wiping tables, then scooted out to the taproom.

Once she entered the public area, she slowed her steps and drew a deep breath. No one liked to be waited upon by a ruddy-cheeked snippet of a skirt. Scanning the room, she frowned. Only two tables were filled. Surely Father could've managed to wait upon these few—

Her gaze landed on her brown-haired hero, and her heartbeat increased to a wild pace. William Barlow leaned forward in a chair, deep in conversation with the fellow seated adjacent to him—his friend, Mr. Fitzroy. Will's presence lit the dull taproom into a brilliant summer landscape simply by merit of his presence—especially when he threw his head back and laughed. And oh, what a laugh. Carefree and merry, as if he'd reached out his hand and pulled her into a jig with the lightness of it.

Mina grabbed a pitcher and filled it with ale, the draw of William too strong to deny. Bypassing the other customers, she headed straight for his table.

"He's invited me to a tea, of all things." His voice, smooth as fresh flowing honey, grew louder the closer she drew to his table. "Can you imagine that, Fitz? A tea. How awful."

A smile curved her mouth as she imagined taking tea with William. Just the two of them. Him in his finest frock coat with a snowy cravat. Her in a new gown. She'd pour a steaming cup for him, and he'd lift a choice little cake to her lips while speaking of his deepest affections. She sighed, warm and contented. "I should think a tea would be very pleasant," she murmured.

Both men turned toward her. Mr. Fitzroy spoke first. "Well, if it isn't the lovely Miss Scott, come to save me from this boorish fellow." He elbowed William.

Will arched a brow at her, a rogue grin deepening the dimples at the sides of his mouth. "I was wondering when you'd grace us with your appearance, sweet Mina."

Sweet Mina. Heat flooded her cheeks. She'd be remembering that endearment in her dreams tonight.

But for now, she scowled. "Mr. Barlow, if my father hears of your familiarity, I fear—"

"Never fear." He winked—and her knees weakened. "I'm a champion with ruffled fathers."

Ignoring his wordplay, she held up the pitcher. "Refills?"

William slapped his hand to his heart. "You know me too well."

Not as well as I'd like to. She bit her tongue. Where had that come from? Maybe Father was right. Maybe she had been reading too many books.

"I'm as intrigued as Miss Scott." Mr. Fitzroy held his cup out to her, for she'd filled William's mug first. "Why would you not want to attend your uncle's tea? As I recall, he's a jolly-enough fellow."

Will slugged back a long draw of his ale and lowered his cup to the table. "Nothing against Uncle Barlow, mind you. And in truth, I was pleased he'd made contact. It's just that, well. . .I am to bring my wife along."

Wife!

The pitcher clattered to the floor. Mina stared at it, horrified. Ale seeped into the cracks of the floorboards, the very image of her draining hopes and dreams. William Barlow had a wife?

Will shot to his feet. "Mina, you look as if you've seen the Cock Lane ghost. Are you ill?"

"I'm f–fine. The pitcher—it slipped, that's all." She crouched, righted the pitcher to preserve the remaining ale, then yanked the rag from her waistband

and mopped up the mess with more force than necessary. The scoundrel! All this time he'd had a hearth and home already tended by a wife? Did he have children as well? She scrubbed harder, grazing her knuckles against the rough wood. Good. She relished the pain and for a wicked moment thought about swishing the spilled ale over William's shoes.

"Wife?" Surprise deepened Mr. Fitzroy's voice also. So. . .Will's best friend had not known either? That was a small satisfaction, at least.

"This is news," Mr. Fitzroy continued. "When did that happen?"

Holding her breath, she ceased her scrubbing, though why she cared indicted her for being naught but a dunderheaded hero seeker. *Silly girl. Silly, stupid girl.*

William sank back to his seat. "Well, I don't actually have one yet. And that's the problem."

"Thank God." The words flew out before she could stop them, and she pressed her lips tight.

William's face appeared below the table. "Are you quite all right?"

"Yes. Just finishing up." She forced a smile, reached for the runaway pitcher, and stood. This afternoon was turning into a novel in its own right. For the first time since she'd met William, she couldn't decide if he were truly a hero or a villain.

Will straightened as well, his gaze trained on her. The sun slanted through the front window, angling over his strong jaw and narrow nose. But it was his eyes that drew her. So brilliant, so magnificently blue, a sob welled in her throat. She swallowed. She truly was a silly girl.

"Say, Mina," he drawled. "You wouldn't be willing to be my bride, would you?"

"I—I—" The words caught in her throat like a fish bone, and she coughed, then coughed some more. Heat blazed through her from head to toe. Surely, she hadn't heard right.

William's grin grew, his dimples deepening to a rakish angle. "Oh, don't panic. It would only be for one afternoon. Surely you could beg off serving for an hour a week from next Thursday?"

Her mouth dropped, but no words came out. What was she to say to that? Everything in her screamed to shout yes, but how could she possibly slip out from beneath Father's notice? And a week from next Thursday? Not that her social calendar was packed full, but something niggled her about the date.

"Oy, miss! Another round over here." Across the taproom, a stout fellow, buttons about to pop off his waistcoat, held a mug over his head.

"I—I don't know," she blurted out to Will and turned.

But William grasped her sleeve. "Please, Mina. Allow me to explain. It won't take but a moment."

She stared at his touch, a frown tugging her lips. Father wouldn't like her dawdling with William, but how could she refuse the man she'd cast as the champion in every story she'd read? With a quick nod and a brilliant smile to stave off the other customer, she turned back to Will. "Make haste. I have work to attend."

"Right, here's the thing." He leaned forward, the excitement in his tone pulling both her and Mr. Fitzroy closer to him so that they huddled 'round the table.

"Uncle Barlow is ready to choose his heir. It's between me and my cousin Percy—"

"Egad!" Mr. Fitzroy rocked back on his chair. "That pompous donkey? I should think there'd be no competition."

"I agree, but my uncle favors a married man. And since I am not. . ." Will tugged at his collar, loosening his cravat. "Well, I gave Uncle Barlow the impression I'd recently wed, or I'd not even be considered."

Mr. Fitzroy let out a long, low whistle.

Mina's eyes widened. "You lied to your uncle?"

William shook his head, the tips of his hair brushing against his shoulders. "No, not outright. I merely led him on a merry word chase, and he arrived at a particular conclusion."

Mr. Fitzroy chuckled. "One day, my friend, your deceptions will catch up to you."

"Perhaps. But not today. Not if you, my sweet Mina"—William captured her free hand and squeezed—"will agree to be my wife for the tea. I could pick you up at two o'clock. What do you say?"

Say? How could she even think with the warmth of his fingers wrapped around hers and his blue gaze entreating her to yield? It would be lovely to live a fairy-tale life if only for part of an afternoon. Take tea in a grand house, finally be a real lady, just like those she so often read about—

"Miss!" the man across the room bellowed again.

—*And* escape the drudgery of serving corpulent patrons who more often than not smelled of goats and sausages.

Pulling her hand away, she smiled at William. "I say yes."

God bless her! For surely her father wouldn't. Before Will could say anything more, she scurried off to fill the other patrons' mugs and drain her pitcher dry. On her way back to the tap, she swerved around a table, and her gown brushed against her hand. Paper crinkled at the contact.

Then she knew.

Setting the pitcher down on the counter, she glanced over her shoulder to make sure no one was looking before she retrieved the note from her pocket. A moan caught in her throat as she reread the instructions:

Sisterhood meeting November 10th
2:00 p.m.

Drat! That was a week from next Thursday. How was she to be in two places at once?

CHAPTER TWO

I have been bent and broken, but—I hope—into a better shape.
Great Expectations

No matter the time of day, London streets teemed as if a great bucket of humanity had been upended and dumped onto the sidewalks. And late afternoon was the worst. Cabs, drays, and coaches filled the cobblestones, forcing pedestrians to travel as far from the gutters as possible, lest they be splashed with liquid refuse of all sorts. William Barlow not only took it all in stride but relished the challenge as well. A good leg stretcher, that's what he needed—especially after the ridiculous proposal he'd just issued to Mina Scott. What in the queen's name had he been thinking?

"Hold up!" Fitz's voice turned Will around—his sudden stop earning him a scowl and a curse from a fishy-smelling sailor who smacked against him.

The man gave him a shove as he passed. "Watch yer step, ye carpin' swell."

Ten paces back, Fitz dodged a knife-seller's cart, one hand holding his hat tight atop his head, and caught up to Will. "I didn't realize this was a race."

"Sorry. My mind was elsewhere."

"Hmm, let me guess. Somewhere back at an inn with a certain blue-eyed beauty?"

Will clouted his friend on the back, and they fell into step together. "You can't be serious. Mina Scott is a sweet girl. Nothing more."

"As I suspected. And now that Miss Scott is out of ear range, how about you tell me the real reason for such a scheme?"

Will shrugged. "I don't know what you're talking about."

"Don't play the innocent with me. Ever since Elizabeth, you've avoided anything to do with women other than lighthearted banter, and you've never given Mina Scott a second thought. Something else is going on here, something mighty powerful to be prodding you to play the part of a husband."

Thankfully, they stepped off a curb to cross Bramwell Street, where it took all of William's concentration to weave in and out of traffic unscathed. And just as well—for he'd rather not dwell in the unforgiving land of memories.

Once across, Fitz joined his side, with only somewhat muddy trouser hems to show for the experience. "You know I won't be put off so easily."

That was an understatement. When Thomas Fitzroy was set on something, there was no turning the man back—a trait that served his friend well down at Temple Court. Even so, Will plowed through a few more pedestrians before he answered. "I told you everything. Uncle Barlow is—"

"Yes, yes." Fitz waved his fingers in the air like an orator making a point. "Uncle Barlow, what have you, and so on and so on. Not that I don't believe every word you said, but I suspect there are a few more words you've conveniently left out. So let's have it."

He snorted. "Perhaps you should have been a barrister instead of a law clerk."

"Perhaps you should get to the point."

Jamming his hands into his coat pockets, Will stared straight ahead. Better that than witness the pity that was sure to fill his friend's eyes once he told him. "It's my mother. She's not doing well. I can barely keep abreast with her medical bills, let alone continue to manage her housing expenses."

"Oh. . ." Fitz's feet shuffled. "Sorry, old chap. I didn't realize. Is she that bad off?"

"Hard to say. You know doctors." He shook his head as the last of October's light faded into the first gloam of evening. "I shall have to move her from France, which will mean setting up a household of my own instead of rooming with you." He sighed. "And that will come with a hefty price tag."

"I see. No wonder this whole inheritance thing is so important to you."

"It is. Don't get me wrong. I don't wish any ill on Uncle Barlow. Quite the contrary. I hope the old fellow lives a great many more years. But were I to be named heir, I'd have the collateral of the position if I must apply to a banker for funds. Lord knows I wouldn't get a penny on my name alone."

His friend's hand rested on Will's shoulder, slowing him to a stop. Will braced himself for the concern sure to be etched on Fitz's brow. But despite his preparation, he sucked in a breath at the sympathy welling in the man's eyes.

"I hope for your sake, and your mother's, that this all works out."

"Indeed." He cleared the huskiness from his voice and forced a half smile. "Let us hope so."

"But I feel I'd be remiss if I didn't mention this." Fitz rubbed the back of his neck. "Miss Scott is a beauty, no doubt. And ladylike. She's been nothing but kind and ever attentive. Yet is she the right sort of woman to impress your uncle as a realistic bride? She is an innkeeper's daughter, after all. Not exactly a highborn miss. And she's nothing like. . . Well, you know."

While it was a champion thing of his friend to voice his misgivings so earnestly, Will cast Fitz's cares aside. Mina Scott would charm Uncle Barlow, perfect manners or not, for she was a perfectly charming sort of girl.

"Maybe so, Fitz, but you have to admit she is a genteel sort of woman, well spoken and well read. And besides"—he shrugged—"there's no one else to ask."

The truth of his words hit home. Pulling away, he strode ahead. There *was* no one else to ask, and if this didn't work, how would he ever pay for his mother's increasing care? Even with Mina Scott's help, it would take a miracle for him to be named heir. He'd not even seen his uncle in over a year—a relationship he'd like to mend but didn't quite know how for the shame that still haunted him.

Last time he'd seen Uncle Barlow was when the man had bailed him out of gaol.

CHAPTER THREE

If there be aught that I can do to help or aid you, name it,
and on the faith of a man who can be secret and
trusty, I will stand by you to the death.
Master Humphrey's Clock

It was a grisly kind of day. The type of gloomy afternoon that stuck in one's craw and worked one's teeth to keep the cold at bay. Autumn was such a fickle friend: warm one day, frigid the next. Today, November's rude manners chased away the remnants of October's warmth. Mina tugged her collar tight against her neck as she dashed down the street.

Two blocks from the Golden Egg, she clutched her skirts in one hand and trotted up the stairs to a grey-stone lodging house. As soon as she ducked inside the entrance hall, she removed her veil and shrugged out of her black cape, hanging both on a peg near the door. The other ladies should already be here and wouldn't notice her dark wraps, or she'd have to field a surplus of questions, the chief one being, Who died? Her mourning cloak and veil would be a good disguise on the street when she later waited for William, but here?

Not at all.

She hurried up the stairs, passed the first floor, and stopped on the second. Halfway down the corridor on the left, she paused in front of a door with chipped paint and rapped thrice—twice—once. The door swung open, and she entered the meeting room of the Single Women's Society of Social Reform—which looked an awful lot like a bedchamber. The occupant, her friend Miss Whymsy, greeted her with a smile. The former governess was a plain-faced woman with steel-grey hair and posture that would make a marine look like a slouch.

"Welcome, my dear." Miss Whymsy pulled her into a prim embrace, smelling of lavender and well-used books. "We were beginning to think you might not make it."

"My deepest apologies." She pulled away with a sheepish smile, for it had been her request that the meeting be moved to an hour earlier than first announced. "Father kept me later than I expected, and it was hard to beg off without rousing his suspicions."

"No apology needed. I am glad you are here no matter the time." Miss Whymsy swept out her hand. "Please, have a seat."

Mina crossed the small room to an even smaller sitting area. Three other ladies perched on chairs near the tiny hearth, soaking in what warmth could be had from the sparse bit of burning coal and from the teacups clutched in their hands. Mina took an empty chair next to Effie Gedge, one of her dearest friends. Her skirt hardly touched the seat before Effie leaned toward her and whispered, "I so hate to see another one go."

"Me too." Mina's gaze landed on the woman across from her, and she couldn't help but wonder how Mary Bowman was holding up, this being her last meeting. Apparently, not too well, for after naught but a flickering smile, Mary stared into her teacup, as if all the courage in the world might be found there.

Miss Whymsy settled on the last remaining chair and lifted her chin. "I call this meeting to order, ladies."

Next to Effie, Miss Minton, every bit as grey-haired as Miss Whymsy, chortled a "Hear, hear" and set her teacup on the floor beneath her chair.

"Now then," Miss Whymsy continued, "as you all know, today's gathering is bittersweet. While we are happy one of our members is soon to be off on a journey of matrimonial bliss, it is always a bit of a sorrow to see one of our colleagues leave. Yet it is necessary if we are to remain the *Single* Women's Society of Social Reform."

"Hear, hear," Miss Minton rattled off again.

Miss Whymsy lifted a brow at her before she shifted her gaze to Mary. "Miss Bowman, you have served the society well these past years, and we thank you for your service."

"Yes, thank you," Mina and Effie said together.

"Hear, hear—"

"Millie." Miss Whymsy skewered Miss Minton with a stare that could knock the fidget out of a child. "You do not have to 'hear, hear' everything I say."

"If it is good enough for Parliament"—Miss Minton bunched her nose, adding wrinkle upon wrinkle to her face—"I should think it is good enough for us."

Miss Whymsy blew out a sigh, and Mina stifled a smile. The two were a cat and dog pair, always scuffling and ruffling, yet, at the end of the day, more often than not were willing to share a saucer of milk together.

"Pressing on." Miss Whymsy cleared her throat. "Miss Bowman, have you any parting words?"

Mary stood, though she was hardly taller than her chair even when she arose. Mina's heart squeezed. She would love to be married—especially to Will—yet when that day came, *if* it came, she would miss this fellowship, and judging by the trembling bottom lip on Mary, she would miss them too.

Bravely, Mary smiled at each of them in turn. "Ladies, it has been my joy to serve with you, and I thank you for the opportunity. I shall never forget any of you, my sisters, and though I will be married"—a lovely flush of pink flamed on her cheeks—"I shall endeavor to always look for ways to help downtrodden women everywhere."

"Well said." Mina smiled.

"I'll miss ye." Effie sniffed.

"Hear, hear." This time Miss Minton challenged Miss Whymsy with an arched brow.

Miss Whymsy ignored it. "Godspeed, Miss Bowman. You go with our blessings."

They all stood, and each one hugged Mary before she exited the room. Mina's gaze lingered on the door long after it closed, conflicting emotions roiling in her stomach. It would be lovely to walk out of here into the arms of a husband. Yet the bonds she'd made with these women would leave a mark once broken.

"Our next, and last, order of business for today is a new project." Miss Whymsy rushed ahead before Miss Minton could utter another *hear, hear*. "I have been approached by the director of the Institute for the Care of Sick Gentlewomen."

Effie's teacup rattled on her lap. "But how would a gent know of us? I thought the whole point o' our society was to remain secret, doing deeds unannounced, just like the good Samaritan."

"Don't worry, Miss Gedge." Miss Whymsy leaned across and patted Effie's knee. "I have taken care to keep all of your identities secret, referring to you simply by the first letter of your last name. You are Miss G, Mina is Miss S, and of course Miss Minton is Miss M."

Mina eyed Miss Whymsy over the rim of her teacup. "Pardon me, but isn't that slightly confusing?"

"Not at all. I can keep you straight, and I don't think it will matter to the director"—her gaze drifted to Effie—"who happens to be a woman, not a gentleman."

Effie gasped. "A lady?"

"Indeed."

Mina's cup tinkled against the saucer as she set it down, the glorious possibility of such a position sending a charge through her. Perhaps life could be more than serving mugs of ale at an inn—for clearly this woman, whoever she was, had found a way to do something important with her life.

"What is it the director would like us to do?" she asked.

"That's just it. I don't think we can possibly manage to do all she asks. The institute is growing at such an alarming rate that they are short on staff, funding, and housing. I am happy to volunteer my services, for the hospital mainly cares for my own kindred—retired governesses—and I suspect, Miss Minton, that you would be perfect for that role as well. Rolling bandages or serving tea and the like."

A smile spread broad and bright on Miss Minton's face. "Hear! Hear!"

This time, Miss Whymsy smiled as well. "Good. That takes care of the volunteering. Mina and Effie, is there any way the two of you would be able to help out?"

"Well," Effie tapped her teacup with her finger, clearly deep in thought, then stopped abruptly. "I've got it! As ye know, being that I'm a lady's maid, I have a fair amount o' castoffs from my employer. I could see my way to parting with a few. Talk is, Bagley's Brokerage in the Houndsditch Market is the place to sell. I'm sure I can wheedle a fair penny for some gowns."

Miss Whymsy clapped her hands. "Brilliant thinking, Miss Gedge." Her gaze drifted to Mina. "Have you any thoughts on the matter? I realize this may be a bit forward, but I feel I must at least bring it up. . . . Is there any chance of housing some of the women at your father's inn?"

She shook her head before Miss Whymsy could finish, a rudeness on her part, yet entirely unstoppable. Father would never allow such an unprofitable use of space, especially before Christmas. "I don't think that's a possibility."

"I see. . . ." Miss Whymsy's voice tapered to nothing.

The ensuing silence poked her conscience like little needles. The two older ladies would be volunteering their time. Effie could donate money. And she'd offered nothing but a big fat no. Yet what could she do? Oh, that she were a wealthy woman, able to bless others out of a storehouse of coins.

She bit her lip, picturing her tiny crock at home filled with shillings and pence—all the money she'd saved these past three years to purchase a new fob for Father's watch. . .a fob her mother had dearly wanted to purchase before her death. Since a girl, it had been Mina's dream to make her mother's wish come true. Should she sacrifice it for the sake of a request by a director she didn't even know?

But as she looked from Miss Whymsy's expectant face to Miss Minton's, the wrinkles carved into their parchment skin were a stark reminder that other women—*sick* women—were in need of that money. More than Father needed a fob, for had he not lived this long without one?

She sighed and, before she could change her mind, said, "I have a small amount on hand at home that I could contribute."

"Wonderful!" Miss Whymsy beamed. "That covers staffing and funding. And as for the housing, well, let's pray about it, shall we?"

Bowing their heads, they set the needs of the institute before the Lord, primarily the housing concern, then went on to bless Miss Bowman's upcoming marriage.

Miss Whymsy ended with an "Amen," and Miss Minton with a rousing "Hear, hear!"

"I believe that officially concludes this meeting. Ladies?" Miss Whymsy stood and held out her hand.

Each of them rose, forming a small circle, and put one of their hands atop the others' in the center. In unison, they lifted their voices. "To God's glory and mankind's good, use our hands and feet in service, oh Lord. Amen."

Before anyone could speak further, Mina edged toward the door. "As much as I'd love to stay and visit, I have to run. Do forgive me. Good afternoon, ladies."

"But Mina—"

She shut the door on Effie's voice, wincing at her own impropriety. But it couldn't be helped. If she didn't dash out of here now, she'd never make it on time to meet William Barlow's carriage.

But even if she were to run, she'd still be late, for the bong of the downstairs clock chimed two.

CHAPTER FOUR

Oh Sairey, Sairey, little do we know wot lays afore us!
Martin Chuzzlewit

Mina huddled closer to a streetlamp. The cold, iron pole offered little protection against the afternoon's bluster, but her black veil and cape might blend in with the dark pillar so she'd not draw undue attention. Hopefully.

Where was William? She hadn't been that late getting to the corner—only five minutes. Surely he would have waited that long.

Fighting the urge to lift her veil and survey the lane, she forced herself to remain statuesque—especially when pedestrians strode past. She'd taken the precaution of instructing Will to meet her five lanes away from the Golden Egg, but still. . . If one of her friends—or worse, Father's friends—chanced by and recognized her, she'd be hard-pressed to explain why she waited on a street corner alone for an unchaperoned ride with a man. Was she doing the right thing? The twisting of her stomach said no.

But even so, a small smile curved her lips. Though this was a mischievous charade, the forbidden excitement of taking tea with the man of her dreams pulsed through her. Was this how *Bleak House*'s heroine Ada Clare had felt when sneaking off to marry Richard Carstone?

Minutes later, a hansom cab rambled closer, and the jarvey pulled on the reins, stopping the carriage at the curb in front of her. It had to be Will, and though she knew it in her head, her heart still fluttered as he climbed out.

He studied her as he held the door open with one hand. "Mina, is that you?"

"Shh," she warned as she drew near, casting a look over her shoulder. Thankfully, no one stood close enough to have heard her name. "Yes, it's me," she whispered.

He offered his hand and a brilliant smile. "Then shall we?"

His strong fingers wrapped around hers as he boosted her into the cab. Once they were both seated, he rapped on the roof, and the carriage lurched into motion.

Sitting this close to Will, she fixed her gaze straight ahead. One peek at him would only add to the jitters in her stomach. Simply breathing in the scent of his bergamot cologne and bumping into his shoulder upped her pulse.

"I understand your desire for disguise, but. . ." He tugged the hem of her veil. "Uncle Barlow might get the impression ours is not a happy marriage."

Leaning forward, she scanned the street to make sure none of the figures they passed looked even remotely familiar, then she sank back against the seat. "I suppose I could take it off now."

She lifted the lacy fabric from her head, then worked to tuck the veil into her reticule. The small pouch strained at the seams, and the drawstring fought against her as she tried to tighten it. Perhaps she ought to have made sure the head covering would fit inside her bag before she'd left home. What would William's relatives think of her with such a lump hanging from her arm?

"I appreciate you going along with me." The warmth in Will's voice stilled her hands. With him beside her, would it even matter what his relatives thought?

"I hope this meeting won't prove too uncomfortable for you," he continued.

She faced him, and her heart rocked every bit as much as the cab's wheels juddering over the cobbles. This close up, his eyes were bluer than she'd credited, like a sea without shores, endless and sparkling. Half a smile softened his clean-shaven jawline, and for the first time, she noticed a slight tilt to one of his front teeth—an endearing little flaw.

"Don't fret about me." She clutched the seat to keep from banging against him as the cab turned a corner. "If I can manage a taproom of clerks and solicitors, I am confident I can manage your uncle."

"That's the spirit." His grin faded, and he looked away. "Though it's not my uncle I am concerned about."

At least that's what it sounded like he said. Hard to tell the way he'd spoken under his breath. She leaned toward him, ears straining. "What was that?"

"Oh, er, I was just wondering. . ." Once again, his blue gaze met hers. "Have you been to Purcell's before?"

"Purcell's? Oh, my!" Immediately her hand shot to her hair, tucking in strays and straightening her bonnet. How often she'd fancied a visit to the famed literary haunt, rubbing shoulders with some of her favorite authors, and now she was to actually patronize such a place? Why was God so good to her?

Clenching every possible muscle to keep from bouncing on her seat in anticipation, she smiled at Will. "Do you think we might spy Mr. Dickens or Mr. Tennyson? Maybe even the Bells or Mr. Melville?"

"I doubt I should recognize any of the fellows you just mentioned."

Her smile faded a bit. "But surely you've heard of them?"

"No, not a one. Should I have?"

Her smile disappeared altogether. He seriously didn't know such august names? Did William Barlow not read? Her throat closed, and she swallowed back the lump clogging it. This was a definite chink in her hero's armor.

"Mina? Is something wrong?"

Alarm deepened his voice, and she determined not only to forgive him for his ignorance but to introduce him to the wonders of literature as well. "No, nothing. That last bump didn't set well with my stomach, is all."

"Well, then thank goodness this ride is over"—the cab stopped—"for here we are."

Will opened the door and helped her out. While he paid off the jarvey, she forced the strap of her unwieldy reticule onto her wrist and looked up at the renowned establishment. Mist settled on her face and eyes, and she blinked so much it was hard to read the fancy name shingle with PURCELL's painted in gilt.

"Let's get you out of this dreadful weather." Will offered his arm.

She wrapped her fingers around his sleeve and walked into heaven. Inside the large reception area, her feet sank into a thick Turkish carpet. Wall sconces flickered, and a massive overhead chandelier glittered light like fairy dust over all. Beyond the podium, where a concierge stood as a sort of gatekeeper, the drone of voices hummed. How many stories were being hatched even as she stood here? How many clever ideas? What kind of great minds fortified themselves with tea while working out plots and characters and all manner of epic tales?

Will approached the concierge. "The name is Barlow, meeting with a Mr. Charles Barlow."

The man ran his finger along a document. Halfway down, the motion stopped, and he looked up. "Ahh, yes. One moment, please."

As the man turned to summon a porter, the front door opened. A gust of wind howled in—accompanied by a woman's strident voice remarking on the excessive chill of the day.

"Well, well, look at this. William already here and on time, no less." A man's voice attacked them from behind. "My fine cousin appears to be all cleaned up and with a pretty little bauble on his arm. How on earth did you manage either of those two miracles?"

Beneath her touch, Will's muscles hardened to steel. He blew out a low breath, then winked at her. "I hope you're ready for this."

Without waiting for her response, he guided her around to face two scowls. The woman in front of Mina was dressed head to toe in midnight blue and ornamented with an extravagant amount of black lace. Her blond hair was coiffed into a coil beneath a feathered hat and pierced through with a silver bodkin, as was all the rage. She was curvaceous, pretty, tall. All in all, quite striking.

Yet something wasn't right about the woman, giving Mina a queer feeling in her stomach. She edged nearer to Will. Nothing appeared untoward about the lady. Every button and thread was in place. No. . .it was more of an invisible atmosphere that clouded about her. A kind of foreboding. Like being alone in a big house and hearing a door slam—and knowing that something was coming for you.

Swallowing, Mina shifted her gaze to the man. He was shorter than the woman but every bit as snappily dressed in his dark grey suit with a white, high-stock collar. His round spectacles enlarged his eyes to dark marbles, and his black hair was pasted back with pomade. He might be a businessman. Or a lawyer. But the longer Mina stared, the more she suspected he might be better suited as an undertaker, so emotionless and coldly did he look upon her.

"Percy, Alice, good to see you." Will's voice strained on the word *good*.

The woman—Alice—sniffed as if he'd offered her a plate of rotted cabbage. "A pig in a suit does not a gentleman make, exemplified in your lack of introductions." Her head swiveled to Mina. "I am Alice Barlow, Percival's wife. And you are?"

Mina tensed. *These* were William's relatives? No wonder he spent most of his nights at the Golden Egg instead of taking part in family affairs.

Will placed his hand on the small of her back in a show of affection. "This is my. . .this is Mina."

Alice's upper lip twitched. "Mina? What sort of a name is that?"

"It's, uh. . ." Mouth suddenly dry as bones, Mina licked her lips, hoping to grease the way for more words to slip out. "It is the shortened form of Wilhelmina. My father's side of the family has Dutch roots."

"Oh." Alice said no more, but she didn't have to. The tone put Mina in her place—on a ladder rung clearly beneath Alice's jewel-toed shoes.

"Uncle mentioned you'd taken a wife." Percy's gaze drifted from Will to Mina. "My condolences."

Mina blinked. Were these people flesh and blood, or were they some of Mr. Dickens's villainous characters?

"Mr. Barlow," the concierge called out. "You may be seated now."

The man barely finished speaking before Percy and Alice shot into motion, nearly knocking her sideways were it not for Will's strong arm behind her. Her reticule swung wild, smacking into Alice as she passed—and earned Mina yet another glower.

Mina peered up at Will as his cousins disappeared through the door. "Are they always this way?" she whispered.

"No." A devilish grin tugged his lips. "Usually, they are worse."

But as she stepped into the grandeur of the tearoom, all thoughts of Will's cousins vanished. Walking beside her handsome prince, it was easy to pretend she was royalty. White linen tablecloths with fresh flowers adorned every table. Men and women of stature lifted dainty cakes to their lips or sipped from fine porcelain cups. The whole room twinkled as light shimmered off the gilded stripes on the pale blue wallpaper.

Slowly, the tight knots in her shoulders loosened, and she lifted her chin. This was where she wanted to belong, not slaving away in an inn that reeked of ale and grease. If she lived in such a world of opportunity and wealth, she could actually do something worthy with her life. Instead of scraping up saved coins to benefit the likes of the institute, she could give so much more. Do so much more. *Be* so much more, a benefactress that would really make a difference to others.

By the time they reached a table in the back corner, Will's cousins had already taken their seats, but yet standing was a thin fellow, dressed all in brown. White hair circled the man's head like a crown, tufting out at the sides near his ears. His face was a road map of years. Grey eyes—as piercing as Will's—twinkled with humour and something more. . .an innocence of sorts. As if, were the lines and grey hairs taken away, he might be naught more than a schoolboy looking for a good game of cricket.

"Uncle Barlow?" Will stared at the man. "Is it really you, sir?"

"Posh! Such formality. Of course it's me. Though I suppose I am quite a few stones lighter than when you last saw me." A cough rumbled in his chest, and he pulled out a handkerchief, holding it to his mouth until the spell passed.

Mina frowned. Will hadn't said anything about his uncle's frail health.

"Sorry." The man tucked the cloth back into his pocket with a wink reminiscent of Will's. "The past year has not been kind to me, but no cause for alarm. My doctor assures me I am on the mend. Now then." He pulled Will in for an embrace with a hearty pat on his back, then released him, chuckling. "This may be the first occasion you've ever arrived on time, my boy." His gaze swung toward her. "Surely you have wrought great miracles in my nephew."

She ought to answer him, truly, especially with the expectant tilt to his head, but her tongue fell flat. Facing this dear old man, posing as William's wife, suddenly stabbed her in the heart.

"Uncle," Will cut in, "allow me to introduce my. . .well, this is Mina. Mina, my uncle, Mr. Charles Barlow."

Uncle Barlow reached for her hand and bowed over it with a light kiss. "Welcome to the family, my dear. I look forward to getting to know you."

Her heart twisted, and she drew back her fingers. The old fellow would not say such things if he knew he held the hand of a deceiver.

She glanced over her shoulder, judging the distance to the door. She never should have agreed to this. Would Will forgive her if she dashed out of here now?

CHAPTER FIVE

There are strings. . .in the human heart
that had better not be vibrated.
Barnaby Rudge

Will tugged at his collar, despising the cravat choking his neck. Thank God this farce would soon be over. How could he have imagined this would work? He didn't have the slightest notion of how a husband should act, though he should have by now if Elizabeth hadn't—

He reached for his tea and slugged back a scalding mouthful, welcoming the burn. Anything to keep from remembering. He'd sworn to never again allow a woman access to his heart. What had possessed him to playact such a scene?

Beside him, Mina sipped her tea as she listened to one of Uncle's stories. Ahh, but she was a good sport and a true friend. Not to mention brave. He barely had the fortitude himself to sit here and endure Percy's remarks and Alice's thinly concealed glowers.

Across the table, Percy looked down his nose at him, a smug lift to one brow—the same look Will had received that Christmas years ago when, as lads, Percy had caught him with Uncle's snuffbox hidden behind his back. Percy never had been able to prove that he'd pinched a wad, but that hadn't stopped his cousin from trying.

Will snuck a covert glance over at Uncle Barlow. The old fellow seemed to be enjoying Mina, and he hadn't made one remark yet on Will's jaded past. At the very least, perhaps this tea would mend the relational fences Will had broken as a young fool. Even now, thinking of his past rebellious ways sickened him.

"Excuse me, Mina, is it?" Alice impaled Mina with a cancerous gaze. For a moment, she didn't speak, but twirled one finger around a silver locket. "What did you say your maiden name was?"

Mina, God bless her, smiled at the woman. "It is Scott."

"*Is?*" Alice's fingers froze midtwirl, and she lowered her hand.

Will tensed. A slip like that was enough rope in Alice's hand to string up

Mina and hang her with her own words. He forced a small laugh. "You'll have to excuse Mina, for you see, the name Barlow is still so new to her."

"Speaking of which, how long have you—" Uncle set down his teacup and once again pulled out his handkerchief as another coughing spell overtook him.

Will frowned. Was Uncle Barlow truly getting better? Perhaps he ought to press the man to get a second opinion from a different doctor.

The hacking faded, and Uncle tucked his kerchief away. Leaning toward Mina, he smiled at her. "As I was saying, how long have you known my nephew, my dear?"

She exchanged a glance with Will before she answered. "Nearly a year."

"Really?" Percy's eyes narrowed. "That seems a rather whirlwind courtship from start to finish. How long did you say you've been married?"

"Tell me, Percy," Will cut in, hoping to divert the man. "I've been meaning to ask, has your bout of the itch cleared up yet?"

Red worked its way up Percy's neck. "I will thank you to keep my personal information to yourself."

Alice swung her gaze to Will, apparently impervious to her husband's distress. "At least your wife's former surname is not an unpronounceable bit of French twaddle like your mother's was."

Beneath the tablecloth, his hands curled into fists. He should've known his mother would have been shaken out and hung to dry at some point in today's conversation. She always was—which was why they could never know she was still alive. Working his jaw, he forced his tone to remain light. "My mother has nothing to do with this."

"I should think she does." Percy faced Uncle Barlow, nearly blinding them all as chandelier light reflected off his glasses. "Surely you would hate to see the wealth of your English forefathers tainted by someone with French blood."

"My husband is right." Alice sipped her tea as she eyed Uncle Barlow. "Percy has solid investments lined up with men who have bloodlines that go back to King Richard. Dear Uncle, there should be no more delay in getting your will and property signed over to Percy."

Uncle grunted, then drifted sideways toward Mina. " 'Something will come of this. I hope it mayn't be human gore.' "

She clapped her hands together with a laugh at Uncle Barlow's quotation. "Simon Tappertit is one of my favorite characters in *Barnaby Rudge*."

"Oh? A Dickens admirer, are you?" Uncle Barlow leaned back in his chair, surveying the breadth of the tearoom. "Look, there he goes now. Posh it! I should have liked to have introduced you."

Will followed his uncle's gaze to see a long-legged man in a houndstooth dress coat clap a bowler atop his head and stride out the door.

"You know Charles Dickens?"

The awe in Mina's voice drew his gaze back to her. She stared at Uncle, wide-eyed and pink cheeked, respect and admiration radiating off her in waves. What would it feel like if she looked at Will so? His chest tightened. Even during their best moments, Elizabeth had never paid him such due.

"I should say so," Uncle answered. "Charles and I go way back. Let me tell you of the time—"

"Enough nattering of folderol." Percy clinked his teacup onto the saucer, jarring them all. "Back to the matter at hand."

"I agree." Picking up her napkin, Alice dabbed her lips, apparently finished with her refreshment and the whole conversation. "I see no reason to delay this affair."

"Especially since it appears you've already spent Uncle's money on some ridiculous investments," Will shot back.

"Why, I ought to—"

"Oh, pardon me. Did I say that aloud?"

"Listen, *Cousin*." Percy shot the word like a poison arrow. "You are unfit in every respect to inherit Uncle Barlow's estate. My wife is perfectly astute in her observation. I see no reason to postpone the paperwork whatsoever."

"Take a care, Cousin. You are dreadfully close to suffering an apoplexy." Will stifled a smile at the slight tremor rippling across Percy's shoulders. Truly, it was wicked of him to prod the man so, but ever so satisfying. Were Fitz here, he'd be rolling on the floor, laughing in spasms.

Alice gasped such a sharp intake, her corset strings were likely in danger of snapping. "I never! Such a lack of manners. Such ill-bred, uncouth—"

Soft laughter and a bass chuckle drew all their attention. Mina and Uncle Barlow conspired over their teacups like bosom companions, alternating between whispers and laughter.

Uncle wiped the moisture from his eyes with his knuckle. "William, you could not have married a more delightful young lady. I am pleased that you have mended your ways and become a man of honour. It seems you've taken full advantage of the second chance I offered you a year ago, and I couldn't be more proud."

Will's gut churned, and a sour taste filled his mouth. Those were exactly the words he'd hoped to hear, the sole reason for asking Mina to attend this tea. But now that the victory was his, he didn't want it. Not like this.

Averting his gaze, he hung his head. "Thank you, sir."

Alice blew out a snort. "Pish!"

Uncle Barlow held up a hand, cutting her off. "As you all know, I am soon to announce an heir for my estate, and I've given much thought to it these past months. Therefore, I should like to name—"

Will looked up. Alice and Percy leaned so far toward Uncle, their chairs might go under at any moment. Even Mina quieted.

"—a date two weeks hence," Uncle continued. "Yes, in exactly a fortnight, I think. We shall meet over dinner the Thursday following next at my town house. Eight o'clock. Is this agreeable?"

"Yes." Will's voice chimed in unison with his cousins', offset by Mina's, "No."

Will draped his arm around Mina's shoulder, ignoring the tension his touch created. "Mina is right. We should first check our calendar. Yes, my sweet?" He gave her a little squeeze.

And a sharp kick jabbed him in the leg. The little firebrand. He drew back his hand.

"Well, well, William. I must say I am impressed with such forethought." Uncle Barlow stroked his jaw. "You will let me know at your earliest convenience, will you not?"

"Of course," he said before Mina could speak.

Ignoring the sneers on his cousins' faces, he blew out a long breath. That crisis had been averted, but he'd soon face an even bigger one—what to do about the dinner in two weeks.

CHAPTER SIX

Accidents will occur in the best regulated families.
David Copperfield

Dinner. Two weeks. In a fine London town house.

Uncle Barlow's invitation sank to Mina's stomach like one too many biscuits. As much as she was growing to like the man, there was no way she could attend. All the bright beauty of taking tea at Purcell's faded as she glanced at Will. How she hated to disappoint him, but stealing away for an hour in the afternoon was altogether different from being gone an entire evening for hours on end. And now that she'd met his dear uncle, the thought of continuing their charade pricked her conscience.

The touch of Uncle Barlow's hand atop hers pulled her gaze back to the old fellow, and her heart twisted at the affection shining in his grey eyes. Will's uncle reminded her far too much of her grandfather, God rest his soul. Grandfather had been the only man to understand her love affair with literature. . . until now.

"It has been a delight to meet you, my dear. I look forward to seeing you again." Uncle Barlow leaned closer, speaking for her alone. "When 'all the knives and forks were working away at a rate that was quite alarming; very few words were spoken; and everybody seemed to eat his utmost in self-defense, as if a famine were expected to set in before breakfast.'" He reared back in his seat and challenged her with a tip of his chin. "Can you name that one?"

She couldn't stop the smile that stretched her lips. "*Martin Chuzzlewit.*"

Uncle Barlow's shoulders shook with a great chuckle. "Ahh, but you do a heart good." Then he pressed his hands on the tabletop and stood. "And now, I bid you all adieu."

Their chairs scraped back as one. "Good day, Uncle Barlow," she said along with Will.

But Percy and Alice immediately swarmed the man, hooking their arms through his. "We shall be glad to escort you to the door."

"No need." He shrugged them off. "I may have a cough, but I am not feeble."

Collecting his cane, he threaded his way through the tables and disappeared out the door.

Will offered Mina his arm, then squared off with Percy. "Until next time, Cousin."

Percy scowled. "Indeed."

As she and Will crossed to the door, Mina memorized every last inch of the tearoom, for she'd revisit it in daydreams to come. In the foyer, Will helped her into her coat, and when they stepped outside, she left Purcell's behind feeling a curious mix of lightness and heaviness. That she'd have to tell Will she couldn't attend the dinner weighed her down. So did the thought of the disapproval in Uncle Barlow's eyes when he discovered the truth.

But regardless, as she stood next to Will while he hailed a cab, she couldn't stop from curving her lips upward. It had been lovely to be a lady for an afternoon, so much so that if it weren't improper, she would have thrown up her arms and twirled. . .but wait a minute. Her gaze shot to her arm—which lacked an overly stuffed reticule.

"Oh!" She laid her fingers on Will's coat sleeve. "I'm afraid I left my bag back at the table."

"Not to worry. I'll retrieve it in a trice—"

"No." She shook her head. "I'll dash off. You hail a cab. If I stay any later, Father will get suspicious."

Will's brow crumpled, but at last he consented. "Very well."

Turning on her heel, she darted back into Purcell's and stopped at the concierge stand. "I'm sorry, but I believe I left my bag at the table."

"It may have been cleared by now," the fellow answered. "Yet you are free to take a look."

Murmuring a thank-you, she hurried into the tearoom, trying not to look conspicuous as she rushed to the table in the rear corner. But the dishes had been removed. A new cloth awaited the setting of a fresh tea set, and no black knit bag sat beneath the chair where she'd laid it.

She pursed her lips. *Oh, bother.* Though the small pouch contained only her veil and no money, still, it was a good veil. Her only one. And she'd be sorry to lose it.

Retracing her steps, she worked her way to the side of the large chamber, where she'd have a straight shot back to the foyer. She'd barely made it when Percy and Alice appeared from the necessary rooms. Drat! Facing them with Will at her side had been hard enough. Alone she was no match. In two clipped steps, she flattened behind a large potted plant, using the greenery for cover.

As Will's cousins drew close, Alice's voice travelled a layer above the din of tea chatter. "There is no time to waste, especially if your uncle is to name the heir in two weeks. You must line up an appointment with the doctor and the administrator."

"Yes, of course." Percy grumbled. "Once the paperwork is signed, I'll make sure Uncle goes the way of Aunt Prudence. Though William will no doubt put up a fuss once he finds out."

"That is a problem. . .but what if he doesn't hear of it? What if we simply lead him to believe your uncle is retiring to his country estate? William hasn't visited there in years. I don't see why he should start now."

"He might, now that he's got a wife."

Their voices started to fade, and Mina wavered. It was wicked to eavesdrop, but judging by what she'd already heard, Will's cousins meant some kind of harm to Uncle Barlow—harm that perhaps she could prevent. Edging away from the plant, she angled her ear to catch the last drift of their conversation as they moved toward the foyer.

Alice snorted. "Then we'll tell your cousin that Uncle isn't feeling up to company. Something about his cough or other such tale. Besides, once your uncle is committed to an asylum, he won't last long. We'll be the owners of the estate, and Will and his bride can go to kingdom come."

"You are delightfully devious, my dear."

Alice's purr disappeared with her out the door, leaving Mina behind with a pounding heart and a righteous anger. Will's cousins didn't just want Uncle Barlow's money. They wanted to destroy him.

And in the worst possible way.

CHAPTER SEVEN

The plain rule is to do nothing in the dark,
to be a party to nothing underhanded or mysterious,
and never to put his foot where he cannot see the ground.
Bleak House

Sneaking a covert look into the foyer to make sure Will's cousins were gone—and finding it empty—Mina dashed out of the tearoom.

"Miss!" The porter's voice stopped her retreat.

She stared at the reticule sitting on his upturned palm, but all she could think of were Will's horrible cousins and their threat to Uncle Barlow. Would they truly shut the old fellow away? And if they did, how long could he possibly last?

"Is this your bag, madam?"

The man's question rattled her from her dark thoughts, and she reached for the black pouch. "It is, and I thank you."

Without another word, she whirled and dashed out to where Will waited at the side of a cab.

He offered his hand to help her step up, then looked closer at her face. "Are you all right? You look as if you've. . .hold on. Did you have to square off with Percy and Alice?" He shook his head. "I should've gone to retrieve your bag. Forgive me?"

She frowned. If only it were something so trivial. "There is nothing to forgive," she murmured.

Clutching his hand, she desperately tried to figure out how to tell Will all she'd overheard. She settled her skirts on the cab's seat, trying not to inhale overmuch. It was going to be a long ride home in a hackney that reeked of sardines and cigar smoke. As Will climbed in and shut the door, not even his pleasant bergamot scent could beat back the rank odour—or stop the sickening twist of her heart. Poor Uncle Barlow.

As soon as the cab rolled onward, she turned to Will.

But his words came out first. "Thank you, Mina, for everything. I daresay my uncle is completely smitten with you."

A small smile trembled across her lips, for the feeling had been completely mutual. Not only had the old fellow quoted from some of her favorite books, but he also kept company with authors she longed to meet. "Your uncle Barlow is a dear old man. I see where you get your good humour. But there's something I must tell you."

He humphed. "Would that Percy might have gotten a smidgen of Uncle's humour as well, hmm?"

She bit her lip, stopping the agreement from flying from her lips. Will's friend Mr. Fitzroy couldn't have been more right when he'd deemed the fellow a pompous donkey.

"Come on." Will nudged her with his elbow. "Admit it. My cousin is an odious beast."

"Your words, not mine."

"Yet you thought so, did you not?"

"Well. . .I do not normally like to speak ill of people, but there is something—"

"Something?" His brows rose. "That's putting it mildly. There's far more than something wrong with Percy. Since we were children, he's done nothing but browbeat me or anyone else who crosses his path. A learned trait, I suppose, from his father. But you, Mina," his voice softened. "You were a terribly good sport about the whole thing. Still, I am thankful it's over. I'll never expose you to Percy or Alice again."

"But what about the dinner?"

"I'm not sure yet, but I'll have a few days to figure it out. At the very least, I could say you simply weren't feeling up to attending, which wouldn't be a huge stretch, for Lord knows even I never feel up to rubbing elbows with Percy."

"But I—"

"No buts about it. I cannot ask you to do more. You've been a good friend."

Friend? Oh, how she wished to be so much more. The cab clattered along and her darker thoughts returned, rattling her as much as the jarring ride. Would her lack of appearance at that dinner cause Uncle Barlow to name Percy his heir? And if Percy were named. . .she shuddered as his words surfaced in her mind.

"Once the paperwork is signed, I'll make sure Uncle goes the way of Aunt Prudence."

"Will." She shifted on the seat and faced him. "Tell me what happened to your aunt Prudence."

His eyes narrowed. "How on earth do you know her name? Did Uncle mention something about her?"

"No. I overheard Percy and Alice speaking of her when I went back to find my reticule."

"Did you?" A glower shadowed his face, and suddenly the cheerful man she adored vanished. "What did they say?"

Plagued by a sudden bout of nerves, she licked her lips. Did he think ill of her for eavesdropping, or had the mention of his cousins darkened his brow?

"Alice said something about paperwork being signed and your uncle going the way of Aunt Prudence. I pray I am wrong on my assumptions, but I must know. What happened to your aunt?"

Lightning flashed in Will's eyes, and she edged back—which was a trifling distance in a cab of this size.

"What is it?" she whispered.

"My aunt Prudence," he gritted out, "was committed to an asylum. At the time, Uncle Barlow acted on advice from her physician. Yet she was horribly mistreated in the name of medical science, and by the time he finished the paperwork to have her released, well. . .it was too late."

Breathe. Just breathe. But no good. Though Mina tried to ignore them, ghosts from the past rose up and squeezed the air from her lungs. She flung out her hand to grip the side of the cab.

"Mina? Are you ill?"

She trained her gaze on him, slowly bringing him into focus until she could shake the memory of voices screeching to her from across the years. "You *cannot* allow anyone to put your uncle into an asylum," she said finally. "You must go to him and reveal what your cousins are plotting."

He assessed her in silence for a long moment, his jaw grinding the whole while. "I don't think Uncle Barlow will believe me. My reputation is not pretty in his eyes. He'll see the attempt as nothing but a scheme to put Percy out of the running."

She jerked sideways to face him, dropping her reticule and spilling her veil onto the cab's floor. How was she to make Will realize how important it was for him to take a stand against such an atrocity? "You must try! Your uncle's life may depend upon it."

Will stared at her, and only God knew what went on behind those blue eyes of his, now turned to ice. Had she said too much? Been too forceful? Crossed some sort of line she ought not have?

He bent and retrieved her belongings, taking time to brush off a bit of mud from the veil before handing it back. "Trust me, Mina." His voice was low and weighted with a burden she couldn't begin to comprehend. "I understand the severity of the situation. My cousins would only deny it should I bring the charge against them. Scraps of overheard whispers are insufficient evidence in a court of law."

She sank back against the seat, clutching her bag. He was right of course, but that was no comfort. Slowly, she smoothed out the wrinkles in her veil, then forced a steadiness to her voice that she didn't feel. "Do you not believe me?"

"Nothing of the sort. I know better than most the deviousness of Percy's character. Blast it!" Lifting his hat, he raked his fingers through his hair. "I need proof, Mina. If I hope to convince Uncle Barlow of Percy's intent, I'll need something more concrete than mere hearsay."

"But if your cousins succeed and put your uncle into an asylum, he won't survive. The cures used in the name of medicine are enough to kill a healthy person. You heard your uncle's cough. Shutting him away in a draughty institution would be the end of him."

Will's hands curled into fists on his thighs, so unlike his amiable self. "I know," he breathed out.

She heaved a sigh herself. Of course he'd need something more valid than what she'd overheard. But how else could his cousins be stopped?

The cab slowed, and she pressed her hand to the door, as though by so doing, she could delay her decision. She met Will's gaze, afraid to hope—yet more afraid not to. "Do you think. . .is there a chance your uncle Barlow will name you heir at his dinner?"

Will scrubbed his hand over his face. "As much as I'd like to say yes, the truth is I do not know."

"Are there any other options if Percy is your uncle's choice? You are a law clerk. Are there not statutes in place to prevent such a heinous act?"

"None." His mouth twisted into a rueful smile. "I'm afraid the legal system is in need of an overhaul in more than one way."

Why did everything seem to be against that dear old man? She shoved open the door, debating what to do all the while, then faced Will. Icy rain pelted in from outside, and she shivered, though less from the chill than from her decision. "Well then, we will just have to make sure your uncle chooses you over Percy at that dinner."

Will's jaw dropped, and for a moment no words came out. "You. . .you want to go through with this?"

She lifted the veil and covered her face, then clutched her reticule with a death grip.

"We must do everything we can to keep your uncle from being committed to an asylum. No one should ever have to suffer what my mother did."

CHAPTER EIGHT

These sequestered nooks are the public offices of the legal
profession, where writs are issued, judgments signed,
declarations filed, and numerous other ingenious machines
put in motion for the torture and torment
of His Majesty's liege subjects.
The Pickwick Papers

William stared at the stack of documents in his hands, but he didn't see them. All he could focus on was the haunted glaze in Mina's eyes as she'd run out of the cab yesterday. A look so ripe with heartbreak and sorrow, he'd wanted to pull her into his arms and protect her from it—and that was a feeling so new and foreign he still didn't know what to do with it. Thunderation! He never should have allowed Uncle Barlow to believe he was married. What a tangled web he'd woven.

Giving himself a mental shake, he reached for the bell on his desk and rang it. No sense dwelling on what couldn't be made right—not yet, anyway. As he waited for a runner to leave the cluster of other errand boys near the door, he determined to go to the Golden Egg as soon as the workday was over and put a smile back onto Mina's face. It was the least he could do for having troubled her with his family affairs.

Satisfied with his plan of action, he tucked the papers into a courier bag and inhaled his first relaxed breath of the morning. The Temple Court clerks' room hummed with quiet activity. Papers shuffled. Pen nibs scritch-scratched like little feet running across so many pages, and the hushed whispers of conferring clerks circled the room, as dry and rustling as leaves caught up in an eddy.

A ruddy-cheeked lad, flat cap set low on his brow, approached his desk with his hand out. "Where to, sir?"

"Barrister Dalrymple, King's Court Chambers." He started to hand over the packet, when Thomas Fitzroy reached out and snatched it away.

"Are you out of your mind?" Fitz rumbled, garnering a black look from the clerk seated a row ahead.

"Are you out of yours?" Will whispered back. "This Jarndyce brief needs to get to Barrister Dalrymp—"

He stiffened. Great heavens! Fitz was right. He'd nearly sent the paperwork to the wrong barrister.

"Thank you, Charlie. That will be all for now." Fitz dismissed the runner with a nod of his head, then frowned down at Will. "What's going on? That's the third error you've made in the past hour, and this one could have cost you your job."

"I know. I. . .well. . .it's complicated." He laced his hands behind his head and looked up at Fitz—his true friend. His only friend, really, since his fall from grace.

"Complicated?" Fitz snorted. "It always is with you. Let's have it."

Will shoved back his stool. Perhaps his friend had a useful thought or two on his current conundrum, for if nothing else, Fitz always had an opinion. "Very well. Come along."

He wove past their fellow clerks, beyond a wall lined with bookshelves, then skirted the collection of runners waiting for the chance to deliver documents. Out in the corridor, he stopped halfway down and leaned against the wall.

Fitz pulled up alongside of him, practically bouncing on his toes. "I can't wait to hear this. What is it that has you so befuddled?"

"Remember that tea I told you about, the one Mina Scott agreed to attend with me?"

For a moment, Fitz's brows drew into a line, then suddenly lifted. "Ahh. That's right. I completely forgot to ask you about it. I'm afraid it was a late night for me with the King's Court boys last evening." He winced and massaged his temple with two fingers. "How did it go?"

Before Will answered, he listed aside and scanned the passageway beyond Fitz's shoulders. The walls of Temple Court contained an overzealous penchant for gossip—and he'd rather not provide fodder for this week's feast. Thankfully, this early in the day, most clerks were still readying their papers for delivery, and none lurked about here. Even so, he lowered his voice. "Not good at all. Uncle Barlow's life is in peril if my cousin Percy gets his hands on the old man's estate. Mina overheard Percy threaten to have Uncle committed to an asylum should he be named heir."

A growl rumbled in Fitz's throat. "Your cousin always was a conniving cur."

"Indeed. And unless I convince Uncle that I am the more deserving beneficiary, there will be nothing I can do to stop him. Knowing Percy, he's likely already got a physician in his pocket, ready to sign whatever papers are needed to have my uncle committed."

"Hmm." Fitz folded his arms. "Then we'll have to fill your pocket as well."

He narrowed his eyes. "What do you mean?"

"Even if what you say is true, and your cousin has people in place, that shouldn't stop you from finding other people to counteract his devious plan. Perhaps there is a loophole in the committal process that can be found. Or maybe there's some kind of reversal application, or well, I don't know. But I do know someone who would. Old Kenwig's the man for you."

Kenwig? Of course. He should have thought of the elderly barrister himself. The man was more ancient than half the laws on the books. Will rolled his shoulders, the tension in his muscles already loosening. "Is he in today?"

"Only one way to find out. Go on." Fitz clouted him on the back. "I'll look over that Jarndyce brief while you're at it."

"Thanks. I owe you one." He took off down the passage.

And Fitz's voice followed. "I'll be sure to cash in on that. Tonight. The Golden Egg."

Will trotted up the stairway. The corridor at the top was far better decorated than that to which the clerks were delegated. His shoes sank into a rug instead of thudding against wooden planks, and light glimmered from brass sconces, not tin. This was a world of silks, not woolens—the world of wealth Elizabeth had aspired to. . .and won.

Shoving down bitter memories, he strode the length of the corridor, and found the door to Barrister Kenwig's receiving room open. A good sign, that. He entered, expecting to persuade Kenwig's personal attendant for an interview with a smile and a coin, if need be. But the tall desk inside and the stool behind it sat empty. Beyond that, the door to the barrister's inner chamber yawned open. Perhaps the clerk had ducked in to have a word with the old man. Will stepped nearer, straining to listen, but no conversation drifted out. Emboldened, he strode to the threshold and peeped in.

On the other side of a massive desk sat a bulwark of the English legal system. Barrister Kenwig lifted a document in one gnarled hand and a magnifying glass in the other—making one eye appear larger than life, slightly milky but bearing keen intelligence. He wore his wrinkles like a garment, the deep creases on his face in sore need of a good ironing. Though the morning was well advanced, he hadn't yet donned his black silk robe.

Will rapped on the doorframe, thankful the man hadn't left for court already. "Pardon me, Barrister. I wonder if I might have a word?"

Kenwig lowered the magnifier and squinted at him. "Ahh, young Master Barlow. Come in. I can spare a few moments."

"Thank you, sir." He crossed the length of the chamber, inhaling the scent of musty books and beeswax, and as he drew nearer the man, breathed in an underlying odour of mothballs. He sank into the leather high-back in front of the barrister's desk. "I shall be brief. There is a hypothetical situation I was discussing with another clerk, one on which I should like your counsel."

"Very well." Kenwig reclined, his chair creaking—or maybe his bones. Hard to tell.

Will leaned forward. "Let's say an elderly gentleman who's never sired children of his own signs over his estate to another relation. This potential heir is a deviant at heart and has the old man committed to an asylum, thereby effectively taking possession of the man's money before he is deceased. And this brings me to my question. Is there any way to counteract or reverse that committal before it's been completely processed?"

The barrister's gaze drifted toward the ceiling, as if an answer might be found in the carved plaster moulding. The mantel clock ticked, and the coals in the grate sank, but Kenwig said nothing.

Nor did Will. He'd learned long ago the best route with the old fellow was to allow him to roam the long corridors of his learned mind.

At length, Kenwig's gaze lowered to his. "Not before it's been processed, but afterward, there are two ways. Discharge of a patient can be initiated by the medical superintendent or at the request of the family."

"Truly?" He stifled a laugh. All he'd have to do was file counter-paperwork? Thank God! A smile twitched his lips.

"It appears this was not so hypothetical after all, hmm?" The barrister tapped a bony finger atop his desk. "Do not tell me you're the deviant, Mr. Barlow."

"No, sir." He glanced back at the door, on the off chance the attendant had returned. The threshold remained empty, but he scooted to the edge of his chair and tempered his tone. "It is my cousin, sir, though he's not yet officially been named heir. I may still have a chance at that. But if not, at least I know that I would be able to get my uncle released with a simple request."

Far lighter in spirit than when he'd first entered the chamber, Will stood and dipped his head in a respectful bow. "Thank you for your time, Barrister, and your sage wisdom. A very good day to you."

"Oh, Mr. Barlow." The old fellow lifted his finger. "One more thing."

Will paused, trying to ignore the foreboding twinge in his gut. "Yes, sir?"

"I should mention that while a discharge can be initiated by you, there is no guarantee it shall be granted. That kind of paperwork also needs the signature of the parish magistrate."

"That shouldn't be a problem. Should it?"

The barrister's thin shoulder lifted in a shrug. "Deviancy is not limited to unscrupulous family members. Tell me, what parish are we speaking of?"

"My uncle's town house is in St. James. His estate, in Harlow."

"Hmm." The word vibrated through the room like a faraway roll of thunder.

"Sir?"

"Well, I suppose it would depend upon where the paperwork is drawn up. I cannot speak for Harlow, as I am not well versed in the ethics of Essex law keepers, but I can tell you that the St. James magistrate is not known for his stalwart morals. I've heard rumours he is a man for hire. Tell me, Mr. Barlow, on the off chance the Harlow magistrate is of the persuadable variety, who has deeper pockets, you or your cousin?"

Blast! His fingers curled into fists. If Percy inherited, he'd have the larger purse—and the upper hand.

CHAPTER NINE

In a word, I was too cowardly to do what I knew
to be right, as I had been too cowardly to
avoid doing what I knew to be wrong.
Great Expectations

Mina strolled down Whitewell Street with her friend Effie Gedge. A brisk November wind pushed her from behind. But even so, her steps slowed as she neared the spot where she'd fled from the cab that rainy afternoon a week ago now—*before* Will could ask about her mother. A heroine would've given him some kind of explanation instead of running off like a coward. Oh, what a humbling truth.

Next to her, Effie rattled on about something, but it was hard to focus on her friend's words with so much guilt muddling her thoughts. Will had stopped by the Golden Egg the day after the tea, and the day after that. . . and, well, every day. But she'd avoided any sort of detailed conversation with him. The questions in his eyes ran too deep and many. She never should have mentioned her mother. Though she'd been hardly more than seven years old when Mother had died, it was a memory she didn't often revisit and rarely shared with anyone. What was the point of lifting a rock and staring horrified at the creepy-crawlies beneath?

Oh, Mother. What would it be like to have a soft shoulder to share her burdens with instead of a father who could think of nothing other than the upcoming Christmas Eve party or how to marry her off? She heaved a long, low breath. She'd never know, she supposed, and that was a perpetual ache.

Effie threaded her arm through hers. "That's the fifth time ye've sighed since we left the ribbon shop, love."

She matched her pace to Effie's and glanced sideways at her friend. "Hmm?"

"Have ye heard a word I've said?"

"Of course. You were saying how Mrs. Lane's new babe is the most adorable thing you've ever seen."

Effie frowned. "That was *before* the ribbon shop."

"Then you remarked on how exceptionally attentive Mr. Lane is to his wife and new son."

"That was *inside* the ribbon shop."

"Then you said that baby Benjamin is the sweetest thing ever and. . .er. . .something more about your employer." She released Effie's arm and lifted her skirts to avoid the mud. Effie followed suit, and they parted ways to maneuver around a puddle.

As soon as they drew together on the other side, Effie rummaged in her reticule and pulled out an old coin, then reached for Mina's hand and dropped it into her palm.

What on earth? Mina lifted the piece of gold to eye level. The edges were jagged in a few places. On one side, a big X—or maybe a cross—was embossed. Hard to tell for the wear. How many fingers had rubbed against this bit of metal? The other side sported foreign words, circling the perimeter, unlike any she'd ever seen. "What is this?"

"A second-chance coin. 'Twas once given to me by Mrs. Lane."

"A what?" She scrunched up her nose at her friend.

"Why, I'm giving ye a second chance, love."

She studied her friend's face. Brown eyes the colour of a stout cup of tea peered back at her. What was Effie going on about? Maybe she should have been paying closer attention. "For what exactly do I need a second chance?"

"To tell me what's really on yer mind." A passing dray lumbered by, nearly drowning out Effie's words with its grinding wheels. Her friend stepped nearer. "Ye've not been yourself the entire hour we've been together, and ye've very niccly danced around all my questions. I haven't much time remaining a'fore I must return to Mrs. Lane with this new lace." She patted her small parcel. "So, ye best talk fast, my friend."

The coin warmed against her skin, yet she wasn't so sure she wanted a second chance to reveal the snarly mess inside her head and heart. Still. . .it would be a release of sorts. And she hadn't a truer friend than Effie. She wrapped her fingers tight around the coin for strength. "Very well, but you mustn't breathe a word of this to anyone. Not to Miss Whymsy and especially not to Miss Minton, for she'd 'hear, hear' it all over town. Promise?"

Effie nodded, more solemn than the Reverend Mr. Graves on a Sunday morning. "Upon my word."

Mina tugged her friend aside, pulling her close to the glass window of Truman's Tinctures and Powders, well out of the path of pedestrians or curious ears. Even so, she lowered her voice so only Effie might hear. "You know that patron I've remarked on a few times over the past year?"

"If ye're speaking of the dashing Mr. Barlow, your figuring is way off. Few? Pah!" Effie chuckled. "If I only had a farthing for each time you sang the praises of the man, I'd be wealthy as a—"

"You see?" Mina cut her off with a glower. "This is why I haven't told you anything, for you can't manage to keep from teasing."

"All right." Effie's mouth rippled as she tried to stifle her grin. "I promise. Not another word."

With a glance past Effie's shoulder, she scanned the lane. Several men strode past on long legs, each carrying a paper-wrapped parcel. A stoop-shouldered lady in black shambled by, leaning heavily on a cane. Yet no one appeared to take an interest in her or Effie, so she faced her friend. "Mr. Barlow asked me to attend a tea with him and his uncle. That's why I had to ask to change our society meeting time last week."

"Aha! When you slipped out o' there like a wisp o' the breeze, I knew something weren't right." Effie arched a brow. "Will you soon be going the way of Mary Bowman then?"

"Of course not." But the thought of such pulsed through her. Despite the shortcomings she'd started to detect in Will, to be his true wife instead of a faux was a dream she wasn't yet willing to depart with.

"His interest in me isn't like that," she continued. "Mr. Barlow is in line to receive an inheritance from his uncle, especially if his uncle Barlow believes him to be happily married and settled down."

"And you went"—Effie's eyes widened—"as his bride?"

"I did. And my! How grand it was." She closed her eyes, reliving the magnificence of Purcell's—until Will's cousins' faces surfaced, along with their threat against Uncle Barlow. Her eyelids popped open. "Well, it was mostly all grand, except for Will's awful cousins. Oh, Effie, they are conspiring to commit the dear old man to an asylum."

Speaking the words aloud breathed life into the monstrous possibility, squeezing her heart. "And you know as well as I what might happen to him there—" Her voice cracked, and she pressed her lips tight.

"There, there, love." Effie patted her arm. "I know that's a blow, considering yer mum—God rest her. But what can ye do?"

"That's just it. There is something I can do to help, but I'm not sure it's the right thing." She heaped another sigh onto her accumulating pile. "Uncle Barlow has invited us all to his town house for dinner next week.

For the sake of William getting that inheritance, and thereby sparing his uncle from such a fate, I agreed to go. Apparently Uncle Barlow will only see fit to award his estate to an heir who's firmly rooted in faith *and* family. I am Will's family, of sorts, leastwise in Uncle Barlow's eyes. But how shall I tell Father? He'll never allow me to attend, especially if he discovers I am posing as Will's bride. Yet if I don't go, then Will's cousin might very well become the heir. . .and Will's uncle would be committed. It seems there is no good solution."

"Hmm," Effie murmured. "That is a dilemma."

The door to Truman's swung open, and both of them fell silent until the woman exiting strolled past them.

"I've got it." Effie beamed. "Why don't ye and Mr. Barlow simply go to his uncle and tell him the truth? If ye reveal the cousins' wicked plot, why, his uncle is sure to name your Will as heir and be glad of it."

Her Will? The idea of William Barlow belonging to her alone quickened her breath—but now was definitely not the time for fanciful dreaming. She shook her head. "I said as much to Mr. Barlow, but he thinks we need more evidence than a snippet of overheard conversation."

"He might be right, I suppose." Effie pinched the bridge of her nose, and Mina desperately hoped the action would coax out some golden wisdom for her to follow. But Effie merely lowered her hand and angled her head. "Ye'll just have to tell yer father the truth of things, love."

She sighed—again. If she kept this up, she'd have no air whatsoever left in her lungs. "I was afraid you'd say that."

"Mina." Compassion infused her friend's tone, far warmer than the November chill working its way into her bones. "Ye didn't really need me to tell ye what to do, eh?"

"Yes—I mean no. I mean. . .I suppose not." Shoving back another sigh, she straightened her shoulders. Effie was right. Deep down in her gut she'd known the correct course of action but, until now, had been trying to ignore it. And that's what she loved most about her friend. Effie had a magical way of giving her the courage to look within and dare to hold hands with what she knew to be right.

She lifted her chin, then grabbed for her hat as a brisk breeze nearly lifted it off her head. "You're right. I shall go to Father at once and explain the situation. If he allows me to attend the dinner for the sake of Mr. Barlow's uncle, then I shall. If not, well, either way I must leave this in God's hands."

Effie grinned. "I knew ye'd do the right thing. Shall I come along?"

"No. I fear I've made you late enough as is. Thank you, my friend, and I'll let you know how things turn out." She whirled to go, then as suddenly turned back. "Oh, I nearly forgot."

With a heavy heart, she retrieved a small purse containing all her savings for Father's watch fob. Though she tried to smile as she held it out, her lips didn't quite cooperate. "Here is my donation to the Institute for the Care of Sick Gentlewomen. I thought you might add it along with yours and see that Miss Whymsy gets it."

Effie eyed her as she collected the offering. "I suspect this is costing you more than some coins."

"It is." She nodded toward the pouch. "That was my sole funding to purchase Father a new fob for Christmas."

"Ahh, love." Effie shoved the purse back toward her. "Surely betwixt the two of us, we can come up with some other way to help the institute."

"I have thought of another way, for the fob, that is. Would you stop over when you've some free time and help me cut my hair? As inconspicuously as possible. I plan to fashion a braided twist for Father to use. It won't be as dashing as a gold chain, but it will be better than none."

Tucking the pouch into her pocket, Effie then straightened her shoulders and saluted. "My scissors are at yer command."

"Oh! One more thing." She held out her other hand, offering back Effie's second-chance coin on her open palm. "Here is your coin."

Effie curled Mina's fingers back around the gold piece. "I'll see yer contribution gets to Miss Whymsy, but you keep that coin. Tuck it in a pocket and carry it with you every day. When the right situation happens along, I'm sure ye'll know just when to use it. And in the meantime, when ere yer fingers rub against the metal, think on more than just the second chance I gave you. Think on the second chance God gives us all, eh love? Now, off with ye."

"Thank you, my friend. I shall see you next week." Turning on her heel, Mina tucked the coin into her reticule, then dashed down the lane faster than decorum allowed. But it was not to be helped. If she didn't get this over with soon, she might lose the pluck to tell her father.

At this time of the afternoon, only a few patrons sat with mugs in hand inside the taproom. It was the off-hour, the lull she would've taken advantage of to sneak off with her book if Father hadn't confiscated it again. At this rate, she'd never finish *David Copperfield*.

She strode directly to his office and rapped on the door before pushing it open. "Father?"

Behind his paper-strewn desk, Father's chair sat empty. Neither did the sweet scent of Cavendish tobacco waft in the air.

Shutting the door behind her, she dashed to the kitchen. Perhaps he indulged in a bite of one of Martha's meat pies.

"Father?" She swung into the kitchen and stopped inches in front of Martha.

"Peas and honey!" The cook retreated a step, a sprinkling of flour taking flight from her collar at the sudden movement. "Take a care, child."

"My apologies." She offered the woman a sheepish smile, all the while knowing it was a poor show of contrition. "I am looking for my father. Have you seen him?"

Martha swiped the back of her hand across her cheek, leaving behind a dusty smear. "He's gone."

"What do you mean, gone?"

"La, child!" Cook's lower lip folded. "Don't tell me ye've forgotten what day it is. Yer father left not an hour ago for his annual trip to Colchester to find this year's best oyster seller. Can't rightly have his famous stew for the Christmas Eve party if he don't have the best oysters."

"Oh, dear," she breathed out. She'd been so caught up in her own worries she hadn't given a second thought to the date—or Father's party preparations.

"Now, now. 'Tain't all that bad. He'll be back in little over a fortnight." A stray hair escaped from Martha's cap, and she blew the rogue away. She edged a step nearer, lowering her voice. "I suppose you should know, though, that your father arranged for Mr. Grimlock to come by on the morrow to manage things while he's absent."

Mr. Grimlock? She stiffened.

"Thank you, Martha," she forced out, then spun away before the cook could read the disgust that surely coloured her cheeks. Now not only would she not be able to tell Father about the dinner at Uncle Barlow's, but she'd have to dodge Gilbert Grimlock's perpetual advances. The man had proposed to her twice already. Of all the men Father could have chosen to tend the inn for him, it had to be Gilbert Grimlock? She narrowed her eyes.

Or had Father chosen the man on purpose as part of his never-ending scheme to marry her off?

CHAPTER TEN

The civility which money will purchase
is rarely extended to those who have none.
Sketches by Boz

Mina pressed her back against the corridor wall before she reached the kitchen, shrinking farther into the shadows as Gilbert Grimlock strode out the door. *Please don't come this way. Please don't even look.*

She'd spent the better part of the past week dodging the fellow. Despite her efforts, he'd occasionally caught her off guard. Such had been the case earlier today. After suffering a morning of the man's ego and innuendoes, she'd begged off with a headache. Which was no lie. His thinly veiled talk of marriage and continual boasting of his accomplishments never failed to throb in her temples.

Just past the threshold, Mr. Grimlock paused, the great hulk of him a dark, unmoving blob. She froze. What would she say if he turned back around and found her skulking about in her finest dress when he thought her abed? *Think. Think!*

But as unexplainably as he stopped, he once again set off, creeping toward the taproom like a giant spider.

She waited until he disappeared, and her crazed heartbeat slowed. Pushing away from the wall, she padded the rest of the way down the passage and slipped into the kitchen. Thankfully, Martha bent over a pot on the hearth, humming a folk tune and stirring up a frenzy. Mina shot toward the back door and eased it open and shut before Cook noticed.

Outside, brisk evening air slapped her cheeks, and she shivered as she dashed to the back gate of the small courtyard. She yanked it open, and when Will turned toward her at the creak of the hinges, the night lost its chill.

"Good evening, Mina. Though I can't say I like this stealthy business, I am happy you came." He offered his arm. "Shall we?"

"We shall." She smiled. How could she not? The gleam in Will's eyes pulled her into the adventure of the evening, erasing the smudge of Gilbert Grimlock on her day and easing the tension of trying to slip out unnoticed.

Together, they stepped into the evening throng of London's streets. The aged thoroughfares never slept. Gas lamps glowed like miniature suns, lighting their way. They strolled past shift workers going to and from factory jobs, washerwomen scurrying home to feed their families, and even a few children peddling matches or candle stubs.

Down at the next corner, William hailed a cab, twice the size of the one they'd ridden in when they'd gone to tea, with four wheels instead of only two.

She grasped Will's hand and climbed into the carriage. But this time when he shut the door, sealing them in shadowy possibilities, her high spirits faltered. If Father knew what she was about, his wrath would be unbearable. And well deserved. This was scandalous. *She* was scandalous. But was not man's life worth a ruined reputation?

Will sank onto the seat across from her, and she edged into the corner, as far from him as possible. What a sorry tale this might turn out to be were William Barlow not a man of integrity, which he was. Wasn't he? She swallowed. What did she really know of him other than her inflated imaginary image?

"Mina, I . . ." Spare light crept in as they passed near a streetlamp, highlighting a strange look on his face. He worked his jaw as if he struggled for words. Did he feel the gravity of their charade as much as she?

But then half a smile quirked his lips, and a familiar twinkle reignited in his eyes. "What I mean to say is that I appreciate you coming along for the sake of my uncle. I realize I've put you in somewhat of a compromising situation, and I will strive to protect your reputation. I vow I shall have you home at a decent hour."

So, he did understand. Warmth flared in her chest. Will was gallant after all, a true hero, and she chided herself for having doubted him. "Thank you. And yes, if you don't mind, as soon as your uncle names his heir, I really must return to the inn."

"Understood." He nodded. "Let's hope it's not a fourteen-course meal, hmm?"

Fourteen courses? How long would that take? She sucked in a sharp breath. "Oh! Do you think—?"

"It was only a jest, Mina, and a poor one at that. Forgive me?" A lopsided grin played across his face. "You shall return to your regular life in no time and not be bothered with mine."

She turned her face to the window. His words echoed like a death knell, clanging loud and deep in her soul. Once this night was over, they'd go back to their lives. He stopping by for a pint now and then, and she pressing her nose to the glass each time he left. Endless hours of serving customers and dodging pinches. Helping Martha shell peas or Father manage deliveries. A regular life? How dismal.

But there was no sense dwelling on such melancholy thoughts now, especially when some good may come of this evening, *if* Will were named heir. And if nothing else, she'd have gotten to share a cab with a handsome gentleman and attend a fancy dinner, just like in one of her novels. As the wheels of the carriage bumped over cobblestones, she straightened in her seat and determined to enjoy the ride, no matter what the next hours might bring.

The cab halted, and when her feet touched ground, she stared up at a magnificent, three-story building. It was hard to tell if the bricks were brown or deep red in the darkness, but regardless, the proud structure stood like a soldier on parade. Candles burned in every window, and merry gas lamps flickered on each side of a grand front door. It was a jolly sight. Like a new friend bright eyed at the prospect of meeting her. She followed Will up the stairs and onto the landing, where he rapped a lion-headed knocker against the door.

Moments later, golden light poured out the opening, draping a luminous mantle on the shoulders of a butler in a black suit. He bowed his head and swept out his arm in invitation. "Good evening, Mr. Barlow. If you and your lady would step this way."

Leaving behind the chill November night, Mina stepped into a June morning—or so it seemed. Brilliant light bathed the large foyer, and long-fronded ferns and other plants sat on pedestals of varying heights around the perimeter. How magical! She might almost imagine herself at the center of an enchanted garden.

Will helped her from her coat and handed it over to another servant, then doffed his as well. The butler led them to a sitting room, where Uncle Barlow rose from his seat the moment she met his gaze. Beside him, perched on the edge of a settee, Percy and Alice pouted, or maybe frowned. It was hard to tell. A surprising twinge of pity squeezed Mina's heart. How awful to go through life with a perpetual sourness festering inside.

Uncle Barlow clapped William on the back with a "Happy you made it, my boy." Then he stopped in front of her. His big hand gathered her fingers, and he pressed a light kiss atop them. "'The pain of parting is nothing to the joy of meeting again.'"

She grinned at his Dickens quote. How sweet that he'd remembered her love for *Nicholas Nickleby*. "Thank you, sir, but the pleasure is mine."

He released her and chuckled. "I didn't think it possible, William, but your wife's charm outshines yours."

Will's gaze sought hers, and a strange gleam deepened the blue in his eyes—a look she'd never before seen from him.

Will cleared his throat, and in a flash, the look disappeared, replaced by a familiar playful twinkle. "She is rather brilliant, is she not?"

Across the room, Percy rose like a black cloud of doom, pulling Alice up along with him. "We are here for dinner, I believe. And I, for one, am famished, Uncle."

"Well then." Uncle Barlow rubbed his hands together. "I suppose we shall have to remedy that, eh?"

He led their entourage out of the sitting room and into a corridor lined with oil paintings and crystal wall sconces. Mina soaked it all in as she walked at Will's side, memorizing the way light played off the gilded frames and the softness of the thick Persian runner beneath her feet. She blinked, praying the dream would not fade. This was a storybook palace, and she was a princess strolling next to her prince.

"Look at that gown." Behind her, Alice's ugly whisper stabbed her in the back. "Puffed sleeves went out of fashion at least three seasons ago. And not a glimmer of jewels, not even some simple earbobs."

"Knowing my cousin," Percy rumbled in a low voice, "it's the best they can afford. Elizabeth Hill did right when she cut him loose, for he's likely neck deep in debt. Obviously this woman was too dull witted to credit his faults and pull out before it was too late."

"I'd say she is a drab."

The venom in their remarks worked a slow burn up her neck, dimming some of the grandeur of Uncle Barlow's fine home. . .and who was Elizabeth Hill?

Will leaned close, his breath warm against her ear, making her forget about his cousins' jabs and a woman named Elizabeth—especially when he whispered for her alone, "Ignore them, Mina. You look lovely and would even had you worn your taproom apron."

Oh, dear. Now heat flooded beyond her neck and spread in a flame across her cheeks. She dipped her head as they entered the dining room, lest he see the effect.

Uncle Barlow stopped in front of a large table draped with white linen and sporting silver-edged place settings. "I've taken the liberty to arrange seating. Percy and Mina on this side." He lifted his right hand. "Alice and William, opposite, if you please."

Percy skirted past her to grab the chair nearest Uncle Barlow's, then backed off at the grim shake of Uncle's head. Uncle Barlow advanced and held the chair out for Mina. Across from her, William did the same for Alice.

As soon as all were seated, servants entered, placing domed platters atop the table. When they lifted the lids, Alice and Percy leaned forward, eyes narrowed at the food.

Mina settled her napkin in her lap. Whatever Will's cousins were concerned about now, at least they weren't scrutinizing her, and she could go back to reveling in her fairy-tale night. Uncle Barlow slid a browned piece of roasted fowl from a serving platter onto her plate, then spooned an accompanying gravy atop it. The savory scent rained drops at the back of her throat. If she could remember everything about this dish, perhaps Martha might be able to copy it.

Across from her, Alice sniffed and stared at Uncle Barlow. "Is something the matter with your cook?"

"No, nothing at all." Uncle speared a large bite of his meat and chewed with such gusto, the tufts of hair near his ears jittered. "Why do you ask?"

"No soup? No fish course? We begin with naught but a main dish?"

"Do you object to fowl?"

Alice's lips puckered for a moment. "No."

"Then why not enjoy what has been served?" Uncle Barlow chuckled. "I assure you, it is by no mistake I have chosen to reduce the courses. A year ago now, my physician suggested my gout might improve should I lose a stone or two. It has, and so I continue to eat a lighter fare."

A rumble sounded deep in his chest, and he pulled out his handkerchief. His cough wasn't as hacking this time though, and for his sake, Mina hoped he was truly on the mend.

"Humph," Alice grumbled, then looked down her nose at Mina. "I suppose this is a feast for you."

She smiled, ignoring that somehow Alice meant her words as a cut. But how could they be? This *was* a feast, for she'd never sampled anything like it. The rich aftertaste of her first bite yet lingered in her mouth. "It is quite delicious."

"I agree." Across the table, William winked at her.

From the corner of her eye, she noted that Percy didn't eat his meal. Odd, for was he not the one who'd declared himself famished? He pulled out a slip of paper and a pencil from his pocket then scribbled down some sort of note, all beneath the cover of the table. The others couldn't see, but she did. Why would he be writing instead of eating?

"Mina." Uncle Barlow tapped a finger on the table, drawing her attention. "Do you remember the scenes in *Bleak House* when old Smallweed demands Judy to 'shake him up'?"

"I do." She set down her fork, a grin spreading. "I own that we are supposed to loathe the man, but secretly"—she inclined her face toward Will's uncle and lowered her voice—"I rather liked him."

"Ha ha! So did I." Uncle Barlow raised a fist in the air and gruffed out in his best Smallweed imitation, " 'Shake me up, Judy. You brimstone beast!' "

Mina laughed, not just from the man's antics, but also from the raised brows on both Will and Alice.

Percy turned slightly away from them all, scribbling furiously. Mina's laughter faded. Whatever Percy was taking notes on couldn't be good, not if he must hide the contents.

"Tell me, William," Uncle Barlow's voice rumbled. "Has your wife made a reader of you yet?"

Her face shot to Will's. The reminder that Uncle Barlow thought them married was an unpleasant jolt, and worse, that it was their deception alone that had earned her a seat at his table.

The tips of Will's ears reddened. "Not yet, sir."

"Well I," Alice interrupted, "find reading tiresome. Tell me, Mina." She dabbed her lips with a napkin, as if speaking her name was a stain to be rubbed off. "Do you not find it hard to distinguish fact from reality after immersing yourself in falsehoods? For that is what novels are, are they not? A great collection of fabrications and imaginary people?"

Falsehoods! She ground her teeth so hard, her jaw crackled. Even if she had thought to bring along Effie's second-chance coin, the anger simmering in her belly would've made it impossible to extend Alice such a charity.

Uncle Barlow leaned sideways and patted Mina's arm. "Pay her no mind, my dear. I should much rather live in a world of unicorns and fairies."

Next to Mina, Percy's small pencil flew with a life of its own. She opened her mouth to call him out, but then servants descended, removing their plates and setting before each of them a steamed pudding decorated with laurel leaves.

Clove and cinnamon wafted up in a heavenly cloud, and she couldn't help but bend and inhale a great, spicy breath. Ignoring Percy, she took a bite. Sweet apples in a thick sauce had been baked within sponge cake, all soaked in some kind of mulled liqueur and lightened with dollops of cream. Absolute perfection filled her mouth. Martha would never be able to re-create this.

Uncle Barlow shoved his dish away after only a few bites. For a moment, Mina held her spoon in midair. Was it proper etiquette to continue eating if the host had clearly finished?

But across from her, Will's spoon dipped into his pudding, and he took another big bite, paying no mind whatsoever to his uncle's obviously sated appetite. She'd have to ask him about it later—on the ride home, perhaps— because for now, she determined to finish every last bit of her dessert.

Percy's pencil flew from his hand, landing on the carpet next to his chair. He shoved his paper back into his pocket then bent to retrieve the pencil, but in his haste, he hadn't tucked the note in deep enough. The small slip of paper fluttered out and landed near the edge of the chair, teetering on the cushion. Any minute and it would plummet to the floor.

Without thinking, Mina snatched the thing, curious as to what he'd been documenting; but as the paper came away in her fingers, guilt churned the sweets in her stomach. Was she now a thief as well as a deceiver? What had gotten into her?

She reached to return the slip, but just then Percy straightened. Any further movement on her part, and she'd be caught red-handed.

She froze. What was she to do now?

CHAPTER ELEVEN

What lawsuits grow out of the graves of rich men, every day;
sowing perjury, hatred, and lies among near kindred,
where there should be nothing but love!
Martin Chuzzlewit

Will studied Mina across the table—as he had been doing all night when she wasn't looking. Fine, white teeth worried her lower lip, and an endearing little crinkle weighted her brow. What on earth was she puzzling over?

He looked closer. In the past year as he'd frequented the Golden Egg, why had he never noticed the sweet, tiny freckles sprinkled over the top of her nose? Or the flaming streaks of copper in her hair? When had she grown into such a beauty?

"Now that dinner is finished," Uncle Barlow said while folding his napkin, "I suppose we should be about our business, eh?"

"Finally," Alice gruffed out beneath her breath, then in a louder, more syrupy tone, "Dearest Uncle, should you like Mina and me to retire to another room so that you men may confer in private?"

"No need." He held up his hand, staving her off. "It is my experience that wives are an integral part in how a household is run, and it is the running of my household that I am most interested in."

"Even so, Uncle Barlow, if you don't mind, I must plead a moment for myself." Mina pushed back her chair and shot to her feet. "Will you excuse me?"

Will cocked his head. Why the sudden need to escape?

"Of course, my dear. The necessary room is the third door on the left." Uncle stood.

So did Will.

But Percy was too busy fumbling with something in his pocket to pay Mina any such respect. Or did the scoundrel feign the preoccupation just to snub her? Oh, how he'd love to reach across the table and yank his cousin from his chair, but he forced his feet to remain still. Schoolboy theatrics probably didn't fit the type of behaviour Uncle was looking for in an heir. Swallowing his disgust, he lowered to his seat as Mina disappeared out the door.

Uncle Barlow planted his elbows on the table and steepled his fingers, tapping them together. "I have one simple question for each of you." His gaze swung to Percy. "I shall ask you first, Percival, being you are the eldest by several months. Should you be named heir, what do you intend to do with the estate once I am gone?"

A shrill titter squealed out of Alice, like that of a rabbit being stepped upon. "Oh! My husband is brilliant when it comes to finance. Wait until you hear his plans. He's going to—"

"I believe I asked my nephew." Uncle curbed her with a glare from beneath his shaggy brows. "If you don't mind?"

Her mouth puckered into a clam ripple. "No, of course not."

Will coughed into his hand, stifling a grin. Between Alice and Mina, there was no contest as to where Uncle's affections lay, and increasingly, his. Bless Mina's heart. She was a sunbeam to Alice's heavy, dark cloud.

Percy straightened in his seat, resettling his glasses just so on the bridge of his nose. After a quick smoothing of any wrinkles on each coat sleeve, he faced Uncle Barlow as if addressing the prime minister.

"The fact of the matter is that my wife is correct." Percy tilted his head in a superior manner. Gads! If he lifted his nose any higher, a nosebleed might follow.

"You see, Uncle Barlow, there are not many men more well versed in finance than I. That being said, I believe that the future lies in rails. With the innovation of the steam engine, and the largest station in all of Europe recently opened right here in London, it's obvious that railroad investment is the way to go."

Uncle Barlow grunted. "Perhaps."

Will folded his arms and leaned back in his chair. Judging by the rise of Percy's chest, the man was about to launch into one of his unending soliloquies.

"There is no perhaps about it." Reaching inside his suit coat, Percy pulled out a sheaf of papers.

Will gaped. How had the man concealed such a thick wad of documents?

"I have taken the liberty of running up the numbers. If you'll just look here." Shoving aside the dishes, Percy spread the papers onto the table and stabbed one in particular with his index finger. "This graph shows that railroads are soon to be the lifeblood of commerce. According to a recent tabulation comparing canals to roads to rails, the upswing is soon to be steam engines. In fact, out-of-pocket expenses pale in comparison to. . ."

His cousin droned on, but Will was more interested in what his uncle might think of the presentation. Was he wearied with Percy's statistics or eager to find out more? He slipped a covert glance at the old fellow, but his uncle's grey eyes neither drooped with boredom nor shone with interest. Only once did Uncle reach for his handkerchief to accommodate a short coughing spell.

Beyond Uncle Barlow, a shadow appeared on the threshold. Will leaned back farther in his chair for a better look. Mina hovered like a spectre, neither entering nor retreating. She lingered, her eyes wide and beseeching his. In ghostlike fashion, she crooked her finger and beckoned him. What the deuce?

"—William?"

He jerked his gaze back to Uncle Barlow, who stared at him in expectation. "S—sorry?" he stammered.

"I said I've gathered enough information from your cousin. It is your turn, my boy, to make clear your position. What are your intentions should you inherit my estate?"

In the doorway, Mina swept her entire hand toward the corridor, pulling his attention once more back to her. Clearly, she signaled him to join her, but why now? Did she not realize—

"Well William?"

He jerked his face back to Uncle. "Nothing," he answered.

Alice and Percy gasped in unison.

"Nothing?" Uncle Barlow repeated.

Behind his uncle, Mina upped her frantic gesturing.

Sweet heavens! What was he to do? Whatever Mina had to say was clearly urgent, but this was his chance—perhaps his only one—to persuade Uncle and thwart Percy's wicked scheme. He straightened his shoulders. Mina would have to wait. "What I mean to say is that I intend to move into your country estate and run things as you always have. Your tenants rely upon the land for their livelihood, and I can't see putting them out of their homes." He narrowed his eyes at Percy. "Not even for the sake of investment."

Red crept up his cousin's neck. "If the master prospers, so do the servants."

"Yet if the master is ruined, so are the tenants," he shot back.

"If one does not risk," Alice's shrewish voice cut in, "one does not gain."

He frowned at her. "But gains are not always positive. Unwarranted risk often reaps ills such as sorrow, debt, prison, or worse."

"Which you know firsthand." Percy leveled the words at him like a loaded rifle. "But I wonder, Cousin, if you have learned your gambling lessons, or would you even now wile away Uncle's money at a gaming table without a second thought?"

Uncle Barlow shifted in his chair, and Will clenched his jaw. Blast his cousin for reminding the old man of his ignoble past.

Mina yet bobbed in the doorway, but he couldn't very well join her now and leave Percy to fill Uncle's head with more reminders of his questionable history. If Uncle Barlow based his decision on the exploits of his younger years, he'd never be named heir. But how could he prove he wasn't that man anymore and that his pompous cousin didn't deserve to— Pompous? That may be the key. Were he to humble himself, perhaps Uncle Barlow might extend some grace, for the man did have a merciful side to him.

Disregarding the sneer twisting Percy's lips, Will turned to Uncle. "Percy is right. As you well know, I have experienced the degradation caused by my own poor choices. I offer you no excuse whatsoever for my reckless past and am, in fact, shamed by it. Yet I am not the man I once was, thanks to you—and God—for giving me a second chance when I was at my lowest point. I assure you, Uncle, that I have mended my ways. Whether or not you choose to believe such I leave in your hands, for I trust you to make a sound decision."

A smile curved Uncle's mouth, crinkling his skin well up to the corners of his eyes. "Well said, my boy. Well said."

Alice reared back her head, barely disguising her breathed out "Pish!"

Percy collected his papers, stacked them in a neat pile, then shoved the whole thing toward Uncle. "Facts over sentiment, I always say. Read for yourself, on this top document right here, you will see—"

"Excuse me. I won't be but a moment." Will pushed back his chair and stood before Percy launched into a lecture on the merits of steam engines. With his cousin so diverted, this would be the best time to safely see to Mina.

He strode out of the dining room, and as soon as he stepped into the corridor, Mina urged him away from the door with a tip of her head. Intrigued, he followed.

"I must speak with you," she whispered. "Alone."

Something dreadful crept in from the edges of her voice, and he reached for her hand. "Very well. Come along." He led her down the passage and pulled her into the sitting room.

"What is it?" He spoke low, her clear desire for secrecy tempering his tone.

"I think I have your proof." She held out an unfolded slip of paper.

Collecting it, he scanned the words.

Picks at his food.
Wishes to live with unicorns.

Believes in fairies.
Outbursts claiming brimstone beasts.

He frowned at the gibberish, then met Mina's gaze. "What is this?"

"Your cousin Percy has been taking notes all evening. Every time your uncle does something questionable, he writes it down. Oh, Will—" Her voice frayed to a ragged thread. "I think he's documenting things out of context to incriminate your uncle, preparing even now to have him committed."

The truth of her words punched him hard, and a growl rumbled in his throat. What a cur! What a wicked, grasping cur. The confirmation of Percy's true intent tightened his gut, and the paper shook in his hand. This had to stop, here and now. He wheeled about and strode to the corridor.

"Will?" Mina's voice trembled behind him—and he hated the fear he'd caused by his abrupt departure. But it couldn't be helped. He never should have dragged her into this.

"What are you going to do?"

He upped his pace, not daring to give her an answer. What he'd like to do would land him behind bars.

Chapter Twelve

If our affections be tried, our affections are our consolation
and comfort; and memory, however sad, is the best
and purest link between this world and a better.
Nicholas Nickleby

Mina sped after Will. She'd never seen him take such a warrior stance—and a shiver slid across her shoulders. She'd hate to be on the receiving end of the wrath she'd witnessed hardening his jawline.

Will stalked into the dining room and slammed the note down in front of Uncle Barlow, the movement knocking loose a pile of papers she'd not seen before she'd excused herself from the room.

"What do you think you're doing?" Percy scrambled to collect the fluttering pages.

"There is one paper my cousin neglected to show you, Uncle." William jammed his finger at the note. "Read it."

"What are you going on about—" Alice's words crashed to a halt as her gaze landed on the scribbled writing in front of Uncle Barlow. She reached to snatch the incriminating paper away, but Will's uncle beat her to it.

Uncle Barlow's lips moved as he read over the words, then he frowned up at Will. "What is the meaning of this?"

"The meaning, sir, is that my cousins intend to have you committed to an asylum."

Mina held her breath. The sudden silence in the dining room was a living thing. A breathing monster. The kind that writhed and nipped. She huddled closer to Will. Were this a novel, she'd skip to the next chapter to see how things turned out.

Percy shoved his glasses tight against the bridge of his nose, as if battening down the hatches before a great storm. Then he threw back his shoulders and faced Uncle Barlow. "I assure you, Uncle, whatever doubts my cousin is trying to implant in your head can be nothing but a scheme to garner himself the inheritance."

Uncle Barlow grunted. "Did you write this note, Percival?"

"I did."

Mina blinked. How stunning. He admitted to the offense without hesitation?

But even more stunning, Percy slid his narrowed gaze to her. Lamplight flashed off his spectacles like lightning bolts. "The real criminal here is William's wife, for she stole the paper from my pocket."

"Mina?" Uncle Barlow turned in his seat, the questions in his gaze driving her back a step. "Did you pick Percy's pocket?"

"I—I. . .no!" She gasped. How had things gotten so turned around? "I took nothing from his pocket. The paper fell out and was about to plummet to the floor, when I simply caught the thing. I thought to give it back, but I—I—"

"There is no need to defend yourself for retrieving a fallen paper, Mina." Will reached out defiantly and entwined his fingers with hers. "The only crime here is Percy's clear indictment of you, Uncle."

"Indictment? Flit!" Percy swatted his hand in the air as if slapping away an annoying black fly. "Such skulduggery can only be imagined in the mind of a deviant. I was merely keeping notes of this momentous evening for posterity's sake."

A snort ripped out of Will. "You seriously expect us to believe that?"

"I should think my word is of more value than that of some law clerk wastrel and his no-account bride. Her ill breeding was apparent even before she resorted to thievery. She suits you though. Far better than Elizabeth ever did. Two unscrupulous peas in a pod, I'd say."

"Enough!" Uncle Barlow roared, and all eyes swung his way. He stood and slapped both palms on the table. "I can see my decision will require more effort than I first anticipated, as you've all given me quite a lot to think about. In light of such, we shall reconvene at my country estate over Christmas. Arrive the week before. Until then, I bid you good night."

Uncle Barlow strode from the room, leaving them agape with the sudden departure. So many questions tumbled about in Mina's mind that she was glad for Will's strong hold of her hand, grounding her. Of course she couldn't possibly go to Uncle Barlow's country estate. How would Will explain that? And who was this Elizabeth that kept getting mentioned?

Percy jumped to his feet, his chair teetering on two legs. He stalked toward Will and speared his chest with a podgy finger. "This isn't finished, Cousin." He emphasized each word with a jab.

"No, it is not." Will spun, his grip on her hand pulling her with him. "Come along, Mina."

Her feet double-timed to keep up with his long stride, though she couldn't blame him. She wished to leave Percy and Alice behind every bit as much as he. In the foyer, a servant waited with their wraps, and Will helped her into her coat before he donned his. By the time Alice's and Percy's footsteps clipped onto the marble floor, Will led her out the front door.

At the bottom of the stairs, he turned to her. "Mind if we walk a bit before I hail a cab?"

She glanced back at the town house. No sign of his cousins yet, but they were sure to appear soon. "Well, I don't fancy waiting here."

He didn't say anything, but the approval in his eyes warmed her in the brisk evening air. They didn't stroll far before a hansom rolled along and Will flagged it down. He opened the door for her and helped her in, then hopped up himself, calling out to the jarvey, "The Golden Egg Inn on Chicory Lane."

She settled her skirts on the seat as the carriage lurched into motion, springs squeaking and bouncier than normal.

Across from her, Will took off his hat and raked his fingers through his hair. The glow of a streetlamp shone in the window, tracing a grimace on his face. "I am sorry, Mina, about the whole evening. I should not have exposed you to my family in the first place. Percy and Alice had no right to say such ghastly things about you."

Despite the chill of the evening, his defense of her wrapped around her shoulders like a warm embrace. "Well, if nothing else"—a small smile ghosted her lips—"this evening has made me realize that perhaps life at the inn isn't as bad as I imagine it to be. Father is strict, but at least he is not spiteful. Our cook may be outspoken, but her words are kind. And"—her smile grew—"I did get to dine in a London town house just like a real lady."

"Oh, Mina, you are a real lady. You are—" His voice cracked along the edges, and he cleared his throat. "You are something special. Very special. I hope you know that."

"Thank you," she murmured, unsure if he could even hear the words for the way her throat closed around them.

Will blew out a disgusted breath. "But blast that Percy for being a scoundrel. To have such blatant evidence brought against him and then turn it around that way. The devil could learn a trick or two from him."

His head hung, and her heart broke. Gone was the carefree man laughing over a mug with his good friend. This William Barlow was a stranger, with his shoulders bowed by the weight of how to rescue his uncle. That he loved the old fellow was more than evident.

Her admiration for him grew, as did her pity. "What will you do now?"

He straightened, yet said nothing more. For a while he looked out the window at the passing streetlights, then eventually heaved a sigh. "I don't know. There's nothing to do but look for more evidence, I suppose. Christmasing at Uncle's estate ought to give me ample time to find something." He turned his face back to her. "Mina, if you are willing, and if I approached your father, do you think he'd give you permission to travel with me?"

"Over Christmas?" The words squeaked out of her. What a dream that would be. Snowflakes and sleigh rides and an estate swagged with greenery. What a story to live inside of! But as the carriage juddered along the cobbles of London's streets, reality smacked her hard. What was she thinking? Father would never let her go. And besides, continuing the charade would only cause more harm than good, for surely they'd be found out. An afternoon tea or an evening dinner was a far cry from spending an entire week together.

She shook her head. "I don't think so. It may be time for you to tell your uncle the truth of us. Surely if you explain we were only trying to save him from the possibility of an asylum, he would understand."

Will grunted. "He would have, had I not ruined my testimony in my younger years." His haunted gaze met hers. "I came up with some fancily embroidered lies in the past in order to gain my uncle's money. I am certain he cannot help but wonder if I have changed. Sometimes I wonder myself."

His mouth twisted as if he sucked on bitter whortleberries; then he sank back against the cushion and rode in silence the rest of the way, apparently lost in thought.

So did she. How did one make someone believe the truth when the truth had been based on a lie? The question played over and over in her head until the cab jerked to a stop. Will helped her out and faced her. Even in the darkness, a strange light gleamed in his eyes, and he stepped closer.

"Mina. . ." Her name on his lips was like a kiss, and he bent closer.

The space between them came alive with promise. Her heart pulsed in a crazed beat, throbbing in her wrists, jittering her knees. If he leaned, just barely, his mouth would be on hers.

She swallowed. What was she thinking? He was a man of means and possibly a future heir to an estate. She was nothing but a girl who ran mugs of ale and plates of sausages to hungry men. It had been a lovely dream—but one built on a lie. It was time to be done.

"Good night, Will," she blurted, then whirled toward the front door.

Her fingers pressed against the wood, about to thrust the thing open, when she froze. She couldn't very well waltz into the taproom wearing her best coat and gown and not expect to meet a few tawdry remarks. Or worse—run straight into Gilbert Grimlock.

She hesitated, waiting for the cab door to close and horses' hooves to clop off, then darted around to the back. What a ninny. So many things had happened tonight that she hardly knew what to think.

Shoving open the courtyard door, she slowed her breathing, then crossed to the kitchen entrance. She eased the latch handle open, releasing the lock. If God smiled upon her, Martha would either be dozing in her corner chair or absent altogether.

Slowly, she nudged the door open, bit by bit, then slipped inside. A single lamp glowed on the counter. Clean dishes sat atop cupboard shelves, and scattered on the worktable were Christmas pudding moulds of various shapes and sizes—most dented, all tarnished. The sight pulled her brows into a frown. No doubt Uncle Barlow's kitchen contained moulds that shone like an August sun.

Holding her breath, she slipped her glance to the corner—but no Martha. No "peas and porridge" or "peas and anything," for Cook's chair sat empty. Her gaze drifted to the work clock ticking away on the wall. Eleven o'clock? By faith! It was later than she'd accounted.

A slow smile twitched her lips. Why hadn't she thought of that before? Mr. Grimlock was surely abed by now. She needn't have rushed the evening after all.

The tension in her shoulders unwound, and she turned to secure the door. She'd just have to take care when she climbed the stairs and passed by his chambers on her way to her own. The floorboard in front of his door was notoriously squeak—

"Mina?"

She whirled. A gargoyle stood on the threshold, beak nosed and beady eyed, blocking the escape to her room.

Gilbert Grimlock.

CHAPTER THIRTEEN

Moths, and all sorts of ugly creatures. . .
hover about a lighted candle. Can the candle help it?
Great Expectations

Mina clutched her hands in front of her, vainly seeking some kind of support to withstand the malignant gaze of Gilbert Grimlock. Riffling through a hundred excuses she could offer the man, she discarded each one in turn, even while knowing the longer she stood there without saying something, the guiltier she appeared to be.

"I—I thought you to be abed, sir. I. . ." Her words languished. Apparently opening her mouth and expecting some sort of alibi to slip out wasn't the most brilliant of strategies.

Mr. Grimlock stalked from the doorway, advancing toward her. He was a boggy sort of fellow, with his ever-present sheen of perspiration winking on his brow and coating his upper lip. The fabric beneath his arms darkened in circles, lending to his appearance of being perpetually moist. The man was a fungus. A black mould, the kind that if inhaled would settle deep in the lungs and force one to cough out the violation.

He stopped inches in front of her, far too close for propriety, bringing with him the sickening smell of potatoes left too long in a cellar. "There are still a few patrons in the taproom. My duty is the management of this inn during your father's absence. I can't very well do that with my eyes closed." Bending, he studied her, his dark gaze spreading over her skin like a rash. "I thought you suffered from a headache?"

"I do—I mean I did." It took everything in her to keep from fleeing out the back door. Instead, she forced her hands to smooth down her skirts, hating that her palms had acquired the same moistness that Mr. Grimlock embodied. "My headache is much better now. Thank you for inquiring, and I am sorry if I disturbed you. Good night, Mr. Grimlock."

She edged past him.

But he sidestepped, blocking her, and grabbed her shoulders. "Your coat is cold and damp. Where have you been at this time of night?"

"I—" She froze. What to say? She certainly couldn't admit to romping about the London streets in a carriage alone with a man. "I had a previous engagement I could not miss."

Mr. Grimlock's eyes narrowed to thin slits. Small dots of perspiration glimmered on his forehead from the movement. "What kind of engagement could you have possibly had at this time of night?"

"A private one."

"Private?" With the crook of his finger, he lifted her chin. "I wonder what kind that could be."

She stiffened beneath the touch of his calloused skin, rough and far too heated. "Excuse me, Mr. Grimlock, but it is late, and I should like to retire."

He bent closer, nearly nose to nose, his knuckle drifting down from her chin and tracing a line against the bare skin of her neck.

This was not to be borne! She wrenched away. "How dare you!"

One of his brows arched, and a single, crude drip broke free from the collection of wet dots on his forehead and trickled down his temple. "How dare I? I am not the one roaming the streets at night. Unless you tell me what you've been about, your father shall hear of this."

Fury ignited deep in her belly, shooting up sparks and shaking through her. "I will not be bullied around by you, sir. You can be sure my father will hear of this, for I shall tell him of your untoward behaviour."

She darted sideways.

But his hand shot out, and he grabbed her arm. "Not so fast. You never did answer me, and I will not be put off. Where were you tonight?"

"It is none of your business. Good night, Mr. Grimlock." She jerked aside—and his fingers dug into the tender part of her upper arm, clasping her all the tighter and pulling her to him. Even through the thickness of her coat and gown, the moisture of him seeped into her clothing.

"The business of the inn *is* my business until your father returns." His breath landed hot on her neck, leaving a clammy vapor behind where it touched.

"Let me go! My life is not part of that business."

"It could be, if only you would let it. I have your father's approval. You have but to say the word, and you could be Mrs. Grimlock by Christmas. We will run this inn together someday, you and I."

The thought of marriage to this beast—especially the marriage bed—surged a strong revulsion through her veins, and she yanked from his grip, the force violent enough that they both staggered.

She used the momentum to finally fly past him. "Good night, Mr. Grimlock."

An oily chuckle followed her down the corridor. "See you in the morning, Mina."

She dashed up the stairs and darted into her room, shut and locked the door, then leaned back against it. She'd not be able to hold off Mr. Grimlock for much longer. Closing her eyes, she forced away the awful image of his sweaty visage.

If only Will had asked her to be his real bride.

CHAPTER FOURTEEN

Love her, love her, love her! If she favours you, love her.
If she wounds you, love her. If she tears your heart to pieces—
and as it gets older and stronger it will tear
deeper—love her, love her, love her!
Great Expectations

Will stared at the affidavit on his desk. Which barrister had requested this? Bagley? Whimpole? Snavesgate? As hard as he tried to remember, all that came to mind was a sprinkle of freckles on creamy skin, doe-like blue eyes blinking up into his, and a tremulous smile on lips that had been close enough to kiss. When had Mina Scott become such an enigmatic beauty—one he couldn't get out of his head?

"Come on." Fitz's voice pulled his attention away from the stack of documents. His friend shoved his coat and hat toward him, nearly knocking him backward on his stool.

Will grabbed the things out of reflex and glanced at the wall clock, then frowned up at Fitz. "Where are we going? It's only half past two."

"You need some air." Fitz turned on his heel and strode toward the door.

Rising, Will shrugged on his coat and clapped his hat atop his head, trying to make sense of his friend's words. By the time he caught up to Fitz at the top of the stairs, he truly did need some air—and some answers. "What's this all about?"

Fitz paused with his hand on the doorknob. "You just sent that last runner to Harberry Court."

"So?"

"Barrister Grovener's chambers are on the other side of town."

The wind punched out of his lungs. Sweet heavens! That mistake would no doubt come back to sink teeth into him. Fitz was right. A walk in the air might do him some good. He yanked open the other door and beat his friend outside and down the stairs to the sidewalk.

"I can only assume this is about your uncle," Fitz said as soon as he fell into step. "Wasn't that dinner last night? Oh. . .egad! How callous of me." His friend shot ahead then walked backward in front of him, concern folding his brow. "You didn't get the inheritance, did you, ol' chap?"

Will shook his head. "Uncle Barlow didn't announce it yet."

"Whew. You had me worried there for a moment." Stepping sideways, Fitz pivoted and once again joined Will's side. "You haven't heard from your mother, have you? Has she fallen into a worse state of health?"

"Not that I know of."

"Well, if it's neither of those things, then what has you so addlepated?"

For a moment, he walked in silence, which was easy enough to do with the clamouring of peddlers and passing vehicles making more than enough noise. Fitz's question rattled around in his skull like a penny being dropped into a tin and given a good shake. What was it that bothered him to such a degree?

He glanced sideways at his friend. "I'm not sure, actually. For some reason, I can't stop thinking about last night. I suppose because it was a perfectly awful evening, thanks to my cousins. You should have seen them, Fitz. They were both in rare form. Percy collected bogus evidence I can only assume he plans to use against Uncle Barlow, then he dredged up my past for all to hear. Worse, both he and Alice said horrid things about Mina, behind her back and to her face. Ahh, but Mina. . ."

His pace slowed, and once again Mina Scott's sweet face crowded out the real world. If he listened hard enough, he could still hear the magic of her laughter as she'd bantered with Uncle Barlow.

A tug on his sleeve yanked him sideways, and he barely avoided stepping into a puddle of sewage and ruining his shoes. "Thanks." He gave his friend a sheepish smile. "Looks like I owe you yet again."

Fitz rolled his eyes. "If I had but a farthing for each time you said that, I'd own a matched set of high-steppers and a shiny new barouche. Now then, what about Miss Scott?"

His smile stretched into a grin. "You should have seen her. A champion and a sport. She put up with Alice's jabs and Percy's slights—which as you know isn't easy to do. And she's completely stolen Uncle Barlow's heart."

"Hmm. . .I'm beginning to wonder if she's stolen your heart as well. I didn't think it possible after the way Elizabeth. . .well, you know—"

Fitz continued speaking, but his friend's voice faded, as did the squawking of a nearby vendor hawking apples. All he heard was the rush of blood whooshing in his ears and the echoing repeat of Fitz's words, *She's stolen your heart as well. She's stolen your heart as well.*

His step hitched. So did his breath. Were Fitz's careless words correct? Shoving down the thought, he shuddered. He'd never again hand over his heart to a woman only to have it sliced open and bled out. Once had been more than enough.

"—announce?" The expectancy written on the curve of Fitz's brow hinted he'd missed a question.

"Announce what?" he asked.

"Who's to be his heir." His friend looked down his nose at him. "This little walk isn't helping, is it?"

"Don't be ridiculous. Of course it is. Uncle Barlow has invited us all to his estate for Christmas, so I expect he'll announce then."

Fitz's eyes widened. "How on earth did you get Miss Scott to agree to that?"

"I haven't. Not yet, anyway."

"I see. Uh. . . ?" Fitz hitched his thumb sideways, indicating the open door of the Brass Rail Pub.

Will shook his head. A mug of ale would only muddle his already fuzzy thinking.

Fitz frowned but kept on walking. "I suppose even if Miss Scott does agree, her father wouldn't allow it. It's not like you're her beau or. . .well, there's a thought for you, eh?"

"How can you even suggest such a thing? No, I shall simply have to persuade her father, that's all."

Fitz cuffed him on the back. "While your tongue is light and quick, I don't think even you can talk your way into gaining his permission to let her go with you."

Tugging the brim of his hat lower, he looked up at Fitz. "You're right. Maybe I do need to become Mina's beau."

"A pretend beau. . .or a real one?"

Exactly. His chest squeezed. So did his breath. "That, my friend, is a question I shall have to think long and hard on."

CHAPTER FIFTEEN

My dear if you could give me a cup of tea to clear the muddle
of my head I should better understand your affairs.
Mrs. Lirriper's Legacy

Tea was life, comfort, all that embodied warmth and fulfillment. . .usually.
But this afternoon, Mina stared into her cup, finding no solace whatsoever. Every creak of a floorboard outside the inn's sitting-room door might be
Mr. Grimlock on the prowl. Each footstep could be his. Dodging the man all
day had stretched her nerves thin, and she just might snap if he dared to breach
her weekly tea with Miss Whymsy.

"What has you so preoccupied, my dear? Is it your father's return?"

"Hmm?" She glanced up at her old friend. "I'm sorry, but what were you
saying?"

"You see?" Miss Whymsy smiled, the skin at the edges of her eyes crinkling
into soft folds. "Your mind is elsewhere."

She stifled a sigh. There was no hiding anything from a former governess
proficient at coaxing truth from naughty children. "I own I am a bit pensive,
though it has nothing to do with my father. Please forgive me?"

Her old friend patted her knee. "There is nothing to forgive, child.
Sometimes life has a way of draping about our shoulders and pressing us
down beneath the weight of it. Is there anything I can do to lighten your
burden?"

Her lips twisted into a wry grin. "I don't suppose you'd want to marry Mr.
Grimlock so he'd stop pestering me?"

"I don't think he'd be very interested in an old governess." Miss Whymsy set
down her teacup, then picked up a book she'd brought along. "Here, this ought
to put you in a better frame of mind."

Mina took the novel and ran her fingers over the red cover with gilt type,
thrilled yet confused. Had the older lady forgotten she'd already read this title?
"Not that I don't appreciate revisiting Mr. Dickens's *A Christmas Carol*, but I
must be honest and tell you I've already read it. Several times, in fact."

"Ahh, but you've not read *this* one." Miss Whymsy reached for the book and opened it to the title page.

"Oh, my." Mina sucked in a breath as she stared at the fine, black penmanship scrolled across the paper. "How ever did you manage to come across a signed edition?"

"It's not mine. It is merely on loan from the director of the institute. Which reminds me..." Setting the book on the cushion between them, Miss Whymsy folded her hands and leaned forward. "I was wondering if you might speak with your father when he returns today. The institute is fair to bursting with women in need, and much to my regret, I have seen several turned away for lack of space. I know I've asked you before, but I feel I must inquire once again. Is there any chance your father would open up a room or two to house those who are ailing?"

She shook her head. "I don't think—"

But her friend cut her off with a touch to her knee. "Allow me to explain. It wouldn't be for those who are contagious but for those who are on the mend and not quite ready to go home yet. By relocating those women here, it would open up beds for other women in need."

An ache settled deep in her soul, not only for the thought of the sick women being turned away, but for the way Miss Whymsy's faded blue-green eyes glimmered with hope. How awful it would be if her friend fell ill and had nowhere to go.

But no. She steeled herself. Father would never allow it.

"I am sorry, my friend, but especially at this time of year, what with the annual Christmas Eve party, there will be absolutely no space whatsoever at the inn. I would love to help, truly, but I am afraid housing women here is out of the question."

"Posh, child." Miss Whymsy sank back onto the cushions. "I figured as much, but on the off chance, thought I'd ask. And don't sell yourself short... you have helped. The money you donated went toward more bandages and dressings. I suppose we shall just have to increase our time petitioning God. Shall we?"

"Of course."

They bowed their heads—but a rap on the door jerked them back up. Mina's heart pounded off rhythm. Had Mr. Grimlock come to further torment her? But surely he wouldn't have knocked. Nor would Father have employed such a courtesy if he had returned.

"Oughtn't you answer that, my dear?"

Miss Whymsy's voice prodded her into action. She stood and crossed to the door.

"Just the person I was looking for." William Barlow, hat in hand, entered, looking far too handsome in his royal-blue cutaway suit coat and buff-coloured trousers. His smile warmed her, as did his gaze. "Good afternoon, Mina."

Across the room, Miss Whymsy cleared her throat.

Mina bit her lip. Had the older lady heard the way he'd spoken her Christian name?

Will turned toward Miss Whymsy. "My apologies, madam. I did not realize Miss Scott entertained company." He dipped his head in respect. "William Barlow, at your service."

"Miss Whymsy." Mina swept her hand toward Will. "Allow me to introduce Mr. Barlow. Mr. Barlow, my friend, Miss Whymsy."

"The pleasure is mine, madam. I am sorry to have interrupted. I promise this shan't take long." His gaze swung back to Mina. "But if you don't mind, might I have a quick word with you and your father?"

Her eyes widened. "My father?"

"Yes."

"I—I . . ." Her words stalled. What in all of God's great goodness could Will possibly have to say to her father? "But he is not—"

"Go on, child," Miss Whymsy interrupted. "Tend to your young man. I shall wait here, for I have a friend to keep me company until you return." She reached for the book.

Will crossed to the door and held it wide. "Shall we then?"

Curious, confused, but mostly nervous Mr. Grimlock might see them, she led Will down the corridor to a small alcove at the end. The space was occupied by a single chair and an end table. A window graced the nook with perfect reading light, and it was a favorite haunt of hers when the weather turned too inclement to be outside.

Will stepped next to her, and she peered up at him, but oh how hard it was to think, let alone speak, when he stood so near. She edged back a bit, until her skirt brushed against the chair. "Why do you wish to see my father?"

He fidgeted with his hat, his fingers playing with the brim. Was he nervous too? "You can't very well spend Christmas at my uncle's estate without your father noticing your absence. So I thought I'd have a word with him."

She shook her head. "As much as I'd like to help with keeping your uncle out of an asylum, there is no chance my father will allow me to go."

"Then I will persuade him, that is unless. . ." He set his hat on the small table then straightened. Gathering her hands in his, he looked deep into her eyes.

Her breath caught in her throat. This was a moment she'd read about in stories. Dreamed about at night. Was this real? The heat of his body standing so near sure seemed it, as did the touch of his fingers against hers.

"Mina, I need to know. Do you want to spend Christmas with me? If you don't, say so, and I shall walk away and not trouble you further."

Trouble? She gaped. Did William Barlow not know the effect he had on her? Could he not feel the trembling in her hands? She did want to be with him, Christmas or any other time of year—but without the lie that both bound and kept them apart.

Swallowing back emotion, she steeled herself for what she must say. "There is nothing I'd like better in all the world, but I cannot—"

"That's all I needed to hear." A brilliant smile deepened his dimples, and he squeezed her hands, pulling her close, wrapping her in his excitement. "Now then, where is your father?"

"He's not yet—"

"Unhand that woman!"

Will turned. She shrank.

"Excuse me." Will's voice hardened, belying the apology in his words. "But the lady and I are having a private conversation, and I will thank you to leave us to it."

Afternoon light highlighted the glisten on Gilbert Grimlock's brow as he scowled at Will. "Who do you think you are, ordering me about?"

Will advanced a step, his jaw clenched. "Not that it signifies to you, but I am Mina's beau."

Her—*what?* She sucked in a breath.

So did Mr. Grimlock. "We'll just see about that," he spat out, then his gaze slid to hers. "Mina, your father has returned."

CHAPTER SIXTEEN

Why, on this day, the great battle was fought on this ground.
The Battle of Life

Will stared at the man stomping away down the corridor. Judging by the pound of his steps, if the fellow had been clutching a gun, Will would be bleeding out on the floor right now. Why such animosity? And why had he allowed that animosity to goad him into such a defense? Declaring to be Mina's beau. Of all things. Not that he hadn't intended to speak to her father about the possibility, but what would this unfavorable start lead to? He'd gone about things the right way with Elizabeth, and that had ended horribly. But this? There was nothing even remotely right about the muddle he'd made of things with Mina.

He turned to where she stood deathly still, her fingers pressed against her mouth.

"Mina?" Closing the distance between them, he gently lowered her hand. Her skin was cold to the touch. "Who was that man?"

Cavernous eyes sought his. "Mr. Grimlock. He manages the inn when my father travels. And if Father has returned—oh, Will!" A little cry caught in her throat. "I am afraid of what kinds of fabrications he'll tell Father."

A surge of protectiveness tightened his gut, and he wrapped his fingers around hers. "Then we must reach your father before he does. Lead the way."

She needed no more encouragement. His legs stretched to keep up with her furious pace. She led him along one passageway, cut through a storage closet with two facing doors, then scurried down a short flight of stairs and turned left, stopping breathless in front of a door—

Where the striped coattails of Mr. Grimlock disappeared.

"I think it best if I go in first." He squeezed her hand then released his hold. "Wait here."

"But—"

"Mina." He pressed his finger to her lips. "All will be well. I vow I shall make things right. Will you trust me in this?"

Her blue gaze held on to his, and slowly, she nodded. The fear, the hope, the shimmer of tears all did strange things to his heart.

"Good girl." He wheeled about. Now, if only he believed his own brave words.

Lord, though I don't deserve it. . . For a moment, his silent prayer faltered along with his step as the truth of his words slapped him. Of course he didn't deserve the ear of God or His help. The Creator of all shouldn't even listen to him after not only being involved in such a great deception but dragging Mina into it as well.

Yet was God not the author of mercy? Of grace? Of second chances?

"Will you trust Me in this?"

The same question he'd asked Mina circled back and punched him in the gut. Either he believed all he'd heard and read of God or he didn't. He wasn't merely standing in front of an innkeeper's office door, but at a crossroads. One that would make or break his faith.

He sucked in a breath and blew out another prayer. "I need Your help, Lord. Make me the man Mina expects me to be—and the man You want me to be. I *will* trust You in this."

He strode into the small room, prepared for battle.

Ahead, Mina's father stood behind a paper-strewn desk, shrugging out of a great, woolen travel cloak. Dried mud caked the hem, and as he hung the garment on a peg, clods of grey dirt fell to the floor.

"This man! This is the very man of which I speak." To Will's left, Mr. Grimlock swung out his arm, aiming his index finger like a javelin. "Not two minutes ago did I catch this man trifling with your daughter. The shame of it! The gall, right here beneath your own roof, sir."

Mr. Scott continued to unwind a long muffler from about his neck, placing the wrapper on the same hook as his coat, and then finally, he turned. When his gaze met Will's, his hazel eyes widened, his brows shooting toward his shock of reddish hair—the same colour as Mina's, albeit shorn and faded to rust. "Mr. Barlow? Can it be you?"

Planting his feet, he nodded. "It is me, sir, the very same faithful patron who's frequented your establishment this past year."

"He's a son of Venus. A rake!" Rage purpled Mr. Grimlock's cheeks, spreading up to his ears. "I insist you cast this villain out immediately for the sake of your daughter's virtue."

Mr. Scott's chest expanded as he looked from Grimlock to him. "Well, Mr. Barlow, what have ye to say?"

"Your daughter's virtue is of my utmost concern—which is why I came here to speak with you today." He paused, heart pounding. Crossroads were notorious for danger, especially this one, for he knew it well. Could he really go through with this again?

How could he not?

Perspiration beaded on his brow, and he had no doubt he looked as moist and quivery as the angry man next to him. Even so, he squared his shoulders and looked Mr. Scott straight in the eyes. "I ask your permission, Mr. Scott, to court your daughter."

Mina's father grabbed hold of the back of his desk chair with both hands. "I can hardly believe it," he murmured.

"Mr. Scott!" Mr. Grimlock ducked his head like a bull about to charge. "I insist on my right of first claim to your daughter's hand. We have a verbal agreement, do we not, sir?"

Will stiffened. Why had Mina never mentioned such a thing? Unless, perhaps, she didn't know? He slid his gaze from Grimlock to Mina's father, thinking on all the times the man had not quite filled his or Fitz's mugs to the brim though they'd paid for fulls. Or the times the ale had tasted distinctly watered down. Mr. Scott was a shrewd businessman—but would he have cut such a deal with the boorish Mr. Grimlock?

"Well. . ." Mr. Scott blew out a long breath, his cheeks puffing, then lifted his face to Mr. Grimlock's. "I did say if Mina didn't take a fancy to any gent before the end of this year, the girl would be yours."

Will's hands curled into fists. Not that fathers didn't frequently arrange marriages, but from the little he knew of Mr. Grimlock, the man was unsuitable for Mina in every way. Still. . .he might be able to use Mr. Scott's unsavory proposition to his advantage. He dared a step closer to the desk. "It is not yet the end of the year, sir. There are four weeks remaining, and Mina's taken a fancy to me."

Her father shook his head, and it was hard to say which creased his brow more—the fatigue of travel or perplexity. "I never saw it coming," he mumbled.

"Don't be absurd." Mr. Grimlock threw out his arms. "Mina can have no idea who is the better man for her. And clearly I am. What does this toff know of running an inn?"

"It is not the inn I intend to pursue."

"You see?" Mr. Grimlock faced Mina's father, thumping his chest with his thumb. "I *am* the superior choice."

Of all the pretention. Percy might be able to learn a trick or two from this arrogant fellow.

Mr. Scott fell silent. Releasing his hold of the chair, he crossed his arms and stroked his chin, clearly deep in thought. That didn't bode well. Mina's father couldn't seriously be considering the arrogant Mr. Grimlock as her future husband. . .could he?

Will strode forward, a righteous indignation burning in his gut, and planted his hands on Mr. Scott's desk. "Ought not your daughter have a say in this? It is her life, after all, that we are bandying about as if she had no stake in the matter."

"Hmm," Mr. Scott gruffed out. "Perhaps ye're right."

"Absurd!" Mr. Grimlock raked his fingers through his hair, standing it on end.

Ignoring the outburst, Mina's father lifted his chin and bellowed, "Mina? Come in here, girl. I know ye're out there!"

Will edged back from the desk, chest tight and breath stuck in his throat. Mina likely wouldn't choose Mr. Grimlock, but what if she didn't choose him either?

Or worse, what if she did? Elizabeth had at one point too—and he still bore the puckered scars on his heart.

CHAPTER SEVENTEEN

That was a memorable day to me, for it made great changes in me.
But it is the same with any life. Imagine one selected day struck out of it,
and think how different its course would have been. Pause you who read
this, and think for a moment of the long chain of iron or gold, of thorns
or flowers, that would never have bound you, but for the
formation of the first link on one memorable day.

Great Expectations

M ina? Come in here, girl. I know ye're out there!"
     Mina clutched great bunches of her skirt as Father's voice boomed out
his office door. Fatigue harshened his words. The timing of this conversation
couldn't have been worse, for her father was ever ill tempered after having suffered the inconveniences of travel. What would he say? What had been said?
The milk she'd taken in her tea with Miss Whymsy soured in her stomach.
Reading about such intrigues was far different from living it—and she wasn't
sure she liked it. At all.

Leaving behind the safety of the narrow corridor, she stepped into the lion's
den. Mr. Grimlock turned toward her, looking as if he might pounce at any
moment. His hair stood on end in patches where he'd tugged it.

Father paced behind his desk, hands clasped at his back. His clothes were
wrinkled, and he had yet to remove his hat.

And Will, God bless him. . . Will stood tall and proud, an island of strength
in this sea of tension. He stepped aside, making enough room for her wide skirt,
the reassurance in his blue gaze lending her support.

"Mina." Father halted his pacing and faced her. "It's come to this. Ye know
I would see ye married, child. Ye must choose between these two suitors. Will
you have Mr. Barlow or Mr. Grimlock?"

She pressed her lips tight to keep her jaw from dropping. Of course there
was no contest, for Will had ever been her hero since the first day he'd saun-
tered into the Golden Egg. Was her dream really about to come true?

"This is preposterous!" A fine spray of spittle flew out along with Mr.

Grimlock's objection. "You hardly know the man."

"Mr. Grimlock, if ye please." Father skewered the fellow with a scowl. "Mr. Barlow has been a regular patron this past year, is a law clerk of good standing, and I'd wager makes the same amount to care for Mina as you. Am I right, sir?"

"Yes, sir." William nodded. "And there's the distinct possibility I am in line to inherit an estate."

"What a load of tosh." Mr. Grimlock turned to her, the movement wafting a sour odour of mouldered oranges. The stains beneath his arms spread in ever-darkening circles, especially when he threw up his hands. "That young swell could be saying anything to fill your head with fanciful thoughts. I offer you stability. The good Grimlock name. A life of pattern, predictability, and solid parameters. Don't be a fool."

Her hands curled into fists. He knew nothing of Will and even less of her to think she desired to spend the rest of her days in such a lackluster fashion. "Mr. Grimlock," she said through gritted teeth. "I thank you for your offer, yet I choose Mr. Barlow."

She shot her gaze to her father, unwilling to see one more dot of sweat pop out on Mr. Grimlock's forehead. "There, Father, you have my decision."

"No! Impossible." Mr. Grimlock stamped his foot like a petulant tot. "My offer is rescinded. I will have nothing more to do with this inn or you people."

Before anyone could say anything further, Mr. Grimlock whirled and stalked out the door, leaving behind nothing but his ringing voice and a blackened scuff on the wooden floor where his shoe had left a mark.

"Well," Father murmured. "I didn't expect to return home to this."

Mina stiffened. Was he cross that she'd ruined his chances of expanding the inn with Mr. Grimlock as his manager?

Almost imperceptibly at first, a slow smile lifted her father's lips, growing in size until it squinted his eyes a bit. "But. . .I couldn't be happier."

She let out a breath, and her shoulders sagged with the relief of it all.

"Nor could I, sir." William grinned down at her, the gleam in his eyes so pure and brilliant, her knees weakened.

Still. . .she bit her lip. Something wasn't right. While everything in her yearned for this to be real, for William Barlow to be her beau, did he *truly* yearn to be hers? Or was he courting her merely to save his uncle? A good reason, noble and compassionate, but one that left her feeling a bit melancholy. Like a child who received a gift-wrapped box, the exact shape and size of a longed for treasure, yet after untying the ribbons and peeling back the paper, finding the box to be empty.

"Sir." William stepped forward. "I know this is all still new to you, but I request to bring your daughter to my uncle's estate for Christmas."

"Meeting the family, eh?" Father scratched his jaw, his fingers rasping on the whiskers sprouted during his travels. "But not yet. Christmas is a money-maker for the Golden Egg. I cannot possibly spare the time to play chaperone with you two when there'll be patrons aplenty for me to see to. No, no. . .after the holidays is best."

She exchanged a worried glance with Will. After Christmas would be too late. But if Father couldn't travel with her, then who? She'd need someone discreet. Someone available. Someone. . .

She clenched her hands to keep from snapping her fingers. "What about Miss Whymsy? The old dear has no one besides us to make merry with during the holiday. Could she not travel with me, if she is agreeable?"

For a moment, her father said nothing, just narrowed his eyes as if studying her suggestion beneath a magnifying glass. "Aye," he drawled. "If she is agreeable."

Finally he doffed his hat and hung it on a peg, then turned and faced Will. "But ye'll have my daughter back here for the Christmas Eve party. It's tradition, and I will not be moved on it."

Will nodded. "I shall have her returned for your famous oyster stew, sir."

She peeked at Will. He'd made the promise with such ease, but how on earth would he keep it?

"Very well. Off with the two o' ye then." Her father swept his hand toward the door. "I've a handsome amount of paperwork to tend to before dinner. Between the three of us," Father lowered his voice and tucked his chin. "Mr. Grimlock weren't all that skilled at innkeeping."

She couldn't help but grin.

"Thank you, sir." William bowed his head.

"Don't be thanking me. Mina's the one that chose ye." He hitched his thumb at her over his shoulder as he strode back to his desk.

Stunned at the whole turn of the afternoon, Mina padded out of the office and into the corridor, Will on her heels.

"He's right, you know."

Will's voice turned her around, and she lifted one brow. "About?"

"I ought to be thanking you, and I do." The dimples on his cheeks deepened as his grin grew. "This may turn out to be the best Christmas ever."

She smiled at his enthusiasm. Indeed, it could be the best Christmas ever—*if* Will truly cared for her. But her smile waned as she searched his face. Did he really want to court her? Or was this all just a ruse?

Tired of half truths and outright deception, her smile faded altogether. A heroine wouldn't waste away with such doubts but would take a bold stand. She swallowed. Could she be a heroine? Did she even have it in her?

Only one way to find out.

She lifted her chin. "While I hope for your sake, and your uncle's, that this Christmas will turn out for the best, I feel that cannot happen without the truth being spoken. I insist you tell your uncle that we are not married, yet are moving toward such, as soon as possible after we arrive. I cannot stay beneath his roof under such pretense, and in fact, I will not."

She clamped her mouth shut. My, but that had been a bold thing to say. Truly heroic. But what would Will think of her outburst? Would he turn around and march back into Father's office, rescinding his offer as thoroughly as had Mr. Grimlock?

His eyes widened, and for an eternity, he said nothing. Just stared. Eventually, his head dipped an acknowledgment. "You're right of course. I will tell my uncle as soon as I'm able."

"Promise?" she pressed.

"Promise." He bent, and his lips brushed against her forehead.

What he said after that was a mystery. Probably some kind of goodbye, for he strode off and left her standing in the corridor, her knees weak. She lifted her fingertips to her brow, wishing, hoping, *needing* his words to be true.

All of them.

CHAPTER EIGHTEEN

She was truest. . .in the season of trial,
as all the quietly loyal and good will always be.
A Tale of Two Cities

"Are ye sure about this?"

Mina met Effie's gaze in the mirror, purposely avoiding eye contact with the large shears gripped in her friend's hand. Despite Effie's skill with scissors, there would still be patches of shorter hair to have to cover up until it all grew back to the same length. But it was only hair, after all—a trifling thing compared to Mina's other worries. Though she tried not to think on it, she couldn't help but wonder how Will would talk his uncle into allowing them to leave the estate before Christmas. Would it be a long-enough visit to expose Percy's wicked intentions? And the question that really niggled. . .was Will courting her only as a means to an end, or was he truly fond of her?

"Mina?"

"Hmm? Oh, sorry." Shoring herself up by gripping the edge of her chair, she nodded. "Yes, I am certain. Proceed."

"All right then. 'Ere goes."

The scissors snipped, and she shivered.

"Hold still, love. Be bricky for me. Don't want to cut too much."

Long locks of reddish-brown hair landed on the floorboards, and with each one, the world turned more and more watery. *Don't think it. Don't do it.* But despite her mental admonition, the last memory of her mother rose like a spectre, pushing tears overboard and dampening her cheeks. *Oh, Mama.* The thin woman in a mouse-coloured gown had sat on the cold flagstones of the asylum floor, arms curled about her knees, rocking and rocking and rocking . . .the shorn hairs on her head sticking out like pins in a cushion. Had her mother even noticed when her hair had been cut?

Mina sucked in a shaky breath. How different might life have been if Mother hadn't lost the baby, hadn't grieved so hard that both her heart and head had broken?

"There we be. How do ye—Mina?" The shears landed with a clatter on the vanity and Effie lowered to her knees, taking both of Mina's hands in her own. "Are ye all right?"

"Of course." She forced a smile and squeezed Effie's fingers before pulling back, then dabbed away the gruesome memory and the dampness on her face with the back of her hand. "I am fine. Just a bit melancholy, though I've no right to be. This hair will make a beautiful fob for Father's watch, and I am grateful you took the time today to help me snip it. I can't wait to see the smile on his face when we exchange gifts on Christmas Eve."

Effie cocked her head, studying her. Apparently satisfied, she bent and collected the locks from the floor. "So, when are ye goin' to tell me?"

Frowning, Mina angled her head one way then another, studying Effie's trimming. "Tell you what?"

"About your plans for Christmas in the country."

Her hands dropped. So did her jaw. "You know? How?"

Setting the hair on the vanity, Effie lifted a brow at her in the mirror. "I ran into Miss Whymsy late yesterday at the milliner's. She were buying a bit o' lace to dress up her hat. Ain't no call for such fanciness just to be volunteering at the institute, so I got it out of her that she's attending you on a little jaunt to the country for Christmas."

She shook her head. The woman was a wonder. "Effie, you could get a marble statue to spill its secrets."

"Ha! I ain't that good. That's all what she told me. I don't know where yer goin' or why, or how you even managed to talk Miss Whymsy into taking a leave from her volunteering. She just said, and I quote, 'Miss Scott and I are venturing out on a small excursion to the countryside. Do be a dear and check on Miss Minton for me in the meantime.'" Effie picked up a brush and tapped it against one palm.

Mina smirked. "I suppose you won't leave here today without me filling you in?"

A brilliant grin brightened Effie's plain face. "Well, it'll take me a good few minutes to style yer hair, and ye've nothing better to do while ye sit there."

"Very well." She sighed as Effie began brushing. "Remember that dinner I told you about, the one at Will's Uncle Barlow's?"

"Aye."

"I thought that would be the end of it, but it wasn't. Now Uncle Barlow has invited us to share Christmas with him in the country."

The brush stopped midstroke next to her ear, and Effie's wide-eyed gaze met hers in the mirror. "But what of the Christmas Eve celebration here at the Golden Egg? It's tradition! Ye can't miss that."

"You sound just like Father. But not to worry, for I shall return by then. Father insisted, and Will said he'd figure out a way to explain it to his uncle."

"Hmm." Effie ran the brush through the rest of her hair, then set it down and picked up a few pins. "Well, at least you're done with the pretend bride business, eh?"

She bit her lip.

"Mina?"

"Sort of," she mumbled.

"How can ye be a 'sort of' bride?" Effie tugged a hank of hair into place and shoved in a pin. "What has your father to say about that?"

Guilt scraped her soul every bit as much as the jab of Effie's next hairpin. Neither she nor Will had mentioned anything about the charade to Father. She couldn't imagine what he'd say. It had been hard enough trying to convince Miss Whymsy to go along with the sham-marriage story until Will had a chance to speak with his uncle. Once the gravity of Uncle Barlow's situation had been explained—plus the fact that Will had asked her father for permission to court her, moving them in the general direction of matrimony—Miss Whymsy had grudgingly agreed. The old lady had vowed, however, that she'd not lie outright. And neither would Mina.

She sat taller and tilted her head, giving Effie a better reach to finish pinning up her hair. "William promised he'd tell his uncle the truth of things soon after we arrive. . .and he asked my father last Saturday if he might court me. So maybe, perhaps, I might be a real bride in the near future."

"Oh, love! How wonderful."

It was. She kept telling herself that. But she couldn't stop the frown weighting her brow.

Effie stooped, staring face-to-face in the mirror with her. "Why do ye look as if it's not so wonderful?"

A sigh to rip a hole in the universe gushed out of her. Would voicing her doubts make them real? *Oh, God, please no.* But the determined gleam in Effie's brown eyes would not be denied.

"I don't know if it's real, Effie. Does William truly care for me, or is this just an act to save his uncle? Not that I mind saving his uncle, but. . .oh, I don't know. I suppose I feel like a character in a book, not knowing how the plot will twist—and am unable to flip to the last page to find out."

Effie shook her head. "But your story is already written, and it does have a happy ending. Are we not promised heaven when we die?"

"It's not the dying part that concerns me. It's the in-between now and then."

"Ahh, love. . .if we knew how things would turn out, then there'd be no need for faith, aye? My mother—God rest her—always told me to think of eternity, then live backward from that. Such a view has a way o' whittlin' down our current troubles to a size we can crumple up into a ball and toss aside."

The words sank in deep, convicting and healing. Her friend was right. What had become of her faith? *Oh, Lord, forgive me.*

Reaching up, she patted Effie's arm. "Thank you for the reminder. What would I do without you?"

"Well, for one, you might have more hair on yer head." With a purse of her lips, Effie straightened and finished with the last of her pins. "There. What do ye think?"

Tipping her head, she narrowed her eyes and studied every angle. Not one bit of shorter hair remained uncovered. "You are a miracle worker."

"Not really, but I happen to know the Giver of all miracles, and ye can bet I'll be on my knees every mornin' praying for ye while ye're gone."

"Thank you. I have a feeling I'll be needing a miracle or two, especially if I'm going to get this watch fob finished before I leave. That's only a little over a week and a half, and it's not like I can devote all my time to such a project."

"Knowing yer nimble fingers, ye'll have it done in a trice." Effie swiped up the old coin she'd given her weeks ago from where it sat on the vanity. She held the bit of gold out on an open palm. "And for heaven's sake, tuck this coin into yer pocket and carry it with ye at all times. Ye just might need to give someone a second chance at that estate, especially if Mr. Barlow's cousins are to be there as well."

Indeed. She wrapped her fingers around the coin. Taking courage from her friend's words of faith and the piece of gold in her hand, she did feel ready for her upcoming adventure. Mostly.

CHAPTER NINETEEN

The light snowfall, which had feathered
his schoolroom windows on the Thursday,
still lingered in the air, and was falling white.
Our Mutual Friend

Outside the carriage window, snowflakes floated. Some seemed to hang suspended. Others languished to the ground. Mina huffed on the glass, then rubbed away the condensation for a clearer view. She'd never been to Essex, nor witnessed such a magical sight. The road to Uncle Barlow's estate wound through a wooded countryside, slowly being tucked in beneath a light counterpane of white.

Would this be the best Christmas ever?

Will rode on horseback, trotting ahead of the carriage, his words of a fortnight ago yet echoed in her mind as she settled back against the seat. Judging by the fairyland outside, his "best Christmas" was off to a good start.

She slipped a sideways glance at Miss Whymsy, who peered out the window on her side of the carriage. The older lady seemed as mesmerized by the wonderland outside as she.

"God's artistry never ceases to amaze me." Her friend turned from the window. "Though my bones don't appreciate the chill, I can't help but revel in the beauty. Oh, how I've missed this."

"You've been to Essex?"

A curious smile lifted Miss Whymsy's lips, as if she savored the aftertaste of a treasured secret. "I served in a country home not far from here. A bit more north though, I should think. Ahh, but those were happy memories."

Yet as the carriage rolled along, the woman's smile faded to a shadow.

Mina patted her friend's leg, hoping to impart some kind of comfort. "Pardon my noticing, but you don't seem happy, thinking of those times."

"I suppose I should have said bittersweet." The blue green in Miss Whymsy's eyes deepened to a shade of hopeful despair, a contradiction that raised hundreds of questions.

And Mina couldn't keep from letting one slip out. "In what respect? That is, if you don't mind talking about it."

"Not at all, for therein does Mr. Hargrave yet live."

The carriage wheels dipped into a rut, giving her a good excuse for the sudden gasp and grasp of the seat. Had Miss Whymsy a past lover?

"Mr. Hargrave?" Mina rolled the name out like an invitation, hoping the woman would share more. "I've never heard you make mention of him."

"There's never been an occasion, I suppose, until now. Believe it or not, I was young once, like you, and thoroughly taken with a Mr. Roger Hargrave—not unlike your affection for the dashing Mr. Barlow."

Mina shifted on the seat, stifling the urge to fan her face though the air was chill. By faith! Why could she never master the flush that always accompanied the mention of Will?

"But as I was saying," Miss Whymsy continued, "Roger Hargrave was the most dashing gentleman I'd ever met. So handsome. So upstanding. He was the younger brother of the earl in whose home I served."

The older lady leaned closer, eyes twinkling, her trademark lavender scent wafting like summer on this wintry day. "We were engaged to be married."

This time her jaw did drop. "You were married?"

"No. You see. . ." For a moment, Miss Whymsy's gaze drifted back to the window, but Mina got the distinct impression the older lady didn't see the snow-laced trees or wintry landscape. She likely wandered in a far-off land of memory—until the woman drew in a deep breath and once again faced her. "My Roger was a military man, called off for one last stint in the Indies where he succumbed to a fever. . .a week before he was to return."

"Oh!" Mina recoiled, her hat bumping against the back of the carriage. "How dreadful."

"It was, but don't fret on my account." Miss Whymsy lifted her chin, her breath coming out in little white puffs. "Though Roger's been gone these thirty years, I have learned to cherish the pain of his absence."

"Cherish pain?" She shook her head, but even that didn't put any order to the curious thought. "I don't understand."

"You see, my dear, real joy is not found in the best moments of life, but in trusting that God is making the best of *every* moment. . .even those as dreadful as death."

What an odd sentiment. Mina sank deeper into the seat cushion, her thoughts taking a dive into Miss Whymsy's logic. How could it possibly have been the best for her to lose her mother at only seven years of age? Was it best that she'd wept for years on end and her father grieved alone every night? Or maybe—*perhaps*—had she been so caught up in the losing that she'd given no thought to the trusting part of the equation?

"I can see you're puzzled. Let me try to explain it a bit better." The governess inside Miss Whymsy emerged in the straightening of her shoulders. "I believe that when God permits pain, it is for the purpose of allowing something new to be born inside of us. I am not the same person I would be had Roger lived—and I trust my clever Creator that I am the better for it."

"So you're saying," Mina thought aloud, "that if my mother had lived, I wouldn't be the person I am today."

"Exactly. Oh, don't get me wrong, my dear." Miss Whymsy reached over and squeezed her hand. "I am in no way trying to negate how awful it was for you to experience the loss of your mother. I am simply saying that one must cherish all moments in life, happy or sad, for when you are older, memories are ofttimes all you have left."

Mina's heart broke, especially thinking of Miss Whymsy sitting by herself in front of the tiny hearth in her chamber, a tea tray set for one on the small table beside her, alone with naught but her memories. "Is it so very awful, living alone?"

"La!" the old lady chuckled, the ruffled edge of her bonnet bobbing with the movement. "God's children are never truly alone—especially in a world filled with books. I daresay you know that, hmm?"

They fell silent then and remained so until the carriage slowed. The horses stopped in front of a three-story, white-stone building, looking as merry as the snowflakes that danced about it. Vines wrapped brown arms around the structure in a loving embrace, and were it spring, no doubt green leaves would offer a stunning show against the backdrop. As her gaze landed on two bay windows curving out on either side of the front door, her smile returned in full force. What a perfect place to curl up with a book.

She turned to Miss Whymsy and rested her hand on the lady's arm. "Thank you for coming along with me. I hope you shall enjoy your stay here."

"I am sure—"

Just then the carriage door flung wide, and instead of the expected footman offering a hand, Uncle Barlow's grey-tufted head poked into the carriage. "I've been waiting for you—oh? What's this?" His eyes widened as his gaze landed on Miss Whymsy. "*Two* lovely ladies? How grand! M'ladies, my castle awaits." He backed out and held the door wide.

"Actually, my dear"—Miss Whymsy quirked a brow toward her—"I have a feeling I shall enjoy my visit here *very* much."

CHAPTER TWENTY

There is no playing fast and loose with the truth,
in any game, without growing the worse for it.
Little Dorrit

Will handed over his horse's lead to a stable boy, then patted the mount on the neck. The ride from Bishop's Stortford to Uncle's estate had been refreshing, reminding him how much he missed the sweetness of air unsullied by coal smoke and humanity.

"Mind you rub this fellow down good and have his left foreleg checked. He seemed to be favoring it."

"Aye, sir." The boy dipped his head.

Wheeling about, Will strode to the front door of Uncle Barlow's country home, his footsteps muffled by the thin layer of snow. Ahead, Uncle held out both arms, Mina's gloved hand perched on one, and Miss Whymsy's curled around the other. Uncle threw back his head, his laughter jolly in the greyness of the late afternoon.

Following their heels, Will entered the large foyer, already decorated for Christmas, and breathed in the scent of fresh greenery, beeswax candles, and hundreds of memories. Ahead rose the staircase where he and Percy used to race down the banisters on Christmas morn—until the year Percy had fallen and his nursemaid had put a stop to that. To his left, the door to the sitting room. How many summer holidays had he hidden behind the settee to avoid having to ride with his cousin? For Percy had ever been the worst horseman on the face of the planet. All walk and no gallop.

Shoving aside the memories, he caught up to Mina and helped her out of her wraps. Uncle Barlow assisted Miss Whymsy, and they loaded down a servant with cloaks, hats, and mufflers.

"Oh, my!" Mina breathed out as her wide-eyed gaze drifted from the holly-and-ivy garland along the stairway to a bowl of clove-studded oranges on a nearby table. "You've decorated early for Christmas."

Uncle Barlow gathered one of her hands in both of his, patting the top of it.

"I thought that since we'd not be here for the actual holiday, why not decorate now? It was so thoughtful of you, my dear, to have invited us all to your father's Christmas Eve gala at the Golden Egg. I own I've never been there, yet William tells me the oyster stew is not to be missed. And I cannot think of a more perfect venue or time in which to announce who my heir will be."

"Th–thank you," Mina stammered. As soon as Uncle released her hand and Miss Whymsy claimed his attention, she shot Will a narrow-eyed glance and a whisper. "What did you—?"

"Sorry," he whispered back, adding a sheepish smile that he hoped was convincing. "It was the only way I could think of for us to leave here by Christmas."

Her brows pulled together. "But—"

Whatever rejoinder she intended died on her lips as Alice and Percy descended the stairway. Will stifled a smirk. Saved by his cousins. That was a first.

"Well." Percy sniffed as he joined Will's side. "I see you've arrived."

In spite of his cousin's rancor, he couldn't help but smile. Some things never changed. In an odd sort of way, Percy's predictability was at least familiar, like donning a ratty woolen jumper, all scratchy and smelling of mothballs, yet altogether a necessity to the feeling of having arrived home.

"Good afternoon to you too, Percy. Alice." He nodded in greeting.

Alice bypassed him and closed in on Mina. "Good afternoon, Mina. I hope your journey wasn't too taxing, though by the looks of you, it likely was. I see you've brought along your mother."

Pink flushed Mina's cheeks. "Oh, but this is not my mother. This is one of my dearest friends, Miss Whymsy. Miss Whymsy, please meet Alice Barlow, wife of Percival Barlow, Will's cousins."

The older lady bowed her head. "Pleased to meet you, Mrs. Barlow, Mr. Barlow."

"A friend, you say?" Alice's green eyes narrowed as she swept her gaze over Miss Whymsy—and apparently found her lacking, judging by the perfect pout on her lips. She whirled back to Mina. "You brought along an uninvited guest? How bold. One might almost get the impression you felt the need for a chaperone."

An alarm gonged inside Will's head. If Alice continued that line of reasoning, she might draw a very revealing picture. He opened his mouth—

But Uncle Barlow charged ahead, collecting Miss Whymsy's hand and placing it on his arm. "I assure you, Alice, had I known Mina was acquainted with such a delightful lady, I would have invited her straightaway myself. Miss

Whymsy, allow me to escort you to the sitting room, where you can wait for a chamber to be readied."

At her consent, they both disappeared out of the foyer.

Percy sidled closer to Will. "A very clever scheme, Cousin."

Ignoring the man, Will swept out his hand toward Mina. Sometimes the best defense was to change the subject. "Mina? How about I show you the house?"

She stepped to his side.

But Percy blocked their passage. "It won't work, you know."

Afternoon light glinted off Percy's spectacles, drilling a beam into his eyes, and he blinked. Clearly there'd be no putting off the man. "I have no idea what you're talking about."

"Bringing the old lady to distract Uncle. You think she can make up for your dodgy past?"

Beside him, Mina tensed. Blast his cousin for always planting doubt in her mind. "No, I do not," he said through clenched teeth. "But if Uncle enjoys Miss Whymsy's company, why begrudge him a little happiness at Christmas?"

"There is something not right about this." Alice tapped a finger against her lips. "Something I intend to find out."

Mina huddled closer to his side, and he stretched out his arm, drawing her near.

And at that moment, Uncle Barlow strolled out of the sitting room, chuckling. He clapped his hands and rubbed them together. "This shall be the merriest of Christmases. I feel it in my bones." He stopped in front of the group and nodded to Will. "Why don't you see Mina up to the blue room and you can both refresh from your travels. We'll meet for dinner at seven o'clock."

Will waited for further instruction, but Uncle Barlow turned, apparently dismissing them.

"And to what room shall my things be delivered?" he asked.

Without turning back, Uncle waggled his fingers in the air. "Why, the blue room of course."

Percy and Alice gave him a queer look—but their confusion was nothing compared to the apprehension in Mina's large eyes as she blinked up at him.

He tugged his collar, fighting for air. Of course he'd be expected to share a bedchamber with his wife.

CHAPTER TWENTY-ONE

Death doesn't change us more than life.
The Old Curiosity Shop

Mina stepped into paradise.

She'd read of bedchambers like this. Walls papered with blue velveteen. Windows overlooking a wonderland of snow-encrusted tree branches. A merry fire glowed in the hearth, and thick rugs added warmth to the room. On one wall was a mahogany desk with a matching chair. Near the fireplace sat two wingbacks stuffed full enough that one might sleep the night through in them without a crick in the neck. A small table rested against another wall with a full tea set. Against the third wall stood a vanity filled with bottles and brushes and a mirror that bounced back light from the windows. But as her gaze landed on the bed—canopied and ruffled and with mattresses so high, a step stool stood nearby—her stomach twisted.

That bed was clearly meant for two.

Flames shot from her stomach to her cheeks. She whirled to face Will. "You cannot possibly stay in here with me. You must speak with your uncle today. Now!"

"Shh." He lifted a finger to his lips and closed the door behind him. "Percy and Alice weren't far behind us."

She retreated a step. He followed. He wasn't seriously thinking of spending the afternoon with her here? Alone? This was taking things too far. Far too far. A hero would not even think such a thing. "This is indecent."

She sidestepped him, but he blocked her.

"Mina, you have my word. I will tell my uncle as soon as the opportunity presents itself, but he's clearly preoccupied with your Miss Whymsy for the moment. Let's give him time to get her settled. We've only just arrived."

"Well, you cannot remain with me behind a closed door for the afternoon."

"I know." He rubbed the back of his neck. Was he as knotted up about the situation then? "I shall think of something."

"What?"

"I don't know." His hand dropped. "But if nothing else, there's a spare room at the end of this corridor. I'll wait until no one's about, then slip off down there."

"If my father hears of this—"

"He won't. Mina, please." He closed the distance between them and rested his hands on her shoulders, giving them a little squeeze. "We ought not give Percy and Alice anything more to wonder about, hmm? All will be well. I promise. Try to relax."

Relax? When she stood in a bedchamber alone with Will Barlow? Riding in a carriage with the man had been scandalous enough, but this was immoral. She pulled away.

"Mina, I am sorry, truly. I should have seen this coming, and I didn't. Forgive me?" He dipped his head, looking at her through his lashes. A lad with his hand caught in the sweets jar couldn't have looked more contrite.

She sighed. How was she to stay cross with such a look? "Very well."

"That's my girl." His head perked up, and he strode to the door. After a glance into the corridor, he looked over his shoulder at her. "All's clear. Rest up. Your trunk will soon be brought 'round, and I shall meet you downstairs later for dinner. Agreed?"

She nodded, for there was nothing more she could do save storm out of there and tell Will's uncle herself.

As soon as Will shut the door behind him, she wandered the room a bit, trailing a finger over much of the finery. Memorizing it all. Was this how Esther Summerson had felt when she'd first arrived at Bleak House?

A yawn stretched her jaw, and the quilted counterpane on the big bed called to her. After travelling all day, it would be lovely to close her eyes, just for a few minutes.

But by the time a rap on the door jolted her awake and a white-aproned maid peeked her head in, more than minutes had passed. Darkness filled the room.

"Might I help you dress for dinner, ma'am?"

She blinked, fighting the urge to look over her shoulder to see to whom the maid offered her services, though it could be none other than her—and that sent a thrill through her. She smiled at the woman as the servant scurried about the room, lighting lamps. "Thank you, but no need. I shall manage quite well on my own."

"As you wish, ma'am."

The maid was followed by a footman with her small trunk hefted up on one shoulder. He set it down next to a large wardrobe, then with a bob of his head, exited as well.

Mina crossed to her trunk and lifted out her dresses. There were only two—her very best—and she frowned at them both. By the third night, when she'd have to repeat one, surely Alice would have something to say about it. But perhaps by then, the truth would be out, and there'd be no reason to stay any longer.

She hung up one dress, then worked her way into the other. By the time she pinned up her hair, she smiled at her reflection in the mirror, satisfied that she looked her best, leastwise for tonight. After one more visit to her trunk, where she pulled out a small pouch containing the second-chance coin, she tucked the bit of gold into her pocket. She might not need it tonight, but when dining with Will's cousins, one never knew.

Stepping out into the corridor, she shivered. The air was far more chill than her chamber, so she upped her pace and descended the stairs to ground level. Surely the dining room was here somewhere, though she should have asked Will the location.

She passed the sitting room, and near the end of another passageway, two doors stood open. Golden light poured out of each. Could be either, so for no other reason than a whim, she ducked into the door on the right.

Then gasped. Books lined three walls, and on the fourth, at least twenty-five pairs of eyes stared back at her. Drawn toward the gilt-framed portraits, she padded inside and wandered from picture to picture.

One was surely a dark-haired Uncle Barlow with his apple-cheeks shaven clean and face smoothed of wrinkles. She cocked her head. He might almost be. . .yes, with that straight nose and strong jawline, the resemblance to Will was stunning.

To the left of Uncle Barlow's portrait was a shadow-faced fellow with a severe brow and overly large eyes. The man was seated, and beside him posed a bony woman in a brown, empire-waisted gown. Both frowned. Each looked as if they'd prefer to run off to another canvas rather than live immortally together in this painting. Were these Percy's parents?

She sidestepped over to the other side of Uncle Barlow's picture, and her breath hitched as she looked into Will's eyes. The hair on this man was a shade darker, but all the same, the features matched Will's exactly. . .save for one thing. There was a certain sadness to this portrait. The kind that called out from the years like a whisper from a grave. She stepped closer, gooseflesh rising on her arms. Was this Will's father? And if so, why was his mother not featured here as well?

"I thought I might find you here."

A deep voice turned her around, and she slapped a hand to her chest. "Uncle Barlow, you startled me."

"Sorry, my dear, but no need to fear in this house. To my knowledge, there are no ghosts—Christmas or otherwise—roaming about. Once a Barlow is dead, he is well and truly dead." He chuckled as he crossed the rug to stand next to her. "I see you've found William's father, and no wonder, for my nephew is the very image of my brother Edward. Both of them too handsome for their own good."

"He is so young here. He can't be much older than Will is now."

"True, and this is how I shall always remember him. Carefree. Laughter at the ready. Holding the world in two hands and tossing it about like a ball. I admired that about him, though I never spoke it aloud, for elder brothers rarely do." Uncle Barlow cleared his throat, then murmured, "In my quieter moments, I yet miss him keenly."

Sorrow thickened his words. He must've loved his brother very much to still feel such strong emotion. Was that why he'd given Will a second chance, perhaps? Had it been some kind of offering of honour to a lost brother?

Pulling her gaze from the portrait, she turned to Uncle Barlow. "What happened to Will's father?"

"It is a sad story, one best told while seated." He turned and sank into one of the chairs near the hearth, then waited for her to take the other. "Edward was the youngest of us three Barlow boys. And as you know, the youngest often are the wiliest. I suppose they have to be, to keep up with their elders. But Edward was more than that. He was a sunburst on a clouded day, always ready with a laugh, and oh, what a charmer. He could lure a penny from a miser's purse with nothing more than one of his grins."

She smiled. "He sounds like William."

"Indeed." Uncle Barlow grinned as well, but then as memories played over his face, his mirth faded. "He was."

"What happened to him?" she whispered.

For a long while, Uncle Barlow stared into the fire, saying nothing. Did he even know she was still in the room? Just at the point when she was sure he wouldn't answer, he pushed up from his chair and stood with his back to the hearth, flipping up his suit tails to warm his backside. "My brother Edward died not long after your William was born. Both he and William's mother were taken by a fever. It is God's grace alone that little William survived."

"How awful." She pulled the words out of a great storehouse of sorrow. The pain of growing up without a mother was bad enough, but to not have a father either?

"You sound as if you've held hands with loss yourself, my dear."

Shoving down a rising melancholy, she nodded, eager to change the subject. "Uncle Barlow, I wonder if William spoke with you this afternoon?"

"I'm afraid I was a bit indisposed." A chuckle rumbled in his chest. "Your Miss Whymsy is delightful, and I confess to overindulging in her company. I took her on a tour of the entire grounds."

"I see." So, the old fellow *still* didn't know the truth. She pressed her lips flat.

Uncle Barlow returned to his chair. "What was it William wanted to speak to me about?"

Absently, she ran her hands along her legs, smoothing wrinkles from her gown. Would Will be very cross if she told his uncle herself? But was this not the perfect opportunity? And they had agreed he should know.

"Uncle Barlow," she began before she could change her mind. "There is something you need to know about Will and me."

"Oh? And what is that?"

Trying not to think of the disappointment in his eyes when he found out about the deception, she pressed on. "We are not actually—"

"There you are. I thought as much." Percy's voice boomed through the open door, and they turned. Will's cousin frowned at her, then shifted his gaze to Uncle Barlow. "We are all waiting on you, Uncle, and have been for some time."

The old fellow patted her knee. "We shall have to continue this later, my dear." Rising, he held out his arm and winked, speaking for her alone. "It promises to be a lively evening, for I've taken the liberty of seating Miss Whymsy next to me. I don't suppose Alice shall like it, but then neither Alice nor Percy seem to like much of anything, eh?"

She rose and took his arm, fingering her pocket with her free hand. Maybe she would need that second-chance coin tonight after all.

For hopefully she'd get a second chance to tell Uncle Barlow the truth.

CHAPTER TWENTY-TWO

Never close your lips to those whom you
have already opened your heart.
Charles Dickens

The evening stretched into a long, sharp dagger and took a deadlier turn when Uncle Barlow and Miss Whymsy decided to retire early. Something about overdoing the day. Will grimaced as he set down his untouched glass of sherry. After parrying Alice's cutting remarks and deflecting Percy's verbal swipes, he'd had enough. "Come along, Mina. It's been a long day for us as well." He offered her his hand, then glanced at his cousins. "Good night."

"Hmm. Perhaps," Percy drawled.

Ignoring whatever the scoundrel had in mind, Will led Mina from the room more exhausted than he'd ever been. Normally he would have laughed off such vitriol. Dodged his cousins' jabs as cleverly as he might a bucket of slop being dumped out a Cheapside window. But when Mina became the sole target of such venom, he'd had no choice but to usher her out before he popped Percy in the nose.

As they strolled toward the staircase, Mina's gaze sought his. "You know you cannot stay in my chamber."

"Of course not." He winked down at her, hoping the lighthearted action would calm her fears.

"But where will you sleep?"

"Don't fret. I've got things under control." For a moment, he wished he had drunk that sherry, if for nothing more than to wash away the bitter taste his words left in his mouth. Under control? Ha! A spinning kaleidoscope couldn't have been more crazed than this topsy-turvy day.

Mina paused and turned to him at the foot of the stairs. "Do you suppose your uncle would mind if I brought a book with me to bed?"

"I should think he'd be delighted and"—he leaned toward her and tapped her on the nose—"would want to hear your thoughts on it when you're finished."

He wheeled about and led her to the library, where she seemed more than at home. He watched her as she roamed from shelf to shelf, her delight doing strange things to his heart. She belonged here, surrounded by books as if they were old friends. Running her fingers along each shelf, she'd pause with a mysterious twitch to her lips, and for some odd reason, he wished this moment to never end. Was this how it was for God to gaze upon His creation as they enjoyed His gifts?

As she passed near a wall sconce, soft light teased out the coppery glimmers in her hair, all done up and begging for release. How long would those locks fall? How silky the feel? His fingers curled in reflex and—sweet blessed heavens. . .what *was* he thinking?

Finally, she pulled a book off a shelf, and a little coo caught in her throat. Judging by the way she cradled the thing to her breast, she'd found a favorite. As she rambled back to where he waited for her at the door, her smile faltered for a moment—when her gaze slid to the portrait of his father.

"Will. . ." She bit her lip as she drew close to him, bringing the sweet scent of the rosemary water she'd freshened up with. "I hope you don't mind, but your uncle told me the sad tale of your father and mother earlier today."

He stiffened. Father. . .*and mother?* What could the old fellow possibly say about her? "What do you mean?"

"How they died of a fever. I had no idea you grew up without knowing either of them. It was hard enough losing my mother as a child. I can't imagine not having my father around. I am sorry for your loss."

Compassion shimmered in Mina's eyes, and the fish he'd eaten at dinner flipped in his gut. All the deceptions, the secrets, knotted into a great net, trapping him and squeezing the breath from his lungs. This had to stop. Surely he owed Mina some morsels of truth—despite his mother's wishes. Besides, it wasn't as if he were telling Uncle Barlow.

"Mina, there's something my uncle didn't tell you, because he doesn't know it himself. But I feel I must be honest with you, for you've suffered enough untruths at my request. My mother is, well. . .she's still alive, though for how much longer, I am not certain. She is very ill."

"She's not dead?" The words rolled from her lips as if she tasted each one and couldn't decide whether she liked the flavour. "While I am happy for you that your mother is yet amongst the living, why does your uncle think—why do you *allow* him to think—she is dead? I don't understand."

Of course she didn't. He'd barely understood it himself that day six months ago when a solicitor had tracked him down and told him the unbelievable details. Reaching, he kneaded a rock-hard muscle on his shoulder. "It is a complicated story," he said at length.

She merely shrugged. "I am well familiar with such tales, for are not all our lives a tangled heap of joy and sorrow? Still, if you'd rather not tell it, I understand."

The pity in her eyes made his heart skip a beat. Had ever a more compassionate woman graced this earth?

Leaning back against the doorjamb, he folded his arms. He'd already relayed the story to Fitz. There could be no harm in sharing it with Mina as well, for his mother had only bade him not to reveal the details to his family.

"My father," he began, "was the youngest brother and, as such, was indulged. Overmuch. And to his detriment, I might add. Though my grandfather urged him to go into the church, he could not give up his artistic bent or his dream to become a renowned painter. He talked Grandfather—or rather Grandmother—into allowing him to study for a year in France amongst the masters. It was there he met my mother."

Mina's nose bunched. "This doesn't sound so complicated."

"This is where it takes a turn." He sighed. How to put this delicately? "While staying as a guest in the house of one of his former schoolmate's relatives, he became enamored with the gentleman's daughter. He asked to paint her, and she accepted. During those long sessions, alone, his admiration of her turned into an indiscretion."

"Oh." Pink blossomed on Mina's cheeks, and for a moment, he considered if he should continue.

Unfolding his arms, he paced the rug in front of the door. Better to tell the rest without making eye contact. "When my mother told my father she was with child, he knew he had to do the right thing and marry her. But she was French. And in his English family's eyes, that would be a mark against her. Were they to find out she was also bearing his child, they'd both be outcasts."

Mina's breath caught. "So what happened?"

"He brought her home immediately, intending to marry in the Anglican church before anyone knew. But while doing a fitting for my mother's dress, a servant noticed her thickening middle and went straight to Grandfather. Needless to say, it did not go over well. Grandfather allowed the marriage to continue to give the child—me—a name, but he swore my parents to secrecy and banned them from his household immediately following the ceremony."

"How awful."

"It was." He stopped his mad pacing and faced her. "They moved to London, where they took up a shabby existence. My father scrabbled to sell miniature portraits while my mother tried desperately to get jobs tutoring French. Shortly after my birth, my father took ill and died. My mother, alone in a foreign country, with a babe and no means to support herself, decided to bring me back to my father's family and plead for Grandfather to take me in, for she couldn't return to her home with a child born far too soon after their marriage. Grandfather agreed. I was whisked off to be cared for by a hired nurse until I could be weaned and questions wouldn't be asked. He let everyone believe—even me—that my mother had died of a fever alongside my father."

"Oh, Will. . ." Mina's words shivered on the air. "I am so sorry. I shouldn't have asked."

He shrugged. "Well, there is somewhat of a happy ending. I hope, at any rate. When my mother recently fell ill, hanging on to life by a thread, she sent a solicitor to find me, which he did, thank God. I have been to see her, and I hope—and pray—that by moving her here, I can care for her, and she'll soon recover."

"I pray so too." Her blue gaze met his. "Thank you for telling me."

Nodding, he swept his hand toward the door. "It is getting late. I should see you up to your room."

He pivoted and strode past the threshold—and came face-to-face with Percy.

Blast! If his cousin had heard any of his tale. . . His hands curled into fists. "How long have you been standing there?" he ground out.

A slow smile spread across Percy's face. "Long enough. Good night, Cousin."

Percy wheeled about and stalked down the corridor.

"Oh, dear." Coming up from behind, Mina rested her hand on his sleeve. "He'll tell your uncle, won't he?"

His shoulders sagged, but a steely determination shored up his soul. Though his mother had asked him otherwise, there was nothing to be done for it now. "Not if I tell him first."

And he would. He'd seek out Uncle Barlow first thing on the morrow and tell him everything or die in the trying.

CHAPTER TWENTY-THREE

*There is nothing so strong or safe in an emergency
of life as the simple truth.*
Charles Dickens

He'd meant to talk to his uncle, truly he had, but the next day passed in a blur of festive activities—and never once had Uncle been without Miss Whymsy at his side. Morning. Afternoon. Evening. All the events had chafed like a damp woolen muffler, rubbing Will's conscience so raw that by the time he escorted Mina up the stairway to her chamber well after nightfall, he could hardly stand himself. Now that he was finally ready to divulge everything to his uncle, it seemed as if the powers of hell conspired against his bringing the truth to light.

At the top of the stairs, Mina leaned close to him and lowered her voice. "Have you spoken to your uncle?"

"Trust me, I tried, but not yet. It seems your Miss Whymsy is a particular favorite of his. The two were inseparable all day."

"I noticed. I've never seen her so happy, so. . .animated, I suppose." A brief smile flickered on her lips, then just as soon faded. "Though I am sorry you weren't able to corner Uncle Barlow because of her."

"Well, the good news is that Percy wasn't able to either." He offered his arm, and they continued down the corridor toward the blue room. "As near as I can tell, that is."

"Which is a bit strange, I think. Your cousin seems the type to relish a good tattling, no matter if your uncle were occupied or not."

"I know. That does have me concerned." He scrubbed his face with his free hand. Percy had never been able to keep a secret—especially one as tantalizing as this. So why now?

"I pray you'll have better luck tomorrow." Mina smiled up at him. "And I'll try to detain Miss Whymsy for you."

"Actually, I still have a chance to speak with my uncle tonight. It's his habit to record the day's activities in a journal he keeps in his study. I'm not sure if it's the writing he enjoys more or the cherry tobacco he uses in his pipe while composing." He winked down at her—and was rewarded with a blush that pinked Mina's cheeks to a most becoming shade.

"Well, despite everything, it was a lovely day. The sleigh ride. Meeting some of the tenants. Oh, and the drinking chocolate afterwards. Sublime!" Her eyes closed and her mouth moved as if she were savoring it all over again.

He couldn't help but chuckle. Such innocence. Such beauty. A sweet combination of all that was lovely and right. His mirth fled, replaced with a sobering revelation. Not only would he never tire of spending time with Mina—he didn't want his time with her to end.

Her eyes popped open, and she arched a brow. "If you don't mind, I shall have to steal that recipe and bring it home to Martha. What an addition it would be to Father's Christmas celebration. It might even outshine his oyster stew."

He stopped at her chamber door and tapped her on the nose. "No thievery involved. You have my blessing to ask Cook for it."

He opened her door and stood aside, but she hesitated on the threshold, apparently lost in thought. Fine little creases marred her brow.

"A farthing for your thoughts?" he asked.

"I. . .well. . ." She sighed as if the weight of the world were hers to carry.

He stepped closer, alarmed yet instantly ready to fight whatever dragon tormented her so. "Tell me."

She peered up at him, her blue eyes almost greenish, so pure was her anguish. "I am concerned about the Christmas party, what with your uncle and cousins planning on attending. Father doesn't know we've been playing the part of being married, and were they to hint at anything, well. . .if my father finds out, I—"

He laid a finger against her lips, and his knees nearly buckled from the softness that met his touch. "Stop right there. If the rest of the evening goes as promised, I shall have the matter taken care of by morning. You are not to lose one bit of sleep over this. Promise?"

For a moment she wavered, then her gaze brightened back to normal and the trust shining in those blue ponds did strange things to his gut. He lowered his hand to keep from pulling her into his arms.

"I promise." A small smile curved her mouth.

"Right then, off with you. See you at breakfast."

She nodded and crossed into her chamber, then turned with her hand on the door. "Good night, Will."

Ahh, but she was a picture, standing there with lamplight bathing her in an angelic glow. It took him several tries just to get out a simple goodbye. "Good night."

Turning on his heel, he fled down the corridor. It was either that or give in to the urge to kiss her senseless. He upped his pace as he descended the stairs, then swung around the staircase and strode toward Uncle's study. The sooner he got this over with, the better. Bracing himself for a long night of explaining, he stepped through the open door. "Uncle Barlow, sorry to disturb you, but there's something important I need to. . ."

His words stumbled to a halt as two grey heads turned to look at him from across the room. A lively blaze in the hearth cast light on the figures seated on the sofa—his uncle *and* Miss Whymsy. He shoved down a groan. Ought not a woman of Miss Whymsy's age be abed? What on earth could they possibly be talking about now when they'd been locked in conversation all the blessed day?

Uncle Barlow beckoned with one hand. "Come and join us William. Miss Whymsy here is just telling me about her volunteer work at an institute I'd never heard of. Quite interesting. You may learn a thing or two."

"I. . .uh. . ." Clamping his mouth shut, he gritted his teeth. What to do? Stay and listen, wait out whatever the older lady had to say—which could take hours, as elders generally got sidetracked frequently and for long periods? Or leave now and have a go at Uncle first thing in the morning?

"Yes, do come join us, Mr. Barlow. If you're half as enthralled as your uncle at my stories, I daresay I could regale you until daybreak." Laughter warbled past the lady's lips.

Just as he'd thought. The two of them had settled in and would make a very long night of it, and by the time it wrapped up, no doubt Uncle would be too weary for the weight of the sordid truth Will must tell him.

"I thank you, but—" He forced a small yawn. "I didn't realize the hour. Perhaps, Uncle, I might speak with you straight off in the morning?"

"Of course. Any time, my boy. And a hearty good night to you."

The two grey heads turned to once again face each other. Defeated, Will shuffled out of the room. Apparently the truth battle was one he'd have to wage the following day.

He retraced his steps up to the first floor, then stalked down the dimly lit corridor. A light still glowed beneath Mina's door, and he couldn't help but grin as he imagined her taking down her hair and brushing it until the reddish glints shone like fire.

Passing on, he took care to edge toward the far side of the wall as he drew close to his cousins' door. No light glowed in the crack near their threshold.

Good. Then neither Percy nor Alice would hear his footsteps as he stole down to the empty chamber at the end of the passageway.

But just as he padded by, the door swung open.

Will froze, praying he'd blend in with the shadows. As long as whoever it was didn't look his way—

"What are you doing roaming the corridor?" Percy's voice stabbed him in the back.

He turned, heart pounding—then angled his head. Why the deuce would his cousin be dressed head to toe in black, from the tips of his shoes, to his overcoat, to the dark hat clapped atop his head? "I could ask the same of you, Cousin. By the looks of it, you're in deep mourning and are about to go out to haunt the night."

Percy scowled. "Isn't your room there?" He lifted a finger and pointed back toward the blue room. "Why are you going in the opposite direction of your chamber?"

He stared down his nose, challenging Percy with a glower. "Just stretching my legs."

"As am I."

Will narrowed his eyes. Should he call the man on it? Clearly his cousin was up to no good. . .but then again, neither was he. He swept out his hand and gave Percy a little bow. "Enjoy your walk then."

"You as well." The sentiment was completely devoid of warmth, and in fact shivered in the space between them.

Percy turned, defiance hanging as thick and dark in the air as the shadows. Which one of them would discover the other's business first?

CHAPTER TWENTY-FOUR

The beating of my heart was so violent and wild
that I felt as if my life were breaking from me.
Bleak House

Some days were the stuff made of dreams. This had been one, despite the slight shadow that it seemed Uncle Barlow purposely avoided a private conversation with either her or Will. But even so, Mina had still relished her morning stroll outside in an enchanted world of snow, dazzling like a thousand candlelit crystals. The afternoon was equally as magical, spent in a library nook in a greatly overstuffed chair with the time to untether her imagination. And most especially enthralling was catching the man she loved in the act of gazing at her when he thought she wasn't looking.

Mina hid a smile, but she couldn't conceal the pink that surely coloured her heated cheeks. Though Will stood on the other side of the drawing room in conversation with Percy, he always seemed to be aware of her—and that was the best dream of all.

On the settee, Uncle Barlow entertained Miss Whymsy with a botanical book and a magnifying glass—or did Miss Whymsy entertain him? Hard to tell, judging by the way their heads bowed together, sharing a secret laugh. Ahh, but this was a good respite for her older friend, for Mina suspected Miss Whymsy laboured far too hard at the institute. The woman never did things by half measure.

Alice played a haunting tune on the piano, the last minor chords hovering on the air like an omen. Then she looked up and pinned Mina in place with the lift of her brow. "Mina, do come over here, would you? I think I've provided my fair portion of music for the evening. It is only right you share your talents, for I wouldn't dream of overshadowing your abilities."

She froze. The only thing she knew how to play was a short hand of whist, and even at that, her card skills were lacking. But music? Despite the many times she'd begged her father for lessons, there'd never been time or money. "I am sorry. . ." She paused, searching for the right combination of words. "But I

. . .I haven't played in years."

Immediately she bit the inside of her cheek. Was it a lie if she'd honestly not played in *any* of her years?

"A shame. I suppose William hasn't been able to afford a proper pianoforte for you. Even so, I have a remedy." Shuffling through papers, Alice pulled one out and held it up. "Ahh, here it is. I shall play, and you shall sing."

"Oh, I don't know. . ."

Uncle Barlow set down his magnifying glass and closed the book. "There's no need for such modesty here. Amongst friends, one should be able to share anything, especially one's voice."

Had ever a fox in a trap felt so ensnared? There was no possible way to get out of this short of feigning a sudden death.

Straightening her shoulders, she desperately hoped to find courage in good posture, then crossed over to Alice. Unless the woman had chosen a hymn or a pub song, it wasn't likely she'd be able to sing a word. She stopped at the end of the piano as the first chords rang out, each one unfamiliar. The expectancy in Uncle Barlow's eyes gleamed brilliant. Her corset bit into her ribs as she tried to control her frantic breathing. How to salvage this farce? *Think. Think!*

But nothing came to mind, least of all any lyrics. And why should they? She'd only read of ladies and high society. She surely didn't know what they'd sing, which only served to drive home the fact that no matter how much she'd like to, she didn't belong here. Sneaking a glance over her shoulder, she eyed Alice, and a niggling thought crept out like a spider. . .did she *really* want to belong here, or would it turn her into a callous, hurtful woman such as Will's cousin? Apparently wealth alone didn't guarantee her life would have any more meaning than Alice's spiteful existence. Why had she wasted so many years thinking otherwise?

The music ground to a halt, pulling her from her thoughts, and she snapped her gaze to the floor, preferring to study the hem of her skirt rather than witness the disappointment in Uncle Barlow's eyes.

"That was your cue, Mina," Alice taunted from the keyboard. "Yet no matter. I'll begin again."

Unbearable heat churned up from her belly, and humiliation choked her. Suddenly she was eight years old again, standing amidst a circle of girls. Several pointing. Some laughing. All listening to the awful Mary Blake poke fun at her for being the daughter of a lunatic. Tears filled her eyes, blurring the world.

"How about something more seasonal? Alice, do you mind?"

She looked up to see Will wink at her as he strode to the piano keys. He forced Alice to yield the bench by his stare alone. Gently at first, then with more gusto, the opening chords of "God Rest Ye Merry, Gentlemen" filled the room like a gathering of old friends. This she could sing, and her knees weakened when Will joined in, his bass voice adding harmony. Even Uncle Barlow and Miss Whymsy sang along.

By the time the last note faded, Alice frowned. "That was quaint." She looped her arm through Mina's and pulled her away from the piano. "But I am tired of music. Let us take a turn about the room."

Unable to escape, Mina padded beside the tall woman, tongue lying fallow, heart fluttering. Why the sudden attention from Alice? Though she tried, she couldn't shake the feeling that this woman was a tiger hiding in the weeds, waiting to spring.

Alice didn't speak until they passed out of ear range of where Percy had once again cornered Will. "So, Mina, you don't sing the classics. You don't play. Where did you say you were educated?"

"I didn't." She let out a breath. That had been an easy answer.

"You didn't say, or you didn't have an education? Which is it?"

"I didn't say."

"Hmm." Alice eyed her sideways, her powdered face flawless in the sconce light. Maddeningly so. Except for the woman's cruel disposition, Alice overshadowed her in every way. "Where did you and William meet? Who introduced you? Perhaps I know the person."

She forced her arm to remain steady where it touched against Alice's, though surely if God struck her down for lying, her stillness would be in vain. "We met at. . .an establishment, and I doubt very much if you'd know any of our acquaintances."

"An establishment?" Alice pecked at the word like a vulture looking for the tastiest bits of meat. "Interesting. How long did you say you've been married?"

La! What was it Will had told her? A year? Nine months? Though she tried to recall what they'd worked out, the way Alice stared at her obliterated all her thoughts. "I. . .em. . ."

"Let me guess, you didn't say that either. I wonder if you can. A nondescript past, a nebulous engagement, and a mysterious marriage. That is more than intriguing." Alice stopped and turned, folding her hands in front of her as if they chatted about nothing more than ribbon colours or button sizes. "I find it interesting that a young woman so clearly in love hasn't much to say about her courtship or her husband. . .unless of course, he is *not* her husband."

Cold dread washed over her. Alice knew? How in the world? Or was the woman simply fishing for a scandal? Either way, the best option—the *only* option—was to exit as soon as possible. Mina threw back her shoulders, hoping such a regal pose would put Alice off—leastwise for now. "This turn of conversation is absurd. I am feeling tired, and I should like to retire now. Good night, Alice. I will see you on the morrow."

"Good night. Oh, and I won't bother sending William up after you, for I don't suppose it will matter what time he frequents the empty chamber at the end of the corridor, hmm?" Half a smile lifted the woman's lips, but it had nothing to do with mirth or amusement. "Though I must admit I am unsure if I should pity or scorn you for being such a naive little girl. At least Elizabeth knew what she'd been doing when her and Will had been together."

Mina whirled, praying the movement wouldn't be as panicky on the outside as the turmoil churning inside her. Forcing an impossible calmness to her steps, she strode toward the door—fighting the urge to bolt.

But as soon as she cleared the threshold, she raced to the stairs, and tears turned the world into a smear.

Oh, how she longed to go home.

CHAPTER TWENTY-FIVE

Lies is lies. Howsever they come, they didn't ought to come,
and they come from the father of lies,
and work round to the same.
Great Expectations

Will kept one eye trained on Mina while she strolled arm in arm with Alice, all the while listening to Percy blather on about the merits of steam engines. Something wasn't right about Alice's focused attention on Mina—and something was definitely wrong in the way Mina strode to the door with clipped steps and disappeared without a good night to anyone.

"Excuse me." He held up a hand to Percy, cutting him off. "It's been a long day. I bid you good night."

"Oh? Do you need a good leg stretcher tonight as well?"

"I could ask the same of you, Cousin. Any more clandestine meetings to attend?"

A tic pinched the skin at the corner of Percy's right eye. "Keep your nose out of my business, and perhaps I shall return the favor."

Will wheeled about, tired of Percy's games—and even wearier of his own.

"That's it. Run off to your cold bed in the spare room."

Percy's retort stabbed him in the back as he dashed out the door. How like his cousin to hold his cards close to his chest and pull one out at the most inopportune moment. Hopefully Uncle hadn't overheard.

But he'd have to deal with that later. For now, the way Mina flew up the stairway concerned him most. What horrid thing had Alice said to her?

"Mina, wait." He took the stairs two at a time.

She turned at the landing, face impossibly pale. Eyes so wide, she looked as if she'd not only seen a ghost but held hands with one.

On impulse, he reached out and rubbed his hands along her upper arms, hoping to soothe. "What has you in such a state? What did Alice say to you?"

"She knows, Will." A little sob punctuated her words. "At least she suspects. And if your uncle hears it from her—"

"Knows what?"

"That we are unwed."

He shook his head. "She can't possibly know that, not for certain. Please, Mina, don't fret. All will be well. This shall soon be over, I promise."

"I—" Her voice cracked. "I know."

Huge tears welled in her eyes, brimming like raindrops and shimmering in the lamplight. His heart twisted at the sight. Grabbing her hand, he led her away from the landing and into the corridor, out of view should anyone chance to leave the drawing room.

He turned to her well before they reached her chamber door, unwilling to spend another second without easing the burden that drove her to weep. Reaching out, he cupped her face, catching her tears before they dampened her cheeks. "Tell me true, Mina. What is wrong? Did I not say this would soon be over?"

"That's just it! This will *all* be over soon. And then what? We go back to being what we were, me serving you ale once a week while you and Mr. Fitzroy swap jokes?" She threw out her hands, the passion in her eyes far too alluring. "Is any of this even real?"

"It is." Without thinking, he bent, and his mouth came down on hers. The heat of a thousand suns burned along every nerve and settled low in his belly. Everything went oddly quiet. The hiss of the gas lamps. The beat of his heart. There was nothing else but Mina's sweet taste. Her breath. Her softness. A tremor shook through him, and he hungered for more. Every other kiss in his life had been wrong. He knew that now—and would never again kiss another.

"Mina," he whispered against her lips, her jawline, her neck. Lost. Hopelessly, wonderfully lost.

A low moan sounded in her throat, sobering him. What was he doing? He pulled back.

Mina's eyes were yet closed, lashes impossibly long against her cheeks. She lifted a shaky finger to her lips and absently rubbed a mouth yet swollen with his kisses. Was she remembering—or abhorring?

He sucked in a breath. "Forgive me. I shouldn't have taken such a liberty. I don't usually—"

Her eyes popped open, and an unnatural brilliance shone in them. . .a fevered kind of fury.

"Don't you? Did you kiss Elizabeth like that as well?" she hissed.

The question slapped him in the face—hard—and he recoiled a step. "How do you know of her?"

"Your cousins have mentioned her several times." The red glints in her hair matched the colour rising in her cheeks. "Was she another one of your pretend brides?"

He spun away as if struck, tensing every muscle in his body. "No," he gritted out. "She was to be my real bride." The truth hung thick between them.

"I've heard enough. Good night, William."

"Mina, wait!" He pivoted back. "I can explain. Let me explain."

"No. I'm done with your explanations. I can't do this anymore. I can't." Her voice shook. "The twisted truths. The deceit. I. . ." She shook her head, knocking loose a single curl. "I will be leaving in the morning."

"Mina, don't do this." The thought of losing her drove the breath from his lungs. He was as thoroughly sick of deception as she, but dare he voice the truth he could no longer deny? "I. . ." Swallowing, he reached for her and pulled her close. "I love you, Mina. With all my heart."

She stiffened beneath his touch. Blinking. Face the colour of parchment. "I wish I could believe that. I really do." Her voice was a shiver of cold wind. "But I meant what I said. I am leaving in the morning."

Wrenching from his grasp, she whirled, the hem of her skirt snapping against his legs.

"Mina!"

He followed her frenzied pace, but too late. She reached her chamber door and slammed it in his face before he could catch her, the slide of the bolt overloud as it shot into place. He stood alone in the corridor with naught but the echo and far too many regrets.

CHAPTER TWENTY-SIX

A dream, all a dream, that ends in nothing,
and leaves the sleeper where he lay down.
A Tale of Two Cities

Lethargic light, a sickly sort of blue grey, leached through the open drapery like a spreading bruise. Clutching the second-chance coin, Mina shoved off the bed, fully dressed, more wrinkled than the counterpane she'd wrestled with all night. Weary to the very marrow of her bones, she paced to the window and pressed her forehead against the glass. The coldness of it shocked and jarred— and she welcomed the bite.

"I love you, Mina. With all my heart."

Will's words of the night before haunted relentlessly, and she squeezed the coin all the tighter. Did he *really* mean it, or was it his desperate attempt to get her to stay? She'd give anything to believe his love was true, but though she tried, she just couldn't. The coin pressed hard into her skin. She could give him another chance to explain about Elizabeth, but even if she did, how would she know for sure he spoke truth?

She blew out a breath, fogging a clouded circle on the window. Mostly she just wanted to go home. She missed Father's bellowing and Cook's mumblings of "peas and porridge." Life at the Golden Egg was a lackluster existence compared to the eminence and elegance of this country estate, but it was her existence. And more importantly, it was real. Not a charade. Without truth as a base, even living the lifestyle of the wealthy didn't give her life meaning. Maybe—perhaps—true meaning in life had nothing to do with outward trappings but with inward genuineness.

A foreign longing welled to run back to the inn and embrace her dull life. She was done with pretending. And done with casting Will as a hero, for he had been a dream. A fleeting, make-believe man she'd invented—and who'd fallen woefully short. She'd love to blame him, to rage and rail against his shortcomings, but truly, was she not as culpable for expecting more out of him than was humanly possible?

Oh, God. I have been so wrong. Please, forgive me.

Outside, an ember of sun lit the charcoal sky. Across the courtyard, the door to the stables opened, and a young man strolled out, dressed for the day's work of tending horses. Good. Then it wouldn't be too soon to request a ride into town.

Turning from the sight, she hurried over to the dressing table and sank onto the stool. There wasn't much she could do about her wrinkled gown, but she ought to at least see to her hair, especially with a full day of travel ahead.

As she wrangled out snarls, she studied her face in the mirror. Her eyes were too big. Her nose, overly long and dotted with freckles. Her lips were too full and remembered far too well the feel of Will's mouth fitted against them. The hairbrush slipped from her grasp, and she caught it before it hit the carpet. No, not again. She'd spent the entire night trying to forget that kiss.

And failed.

She cast the brush onto the table and poked pins into her hair, grazing her scalp. Had Will spoken the same words of love to Elizabeth? Had Elizabeth been as naive as she to wish they were true?

No more. She shoved up from the table and retrieved her coat, tucking the second-chance coin into the pocket. It was too early to trouble Miss Whymsy's door, but perhaps by the time she finished talking with the stable hand, the older lady would be stirring.

The corridors were yet dim, and she tread as quickly as she dared without bumping into a side table or tripping down the stairway. She paused in the foyer, debating if she ought to use the front door. But no, better to use the back servants' entrance, for that's what she really was despite her pretending otherwise.

Outside, cold air violated the hem of her skirts and climbed up her legs. It wasn't far from the house to the stables, but by the time she ducked inside to the smell of hay and horses, she wished she had thought to grab her muffler.

The same young man she'd seen earlier turned from a workbench at her entrance and dipped his head. "Can I be of service to ye, ma'am?"

"Yes. I was wondering if you could bring around the carriage and drive my travelling companion and me to Bishop's Stortford. We shall be catching the morning train to London."

"Aye, ma'am. I'll bring it 'round within the hour."

"Thank you." Clutching her coat tighter at the neck, she headed back out into the nip of the winter morning. Hopefully Miss Whymsy was up, though it was a shameful task to have to ask her friend to leave so soon after convincing her to come in the first place. In the four days they'd been here, the woman had seemed to enjoy herself, especially when Uncle Barlow was in the room.

Halfway across the courtyard, she paused, wishing to brand into her memory the elegance of the white-stone estate. Would she ever have another chance to Christmas in the country? It had been lovely—while it lasted. Sighing, she swept her gaze from the snow-crusted windowsills of the ground level, up to the first floor, then paused on the nearest window on the second. The drapes were pulled back and a face stared out, framed with white, tufted hair.

She gasped. Why was Uncle Barlow frowning at her? Had Alice already gone to him with her suspicions? Her shoulders slumped as she imagined his disappointment. Good thing she'd arranged for transport, for surely Will's uncle would be asking her to leave within the hour.

With a halfhearted wave at the face in the window, she continued toward the house—but he kept staring at a point beyond her. Had he never really been looking at her to begin with? She turned, then squinted for a better look.

On the side of the road leading into town, two dark shapes stood in conversation near a horse swishing its tail. One man wore glasses—easy enough to identify as Percy. The other was a rotund fellow, nearly twice the breadth of Percy, and wearing a ridiculously tall hat. Did he think that made him appear any less roly-poly than the great ball of black wool that he was? An odd time for a conversation and an even odder place in which to conduct their business.

But it was no business of hers. Not anymore. She ducked her head into the cold breeze and pressed on toward the house. It was time to rouse Miss Whymsy—and leave all this behind.

CHAPTER TWENTY-SEVEN

*If our affections be tried, our affections are our consolation
and comfort; and memory, however sad, is the best
and purest link between this world and a better.*
Nicholas Nickleby

Will descended the stairs two at a time. Was he too late? Was Mina already now on her way back to London?

His foot landed crooked on a step, and he grabbed for the balustrade. Falling headlong would slow his pursuit—but not end it. If he had to run through the snow all the way to the Golden Egg, he would explain the full truth to Mina. He owed her that. He owed himself that. And most importantly, he owed it to God.

Both his feet landed on the foyer floor, and the sound of swishing skirts turned him. With one hand yet on the railing, he memorized Mina's graceful shape—for she'd likely never want to see him again after this. "Thank God you're still here," he spoke more to the heavens than to her.

"Not for long." She stopped at the foot of the stairs and lifted her chin. "Goodbye, Will."

Her words were cold. Final. Like nails being hammered into a coffin.

He reached out and grabbed her arm, gently yet firmly. "Mina, listen, just for a moment, and then you may be on your way."

She stared at his fingers on her sleeve. "There can be nothing more to say. You will not talk me out of leaving."

"I don't intend to. I simply want to explain about Elizabeth. That's all. I swear it."

Pulling from his touch, she met his gaze, her blue eyes a sword, seeking to cleave away any more lies. "You don't owe me an explanation. It is your uncle you should be talking to."

"I know. And I will." He plowed his fingers through his hair, the movement as wild as the beat of his heart. "But a word with you first, please."

With a sigh, she leaned her back against the stair rail, resignation bending her brow. "What is it you have to say?"

He widened his stance, for speaking the past aloud was sure to knock him sideways. Just thinking of it put him off balance. "Though I hate to admit it, in my younger years, I lived solely for wine, women, and making merry. It was then I met Elizabeth Hill, at a house party, for much to my shame, *I* was the life of the party."

His head drooped, and he studied his shoes. Memories twisted his gut. Too much drink. Too many indiscretions. Unknowingly, he'd lived the same debauched life as his father before him.

"You don't have to tell me this," Mina murmured.

"No, I. . ." He jerked his face back to hers. If he didn't get this out now, he never would. "Even then Uncle was gracious, urging me to stop the ribald lifestyle and settle down. I thought taking a wife who enjoyed a good time as much as I might be a way to pacify him while continuing to live unbridled; for you see, Elizabeth loved her social life as much as I did mine. She was agreeable to my proposal, and I even fancied myself in love with her."

Mina's jaw clenched, the fine lines of her throat hardening to steel. "The very words you spoke to me last night."

He drew a deep breath, willing the truth he'd known all along to finally pass his lips. "No. It's not the same at all. You have taught me that there's a great deal of difference between self-love and self-sacrificing love. You didn't have to come here. You didn't have to help me try to save Uncle Barlow, yet you did so, willingly. Elizabeth never would have done such a thing unless she had something to gain for herself."

Mina bit her lip, her teeth worrying the flesh, almost in time to the corridor clock ticking away.

And Will prayed, pleading for truth to win, for past sins to be forgotten. For Mina to give him a second chance.

Stepping away from her post at the railing, she paced a small figure on the rug, and a quick slice of fear cut through him from head to toe. Did she mean to run off now? To turn her back to him as Elizabeth had?

But she stopped, inches from him, her face unreadable. "What happened to her? To Elizabeth, for you said she was to be your bride, not that she *was* your bride."

It wasn't much, but the barest flicker in Mina's eyes birthed a hope in him. Maybe—perhaps—she actually would hear him out and come to believe his feelings for her were true. *Oh, God, make it so.*

"Elizabeth broke off the engagement," he began, "for she'd worked her way into the graces of an earl. I don't blame her—now, that is. I did then. That was a black period. An angry one."

Ghosts of the past curled about him like thick smoke, and he tugged at his collar. "My bitterness drove me to worse sins, chief amongst them gaming. Were it not for Uncle Barlow, I'd still be wallowing in debtor's prison."

Her eyes narrowed. "What do you mean?"

"Uncle Barlow paid all that I owed—and more. He arranged for me to be taken on as a law clerk. God knows I didn't deserve that kind of mercy, and I couldn't understand why he did such a thing. Yet for his sake, I tried to live in a more respectable manner. Shortly thereafter, Fitz invited me to a church service, and then I knew. Funny, is it not, that one doesn't know how bad one really is until trying hard to be good."

Pausing, he revisited that holy day. The sacred union. The wonder of it even now was enough to pump warmth through his veins. A small smile twitched his lips. "Uncle's extravagant act of compassion paled in comparison to the grace God offered me that day. I've never been the same. Oh, how that must sound coming from my mouth. For you know better than most that I am not a saint."

Small, white fingers appeared on his sleeve, and she pressed hope into his arm with a little squeeze. "Thank you for telling me."

A lump clogged his throat and he fought to clear it. "I've been such a fool. I should have left Uncle's well-being to God instead of taking it on myself." Collecting her hand in his, he dropped to one knee and tipped up his face. "I don't deserve it, but will you forgive me, Mina, for pulling you into this deceitful plan of mine?"

Slowly, she nodded. "Of course, but I am still leaving."

"I wouldn't dream of stopping you—"

"A very pretty time to propose now." Footsteps thudded on the floor as Percy rounded the other side of the stairs and stopped in front of them. A smile spread across his face like gangrene, sick and deadly.

Will shot to his feet, but before he could utter a word of defense, Percy continued, "I wonder what Uncle will say when he discovers your deceit."

He threw out his hands. It was either that or throttle the man. "I am not propos—"

"What is this?" Uncle Barlow's voice shook from above, and they all pivoted to see him descending the stairs.

"These two are a fraud, Uncle Barlow." With a fierce sweep of his hand,

Percy aimed his finger at him and Mina, casting them both into destruction. "William and Mina are not married."

Uncle Barlow's footsteps fell heavy on the stairs, and he looked down upon them as God Himself. "I know."

CHAPTER TWENTY-EIGHT

To conceal anything from those to whom I am attached
is not in my nature. I can never close my lips
where I have opened my heart.
Master Humphrey's Clock

Uncle Barlow's revelation echoed from wall to wall, hanging a pall in the air, thick as cream, and smothering the breath from Mina's lungs. *He knew?* She didn't dare look at Will. The devastation on his face would surely match hers, and it was hard enough to maintain her own composure without having to witness his.

Uncle Barlow descended the last stair, his feet landing on the foyer's tiled floor like a crack of thunder. He stood there for a moment, saying nothing, staring at each one in turn, the disappointment in his eyes nearly driving her to her knees.

"I would have a word with all of you. In my study." He turned and strode off, his steps echoing in the stunned silence left behind.

Percy flashed them a wicked smile, then immediately fell into step behind Uncle Barlow. And no wonder he was so eager, for he renewed his tirade slandering her and Will, devoting them to ruin as they trailed him. Percy's words were awful—because they were true. Oh, that she'd never gone along with this scheme to begin with. Her step faltered, and Will reached for her hand.

They entered a wood-paneled room with books lining two of the walls. Directly behind a desk at center, Uncle Barlow sat as judge and jury. Will led her to stand in front of the desk, with him as a buffer between her and Percy. But that left nothing between her and the snarling head of a skinned tiger, lying inches from her feet. The flattened carcass made for a fine rug except for its head, which had been left intact. The fangs gleamed ivory and sharp at the pointed ends and, at the roots nearest the lips, darkened to a brownish, dried-blood colour. How much flesh had those teeth torn into?

"I demand you cast these two sinners out into the cold." Percy's voice snarled, and she jerked her gaze away from the dead danger to the one very much alive. "William has besmirched the Barlow name by taking a woman who's not legally his wife."

"I have not!" Will splayed his fingers, dropping her hand and daring a step closer to his uncle's desk. "Mina's virtue is—and never has been—violated. She is innocent, and I take full blame for the deceit in which I convinced her to partake."

Percy tipped his chin to a pert angle. "One cannot believe the words of a deceiver."

Will spun toward him, jaw clenched so tightly a muscle stood out like a rod on his neck. "Nor can one believe the tales of a schemer."

"Enough!" Uncle Barlow's voice bellowed sharp and black, absorbing all light and air and objections.

Caught between the fangs of the tiger and the three man-beasts roaring in a fury, Mina edged back a step.

Uncle Barlow swung his gaze to Percy. "I also know of your devious plans, Percival. I have had my suspicions all along. Your clandestine meeting this morning with Mr. Greaves merely confirmed them. Very sloppy of you to meet in view of the house."

"Don't be ridiculous! There was nothing clandestine about it."

From this angle, slightly behind Percy and off to the side a bit, the morning light leaching in through the windows outlined his frame—and it shook slightly.

So did Percy's voice. "Fallon Greaves and I go way back. I was merely passing on the prospect of having him join in my investment venture. Nothing more."

Uncle Barlow leaned aside and opened a top drawer, and as he riffled through papers, Will leaned aside as well, whispering for her alone, "Mr. Greaves is the administrator of the Bishop's Stortford Asylum."

"You mean—?"

Her whisper was cut off by the sharp slap of a document landing on the desktop and the stab of Uncle Barlow's finger skewering it in place. "Are you speaking of this venture, Percy?"

In two long strides, Percy snatched the paper from off the desk. The parchment quivered in his grasp as his gaze swept over it. "Where did you get this?"

"Do you really think me senile?" Uncle Barlow leaned back in his chair and folded his arms. "That night at dinner, when you shoved document after document in my face, I took the liberty of memorizing several names. I contacted them, which led me to other names, and eventually on to a devolving list of men who are none too pleased with you at the moment. Apparently you've pledged more investment dollars than you've paid. In short, you are in debt to some very powerful men."

For once, Percy said nothing, though his mouth opened and closed several times like a landed halibut.

"Uncle Barlow," Will broke the awful silence. "My intent was to protect you from Percy's schemes. Please allow me to explain."

The older man shot up his hand, shoving William's words right back at him. "No explanation needed. I have known since you arrived that you were not married. But there is one thing I do not know." Will's uncle turned his grey gaze to her. "Tell me, Miss Scott, what is it you hoped to gain by going along with my misguided nephew and this ridiculous farce? What did he promise you?"

Her corset cut into her ribs. Breathing was out of the question. It would be better to stare at the tiger's fangs than to stand in the glare of such righteous damnation. But she couldn't look away from the furious disappointment glowering out from Uncle Barlow's soul—for she deserved it.

"Nothing, sir." The words squeaked out impossibly small, and she tried again. "I stood to gain nothing at all, save for the chance to hopefully prevent you from being forced into an existence no one should have to suffer. There is nothing but death in an asylum, and I know of what I speak, for my mother suffered such a fate. After discovering Percy's true intent, I couldn't let that happen to you. Yet I confess Will and I went about it the wrong way. It was wrong of me to have deceived you, and for that I am woefully sorry. I can do nothing but beg for your forgiveness."

Tears burned her eyes, for something precious had been lost. Not since her grandfather had she shared so thoroughly her love of literature—not even with Miss Whymsy. Would that Uncle Barlow were in possession of the second-chance coin instead of her.

On the other side of Will, Percy started clapping, the sharp ring of his hands echoing from wall to wall. "Stunning performance, Miss Scott. Where did you say you picked this one up, Will—on Drury Lane, was it?"

"Leave off!" Will moved so fast, air whooshed against her cheek. He grabbed Percy up by the lapels, twisting the fabric until wheezes garbled in Percy's throat. "You are finished disparaging Mina."

Uncle Barlow shook his head, clearly disgusted. "Let go of your cousin, William. Violence solves nothing."

Will let go—but not without a little shove. "Leave Mina out of this, Cousin." Then he turned to his uncle. "I take complete responsibility for having persuaded

Mina to act as my wife. It was wrong. *I* was wrong. Do not blame her."

Will's defense wrapped around her as warm as an embrace.

Percy tugged at the hems of his sleeves, straightening each one. "On the contrary, the woman is every bit as deceitful as my cousin—on par with Will's mother. . .for she is alive. Alive and well and living in France. No doubt packing her bags even this minute in hopes of setting up house here." He spread his arms.

Next to her, Will stiffened.

Uncle Barlow jerked as if he'd been struck. "Is this true, William?"

Mina stared, horrified, at Will. What would he say? Would he deny it or tell all?

His head dropped. His shoulders. Even the very air around him seemed to deflate. "It is true, sir. My mother is alive. But I swear I did not know it until only recently, and she made me vow to—"

"Stop. I've heard enough." Uncle Barlow scrubbed a hand over his face. Again and again. "I think it best that you all leave—and not just this study, but my home. I withdraw my Christmas invitation."

"But Uncle, surely you're not going to listen to a word of such drivel spoken by a liar and a loose skirt." Percy's voice tightened until it cracked. "William is not fit to inherit."

Uncle Barlow shot to his feet and slammed his fists on the desktop. "Neither of you are. Now out!"

Percy whirled, muttering oaths and calling down brimstone upon them all.

Will reached for her hand. "Let us leave, Mina."

She lagged behind, her heart lying in pieces somewhere on the floor back near the tiger's mouth. How abominable this whole thing had turned out. . .and not just for her, but most especially for Will. Lord knows he didn't deserve it, but would Uncle Barlow consider giving him yet another chance? It would take a miracle, an act of God—yet was that not what Christmastime was really all about?

Wrenching from Will's grasp, she turned back and marched to Uncle Barlow's desk. She shoved her hand into her pocket and pulled out the second-chance coin, worn now like a talisman, and set it down on the desk.

Uncle Barlow glowered. "You cannot buy back my good opinion, Miss Scott, and in fact, have only worsened it in the attempt to do so."

"I—I would never think of it, sir. I will only say this. A friend of mine gave me this coin, but I think, perhaps, you have greater need of it than I."

He said nothing, and behind her, William's whisper travelled from the door,

"Mina, come along."

But if she didn't say these words now, she'd never get another chance. She pointed at the coin. "That small piece of gold is a second-chance coin. I've kept it, wondering who to give it to, and now I know. I give it to you and plead that you'll see fit to give William a second chance—again. He's told me of his past, and I don't blame you for thinking ill of him. Yet the man I know now is not the same as the man that he was. He did change after you redeemed him from gaol."

Uncle Barlow's grey eyes hardened to steel. "You will forgive me if I favor the evidence I've seen rather than your word."

"Evidence that is incomplete, for the full truth is that William's mother is sick, and she made him promise not to alert you. He's been using his own funds to pay for her doctor fees and apothecary bills. Her room and board. Will didn't wish to get you out of the way in order to spend your money, like Percy did. He merely hoped to use the collateral of the inheritance to gain a small loan from a banker to continue her care. It had nothing to do with wealth or greed but to hopefully save the life of another human being. As misdirected as it was, Will acted out of love and kindness, nothing more. I will be the first to admit he is a flawed man, but he is a good one, and I hope you can find it in your heart to forgive him."

Without waiting for a rebuttal—for she'd spent all she'd had to say anyway—Mina turned and strode out the study door.

Past a gaping William.

CHAPTER TWENTY-NINE

There ain't a gent'lman in all the land—
nor yet sailing upon all the sea—
that can love his lady more than I love her.
David Copperfield

After a last glance over his shoulder at his uncle's estate, Will descended the final stair and dashed to catch up to the carriage setting off down the lane. The cold tried to nip him, but a white-hot sense of failure burned within. He'd likely never see Uncle Barlow again, and for that he was truly sorry.

"Hold up!" he shouted to the driver.

The man pulled back on the reins with a "Whoa."

Slipping on the snow, Will flung out his arms to keep from tumbling, then slid-walked the rest of the way to the carriage door. It would be a long trek to town should Mina and Miss Whymsy deny his request to board. But even if they consented, the ride would likely be just as long. The humiliation Mina had suffered on his account had been no small matter. He wouldn't blame her if she gave him an earful, or worse—icy silence.

He opened the door and hefted himself up onto the step, sticking only his head inside. Miss Whymsy blinked at him from one seat, Mina from the other.

"I know I'm likely the last person either of you ladies would want to share a carriage with, but my cousins have taken the other coach, and the horse I rode here is lame. May I ride with you into town?"

Miss Whymsy frowned. "You'll catch your death out there. Of course you may ride with us. Come in."

"Thank you." He yanked the door shut and latched it, then jockeyed for the best place to sit. The older lady sat on one seat with a large bag next to her, overflowing with books. He could squeeze between the bag and wall—maybe. It would be a tight fit.

But Mina gathered her skirts and shifted to make room for him. The carriage heaved into motion, and he sat before he fell upon either of them.

The wheels crunched through the snow. Horses' snorts added to the jingle of tack and harness. He turned to Mina, and she to him, but words stuck sharp in his throat. How was he to tell her how sorry he was? How proud he'd been when she'd defended him to Uncle? How he hoped she could somehow forgive him? Regret upon regret heaped into a great pile and sank in his gut. He'd laughed off many things in his life, but here, now, staring into the endless fathoms of Mina's blue eyes, he doubted he'd ever smile again.

Across from them, Miss Whymsy clucked her tongue. "It's rather hard to breathe, what with the elephant taking up so much space in here."

They both turned their heads toward the woman, Mina giving hers a little shake. "What elephant, Miss Whymsy?"

"Posh! I may be old, child, but I'm not blind. There is clearly much on both of your minds." Leaning sideways, she pulled out a thick book from her bag and shook it at them. "I shall be otherwise occupied, so have at it."

She plopped the book onto her lap and opened it with one gloved finger, ignoring them.

The woman was right. He had far too much on his mind, but what to say? Where to begin? He blew out a long breath, creating a frosty little cloud, then turned back to Mina.

"Mina—"

"Will—"

Her name blended with his on the air, and she shrank back.

"No, no." He shook his head. "Ladies first. I would hear what you have to say. All of it. No matter what."

Bracing himself for the onslaught, perhaps even tears, he clenched the seat so hard his knuckles cracked.

But a strange transformation took place. Mina's face softened beneath the brim of her bonnet. Her brows knit, not in an angry twist, but slanted with a bend of compassion. "Oh, Will, I am sorry for the way things turned out. I know money will be a stretch for you, what with your mother's illness. But one thing I've learned from all this is that there are more important things than wealth. Spending time with your cousins showed me that pretty dresses and dining in fine establishments doesn't necessarily bring significance. Significance comes in caring—really caring—for those around us. Please don't misunderstand, I know you do care for your uncle, and I'm not for one minute saying you don't, but you—I—went about it in the wrong way."

She paused, and the fine lines of her throat bobbed. "I can honestly say now that as mundane as my life is with Father, I would rather smile with him over a simple bowl of oyster stew on Christmas than to sit at one more linen-clothed table with Percy or Alice. There's value in that, in the sharing of joy and tears, and that's what makes life worthwhile. Not what we do or what we accomplish. I have you to thank for that revelation, for had you never asked me to be your pretend bride, I'd still be wishing to be someone or somewhere else."

His chest tightened, and breathing turned into a chore. Had ever a more gracious woman lived? She should've railed at him. Cursed him. Blamed him for the beastly way she'd been treated by his cousins. . .and by him, for he was the one who'd dragged her into this situation.

"I know you're disappointed with how things turned out, but at the very least—" A small smile curved her lips. "Your uncle won't be committed to an asylum. And that's what we were working toward all along. It was a hard victory, but a victory nonetheless."

"And for that I am thankful." He attempted to match her smile, but bitter remorse stole his last reserves of humour, and he could do no better than manage somewhat of a grimace. "I regret, however, that I've broken the very thing I'd hoped to mend, namely my relationship with Uncle Barlow. I doubt he will ever speak to me again. Nor should he."

A ray of sunshine broke through the clouds, angling in through the window and resting upon Mina as a halo. "But how could he remain angry with you? The truth of what you did, while draped in duplicity, was for the benefit of him, not yourself. You are a man of integrity, despite how sideways it comes out."

Her words and the admiration shining in her eyes did much to soothe his soul—but could do nothing to erase the stain of his past.

"You give me too much credit, Mina." And she did. God knew he was as big a schemer as his cousin. "If I'd been up front with Uncle to begin with, left everything in God's hands instead of taking the situation into my own, none of this would have happened."

She reached out and squeezed his hand. "I think we both learned a lesson, hmm?"

Without thinking, he covered her glove with his own, sandwiching her hand between his. How small, yet how strong. How would it feel to gather her in his arms and—

The carriage jolted and his leg bumped against hers. Red bloomed on her cheeks, and the thin space between them charged like the air before a lightning strike. He sucked in a breath. So did she. Their gazes met—and held.

"Oh, for heaven's sake." Miss Whymsy slammed her book shut. "Now would be the time, Mr. Barlow."

"The time for what?" he asked without shifting his gaze.

"Love is surely wasted on youth. There is no better time to ask Miss Scott to marry you than now."

Choking on the suggestion, he released Mina's hand and brought his fist to his mouth to keep from spluttering.

Mina's jaw dropped—and a strange light of hope kindled in her eyes.

Lowering his hand, he tugged at his collar. Air. He needed air, and lots of it. As much as he wanted to make Mina his own, how could he possibly take on a wife and care for his mother on a law clerk's salary?

He slipped a sideways glance at the older lady. "You overstep, madam."

"I think not. Clearly the two of you are in love. Do you deny it?"

Heat burned a trail from his gut to his heart—especially when he shifted his gaze back to Mina.

"Your answer, Mr. Barlow?" Miss Whymsy prodded.

Gads! Had the woman been a lion tamer before she'd retired?

"No," he said, staring deep into Mina's eyes. "I do not deny it."

Mina lifted her chin. "Nor do I."

His breath hitched, and for a moment he dared imagine a future of love and life and joy. Of whispers in the dark of night and blue-eyed babies with copper-streaked hair.

But then the carriage wheels dipped into a rut, jolting him to reality. Love, no matter how pure, did not put food on the table or a roof overhead. "Mina, I—" his voice broke, and he swallowed. "I'm sorry. I have nothing to offer you. Once I move my mother here, I'll be sharing a one-room flat with her, and there will still be doctor bills to pay. I cannot ask you to endure such a hardship."

"Of course you can," she murmured.

He leaned closer. Surely he hadn't heard her right. "What?"

"You *can* ask me. One room or ten, it doesn't matter as long as you're in the room with me. I'm done with playing the part of a lady. I've had my tea at Purcell's. My dinner in a London town house. Even a holiday of sorts at a country estate. The only kind of lady I want to be is yours. Truly, that's all I've ever wanted from the minute you first asked me to be your pretend bride."

He gaped. "Do you mean that, knowing all you do about me?"

She beamed. "I do."

Was this real? Had she just agreed to be his wife? As the carriage wheels rattled along, so did a hundred more questions turn round and round in his head.

"For pity's sake, lad," Miss Whymsy scolded. "Kiss the woman!"

Oh, hang it all. Without a clue as to how he'd manage providing for a new wife and an ailing mother, he pulled Mina into his arms and kissed her soundly.

CHAPTER THIRTY

For it is good to be children sometimes,
and never better than at Christmas,
when its mighty Founder was a child himself.
A Christmas Carol

Snugging the bow tight on the small package, Mina lifted Father's gift for inspection as the mantel clock struck six. She jumped to her feet. No time to waste! Guests were likely already arriving, maybe even Will. The thought sent her heart tripping and her feet moving. She dashed over to her chamber door and slipped out.

She'd been right. Merry chatter and laughter wafted up the stairs from the taproom, the sound of "Happy Christmas!" being bantered about. The savory scent of oyster stew filled the entire inn. Upping her pace, she raced along the corridor to Father's room.

She rapped her knuckles against the wood and hid the gift behind her back with her other hand. "Father? It's time."

"Coming, girl."

The door swung open. Father stood with one hand behind his back, dressed in his finest grey serge suit. His hazel eyes twinkled. "I've got something for ye, Daughter."

She grinned. "And I for you."

"Ye ready?" He fairly bounced on his toes, as giddy as a young lad.

Her grin grew. Ahh, but she'd miss this tradition, the private exchange of gifts between her and Father before celebrating with friends. Yet just because she would be married next Christmas, surely that didn't have to mean an end to all her traditions with Father, and in fact, she determined, it would not.

"Ready." She met her father's gaze, and they counted down in unison. "Three. Two. One."

She held out her gift. So did Father—and they both tore into the wrappings, bits of paper flying and falling to the floor like snow.

"Oh, my girl. How thoughtful!" Emotion roughened his voice. "Ye could've bought a fob and yet ye took the time to make me one?" He yanked out his pocket watch and wound the braided twist through the loop. "It's perfect."

Forgetting her own gift, she grinned, wide and carefree. "I am happy you think so. I know Mother always intended to purchase you a gold chain, and I still hope to someday carry out that wish."

"No, child. This is dearer to me than a bit of shiny metal, especially now that ye'll be leaving me." He ran a gnarled knuckle along her cheek. "Now go on. Finish opening yours."

Pulling off the last of the brown wrapper, she sucked in a breath. "Oh, Father!" she whispered.

Fingers trembling, she flipped open the cover of a somewhat frayed copy of *David Copperfield* and caressed the title page. In all her twenty-three years, Father had never once given her a book, and she hugged it to her chest. "I shall cherish this always."

Father's big arms wrapped around her, and he pulled her close. "Just as I cherish you, my girl. Happy Christmas, now and always."

A sob caught in her throat, and she nuzzled her face against his waistcoat. As thrilled as she was to become Will's wife, she would be hesitant to leave her day-to-day life with this man. "Happy Christmas, Father," she murmured.

He gave her a little squeeze, then released her. "Our company awaits. Shall we?"

Sniffling back tears, she looped her arm through his and gave him a wavering smile. "We shall."

Her steps faltered only once as they descended the stairs—when the blue of William's eyes met hers from across the room.

But Father halted her two steps from the taproom floor, so that they looked out over the patrons filling the Golden Egg. A more merry sight she couldn't imagine. The room was draped with holly bunting. Strings of cranberries and nuts and raisins swagged back and forth across the ceiling. Everyone smiled and chattered, and best of all, Will shouldered his way through the crowd toward her, the gleam of love in his eyes stealing her breath.

"Friends!" Father bellowed.

All turned his way, and the din lowered to a muted hum.

"Welcome one and all to the annual Golden Egg Christmas Eve celebration, but before I serve what I know yer all waitin' on—"

"Bring out the stew! Bring out the stew!" The chant started low then grew in intensity.

Releasing his hold on her arm, Father lifted his hands. "Aye! Stew ye shall have. But first, an announcement. Mr. Barlow, if you wouldn't mind joining us."

With a grin and a wink, Will hopped up on the bottom stair and entwined his fingers with hers.

"It is with great pleasure that I should like to announce—"

Just then, the front door burst open, and along with a blast of chill air and a flurry of snowflakes, in bustled a surprising collection of new arrivals. Uncle Barlow's grey hair tufted out from the brim of his hat. Next to him was Miss Whymsy, who walked next to a tall lady with an assured step.

And behind them marched Percy and Alice.

"An announcement, you say?" Uncle Barlow doffed his hat. "Then we've arrived just in time. I should like to make an announcement."

Mina tensed, and Will's hand squeezed hers.

Father leaned close and whispered in her ear. "Who is that?"

"Will's uncle," she whispered back.

"Ahh. Fitting that his family join us." Straightening, Father motioned for the newcomers to work their way to the stairs. "Come, come. We will do this together."

But she couldn't quite work up the same amount of excitement that boomed in Father's voice. What would Uncle Barlow say? Had he forgiven Will? Or her?

Will pulled her close. "Have faith, Mina. We've done all we could. Let us leave this in God's hands, as we should have from the start."

The crowd cleared a space for the entourage, and Uncle Barlow dipped his head toward Father. "Thank you, sir." Then he faced the crowd. "In this season of giving, there can be no better time than to announce to whom I shall give my estate. And so, tonight, amongst family and friends—" he beamed down at Miss Whymsy—"I should like to name the heir of the Barlow lands."

Percy and Alice leaned closer.

Miss Whymsy smiled broadly at the lady next to her.

Mina held her breath. *Please, God, have mercy.*

"I shall place my holdings in a trust, to be used exclusively for the Institute for the Care of Sick Gentlewomen, which is directed by my new friend here, Miss Florence Nightingale."

The lady next to Miss Whymsy clapped her hands with a "Hear, hear!" that would've made Miss Minton proud.

The institute? But how had the old fellow. . .of course. Miss Whymsy must've spoken of it. Mina couldn't help but smile. What a perfectly fitting solution for Uncle Barlow and the institute.

"Yet," Uncle Barlow continued, "I shall need an administrator to live at the estate to manage the funding and all other details. A trustworthy administrator. One who knows the house and lands like none other, and who of course shall be well compensated."

Percy stepped forward.

But Uncle Barlow extended his hand toward Will; the old, worn, second-chance coin resting on his upturned palm. "What say you, my boy?"

Without letting go of her hand, Will reached for the coin with his other. "Only if I may bring my wife along."

Uncle Barlow's gaze swung toward her. "In truth?"

"Aye!" Father belted. "And that's my announcement. Lift yer mugs in toast and honour to the happy new couple. We make merry tonight, and in four weeks' time, shall make merry again with the marriage of my daughter to Mr. William Barlow."

A roar shook to the rafters, followed by a hearty "Bring out the stew!"

Which prodded Father into action. He trotted down the last few stairs then disappeared into the kitchen, where Martha had been the sole keeper of the big bubbling pot for the past hour.

Will tugged Mina down the rest of the stairs and shepherded her over to his uncle. "Thank you, sir. This is no small honour—" Will's voice choked.

And she didn't blame him. What a marvel, how things had turned out.

Uncle Barlow clapped him on the back. "I think we can all thank Miss Whymsy. The whole idea was hers. Oh, except for this. . ." His face sobered. "I have arranged for your mother to be moved to the institute as soon as she is well enough to travel. I hope to make things right by her. No one should have to fear their own family."

The world turned watery, and Mina blinked back happy tears. *Thank You, God, for taking such a twisted situation and straightening it out.*

Will's throat bobbed several times before he answered. "You are more than gracious, sir. I can only hope to someday become the man that you are."

"I'd say you're well on your way, but remember these words, my boy. 'Whatever I have tried to do in life, I have tried with all my heart to do well; . . . whatever I have devoted myself to, I have devoted myself to completely; that in great aims and in small, I have always been thoroughly in earnest.'" Uncle turned his smile toward her. "Can you name that one?"

Joy swelled in her heart and spilled over into a large grin, for in the speaking of a single quote, she knew she'd been well and truly forgiven by Uncle Barlow.

"From *David Copperfield*, sir." She hugged the book tucked beneath her arm all the tighter.

He chuckled. "Spot on. I shall have to work harder in the future to baffle you, hmm?"

"Oh, Mr. Barlow." Miss Whymsy crooked a finger at Will's uncle, beckoning him to her side. "If you wouldn't mind, a moment please?"

"Of course," he answered, then bent his head closer to Will and Mina, speaking for their ears alone. "Mum's the word for now, but don't be surprised if another wedding follows shortly after yours."

The old fellow turned on his heel and darted off before either of them could reply—and a good thing too, for Mina was speechless. How amazing. How happy. How kind of God to have worked out such a perfect ending.

She peered up at Will, memorizing the joy on his face. Who knew what hardships the new year would bring, but for now, she'd live in this moment—in his gaze of love. "Oh, Will. How happy I am—"

"Congratulations, Cousin." Percy brushed past her and stopped in front of Will. "I guess you got what you wanted."

"No, not quite."

Will's words jolted through her. What more could he possibly want?

"There is one more thing that I desire." He held out the second-chance coin. "To give you this."

Percy snatched away the bit of gold in a trice. "What is it?"

"I am the man I am today because Uncle Barlow—and God—gave me a second chance. I'd like to do the same for you. I will speak to Uncle about seeing to your creditors, if you promise to stop your wild moneymaking schemes and get yourself an honest job. In fact, I happen to know of a law clerk position that will be opening up shortly."

Her heart swelled. William Barlow was a hero after all. . .*her* hero.

Percy narrowed his eyes. "What's the catch?"

"There is none."

"Don't be ridiculous. Surely you expect something out of me for such a save." Percy cocked his head like a curious tot. "What is it?"

"I neither expect nor require anything. Don't you see? This is your chance to earn an honest living. Granted, it's not much, but there's opportunity for you to work your way up. Of course you don't deserve it, but neither did I when Uncle first offered me the position. And God knows none of us deserve His mercy—yet it is freely given. I cannot do otherwise. So, what do you say?"

Percy blinked. Then blinked some more. "Well. I. . .I don't quite know what to say."

Grabbing two mugs off a passing tray, Will handed one to his cousin and held up the other. "How about you say Happy Christmas and leave it at that?"

"What's this about?" Alice asked as she joined Percy's side.

For a moment, Percy frowned, then slowly reached with his free hand and pulled Alice close. "Happy Christmas, to our cousins." He clinked his mug against Will's and took a big draw.

With a laugh, Will swigged a drink, set the mug down, and gathered Mina into his arms.

She smiled up at him. "You really are a hero, you know."

"I wouldn't go that far." He kissed the top of her head. "But it seems this has turned out to be the best Christmas ever."

"It is, my love." She nuzzled her face against his shoulder. "That it is. And may we have many more."

HISTORICAL NOTES

Christmas Pudding

Christmas pudding is quite a production, one that begins well before Christmas Day. In fact, it begins on Stir-Up Sunday, the last Sunday before Advent (or five weeks before Christmas). This is why when Mina returns home from dinner at Uncle Barlow's, she sees the pudding moulds on the kitchen table even though it's not yet Christmas.

Victorian Oyster Stew

Oysters have been savored in Britain since the days of the Romans. By Victorian times, industrialization cheapened oysters to the point of them becoming a staple of the poor man's diet, and they were a common fare served in public houses. This, however, depleted their abundance, and by the mid-1800s, the natural oyster beds became exhausted, making it harder to find good oysters. While other foods were served as well on Christmas Eve, oyster stew was as common as goose or turkey.

"God Rest Ye Merry, Gentlemen"

The origins of this song are controversial, with some claiming it dates back to the fifteenth century and others saying it didn't appear until 1760. Regardless, Victorians knew it well. Even Charles Dickens included it in *A Christmas Carol*.

Drinking Chocolate

What we now call cocoa or hot chocolate was called drinking chocolate in the mid-1800s. This beverage was a favorite among Victorian ladies. You can find recipes for it even from the Regency period (early 1800s).

Florence Nightingale and the Institute for the Care of Sick Gentlewomen

Despite opposition from her family, Florence Nightingale became the superintendent at the Institution for the Care of Sick Gentlewomen in Distressed Circumstances in London. Because of her, the facility began accepting patients of all religions, not just those allegiant to the Church of England. She received no salary and was responsible for her own expenses.

Secret Societies

Victorians were intrigued by the idea of covert meetings and secret societies. Many of these "clubs" dabbled in the supernatural, but a fair amount of them pursued social justice. While the norm was fraternal fellowships, there were also sororities or "sisterhoods."

DEDICATION

To Jan Miller—my Effie kind of friend. And as always,
to the One who not only gives me second
chances but oh so much more—Jesus.

ACKNOWLEDGMENTS

There are so many people who had a hand in bringing this story to you, but namely I'd like to thank the best critique buddies a girl could have: Yvonne Anderson, Julie Klassen, Elizabeth Ludwig, Shannon McNear, Ane Mulligan, Chawna Schroeder, and MaryLu Tyndall.

A hearty round of applause as well to Annie Tipton, the awesome editor who took a chance on me in the first place.

And last but definitely not least, much gratitude to my hero husband, Mark, who also happens to be my true BFF.

The Old Lace Shop

September

CHAPTER ONE

Bella
London, 1855

I have long abhorred black. It is a great abyss, sucking in the colours of the rainbow and wringing the life from them. The moniker of death. Nonetheless, I brave the darkness one last time to retrieve something precious. Plunging my hand past heavy gowns of the offensive colour, I rummage deep in the chest. Near the bottom, my fingers bump into a velvet box. Victory! Gripping it, I pull it out, and my throat goes dry. What I am about to do is as rebellious as Jezebel herself.

Inside, my mother's single pearl attached to a silver chain rests on indigo satin. My hand trembles as I remove the keepsake and fasten it around my neck. Shortly after I married, on my very first Christmas as a young bride, Mr. White forbade me to wear my mother's necklace, saying it didn't befit a woman of my elevated station. Fingering the pearl, I relish its coolness, and defiance wells. This year I will celebrate Christmas with holly and laughter and a large stuffed goose instead of dark looks and criticism. Too many years have I spent shut away in a stagnant town house without a morsel of cheer. No more. Today I'm free, finally and completely my own person, leastwise once I sign all the paperwork.

I toss the empty case back into the chest and slam the lid; then I rise—and a genuine smile curves my lips. Is it wicked to embrace such elation? Then so be it. Never again will I cower before a man—a promise to myself and to God.

"Mrs. White?" Betty raps at my chamber door and ducks inside. Her bleached apron is stark against her black servant's gown, and my smile fades. How much would it cost to reissue the staff with pewter-grey liveries instead? Yet another matter to take up with the solicitor when he arrives in an hour.

"Yes, Betty?" I soften my tone. Harsh words make her flinch even now, though it's been a year since my husband raged about the town house.

"My pardon for disturbing you, mum"—she dips her head—"but a Mr. Barlow is here, awaiting you in the sitting room."

"Barlow?" I roll the name around with my tongue and find it a completely foreign flavour. "Who is that?"

The ruffle on Betty's cap trembles where it meets her brow. "Says he's with Smudge and Gruber, mum."

I glance at the clock ticking away on the mantel. Fifty-six minutes remain until I expect Mr. Smudge. A shadow clouds my mind, as dark as the mourning gowns I've laid to rest. Was this Mr. Barlow here with ill tidings? Frowning, I thank Betty and leave my chamber.

Memories bombard me like thrown tomatoes as I scurry down the corridor. There, where the September sun shines through the windowpanes, my husband threatened to push me out the glass. I speed past the vigil lantern that carved a small scar into my neck when he'd swung it at me. And at the top of the stairs, I press my hand to my stomach. How many times had Mr. White said he ought to shove me down the stairway and be done with me?

Ghosts. All ghosts. My husband is well and truly gone. I descend the stairs, hopefully for one of the last times. I cannot leave soon enough this house of horror.

A thick man, hardly taller than I, stands looking out through the sheers at Wellington Street, either enthralled by the day's traffic or lost in thought. I clear my throat. When he turns, sunlight bounces off his spectacles.

"Good day, Mrs. White." He bows his head. "Mr. Percival Barlow, clerk to Mr. Gruber, at your service."

I study his dark hair and somewhat pasty skin, but neither the name nor the face correlate with any memory I can dredge up. I take a seat on the settee and direct him to an adjacent chair. "To what do I owe this visit, Mr. Barlow?"

He settles a leather brief-bag on his lap and unbuckles the straps while he speaks. "Normally I make the rounds for Mr. Gruber. Unlike Mr. Smudge, he rarely leaves the office. However, today I took it upon myself to add Mr. Smudge's clients to my stops as well." He pulls out a sheaf of papers then lifts his face to me. "I regret to inform you your lawyer, Mr. Smudge, took a fall from a horse yesterday and broke his leg. In short, I am here to get your signature on the documents he intended for you to sign."

He hands over the papers, and I page through them. Strange how a lifetime of ambition can be condensed into nothing more than a stack of parchment.

Mr. Barlow offers me a pen. "Each document represents one of your deceased husband's holdings. Sign your name on the bottom lines and the businesses will be sold, the proceeds of which shall come to you."

Surely Mr. White is rolling over in his grave as I write my name on the first page, selling off a dry goods warehouse in Birmingham. He'd married me, a girl five decades his junior, in order to avoid the travesty of dying without an heir—and made me pay with each passing year in which I didn't give him a son.

"You should be very well-off for the rest of your days, Mrs. White." Mr. Barlow's low voice drowns out the scratching of my pen. "I daresay you shall be able to do whatever it is you fancy."

His words slam into me, and my pen hovers above the line on the last page. Whatever I fancy? La! The only fancy I'd clung to the past year was the hope of leaving behind this town house and settling elsewhere, far from London. Escaping the past. Starting a whole new chapter of life. But what? And where? Flight had so preoccupied my mind that I'd neglected to give a thought as to where I'd land.

My gaze sharpens on the heading of the page in my lap. *Nottingham Lace and Hose.* Nottingham? Why not? It's as good a place as any.

I set the pen on the tea table then hold out the unsigned paper to Mr. Barlow. "Tell me of this business, sir."

His big eyes widen as he grasps the page between finger and thumb, and while he silently reads, his lips fold into a pout. "It appears this is a lace manufacturing company, one of your husband's smaller holdings. His possession was at 51 percent, making him the majority owner but not by much. It says here"—he spears his finger midway down the document—"that once you've relinquished your allotment, the co-owner intends to purchase that share for sole proprietorship."

Mr. Barlow shoves the paper back at me. "Not to worry, Mrs. White. There is nothing untoward about this paper. Simply sign it, and I shall be on my way."

I finger my mother's necklace, leaving the paper to dangle from Mr. Barlow's fingers. "Tell me, sir, what happens if I do not sign that document?"

"Not sign?" His head recoils as if I've slapped him. "Why would you not? Surely you do not intend to pursue the majority ownership of some small, dismal manufacturing company in the middle of nowhere. For without your signature on this page, the holding falls to you—an unheard-of position for a woman."

My fingers snap closed around the pearl, the small hairs at the back of my neck bristling. It may be a poor decision, but I've been told one too many times what to do, how to live, when to breathe and eat and walk. A scream wells in my throat, and I use its energy to lift my chin. "Yes, Mr. Barlow. That is exactly what I intend."

His wide mouth parts then closes as if words have bunched up behind his teeth and he's too afraid to let them loose. Finally he sinks back against the cushion. "Are you certain of this, Mrs. White? It's a different world north of here, and manufacturing is a harsh and unforgiving trade. I fear a woman of your stature may not last long in such an environment."

I stifle a smile. Let him oppose me. It only empowers me more. Because even if I suffer, this time it will be due to *my* choice. "I am certain, sir."

His skin greys to the shade of yesterday's porridge, and he fumbles inside his coat pocket to pull out a beat-up gold coin. He holds it out to me on an upturned palm.

I pluck the coin from his hand and hold it to the light streaming in through the window. I've never seen the likes of such. The edges are chipped and gouged. A raised X takes up the most of one side. Words I cannot read encircle the other. I angle my head at Mr. Barlow. "What is this?"

"It's a second-chance coin, Mrs. White." He pushes the paper for Nottingham Lace and Hose back at me across the tea table. "I should like to give you a second chance to reconsider your decision."

I offer back the coin. "No need, sir. My mind is quite made up."

He blows out a sigh, the kind that condemns me for being such a daft female, and rises to his feet, collecting all the papers save for the lace company. "Then I suppose I am finished here. I bid you good day, madam. And good luck."

I rise as well, following. "But your coin, sir."

Pausing on the threshold, he turns to me. "Keep it. I have a feeling you may need it, especially with your new business partner. I only wish I had third- and fourth-chance coins to give you as well."

He pivots, and I am left alone with the piece of cold metal in my hand and a knotted bundle of hope and fear in my belly.

Chapter Two

Bella

Travelling by train, while a novel experience, is a tiresome affair, especially when seated shoulder to shoulder in a car that smells of overcooked pork, sweat, and tobacco. As soon as the great wheels squeal to a stop at the Nottingham Midland Station, both Betty and I are on our feet, eager to get off.

Like ants emerging from an anthill, passengers scurry about the platform, hailing porters, grabbing baggage, greeting friends or family. I clutch my small bag with both hands as humanity swarms. But when Betty turns her brown eyes to me, overlarge and seeking leadership, I straighten my shoulders. I am, after all, a woman of responsibility now.

And besides that, I am running late thanks to a broken steam boiler.

I snap into action and flag down a porter, giving him my claim ticket for all of our baggage. Fishing about in my bag, I bypass the second-chance coin and pull out a crown. I hand it over to the fellow, along with instructions as to where to deliver our trunks.

"Yes, madam." He dips his head with a crisp nod and darts back into the fray of travellers.

I glance at my ever-present companion and offer her a smile. "Ready, Betty?"

Apparently the starch has returned to her spine, for she lifts her chin. "Aye, mum. Let's be off."

Outside on Station Street, the late afternoon sun prods me to hail a hackney. I have no idea as to the layout of the city or how far the factory is. All I know is that the address I give the jarvey represents my future, for better or worse—though in all honesty I cannot imagine anything worse than the past eight years. I ask the driver to drop me off at Nottingham Lace and Hose then to continue on the few blocks farther to leave Betty at our rented rooms. I'd chosen the flat sight unseen for ease of commuting to and from the factory.

Tingles prickle along my arms as I climb into the cab. I have an occupation. Me. A woman who's lived invisibly for twenty-seven years. Excitement jitters through me as tangibly as the lurch of the carriage. With God as my witness,

I will succeed at this manufacturing endeavor, for I will give it my all or die in the trying. Who knows? Perhaps God handed me this opportunity as a second chance to start life over, freed from the oppressive shadow of men.

"Gaff, mum!" Betty's voice is strangled. "Would ye look at that?"

I lean forward to peer toward the curb. My breath catches in my throat as the coach rattles past woman after woman. A few are standing, but most sit with their backs shored up against soot-coated brick walls. Some hold out cans and lift their voices to beg for pennies. Others are silent, their open hands cupped to collect any meager offerings dropped by passing pedestrians.

All of them stare into the distance, unseeing of the world around them, some with milky eyes, others not.

"They're blind, Mrs. White." Betty's words fade to a whisper. "Every last blessed one o' them."

I sit back against the leather cushion, unable to make sense of it. Not that beggars aren't common in London—but all women? And all without sight? What has caused such a surfeit of blindness?

The carriage heaves to the left as we careen around a corner, and I fling out my hand for balance. Though my heart aches for the nameless women so burdened by tragedy, I put them out of my mind. It will not do to greet my co-owner with a trembling handshake or unsettled thoughts. He likely isn't happy about the prospect of working with me anyway—as Mr. Barlow made abundantly clear. So did Mr. Smudge's letter I'd received this morning, pleading with me to reconsider, and I almost did when I learned the name of the man I'd be comanaging alongside. A Mr. Archer. Reading the name had pierced me like an arrow, but surely there were hundreds, if not thousands, of men in England bearing such a common surname.

The cab stops. I step out and pay the jarvey then swallow hard as the carriage rolls off, leaving me alone. The sun darts behind a cloud, and the building glowers at me like a scolding matron, telling me I don't belong here. Coal smut blackens the bricks and coats the windows with a thick veil. For the space of a breath, I am tempted to run after the cab, jump in, and ask the driver to take Betty and me back to the station.

A woman passing by bumps into me. Her head dips low and her shoulders curl as if she carries the weight of dead dreams in a great bundle on her back. "Pardon," she mumbles, before disappearing through an open, wrought-iron gate.

I stare after her. If I leave now, give over the business and rely on my deceased husband's wealth, my own dream of living independently will bend my back every bit as much as that woman's. Spending Mr. White's money is not the same as earning my own—and I desperately need to be on my own for once in my life. So I straighten my bonnet and follow after the woman.

The gate leads into a large courtyard surrounded on three sides by buildings, all connected. A hulk of a dray stands next to a nearby dock where men load stacks of crates. Boys in flat caps dart about, running Lord knows what sort of errands. All ignore me. Not far from where I stand, a door swings shut, the drab hem of the woman's gown vanishing inside. It might not be the main office door—but then again, it might. Worth a try.

Leaving behind the bustle of the yard, I enter an entirely new world—a world of endless noise. Even though the working floor cannot be seen from where I stand, the clank, bang, and ratchet of so many machines boxes my ears. I will hear the clatter of it long after my head hits the pillow this night.

And the air! A fine dusting of winter snow floats through it. No, not snow. Dust from yarn and thread, spinning and whirring and rubbing. It tickles the small space high up in my nose where not even a good sneeze would clear it.

Eager to escape both noise and dust, I find a thin man with wire-rimmed spectacles, who directs me to the office. I ascend the stairs. Not that it helps much. My elevated position deadens the noise only slightly and lessens the dust none. Both cease to matter when I spot a door marked with the name of Mr. Archer and my heart twists in an odd way. Nerves, no doubt, for the fellow will be none too pleased to discover I am here to comanage and not sell out. Or could it be that the name of Archer is branded onto my soul? I pause and close my eyes.

Oh, Lord, go before me.

It's a ridiculous prayer. How many times had I pleaded the same when facing my former husband? I rub a scar behind my ear. But then again, maybe not so ridiculous, for I am here and he is not. Before I can change my mind, I rap my knuckles against the wood and step back, expecting a dark-suited mister with grey hair and a scowl to fling open the door.

It does not open.

I rap again. "Mr. Archer?"

No response.

My brow bunches, and I glance at the watch brooch pinned on my bodice. Half past four. Right on time. Hmm. Perhaps Mr. Archer has been called to the factory floor for some unexpected mishap. Stepping aside, I lean my back against the wall and wait.

And wait.

And wait.

Now and then an office worker scuttles past, and though I inquire after the master of the factory, no one seems to know where he is. For a while, I pace a small circle and entertain myself with grand imaginings of how I shall keep Christmas in a high fashion this coming season, planning a mouthwatering menu and mentally decorating rooms I've not even seen yet.

But the minutes drag on.

And on.

I frown. I cannot be the only one who's had to suffer such an interminable delay in this cramped corridor. My first order of business shall have to be a suitable waiting room for occasions such as this.

By half past five, my feet pinch and my lower back aches. Has this Mr. Archer gotten wind of my sex and decided to prove some kind of point? A sigh rips out of me. Fine. If that's the game he wants to play, I shall simply return first thing in the morning. Leaving the office behind, I turn to descend the stairs.

A black-suited man dashes upward, his long legs eating two stairs at a time. His agility catches me off guard. It makes sense, though, that my late husband would have chosen a younger man to manage in his stead. He'd not have wished to be rallied from London to attend matters here.

Near the landing, the man glances up. Blue eyes meet my gaze with all the intensity of a November sky. He freezes.

So do I. Hundreds of emotions wash over me, too many to name, as if a great, cold bucket of water has been upturned over my head. I gasp for air, and my reticule shakes in my death grip. The connection with my small purse is the only tangible thing buoying me in this dark void of uncharted sea. Because two breaths away from me stands Edmund Archer.

The only man I have ever loved.

CHAPTER THREE

Bella

If skeletons can smile, surely my late husband's skull is unhinged at the jaw with an ear-to-ear grin at my mortification. What cruel hoax is this? Of all the Archers in the world, I am to partner with Edmund? The man who'd whispered intimate promises and kissed my lips until I was senseless, breathless, helpless?

"Bella?" His voice, smooth as a summer afternoon, unearths memories I thought I'd buried deep. Evidently not deep enough. Time rolls back to moon-lit trysts in the garden, dinners and dances and carriage rides in Hyde Park. Countless shared heartbeats and secrets.

"Edmund." Though I'd vowed never to repeat it, his name rolls off my tongue, the traitorous organ. I clear my throat then amend the blunder. "Mr. Archer."

He advances, his hands clenched at his side, a strange mix of familiar and foreign that in one swift swipe cuts me with loss and heals with wonder. His boyish good looks have matured beyond my wildest imaginations. He is dev-astatingly handsome in his prime, taller than I remember, broader of shoulder, all muscle and steel.

What little breath that remains in me whooshes from my lungs.

His brows pull into a line as he studies me, questions swimming in those blue depths like an overburdened pond of pickerel. "What are you doing here?"

Exactly. The question rattles around in my head, shaking my resolve. Of all my late husband's holdings, I chose *this* one to keep?

But it's done now. The rest are sold off. This is my last—my *only*—chance to be my own woman. Inch by inch, I straighten my spine. Holding hands with adversity is nothing new, so whatever may come of this venture, it will not be anything I can't survive. Independence never comes without a cost.

I meet his gaze. "I had an appointment with you at half past four."

"I am aware of no such commitment. And why would you wish to see me?"

"Mr. Archer?" Footsteps pound up the stairs. A man wearing a greasy apron and a frown stops on the top step and hitches his thumb over his shoulder.

"Beg your pardon, sir, but there's a knotted-up swing arm on the floor, halting production on machine number seven."

Edmund turns. "Have Garrety manage it."

"Can't, sir. Garrety's seein' to the broken shaft in the winding room."

With a sigh, Edmund rakes his hand through his hair, pausing to press in his fingers at the back of his neck. The trademark gesture squeezes my chest. It is a reminder, a remainder, a string that yet connects us when I thought I'd severed all ties.

"Fine, I will be there shortly." He offers the man his back and, in two long strides, opens the door to his office and holds it wide. "My apologies, but I am afraid I can spare you only a few minutes, nothing more. Please, have a seat."

I sweep past him, and my step falters on the way to the chair in front of his big desk. The small room reflects Edmund in so many ways. His sense of order shows in the stacked documents on the desktop and the straight line of book spines on the small shelf in the corner. His meticulous awareness of details shines in the spotless window overlooking the production floor. Most of all, his scent permeates the small room, a blend of cedar and freshly picked oakmoss.

He doesn't sit but merely leans against his desk, clearly conflicted between hearing me out or tending to the swing arm, whatever that is. Something flickers in his eyes. Something warm and almost sacred. "The years have been kind to you. You are as lovely as ever."

The words wrap around me in an embrace I haven't felt in years, and for one dizzying moment, Edmund Archer's blue-eyed spell captures me again.

God, help me.

I lift my chin. "Thank you, but I did not come here seeking compliments. I had an appointment with you to discuss—"

"Which reminds me, one moment, please." He reaches back and retrieves a small black leather book. Papers flip then he stops, running his finger halfway down a page. His face lifts to mine, a small frown marring his forehead. "As I suspected, I have no appointments until tomorrow at half past four, with the majority owner of the factory—"

His eyes widen, and he sets the diary back atop the other ledgers. "Ahh, so that is why you are here. Though I must confess I anticipated your late husband's solicitor would manage the paperwork, not you."

I shake my head, trying to order my thoughts as neatly as the contents on Edmund's desk. "There must be some mistake. I was told you expected me the ninth of September, which is today, not the tenth, though it is a rather moot point now, I suppose. Nevertheless, I apologize for the confusion."

"No need." He shrugs. "You are likely not at fault. Communication is not the law profession's strong point."

A sharp rap on the door turns both of our heads.

"Pardon, Mr. Archer." A muffled voice leaches through the frosted glass and grows louder as a stubble-haired man, work cap askew, pokes his head through the opening. "My apologies, sir, but ye did ask me to remind you, come Armageddon or not, about the shipment for Brussels. It's needin' yer sign-off down at the dock a'fore it can leave the gates—and it's been waitin' for ye nigh on an hour now."

Edmund nods. "Hold off just a few minutes more. I shall be there shortly."

"Aye, sir."

The door barely closes before Edmund steps away from his desk and skirts around it to the back side. He pulls out a drawer and lifts a single sheet of parchment then pushes it across the tabletop toward me. "Forgive my haste, but duty calls. Your signature, if you please, then you and I may both be on our way."

More paperwork? Is the entire business world nothing but pen and ink? I collect the document, and as I read the first few lines, my lips purse, unladylike yet altogether unstoppable. It is the same paper Mr. Barlow wanted me to sign—the one relinquishing my majority in this factory.

I snap my gaze to Edmund. "It appears you could not have spoken a truer word, for there has indeed been an enormous lack of communication. I am not here to sign away my husband's portion of the business, but to manage it."

A small smile ghosts his lips, as if I am the one playing a ludicrous prank instead of fate. "You cannot be serious. Simply write your name on that line and—"

"Pardon me, but this is no jest." I stiffen my shoulders, emphasizing my point with stalwart posture. "Like it or not, I intend to act as the majority owner of Nottingham Lace and Hose."

"You? A woman? Don't be ridiculous." A chuckle rumbles in his throat, and the longer I stare at him unmoved, the more his mirth fades, until eventually he plants his hands on his desk and dips his head. "Look, if this is about what happened between us all those years ago, believe me when I say I did what was best for you. Leave the past in the past. Sign the paper."

Best for me? Leaving me brokenhearted and married to a man thrice my age who abused me in every possible manner? My throat closes with the unfairness of it all.

I rise, employing years of hard-learned grace and elegance from attending Miss Eleanor Brighton's School for Young Ladies. Pinching the top of the paper with both forefingers and thumbs, I rip the document down the center then spear him with an arched brow. "Go tend to your business, and I shall be back in the morning to tend to mine. Good day, Mr. Archer."

I drop the torn pieces on his desk and cross to the door.

"Bella, wait!"

Wait? For what? More conversation in which he tries to persuade me to give up my only chance at being a businesswoman?

I shoot him an evil eye over my shoulder. "You will not address me so informally, sir. I am Mrs. White. Your new partner."

CHAPTER FOUR

Edmund

The door of my office slams, and I am alone with chaos and the fading sweetness of Bella's honeysuckle scent. Both annoy me. I hate the idea of partnering with anyone, let alone a woman who has no idea of how to run a lacemaking factory.

"Bah!" I snatch up the ripped halves of the document that was to be my freedom, my future. My hope. The paper crumples in my hand, and I squeeze until my fist shakes. I will not go down without a fight. But by all that is holy, did it have to be Bella I must stand against?

Oh, Bella.

Unbidden memories—long ago buried—resurrect and pelt me like a burst of grapeshot. How small her hand had seemed the first time I entwined my fingers with hers. How sweet her laughter rang, clear and bubbly as a spring stream, when I swept her around the dance floor. How perfectly our bodies fitted together the night I'd kissed her lips.

I throw the wadded document hard against the wall and watch it drop to the floor; then I stalk out of my office, leaving it behind. Leaving it *all* behind. For now.

Like a member of the fire brigade, I sort through which blaze to put out first as I descend the steps. Should I help Garrety with the broken shaft in the winding room? Speed over to the dock and send that shipment on its way? Or deal with the knotted-up swing arm? Ignoring any of them will cut into earnings—and Nottingham Lace and Hose desperately needs to make a profit by Christmas, or the only gift I may give the workers is a termination notice.

Deciding on the swing arm, I shove open the door to the lacemaking floor. As I near machine number seven, its operator, a man in a lint-covered brown coat, steps out and blocks my way. A scar puckers the right side of his mouth, but that never stops Gramble from complaining. If anything, it empowers his right to rally against the unfairness of the world. God only knows what crime against justice he's perceived in my management now.

"Mr. Archer, I—"

"Not now, Gramble." I shove past him. "See me later in my office."

Thankfully, the clack and clatter of the machines drown out any further protest from the man. At the back of seven, Franklin, the best foreman I've ever had, scowls at the busted swing arm.

"Your verdict?" I ask.

He shrugs. "It's broken."

"I can see that." I pull off my coat and hand it to him then push up my sleeves. Swing arms are notorious for ripping or gouging. If I show up at home one more time with a ruined suit coat, Mrs. Harnuckle will have my head on a platter, and a freshly shined one, at that.

Stooping, I run my fingers along the thick piece of metal. Nothing snags. The knob of the bolt rises in just the right place. All appears to be—hold on. I stretch as far as possible and. . .there. Something is wedged near the gear shaft, knocking off the threads with each run. It is jagged on one end. The rest is hard, smooth, and the length of my thumb. An easy-enough fix, but dangerous.

Withdrawing, I face Franklin. "There is a foreign object off-ticking the thread. I'll have to remove it. Toss my coat down, and on my mark, run the loom. Oh, and make sure you start the loom, not Gramble."

Questions crease his brow. "But you would be risking your arm, sir."

"Better my arm than hazarding an ill-met order."

Franklin shakes his head and drops my coat. The fluff on the floor clings to it, and I imagine Mrs. Harnuckle's bulldog glower as if she stands here witnessing the act.

Once Franklin positions himself near the lever that starts the machine, I jockey for a better position at the side closest to the offense. Timing is everything. Sweat moistens my palms, and I swipe them against my trousers. The single beat of a heart stands between freeing the machine's arm or amputating mine. And this is what Bella wishes to take part in? Her delicate frame is not suited for such manual labour.

I shove in my arm, shoulder deep, and nod at Franklin. The beast groans. So do I. One flywheel hums into motion. Another does not. My fingers wrap around the lump, and I pull. The swing arm falls. I yank so hard that I stumble backward. The hem of my sleeve snags and tears, but not my flesh.

Thank You, God.

Franklin jams the lever into neutral and claps me on the back. "That were close, Mr. Archer. What is it?"

I open my hand, fingers shaking. The broken stem of a bone pipe rests on my palm. Rage lights a fire in my belly, and my gaze strays to a brown-coated malcontent leaning against the side of the machine. Stupid Gramble. There's no way I can prove this is his pipe, but all the same, I know it is. If he's been smoking inside the factory walls, one stray spark in this tinder house could kill us all. I ought to grab the slackard by the collar and drive home the fear of God and man.

But instead I wheel about and head for the door. I'll accuse Gramble of reckless endangerment in private, when he seeks me out later. No doubt the snake will just lie—he always does. Were it not for his wife and nine children, most of whom work the floor along with him, I would kick his sorry backside to the gutter. The fine line between compassion and justice blurs. Am I doing anyone a favor by allowing him to remain employed when his careless antics might threaten the viability of the company?

Bella has no idea of the weight her slim shoulders will soon carry if she continues to go through with her mad scheme of comanagement.

I step out into sunshine and fresh September air. Across the yard, four harnessed Belgians stamp and snort, as anxious as the two men pacing the dock. Grinding my heels into the gravel, I make all haste, when a boy darts in front of me, stopping me short.

"Mr. Archer, sir?" He holds out a slip of paper. "For you."

Fishing around in my pocket, I snag a coin and offer it in exchange. "Thank you."

The boy speeds off as fast as he came, and I unfold a note with my name scrawled across the front. Inside, the familiar penmanship of my colleague and friendly competitor, Jack Humphrey, forms six devastating words.

Adams. Birkin. Old Dog and Partridge.

My shoulders sag. For the second time this day, I ball up paper and fling it to the ground. First Bella. Then Gramble and his pipe. Now this. On their own, my nemeses Thomas Adams and Richard Birkin are forces with which to be reckoned.

But if those two are devising grand schemes over at the Old Dog and Partridge, they could put me out of business.

CHAPTER FIVE

Bella

It is magical how a hot cup of tea on a brisk morning can calm the most savage of moods. . .and after a long night of railing against my bedsheets and yesterday's scorn in Edmund's voice, I am sorely in need of such tranquility. Not even my silly little game of planning for Christmas had lulled me to sleep.

Yet today is a new day. A fresh beginning. And as I tie on my bonnet and snatch up my reticule, the jingle of the second-chance coin smacking against the others is a reminder to provide Edmund another opportunity to accept me as his business associate. God's mercies are new every morning. Perhaps Edmund's attitude will be new as well now that he's had a chance to befriend the idea.

"What time shall I expect you back, mum?" Betty stands near the front door, holding out a pair of gloves.

I shake my head at the offering. Is it not presumptuous to flaunt a competitor's wares on my hands now that I own a lace company? "More than likely I will not return until well into the evening. The first of many late nights, I suspect. We shall both be heartily occupied over the next several weeks. You with redecorating"—I sweep my hand toward the drab walls of the vestibule—"and me with learning all there is to know of lacemaking. We will reconvene tonight and decide on curtains and wallpaper, hmm?"

"Yes, mum." She reaches out a tentative hand toward my sleeve then pulls back before contact and ducks her chin. "God bless ye, Mrs. White, on yer first day at the factory."

"Thank you, Betty." A smile curves my lips. "I shall take all the blessings God has to give."

Outside, the streets feel surprisingly like London. Loud. Crowded. Smelling of smoke and horse droppings. Though the sun has hardly rolled out of bed, hawkers already bark from behind their carts, selling everything from sausages to apples to tonics guaranteed to cure gout and lung vapors. I ignore them all and turn onto Bridge Street, then flatten against a stone wall as a troupe of blue-suited young boys march past, two by two, silent and grim faced and following a headmaster in a flowing black robe. Why are they not in school?

Ahh, perhaps a library is nearby. I should like that. Very much! The temptation to fall in behind the last boys and trail them entices for a moment, but I turn away, the brunt of business before pleasure lagging my steps.

As I near Nottingham Lace and Hose, my steps falter altogether. Since I took a carriage yesterday, I did not notice the old building leaning against the factory. It is a carbuncle that ought to be removed before it topples and falls upon an unsuspecting pedestrian. The pile of blackened bricks has boards in place of windows, and above the door, an old shingle hangs by rusty chains. Mould collects in the corners and spreads over the sign like a cancer, nearly blotting out the remnants of lettering that reads OLDE LACE SHOP.

Yet none of that lifts gooseflesh quite as much as the living foundation shoring up the building. Women, five of them, sit with their backs to the crumbling walls, each dressed in varying degrees of rags, from threadbare wraps to naught but strings for shawls. None sport any colour. They are one with the dirt. The refuse. Tread upon by nature and man alike.

And every last one of them stare blankly into space, hands outstretched.

The milk I'd taken with my tea rises sour in my throat, compassion choking me. Why was I so blessed when these women clearly were not?

I yank open my reticule and, bending, give each woman a coin and an encouraging word. The last woman reaches out and grabs my sleeve.

"God bless ye, miss. Will ye stop by tomorrow?"

The hope trembling her words hits me square in the chest. Did no one else ever come this way? Ever open their purse or their heart to such desperation? I pat her hand. "Yes, I shall."

She pulls back, and I stumble away, my own problems having been rightly whittled down to size. Even if Edmund doesn't change his mind, managing a business with a belligerent co-owner is a trifling matter compared to the blind women shrouded in rags and despair.

This time when I enter the factory's wrought-iron gates, I know where to go. And again, this time, I find Edmund's office empty. Fumbling with my watch brooch, I frown at the glass face. Half past eight. He should be here. Then again, perhaps he is elsewhere on the grounds. How much time does he really spend in an office anyway?

I descend the steps, but just before I explore down a corridor, I pause and study the layout. I have no idea what is behind the wall nearest the stair, but were it knocked out, the space might serve as a private waiting area for customers or merchants. A far better prospect than standing in a stuffy passageway without so much as a chair. And if the space proves large enough, with a new wall or two built, I might even have an office of my own. I shall inquire about the possibility today.

That bit of business decided, I stride down the passageway with a bounce to my step. It feels good, this decision-making. Choosing what to do and how to do it. I will find Edmund and share my plans then begin my education in the structure and functions of a lacemaking factory.

I push open a heavy wooden door and enter a Christmas wonderland. Thread dust hovers in the air like so many snowflakes—in *all* the air, even that which I breathe. It goes down tickly and rises up in a cough. But the affront to my ears is worse. Clicking. Clacking. Bang-bang-banging. I lift my hands to cover my ears, so deafening is the noise. The great machines filling the room rumble like monsters, their giant arms reaching and grabbing. Their big black bodies hunch row upon row. Large leather belts and pulleys run nearly floor to ceiling, whirring from wheel to wheel.

In the middle of this chaos, people scurry, tending the beasts. White dust settles on their shoulders and heads. Scarves cover the bottom halves of their faces. I blink. Even were I to find Edmund here, we'd never be able to talk above the din.

Skirting the machines and dodging the slant-eyed looks of workers, I wend my way across the long room and push through another door into blessed silence, comparatively speaking. The area is ill lit and cramped. Three of the walls contain a door. The fourth, a staircase. I lift my hem and ascend.

At the top of the stairs there is only one option: a scarred wooden door. The handle gives easily enough, and the door groans open into a large, narrow room. A row of women in white smocks sit on chairs, back to back, lace pooling on their laps, facing the row of windows high up on either wall. Their heads turn in unison, and they stare at me.

The scrutiny of at least twenty women prickles over my skin as if the needles they hold jab me instead of their lace pieces. Some pause halfway through a stitch. Others lower their hands. None look any too pleased that a strange woman has burst in upon their industry.

The woman nearest me angles her head, her eyes a translucent grey in the shaft of light streaming through the glass. "May I help you, miss?"

Her elbows and shoulders poke knobs in her smock, such a thin waif is she, yet there is something familiar about her frame. Something almost recognizable in the sloop of her shoulders and the fine spray of freckles dotting her face.

Ahh. The woman who'd bumped into me yesterday.

"Perhaps you may." I curve my lips into a pleasant smile. Who knew when the woman had last been treated with such a small kindness? Surely grins were not shared frequently in this group of needles and bones. "Could you tell me where to find Mr. Archer?"

"Oh, he rarely comes up here, miss. No machinery need be tended in the finishing room."

"I see. I am sorry to have disrupted your work, Miss. . . ?"

"No miss about me. I'm Mary. Just Mary."

"Well, Mary." I flash another smile. "I am pleased to meet you and thank you for your assistance."

Mary turns her face back to the light pouring in and once again lifts her needle. The other women, apparently satisfied the show is over, turn as well.

Backtracking, I descend the stairs, all the while incubating a newborn idea. Clearly those women are malnourished. Would it not be to their benefit—and that of the company's—if they and all the other workers were treated to a cup of tea and milk partway through the day? Such a small treat would not only boost production but morale as well. Maybe I could even invite the blind ladies at the Old Lace Shop. I pen a mental note to ask Edmund about it.

At the bottom of the stairs, I turn right and choose another door, which opens into the yard, once again a'bustle with activity, especially near the dock. Perhaps Edmund is overseeing a shipment.

I set off across the gravel, but three steps later, a young boy carrying a package scurries across my path and trips on an overturned cobble. I grab him by the back of his coat before his face smashes into the ground and heave him upward. He can weigh no more than a basket of puppies and is every bit as wiggly.

Cap askew, he peeks up at me from beneath the brim, white fluff clinging to his coat. "Beg yer pardon, miss. Got to run!"

He snatches up the fallen parcel and darts off, kicking up gravel from his flying feet. At that rate, he'll scrape his knees *and* his chin before the day is done. Quite the contrast from the austere schoolboys I passed on the way here, and with that thought, my chest squeezes. That boy should be in school as well, not running errands in a noisy, crowded lacemaking factory. When would he have an opportunity to learn the basics of an education?

Nibbling my lower lip, I proceed toward the dock. Maybe besides installing a waiting room and an office, there might be enough space to include a small tearoom for the malnourished women finishing off lace and a schoolroom for the errand boys.

Gruff laughter pulls me from my plans. I climb three rough stairs and close in on a duo of men with their backs to me. Small puffs of smoke rise above their heads, the scent of green-leaf tobacco wafting out from them.

I stop just behind the fellow in a brown coat. "Excuse me, I am looking for Mr. Archer."

The man stiffens and whirls, tucking one hand behind him. Is he hiding a pipe? But as his gaze meets mine, the question flees from my mind, and I suck in a breath. A scar slices across one side of his mouth, right through the lips, like an earthworm taking a wrong turn on his face.

"Well, well. Are ye now?" He laughs, the sort of ribald chuckle that could heat the cheeks of a harlot. "That's a fine jest, this time o' day."

I retreat a step, though instantly I am aware that is a mistake. One should never back away from a monster lest he think it a game and give chase. How well I know this.

As suspected, the man advances, a keen flash of interest in his gaze. His breath stinks of fish and smoke.

I plant my feet, refusing to cower—a trait that marks me with my own scars. "I assure you, sir, I am in earnest. Do you know where I may find Mr. Archer?"

"His grand house, I suppose."

"What do you mean?"

Turning aside, he litters the ground with a wad of spit then swipes his free hand across his lips. "Master don't never come this early, and why should he when he expects us here at the crack o' dawn, running the business for him."

Disgust thickens his voice. I do not lay blame. Edmund *should* be here.

I tip my head. "Thank you, Mister. . . ?"

"Gramble, miss." He nods. "The name's Gramble."

Clutching my skirt, I tread down the stairs, anger thudding in my steps. I do not know much about business, but not even a household manages without a master to direct it. And as majority owner, I must—I *will*—insist on Edmund's presence. Here. Now.

Even if I must yank him out of his bed.

CHAPTER SIX

Bella

The carriage rolls past the last of the row houses on Nottingham's west side. I peer out the window, curious and slightly irritated as to why Edmund insists on living such a distance from the factory. What if a crisis arises? Have the years so much changed him that he now thinks only of his comfort? His needs? What became of the man who lent me his coat in a sudden downpour or bent to a beggar child and handed over the contents of his pockets?

My brow weighs heavy with a scowl. What a naive woman I am. Such callousness should not be so surprising coming from a man who gave not a whit for my feelings when he walked out of my life.

Why, God? The prayer is my breath nowadays. *Why does it have to be Edmund with whom I must partner?*

Self-pity stings my eyes, and heaving a great sigh, I stare out at an ash tree. Yellow leaves on the farthest reaches of the branches flutter with the first whisper of autumn. The way the morning sun warms my cheek through the window, it is hard to believe that soon winter winds will blow.

We turn off the main road and onto a narrow lane, winding through more trees. What a glorious ride this will be when oranges and reds dapple the greenery.

The carriage stops. Stairs thump-bump into position, and the door opens. The jarvey lends me a hand as I descend.

All my thoughts of Edmund's comfort seeking fade as I stare, a bit slack jawed, at the cottage nestled in this clearing of oak and willow. A thatched roof curls over the whitewashed walls like a prayer. Mullioned windows with flower boxes flank each side of the front door. It is a cozy croft, well kept and welcoming, but better suited to a farm manager, not a factory owner.

I turn back to the jarvey. "Are you certain this is the home of Mr. Edmund Archer?"

He shrugs. "This is the direction you supplied, madam."

For a moment, I nibble my lip, doubt draping over my shoulders like a heavy blanket. Did the clerk at the factory copy it down wrong? Then again, perhaps this *is* the right home. Perhaps Edmund is married to a shrewish wife who wishes to remain separate from the clamour of the city.

I stride to the door and lift my hand to knock; then I freeze. Am I *really* ready to meet the woman who stole the role that rightfully should've been mine?

Nonsense. The past is behind me. I am my own woman now. Majority partner of a thriving business that desperately needs a master at the helm every morning. I rap on the wood.

No answer.

So I pound all the louder.

Moments later, the door swings open to a grey-haired fellow with a round face and a rounder belly. One slight nudge and surely the man will roll away like a great glass marble. He smells slightly yeasty, as if he spends too much time begging buns from the cook.

His gaze sweeps over me. "May I help you, miss?"

I manage a smile. "I am here to see Mr. Archer."

Leaning aside, he gawks past my shoulder. "Your cart overturned, you say?"

Though I'd heard no commotion at my back, his words alarm me. I whirl, expecting to see the carriage somehow tipped on its side. But the coach sits where I left it, the driver perched on the seat and partaking of a pipe.

Confused, I once again face the old man, this time with a raised brow. "As you can see, there is no problem with my carriage. I should like to see Mr. Archer."

"Well, let's have it, then." He stretches out a gnarly hand, his knuckles the size of walnuts. Clearly he expects me to produce something. . .but what?

I can't help but cock my head like an inquisitive tot. "I beg your pardon?"

"The bottle of starch water for Mrs. Harnuckle."

My former doubts rise with a vengeance. Perhaps I truly am at the wrong house. I retreat a step, consider bidding the man a good day, but on second thought decide to give it one more go. "Is this the home of Mr. Archer or is it not?"

The man's outstretched hand rises to his ear, and he cups his fingers while angling his head. "What's that?"

"Is this the home—"

He holds up a finger, disappears for a moment, and then reappears with a cone-shaped trumpet that he holds to his ear. And suddenly the ridiculous conversation makes sense, though why the man answered the door without his hearing aid is a mystery—but not quite as mysterious as why Edmund employs the odd man in the first place.

I step close to his listening device. "I am here to call on Mr. Archer." The words march off my tongue like crisply stepping soldiers.

He shakes his head. "Not possible, miss. Master doesn't take any callers. Good day."

He pulls back, poised to shut the door.

But I advance, righteous indignation filling me with boldness. A business partner ought not be rebuffed as a common beggar, but how to convince this bumbling servant?

"Your master's honour is at stake. Do you understand?" Since he's lowered his ear trumpet, I practically shout.

His lips push into an O. "Honour, you say? Master Archer's?"

I nod. Perhaps this will work. "Please. I need an immediate audience with him."

"Hmm. . ." His lips flatten. Slowly, though, he opens the door wide, sweeping his arm out for me to enter. "This way, miss."

Once past the threshold, he guides me toward the opening on the right side of the small vestibule, bypassing the opposite door that opens into a dining room and ushering me past a short passageway that I can only guess leads to a kitchen.

"Wait here, miss, and do not venture a step elsewhere."

It is strange, this ordering about from a servant. Then again, everything about this venture is strange. Turning from his retreating back, I glance around the room. While it does not meet the standards of a London town house, it is nonetheless a comfortable sort of parlor. A fireplace graces one wall. A bow window with a cushion for sitting looks out on the front lawn, the perfect place to curl up with a good book and a cup of tea on a wintry afternoon.

But I am drawn to a shelf on the opposite wall. There sits a framed mirror on an easel, a cut-glass lamp, and next to it, a small brooch hung by a ribbon from a nail. It is an oval bubble of glass with intricately woven hair inside, creating tiny fern fronds that encircle two initials.

C. A.

My breath hitches. Either this is a memento of Edmund's deceased mother—though I don't recall her first name starting with *C*—or it is a death ornament in memory of his wife. Either way, I feel like an intruder. Such an intimate object is not meant for public viewing. I never should have come. How many times had my husband upbraided me for impetuous acts such as this?

I dash to the door, hoping to spy the old butler before he finds Edmund, when childish laughter draws my gaze down the corridor. A young girl, six or possibly seven, hobbles nimbly with one crutch, shriek-giggling all the way—until she sees me and stops.

My fingers flutter to my lips, stifling a gasp. The girl gazes up at me with eyes the shade of Edmund's yet slightly slanted. Her nose is flattened, her forehead taking up more space than is normal. But for all the oddities, her grin is large and infectious. I cannot help but drop my hand and smile back at her—

Until a shadowy shape emerges behind her and roars, "What are you doing here?"

The rage on Edmund's face is alive, indicting and condemning in one black look. The young girl flinches at his outburst.

Something ugly settles deep in my chest, squeezing the air from my lungs. He is right. What am I doing here? Why did I not confront him in his office instead of in his home?

Sucking in a breath, I package up regret, ignorance, and fear and stow it deep inside my heart to open later in a quiet—and very alone—moment with God. Then I lift my chin. While I do not know much yet about the business ways in the world of men, of this I am certain: a majority owner ought never to cower in front of a partner.

"I came to ask you the same, why you are here instead of at the factory, but now I. . .well. . ." Further words crumble to dust on my tongue beneath Edmund's terrible stare. Everything in me screams for me to flee, to hide, or at the very least to bow my head in submission.

Frantically, I reach for my pearl necklace. The cool gemstone is a tangible reminder of my mother—the woman I want to be. Mostly. Mother was an unapologetic bluestocking, independent of mind but not of means. I wish to achieve both, and so I plant my feet, squashing the urge to run.

"Flora." The harsh lines on Edmund's face soften as he glances down at the girl. "Find Mrs. Harnuckle and tell her Father says you may have a biscuit, hmm?"

"Yes, Papa." The girl nods, and though it's barely possible, her grin widens. "Goodbye, lady!" She maneuvers around and skip-hops on her crutch past her father. His gaze follows her.

"Goodbye, Miss Flora," I murmur.

As soon as the girl disappears down the corridor, Edmund turns to me. The coldness in his eyes makes the scar behind my ear ache. A glance like that from Mr. White usually meant some kind of retribution, like the night he'd thrown a brass candlestick. I should leave now. Back out slow and quiet. My fingers wrap all the tighter around the pearl. God alone keeps my feet rooted to the carpet.

A muscle jumps on Edmund's jaw as he opens his mouth. "You may have a legal right to half the factory—which I *will* contest—but you have no business whatsoever in my home. I thank you to leave, Mrs. White, and to keep to yourself what you have seen."

CHAPTER SEVEN

Edmund

Yesterday's shock of seeing Bella at my office door is nothing compared to the sickening twist in my gut at witnessing her here in my house. My world teeters at the edge of a black abyss.

Seven careful years. Seven! Keeping my head down. Vigilant and tight-lipped to a fault. Living at the edge of nowhere, hidden from eyes and whys and flaming lies. But for all my circumspect ways, with one small breach of obedience, old Baxter has opened the door wide to utter disaster. Indiscreet old man! I ought to send him packing today.

But truly, is the fault not mine?

The question hits me broadside. The day I bought this house, I should have pensioned off the feeble fellow and hired a more capable butler, but oh, how promises to the dead can bind and bite long past the burying of bones.

Bella stares at me, and for a brief moment, her composed mask slips. A sliver of raw terror flashes in her brown eyes. She fiddles with a pearl necklace, clearly nervous, and my gut clenches. Have I become such an ogre as to terrify widows in my own home?

"I am many things, sir, but I am not a gossip. What goes on in your house is your business alone." Her voice shakes. As does the hem of her skirt. Clearly, my offense has cut deep—adding pain upon pain to the wounds I can never seem to quit ripping wide.

I am a beast, but for good reason. *Always* for good reason.

Yet does that make it right, God?

As usual, no answer booms from heaven.

I pinch the bridge of my nose. The damage is already done. There is no sense in furthering this farce. Lowering my hand, I soften my tone. "I did not mean to imply you are a woman of imprudence. I simply meant that you. . ." Words knot my tongue, but which ones to say? What to hold back? How to protect my daughter and Bella's dignity without harming either? Of necessity, my daughter is the greater concern. Bella is a shadow from the past, a woman I no longer know. . .so why the twist in my chest?

"Come." The directive is more of a growl than an invitation, but it cannot be helped. One does not easily recover from a potentially mortal blow.

Please, God, may this not be a fatal blunder.

Reluctantly, I sweep my hand toward the sitting room. "As long as you are here, let us settle our differences once and for all."

Her gaze pings from my face, to my hand, and finally toward the sitting-room door. Without a word, she turns and enters. Thankfully. Had she run out of here with fire in her step, I'd have had to track her down for Flora's sake.

Bella bypasses the sofa and crosses to the mantel then faces me, her hands folded in front of her. Her face, lovely as ever, tips upward slightly. Morning light from the window slips over the curve of her high cheekbones and slides across the determined slope of her nose. Her nostrils flare. She is on edge.

Grinding my jaw, I cast a wild glance about the room, grasping for something—anything—to divert. The cut-glass water decanter will suit. I turn my back to Bella and set about pouring drinks.

"Why did you come?" The question pours as freely as the liquid.

"You were not at the factory. I came to see why."

"Well, now you know." The decanter shakes in my grip as I set it back on the small table. It is in the knowing that all of Eden fell.

Collecting both glasses, I face Bella *and* the moment I dreaded would one day come. "Flora is brighter in the morning, clearer of mind, less sleepy. I grant her an hour of my time before I put in twelve to fourteen at the factory."

Only Harnuckle, Baxter, Nurse, and Cook know this—and in the speaking of it, I am stripped bare. Naked. Cold and ashamed of the stark truth.

"Here." I stalk over to Bella and shove the glass at her. As soon as she grasps it, I retreat to the window. Better to look out at the first decaying leaves of autumn than the gleam of deadly pity in Bella's eyes.

"I did not know you had a daughter." The accusation stabs me in the back.

Mouth suddenly dry, I guzzle down the water and return the glass to the table; then I resume my post at the window. "No one knows. My late wife took the secret of Flora to her grave, God rest her."

"But why keep the girl a secret? I mean, obviously Flora has some . . .em. . .difficulties, but surely—"

"There is no *surely* about it!" I turn away, seething. She can have no idea of the carelessness of her well-meaning words. "If it gets out that I've fathered a cripple, a child of insufficient mental capabilities, I will lose the trust of my buyers. First, for siring such an anomaly, and second, for not having the fortitude to shut her away in an asylum."

My tone rumbles like thunder in the small room, but I do not repent. The vileness of the unjust situation merits such a severe affront.

Bella gasps, her fingers fluttering to her chest. "But that would be wrong in every sense of the word. You are her father! Obviously you love her. There can be no shame in that."

A bitter laugh rises like bile and spills from my mouth. "Have you yet to learn that life is not so simple?"

Her lips tremble, and she reaches to rub behind her ear. "Yes, I suppose that I have."

Of course she has, after being ordered about by her father until the scoundrel married her off to the highest bidder. Bella is a smart woman. It doesn't take long for a pawn to realize its lesser value. And that's what we are. Naught but playing pieces the powerful move about at their whim. Would to God I'd learned that sooner.

But the game ends here. Now. Leastwise for Bella, if I have any say in the matter. No one will accept a woman as a co-owner anyway, and one misplaced word about Flora—wouldn't Adams and Birkin delight in playing that card against me. No. If Bella returns home to London, it will save us both a world of pain.

I reach out tentatively and lightly rest my hands on the upper part of her arms. She stiffens but does not turn away.

"The business world is a ruthless master, dictating even to the point of who you may love and who must be cast aside. Go home, Bella." I rub my hands up and down, hoping to impress my words upon her heart with a soft touch. "Go back to London. I am sorry for the loss of your husband, but grasping on to this business holding of his will not bring him back."

"Back?" She yanks away from me, an unrecognizable hardness glinting in her eyes. "I would not wish that man back for all the queen's jewels." She whirls, her whole body trembling. "I *grasp* this business, Edmund, because I *need* this business. Need this job." A sob chokes her words. "Desperately."

Need? I knew the tightfisted Mr. Venerable White to be shrewd and conniving in his politics and domineering in his management style, but had he truly left Bella nothing but one small business and expected her to run it as a man? What kind of brute had she been living with these past eight years?

I stifle a growl. Blast Bella's father! The selfish, greedy goblin. Giving her away to such a monster for the sake of his own political maneuvers.

Once again, I reach for Bella, but before my fingertips touch her sleeve, I pull back. Am I not every bit as culpable for having listened to her father in the first place all those years ago?

"Very well." Defeat rises thick up my throat. "Though I do not know why God has seen fit to bring our partnership about, I confess that His ways are beyond what I can fathom. But here we are, for better or worse, though I suspect there is a whole lot of worse headed our way."

She turns, wonder lifting her brows. "Y–you will not contest the legality of the situation?"

I could. I should. But what kind of life will Bella have without the means to support herself as a widow? I pin her in place with a fervent stare. "Will you not breathe a word of Flora's existence?"

"I will not." A smile grows on her face, and she offers her hand. "Partners?"

I hesitate. This is either the biggest mistake I've ever made or possibly my—our—salvation. Her fingers fit small inside mine. "Partners."

But as I pull away, doubt assails me, warning me that I will once again fail her. Fail myself. Fail all those in my employ who are counting on my provision. Which would mean the workhouse for me and Bella.

And the asylum for Flora.

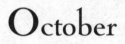

October

Chapter Eight

Bella

Three weeks later, the tentative truce between Edmund and me has solidified into a peaceful sort of pact. I don't mention Flora—though my curiosity grows stronger with each passing day—and in return, Edmund endures my regular visits to the factory. Though he turned down my idea to institute a tea time for the workers, he grudgingly approved transforming a former storage closet into a small receiving room. It is not as grand a space as I envisioned, but it's still an improvement over asking customers to stand in a cramped corridor.

The sun shines radiantly as I walk to the factory this morning, though the breeze carries a chill that cuts through my woolen cape. I tighten my grip on the ledger I carry and turn onto Hollowstone.

Two streets down, I veer to the right. Ahead, by the Old Lace Shop, are the five black lumps of rag and bone that I've come to care about. My steps quicken as I pull out some coins. The next gust of wind bows the women's heads and flutters their tatty old bonnets. Winter will arrive soon, and these ladies will sit covered in snow, shivering. My heart twinges. I could gather them into my home during the day, but then they'd have no means by which to earn money. What a cruel career these women labour in, relying on the good graces of others in the cold and shadow of the very industry that blinded them in the first place, for each had at one time been a mistress of hand-finished fancywork. All the countless hours they'd spent working in poorly lit factories, squinting at the fine weave of impossibly thin threads, not only stole their youth but their vision as well.

But if lodging them is out of the question, I can at least offer a meal.

I pause near the first woman. "How are we today, ladies?"

Several faces turn toward me. All murmur a greeting. Martha, the one closest to me, adds, " 'Tis always a better day when you pass by, Mrs. White."

"God bless you, Martha." I drop a coin into her outstretched palm and pass along the row of women, giving each a farthing and hopefully some measure of dignity by recognizing them individually. "Dorie, Alice, Anne."

My feet stop at the last woman, and I stoop to clasp Hester's hand in my own. She reminds me of my dear aunt, long since gone, with her enigmatic smile and paper-thin skin. "God bless you as well, my friend." I wrap my fingers around hers, securing the coin inside her grasp.

With her other hand, Hester reaches and rubs the lace of my sleeve hem between her thumb and forefinger, gently, slowly, her face puckering the more she feels along its length. Her eyes—one milky, one not—seek mine as if she can see. "I'm grateful as always, missus. You know I am, and I don't mean to offend, but there is something I must tell you."

I pull away, frowning. "What is it, Hester?"

"There's a flaw there, in your lace hem. Oh, it's a fine bit of piecework, don't get me wrong, dearie. But one of the threads ain't quite right."

Narrowing my eyes, I lift the offending lace and inspect it. Cream-coloured threads weave in an intricate pattern, one of the finest samples Nottingham Lace and Hose produces. I requested the piece from Edmund. But I see no hole in the delicate design. No knots or. . .wait a minute. There. One fine thread is joined with another where it should be casting a line on its own. How in the world had Hester discovered the nearly invisible blemish?

"You are right, Hester, though I can barely see it." The wonder in my voice comes out breathy. "I confess I am amazed you can detect such a small imperfection."

"I thought I noticed it yesterday." She taps her temple, near her eyes. "The sight may be gone, but we can still spot flaws a mile away, right, girls?"

The other women chirrup an agreement, and my jaw drops. They all possess the same skill? The first stirrings of an amazingly wonderful idea unfurl in my mind. Naturally, Edmund will not be easy to persuade, but I have years of experience in facing conflict.

I rise, buoyed by the prospect of bettering these women's lives, now and in the future. "Ladies, I should like to invite you to my home for a hot meal each day at noon."

Surprisingly, Martha looks away, a few whisper amongst themselves, and Hester frowns up at me. "We might take yer coin, missus, for such is our employ at the moment." Her chin lifts, a stray whisker poking out as bristly as her tone. "But we pays for our food."

My fingers fly to my necklace, and the rock-hard pearl reminds me of my own grasp for self-respect. How callous of me to think I can play God.

"Forgive me, Hester. You are right. I shall see you tomorrow then, hmm? Good day, ladies."

Their farewells follow me as I set off for the open gates of the factory and head toward Edmund's office. I am not to have an office of my own. Edmund thinks the workers—especially the men—will not take kindly to a female master. I hate to admit it, but I suspect he is right.

Just as I am about to reach for the door, I hear a familiar low tone and turn my head. Striding across the yard from the loading dock, Edmund converses with another man—his foreman, if I remember correctly. But it is not the foreman who garners my attention. It is the tall, fine figure that Edmund cuts in his brown coat and long-legged trousers. Even after all these years apart, my pulse races at the sight of him. Apparently the feelings I thought dead and cold are simply banked beneath ashes and time.

Both men dip their heads in greeting as they near me. Only Edmund speaks. "Good morning, Mrs. White."

"Mr. Archer. Mr. Franklin." I nod to each in turn.

Edmund faces his foreman, cuffing him on the back. "That'll be all, Franklin. Oh, and keep a keen eye on Gramble. The fellow's up to something, if I don't miss my mark. And if you see that Moffit Scruggs slinking around near the gate, send him packing. I've had enough of his scavenging boys picking through what isn't refuse."

"Aye, sir." Mr. Franklin glances at me. "Good day." Then he bypasses me and enters the scarred factory door.

I offer the ledger to Edmund. "Just returning this. I believe I am up to date for this year now."

His fingers brush against mine as he retrieves it, and heat flares up my arm from his touch.

"I trust you found everything in order."

"I am not here to find fault."

A sheepish smile curves his lips. "Forgive me. I am not used to sharing my records on such a regular basis."

"I don't suppose you are. Mr. White was not one to be overly attentive as long as things were running smoothly."

A gusty breeze trails my words, shivering across my shoulders—or is it the unwelcome memory of Mr. White that chills my blood? It is hard to shake his brutal rage for any inconsequential error of mine. My gaze drifts to the puckered skin across my knuckles from the strike of a fire poker when I'd forgotten to have his brandy warmed. And that was but a trifle compared to my great failure at being unable to conceive. I fold my hands, hiding the scars, and stare at the gravel, desperately wishing to forget.

"Were the years with him so very terrible?"

Edmund's voice is a sweet caress, but I cannot stop my fingers from inching up to my ear. I have no answer for him. Terrible doesn't begin to describe the hellfire I'd lived through, and a bitter laugh surfaces. "Suffice it to say he was harsh."

"Blast it." Sorrow thickens his tone, and he gently pulls my hand away. "If I had known what kind of husband he was, I never would've left you to his devices."

Sudden fury burns hot in my belly, and I yank away from his touch. "Why did you leave? You never even said goodbye. What kind of man does that?"

A muscle jumps on his neck, sticking out like a rod of steel. "I couldn't. It was part of the agreement."

"What agreement?"

"Are we really having this conversation now?" He flings out his arms. "Here?"

He's right. The door could open at any time, ushering out curious ears, and if our voices rise any louder, the words will travel over to the loading dock where men heave crates into a dray.

Even so, I jut my jaw. Too many questions have festered for too many years, and now that the wound is opened, it is better to purge the poison, no matter where it might spill. "Yes."

He blows out a breath, then with a light touch to the small of my back, he guides me to a quieter corner near the gate. When he faces me, pain etches lines in the squint of his eyes. "Very well, if you will not be put off. The night of the Watsons' Christmas ball, do you remember it?"

My breath hitches. How can I ever forget the magic of that evening? Dancing with none but Edmund, finding a shadowy nook where we stood beneath a ball of mistletoe, drinking mulled wine until both our tongues loosened and we whispered words of love. I've tried to evict the image of him gazing at me with such passion, all golden and heady in the light of the Christmas tree candles. Lord knows how I've endeavored to banish the endearments he'd spoken against the curve of my neck, his lips hot against my skin. . .but to no avail. That Christmas is branded on my heart.

"I've relived that night a thousand times since," I murmur.

"Me as well, but I suspect for different reasons." He plows a hand through his hair and looks away. "When I returned you home and you went off to your chamber, your father called me into his study and gave me an ultimatum. If I continued to pursue you, he vowed to pack you up and send you to your aunt in Belgium. Then he threatened to systematically destroy my good name in every manner possible. I would lose everything, and while I cared nothing about my ruin, my ward at the time was my sister, if you remember. Destroying me would have destroyed her as well." He glances back at me. "Without my provision, Amelia would've been on the streets, or worse, the workhouse."

I shake my head, horrified. "I had no idea."

His face hardens into a haunted mask. "I am not surprised. Your father was a master at his deceitful games."

I bite my lip. I'd known my father to be conniving in his business dealings, but this? It sounds rather extreme, even for one as wily as he. I lock gazes with Edmund. "And if you left—which you did—what did you gain?"

He snorts, clearly disgusted. "You make it sound so easy, like part of my heart, my soul, wasn't lost in the bargain." His nostrils flare. His jaw clenches. And for some odd reason, this difficulty in telling me the truth endears him to me all the more.

"I gained the promise of your father that your happiness and prosperity would be ensured by your marriage to a member of Parliament, but apparently your father was the biggest winner. He gained legislation opportunities that benefited his pocket."

My blood drains to my feet, and I sway. Edmund bolsters me up with a grip to my arm.

"Are you saying"—the words quake out of me—"that my father married me to that monster for his own benefit?"

Oceans of pity swell in Edmund's blue eyes. "As I said, I never would have left you had I known."

I pull away from his touch. "And you? How did Father reward you?"

"You're standing in the midst of what I gained. Forty-nine percent owner-ship of Nottingham Lace and a yearly stipend for my sister until she married. There you have it. All of it. The whole sordid truth. I don't blame you if you hate me now more than ever. God knows I deserve it."

He's right. Hatred does nip its fangs into my heart, not for Edmund, but for a father who should've protected instead of exploited his only daughter. Tears well and the world turns watery, but I fight to hold the tears back as I peer up at Edmund. "As much as I have wanted to, I have never hated you. Not once."

His brow folds, and emotions too many to name flash in his eyes. The hum of the factory yard fills in his silence until finally he speaks. "Your words tempt me to hope."

I shake my head. Perhaps he truly had loved me once, but surely that faded when he took to wife another woman.

"You married," I accuse.

"I did, yet it turns out I was duped every bit as much as you." A shadow darkens his face. "Catherine was not the person she led me to believe before we wed and was nearly the downfall of me and my business. It is a mercy in more ways than one that she did not suffer long before succumbing to a fever. As cruel as it is to speak such words, I daresay Flora and I are better off without her." He turns on his heel, abruptly ending the conversation. "There is an issue with a boiler I must attend," he clips out.

Stunned by his candid revelation about his wife, I stand mute, watching the back of his coat. How different might life have been had we bucked conformity and married all those years ago.

The next gust of wind shivers through me, shaking me from what-ifs and could-have-beens and reminding me of my mission for the blind women. I scurry to catch up with Edmund and stop him with a touch to his shoulder just before he opens the door to the factory. "One more moment, please. There is a matter, not of personal nature, that I wish to address, something that will increase quality for a minimal amount of output."

Slowly, he turns back. "Careful. You're starting to sound like a businesswoman."

I smile. He can have no idea the yearning those words feed. "I shall take that as a compliment."

He humphs. "So what is this matter?"

"The blind women who beg outside the Old Lace Shop, I think we can use them. Actually, they could benefit all the lacemakers hereabouts."

His mouth twitches, not quite a smirk, but enough to reveal his skepticism. "You've said it yourself. The women are blind. How can they possibly be of use?"

"Their sight is gone, but their skills are not. Look at this." I hold up my lacy sleeve hem for him to examine.

Scowling, he glances at the offering. "I don't understand."

"There is a flaw, one I'd not detected, but Hester's nimble fingers did."

He bends closer, his blue eyes travelling the fine lines of the piece until finally he breathes out a small *ahh*. "What has this to do with anything?"

I lower my arm. "I propose we hire those women for quality control, obviously for only the most important orders, and set them up in a room of their own."

"No." He shakes his head.

"But you've not heard me out."

His jaw firms, and he scowls. "I believe I made myself more than clear when we discussed the receiving room several weeks back. The buildings have not grown since then. I cannot spare one more square foot for another of your improvement ideas."

"What about the old warehouse over there?" I point across the yard at the only building where no workers buzz about.

Edmund sighs. "It's not a warehouse. Those are former sorting rooms that have been unused for years. It wouldn't be a safe place to bring you, let alone elderly women with no sight."

"Couldn't you—"

"No. It's too decrepit, and there is no extra money to refashion the space. I'm debating if I can even use it for storage without endangering somebody's life."

I blow out a long breath. Being the majority owner, I could simply order him to acquiesce, but given the fact that he knows these buildings and grounds more intimately than me, I feel I must bow to his wisdom.

But that doesn't mean I'll give up so easily.

I look him square in the eyes. "There must be some small space in which to house five old women. They could offer their services to any and all, and in the process, generate income to provide for their needs."

"I grant you it is an innovative idea, but. . ." He grabs the back of his neck and kneads a muscle. I know I'm adding to his tension, but it's worth it if it brings the old women out of the cold.

Finally, he lowers his hand and shakes his head. "As much as I want to help you, I cannot. We will have no customers at all if we do not produce the lace in the first place, and lace is not produced by reducing available work space."

His words sink like a rock to my stomach—until a new idea springs up.

Edmund grunts. "I know that look. What are you thinking?"

"The Old Lace Shop, the building." I snap my fingers. "There is plenty of space in there, and it's not in use."

"Because it needs to be pulled down!" A bitter chuckle rumbles out of him. "No, absolutely not. I'll not spare one penny of company money to tear down that pile of bricks and rebuild."

"Fine. Then I'll raise the money myself."

Both our brows lift at my bold words.

"And how do you propose to do that?" he asks.

Exactly. What do I know of soliciting for funds? The next gust of breeze snatches my bonnet ribbons and slaps me in the cheek with them. But the bitter truth is that I've got to do something or those women will be sitting out in the cold. Hester already has a cough. She won't survive a frigid winter. I could easily withdraw money from my husband's estate. . .but no. I will not rely on Mr. White—dead or not—for even one penny. This is something I must do on my own, as much for the women as for myself. Leastwise, I have to try it as a first resort, not a last.

"If I manage to acquire the money and take care of the renovations on my own"—my gaze rises to Edmund's—"will you hire those women for your premium orders?"

A sigh deflates his chest. "If those women are truly as valuable as you say they are, then yes."

"Well then, I'd best get busy."

But busy doing what? I turn lest he see the creasing of my brow. Where does one begin to solicit funding? I know nothing of this undertaking, but I do know this. . .I am more than determined not to use a penny of Mr. White's money for the venture.

This is something I have to do on my own.

Chapter Nine

Bella

The next day, I stand in a receiving room at Adams' Lace Factory on Stoney Street, facing a pug-nosed bulldog of a clerk who sits behind his desk like a hound guarding a bone. He even smells of damp fur.

"Good day." His upper lip curls as he speaks. "How may I help you?"

Though the man admittedly is a pile of muscle on a stool, there is no reason I should be cowed by him. But I am. Years of intimidation are hard to forget—yet this is the course I have plotted and I *will* see it through, on my own terms, and not be ruled by my past. Ever so determined, I clutch my reticule in a ridiculous grasp for courage. "I should like to meet with Mr. Adams, please."

He taps one finger on the desk, keeping time with his words. "Your name and purpose, madam?"

"I am Mrs. White." I toss back my shoulders hoping to impress, for surely the name will mean nothing to the clerk or to his master. "I am come on a matter of charitable opportunity."

The clerk shakes his head, his long jowls swaying with the movement. "Mr. Adams already gives to the church and hasn't the time or resources to entertain anything more."

He reaches for a pen and dips it into an inkwell, dismissing me with the scratching of his nib against the parchment. There are other assorted documents littering the desktop, one of them with sketches of cogs and gears. . .and my interest is piqued when I see *Nottingham Lace* written in the corner. I narrow my eyes. The small text says something about the possibility of being ten times the power of—

The clerk snatches the paper and shoves it in a drawer. "If you do not leave this instant, I shall be forced to contact a constable." He plants both of his meaty hands on the desk and rises. "And so I bid you good day, madam!"

I flinch, and the scar behind my ear throbs. This is not going well. Not at all. Perhaps I ought to try here again another day, preferably one when this disagreeable man is absent. With a last glance at the closed door leading to Mr.

Adams's office, I turn and flee, disappointed but not hopeless. I've learned from this experience. Charity does not gain an audience with a businessman.

The next factory is just down the street, and for a moment, I gawk up at the formidable redbrick structure. It outshines any building I've visited in this part of Nottingham. Inside, the noise is still unbearable and thread dust hangs heavy in the air, but it is a spacious affair. Wide corridors, a receiving room with plush seats—it even sports a settee in front of a coal fire. The clerk here wears a jolly aquamarine cravat and a smile.

He tips his head courteously. "Good morning, madam. How may I be of service to you?"

"Good morning." I step up to his desk, grateful for his greeting. Little creases spread out from his eyes as if he laughs a great deal. At once I am at ease, and the sting is removed from my earlier encounter with Mr. Adams's dreadful clerk. "I request an audience with Mr. Birkin, please."

"Name and purpose?"

"I am Mrs. White." I flounder. Charity doesn't work, but what will? On instinct, I reach for my mother's pearl necklace—and am instantly fortified with a new idea. "I have come on a matter of dignity."

"Dignity?" His brows shoot to his receding hairline. "That's a new one."

Pushing back his chair, he rises and crosses over to the frosted glass door separating the master from the masses. After two taps, the clerk pushes the door open wide enough to poke in his head. "There's a Mrs. White to see you, sir. Says it's a matter of dignity."

A low voice rumbles inside, too indistinguishable for me to make out any words.

"Very good, sir."

I press my lips tight. Did that mean very good, the man would see me, or it would be very good to have me dismissed?

The clerk swings the door wide and nods for me to enter. Apparently, dignity is an easier sell than charity.

Mr. Birkin's office smells of cheroots and lemon balm, an interesting combination. The man himself rises from his seat behind his desk and waits until I sit before he lowers to his chair. He is an older fellow. Craggy lines carve into the puffy skin beneath his eyes. His silver-streaked hair is slicked back with pomade—which may account for the citrusy smell in the air—and his mutton-chops splay out wild and bushy near his collar. While fashionably dressed, he seems the sort that wouldn't mind cozying up to a fire and swapping a tale or two over a cup of tea.

I can't help but smile into his warm brown eyes. "Good day, Mr. Birkin. I am Mrs. White."

"Pleased to meet you, madam." His voice is distinctive, somewhat raspy, like the scrape of an old desk drawer that's hard to open. "How may I be of service?"

"I realize you are a busy man, sir, so I will get straight to the point. I am sure you have noticed the plight of the blind women of Nottingham. I feel that helping them is a civic duty and a matter of honour. Granted, helping them all would be an overwhelming and expensive task, but doing nothing is unacceptable. That being said, it is my mission to solicit leading businessmen such as yourself to contribute toward providing a place for five of these women where they might labour to support themselves before winter sets in."

He leans back in his chair, a twinkle in his gaze. "I beg your pardon, madam, but what exactly have these blind women to do with my dignity?"

Hmm. Have I not made myself abundantly clear?

I smooth out a wrinkle in my skirt while searching for the right words. "Being that you are a factory owner yourself, I thought, perhaps, that you might extend some assistance toward those poor souls who were ruined by the business, restoring *their* dignity."

"I see." He sniffs and angles forward in his chair, his brown eyes staring directly into mine. "In your own words, madam, I am a factory owner. I do not run a charity but a business, which I should be tending to now, and so I bid you good day."

Oh, dear. This isn't going at all like planned. I scoot forward in my seat, desperate to make him understand. "This has nothing to do with charity. These women can provide a valuable skill. Their eyes no longer work, but their fingers do, and they are able to find the tiniest of flaws in a piece of lace. I propose you donate money to the renovation of the Old Lace Shop. It's a perfect space for them to take in your finest pieces. With a guarantee of perfection, you can sell that lace for a higher profit."

"Hmm." He reaches for a wooden box on his desk and pulls out a cheroot then rolls the thing between his thumb and forefinger. Is this a stalling tactic? A nervous tic? Or is he truly considering my proposition?

"Tell me, Mrs. White, what of the money I give up front for the renovations? How does that get paid back?"

I blink. Does the fellow have no understanding whatsoever of an endowment? "It doesn't, sir. Such is the nature of a donation."

Lifting the tobacco to his nose, he sniffs along the length of it then levels his gaze at me. "I am sorry, madam. Once again I must repeat, I do not run a charity. Good day."

My lips part, and though I must look like a landed halibut gasping for air, it cannot be helped. How can such harsh sentiment come from such a mild-looking man?

"Excuse me, Mr. Birkin," I try again. "If you would just—"

"I said good day, madam. Bates!"

I jump, surprised at the deep bellow from the grandfatherly fellow. How could I have been so wrong about him?

The clerk pops his head inside the door. "Yes, sir?"

Before Mr. Birkin can respond, I rise. Righteous anger kindles hot in my chest. Will this man of means spare not even one coin? What else can possibly persuade him? Must I throw myself at his feet or—that's it.

"Mr. Birkin," I clip out. "What if you were to be recompensed not by money but by service?"

He lowers his cheroot, interest flickering in his eyes. "How so?"

"I am good with numbers and organization. Perhaps you need a hand with your ledgers? Or I could take a look at your warehouse and suggest ways in which you might better utilize the space. Why, just recently I was able to insti-tute a new receiving room over at Nottingham Lace and Hose, providing a comfortable waiting area to improve customer satisfaction."

"At Archer's place?" His eyes narrow. "What exactly, madam, makes you qualified to offer such services? What could you possibly know of lace manu-facturing and the intricacies of business?"

"As the majority partner at Nottingham Lace and Hose, I have learned—"

"You're a spy!" he bellows. "Of all the bold-faced moves!" Red flares in splotches up his neck as he turns to the clerk. "Haul this snippet of a skirt out of here and see that the gate is locked behind her."

His terrible gaze swings back to me. Gone is the mild-mannered elder, replaced by a fiery-eyed titan. "And you tell that no-account Archer this act of war will be well met."

Chapter Ten

Edmund

B last!"
The ratchety clanking and incessant bang-grinding of the machinery mutes my expletive but not the throbbing in my fingers. I pull back my hand and inspect the knuckles split wide and bleeding, devoured by the bite of the gear teeth on machine number seven. Ever since the pipe stem incident, this beast has acted up something fierce.

"Pardon, sir!" Behind me, Clerk Baggett's voice strains to be heard above the din. "Someone here to see you."

I yank out my handkerchief and growl a response as I wrap my hand. "I can't be bothered now."

"It's Lord Hampton, sir."

Surely I've not heard right. No earl would deign to visit such an industrial part of town. Stooping, I back out of the guts of the machine, and a hank of hair flops down into my eye. With the back of my uninjured hand, I swipe it away along with the sweat on my brow.

Then I turn and face Baggett. "*The* Lord Hampton?"

"One and the same, sir." Baggett's head bobs as if a bolt has loosened. "I took the liberty of seating him in your office."

Interesting. Machine seven will have to wait, for a peer must never be kept caged in an empty office for long—or anywhere else, for that matter.

"Very good, Baggett." I wheel about.

"Hold up!" The clerk's shout pulls me back.

Baggett holds out a handkerchief of his own. "Your brow, sir."

"Thanks." I swipe the cloth over my forehead, and it comes away stained with grease. Mrs. Harnuckle is sure to glower at not one but two ruined handkerchiefs to launder. I tuck the offense into my pocket as I stride down the narrow aisle on the workroom floor.

My suit coat hangs on a peg in the corridor. Thank God I'd thought to remove the thing before I set to work this morning. I brush lint off the shoulders, and as I trot up the stairs to my office, I roll down my shirtsleeves and shove my arms into the coat. A frown weights my brow as I reach for the knob. Blood taints the cloth covering my knuckles. Not a good impression for a businessman. I open the door, hiding my injured hand behind my back and offering the other, which is thankfully my right. "Lord Hampton, sorry to keep you waiting."

The man turns, wafting the scent of bergamot shaving lotion and lots and lots of money. He is my height. The same build and hair colour. But we are nothing alike. This is a man of power, centuries of breeding, and more wealth than I will ever see.

"Not to worry, Mr. Archer." He grasps my hand and gives it a firm shake. "The longer I'm about town, the less time spent in the company of my dear wife's sister, who's come to stay with us for a time. Too long of a time, if you ask me."

I offer the man a small smile that tastes bittersweet. While I never experienced in-laws who chafed, many were the times I spent working long hours to avoid going home to a wife who complained and belittled like none other.

"Please, have a seat." I sweep my arm toward a chair, and while his back is turned, I slide into my own seat behind my desk, grateful to hide my wrapped hand in my lap. "How may I be of service to you?"

"Actually, I'm not sure that you can be." He sniffs. Hopefully he's brought his own handkerchief should he need one. "But I thought to give you a try first."

I tilt my head, beyond curious. "Sounds like a challenge."

"It may be, considering the size of your factory."

"I am intrigued." I truly am. What on earth does the size of Nottingham Lace and Hose have to do with an earl and his whims? I lean back in my chair. "What is your proposition?"

Once again he sniffs. Indeed, he will be in need of a cloth sooner or later. Silently I pray that it is much later.

"My lady wife finds your lace to be of supreme quality, and with her sister in residence, the two of them have conspired to regarb the whole of Warburton House." He reaches into his pocket, produces a white square of cotton, and then sneezes into it.

My shoulders sag with relief at God's faithfulness.

"Pardon." He tucks the cloth away. "Now then, where was I? Ahh…yes. The refashioning. There are fifty-two windows at Warburton House, all suddenly in need of new lace panels, unique yet identical and without flaw. Are you up to the task, Mr. Archer?"

I blink, stunned. An order of this magnitude will give me the edge over Birkin and Adams. I suck in a breath, hoping to keep my voice at an even keel. "Absolutely, my lord. I would count it an honour."

"Very good." He rises. "Have your clerk write up the paperwork and deliver it to my steward; then send someone out for measurements."

I shoot to my feet and scramble to the door, holding it wide for him while keeping my injured hand concealed behind my back. "May I ask when exactly you expect the panels to be delivered?"

"Oh, yes, I suppose I should have made that clear." He claps his hat atop his head. "The curtains must be installed no later than the morning of Christmas Eve. Apparently we are to throw quite the gala on Christmas Day." A shadow darkens his face. "Yet one more conspiracy of my wife and her sister. I can only hope that it will not bring more relatives to reside beneath my roof. Good day, Mr. Archer."

"Good day, my lord."

I close the door behind him then wander back to my desk. Christmas Eve is but ten weeks away. There is thread to order, a pattern to be decided upon, new templates to make. . .and that's just the beginning. I sink into my seat and pull out pages of blank parchment. Dipping the pen into ink, I begin scratching out calculations. Is there enough money to spare to hire another worker or two? Are there enough funds to expedite a shipment of bearing grease? I don't look up until a rap at my door breaks my concentration.

Baggett pokes his head in. "Gramble to see you, sir."

"Gramble?" I frown. "Why is the man not working?"

"It's after six, sir. Quitting bell rang a quarter of an hour ago."

I glance out the window. Sure enough, twilight falls as heavy and thick as the stack of paper I've managed to pile onto my desk. No wonder a headache throbs behind my eyes. I should have lit a lamp long ago.

"Very well. Send him in." I rise and set a cheery flame aglow in the oil lamp on my desk.

"Mr. Archer, sir." Gramble enters, hat in hand, his small eyes appearing all the more like black beads until he steps into the circle of light radiating out from the lamp.

"Gramble." I drop back into my chair. "What brings you here?"

"I been tryin' to have audience with ye, sir, for the past month." He fiddles with the hat in his hand, edging his fingers round and round the brim of it.

"So I've noticed, yet you have a talent for seeking me out at the most inopportune times. What have you to say?"

The man puffs out his chest, and his gaze floats upward, as if he's about to recite a monologue from memory. "I been here nigh on five years now, Mr. Archer, long enough to see my wages increased." His gaze drifts back to me, his eyes narrowing slightly. "Only all's I seen is naught but a mere tuppence extra an hour."

So this is about money. I should've known. It *always* is. Yet judging by the reek of sloe gin and burley tobacco that radiates off him, he'd have significantly more pennies in his pocket if he'd quit drinking and smoking.

I shake my head. "You know as well as the rest of the workers that I offer the fairest wages possible. Most count themselves lucky to be in my employ."

His hat circles faster in his hands. "Be that as it may, sir, I insist upon a raise."

"And so you shall have it. I will give you a raise—in your hours, which, in essence, will increase your earnings."

His hat stops moving. "How's that?"

"Starting tomorrow, the twelve-hour workday shall be increased to fourteen between now and Christmas. That will give you two extra hours' worth of earnings."

"Fourteen hours!" The scar ruining his face deepens to purple. "That's inhuman, that's what."

"Take it or leave it." I shrug. "There are plenty on the street who will gladly fill your space."

His lips twist into a sneer. "Ye'll get yers one day. I'll see to that."

I rise, skewering him with a murderous gaze, and lower my voice to a dangerous growl. "Is that a threat, Mr. Gramble?"

He retreats a step and suddenly finds something very interesting on the floor to study. Cagey man. Only God knows if his repentant stance is genuine.

"No, sir, Mr. Archer. Not a threat," he mumbles. "Not from me."

"Then I bid you good night."

"Good night." He jams his hat atop his head—brim now crushed on one side from where he'd white-knuckled it—and stalks out the door.

I roll up my sleeves with a sigh then follow. It will be a long night.

At the bottom of the stairs, Clerk Baggett turns to me where he's just about to exit the front door. "Good night, sir."

I nod as I pass him on my way to the workroom floor. "It will be if I can get seven back up and running."

And if I can't, fourteen-hour days or not, I'll never make the deadline for Lord Hampton's lace panels.

CHAPTER ELEVEN

Bella

What have I done?

The question bludgeons me as I stand in the middle of a disaster. The Old Lace Shop might have been a grand work space at some point in time, but now? I clench my skirt and pull it higher lest the rat droppings on the floor damage the hem. I ought to have visited here long before I decided to use my own funding and hire Mr. McGreary to renovate the place. But after a week of suffering refusals from nearly every businessman in Nottingham—combined with five solid days of icy rain and nipping winds—I felt I simply must get moving on the matter for the sake of the dear old women who even now are sitting out front, braving October's assault.

Mr. McGreary walks the perimeter of the big room, shaking his head. Courageous man. I am too horrified to move away from the door.

Streaks of sunlight reach in through the cracks of the boarded windows. The creepy contrast of brilliance against shadow is unnerving, especially where it highlights the many spiderwebs. Ceiling timbers hang down like dead men suspended from a gallows. Great chunks of plaster have fallen and broken into powdery bits, and mould blackens what was once white. Many floorboards are missing, and the whole place smells of dampness and death.

This is not at all what I expected.

But when Mr. McGreary completes his circle and stops in front of me, I stand tall and force a pleasant tone to my voice. "Well, sir, what do you think?"

"God's honest truth?" His bushy brows climb high on his forehead. "I think it ought to be torn down, lass."

His verdict echoes what Edmund has told me, and my stomach sinks. Absently, I toy with the pearl at my throat. True, this place is a ruin, but how much more so is the indignity of sitting out on the street, relying on the graces of passersby? No, for the sake of the ladies, I cannot—*will* not—accept Mr. McGreary's dire opinion, and I look him straight in the eye. "Surely removing what is here and rebuilding will take longer, will it not?"

"Aye." He scratches his jaw, his fingers rasping against his grey whiskers. "But as it is, it canna be done in the month ye were hoping."

Drat! Putting off the completion only ensures the women will suffer frigid weather. I peer up at him, almost afraid to ask. "How long, then?"

"Three, maybe four months."

Just then a gust of wind rattles the boards on the windows, strengthening my resolve. "Make it two, and I will pay you extra to have it finished by Christmas Day."

"Oh, I dunno, lass." He glances over his shoulder at the decrepit sight.

Please, God, make him say yes.

Shaking his head, he swings his gaze back to me. "That be a hard order to fill, what with my workers already tied up in finishing the new Birkin warehouse."

I want to stamp my foot and scream at the unfairness of building accommodation for threads and lace when old women are left outside to freeze. My heart squeezes and. . .wait a minute. If I can appeal to this man's heart, perhaps he will find a way to help me.

"Tell me, Mr. McGreary, is your mother still alive?"

"Aye, lass." He nods warily. "By God's great mercy and pure Scot's blood."

"I am glad to hear it, and I have no doubt you are a dutiful son. But can you imagine if she had no one to care for her? If she had to live by her own means? Forgotten, hungry, perhaps even blind, such as the women you saw on your way in here." I edge a step nearer to him and soften my tone. "Would you not do everything within your power to provide your mother with shelter from the cold and a means to support herself?"

A slow smile lifts one side of his mouth, and a chuckle rumbles in his throat. "Yer a shrewd one, lass, I'll give ye that. But I canna come up with extra workers out of thin air, not even for my auld mother."

He's right. Work won't get done without muscle. But as majority owner of a factory, do I not have labourers under my employ that I might lend? After all, this building is part of the lace factory. I don't want to force Edmund or remove workers without his knowledge, for I am woefully aware of how much I have to learn about the business, but I am willing to risk an argument with him over the matter.

"What if I provide two men from the factory to help? Will that be sufficient?"

Once again Mr. McGreary's gaze drifts around the room. "Hardly," he mutters; then he folds his arms and widens his stance. "But I'll do my best for ye—and my dear mother—to see about getting it done."

Victory at last. I can't help but grin. "Thank you, Mr. McGreary. I have full confidence in your capabilities."

I exit, leaving him to figure out what to be done first, but as I cross the threshold, a bark of a cough assaults my ears. At the end of the row of ladies, Hester lifts a scrap of cloth to her mouth. I speed to her side and crouch. "Are you ill?"

She clears her throat once, twice, and then lowers a yellowed handkerchief and lifts her face to me. "Just a bit of a tickle, that's all, missus."

Liar. I'd heard that sort of hack the month before Mr. White died. I could be wrong, and I pray to God that I am as I rummage in my reticule. Bypassing the second-chance coin, I pull out a wrapped ginger drop. I press Hester's fingers around my offering. "Here is a lozenge."

"Thank ye, missus, oh—I've something for you as well." She reaches inside her coat and pulls out a small package. What in the world?

I unfold a parcel that is no bigger than my palm. Inside there is a delicate piece of lace, and I hold it up to examine the intricate pattern in the sunlight. Tiny lords and ladies, the size of a child's fingernail, are part of the lacy pattern. One plays a mandolin. Another a cello. One drinks tea and another sits at a pianoforte. There are embellishments and flowers, whorls and curlicues. I've never seen the likes of it, not even in the finest shops on St. James in London.

"Oh, Hester," I breathe. "This is absolutely stunning. Don't tell me you made this?"

A smile dawns on the old woman's face, and suddenly she is a young maiden again, lovely and carefree. "I did." She turns to the other women. "We were all capable of such beauty at one time, right, girls?"

A chorus of agreement rises.

I rise as well, speaking for all to hear. "And you shall use those talents again, ladies. I am pleased to announce that the Old Lace Shop will soon be put to rights, and Mr. Archer has agreed to hire you on."

"Law!" Hester slaps a hand to her chest. "But we can't see!"

"Ahh, but your fingers can. Remember that flaw you found on my sleeve? Your skills at detecting defects can be used on the most important orders for Nottingham Lace and Hose, which will put our quality far above the rest of the competition. Are you willing?"

Some of the women put their heads together, whispering. Alice's jaw drops. Hester's voice shakes with wonder. "Why, I think I speak for us all when I say yes!"

Dorie, Alice, Anne, and Martha all nod vigorously.

Despite the cool breeze, warmth spreads in my chest. "Then it is settled. The

Old Lace Shop shall open on Christmas Day with a dinner for all, beginning a new year of prosperity for this new business venture."

Hester's mouth pinches for a moment, no doubt struggling with the offer of a free dinner, but how can she refuse a Christmas Day feast?

She can't. Her voice rises above the *clip-clop* of a passing horse and rider. "Glory be!"

The other women join in with their own shouts of cheer.

For the first time in years, the scold of my dead husband raging about how useless I am fades to naught but a whisper. I bow my head, thankful for this opportunity.

Then, rewrapping Hester's lace, I stoop and offer it back. "Thank you for showing me this."

"Weren't showin'." Hester shakes her head. "I were givin',' missus."

"Oh! But this is too precious."

"I want ye to have it, Mrs. White. Ye've given us back our dignity, ye have."

"While I appreciate your kind words, your dignity has nothing whatsoever to do with me. You've had it all along, for you are made in the image of God." The words spilling from my own lips surprise me, and even more astonishing is that I believe them. The short time I've been here, setting up my own household, learning the ways of my own manufacturing business, has been a balm to my battered soul, restoring me in ways I did not realize needed mending. Has God wrought such a miracle in the little over a month that I've been here?

"God bless ye, missus," Hester rasps. Not a cough, but not clear breathing either.

"You as well." I squeeze her hand then straighten and head toward the big gates of the factory. The sooner I speak with Edmund and acquire two labourers to help Mr. McGreary, the sooner Hester and the women will be out of the elements.

CHAPTER TWELVE

Bella

Just past the factory's iron gates, on the wall near the main entrance, a daring tendril of ivy clings to the blackened stone. Red leaves blaze against the cold backdrop. It is a barren place for this plant to have settled its roots, yet here it thrives, amidst workers too busy and indifferent to notice its beauty. I bend and pick a single, vivid leaf, yearning to possess the same sort of resilience.

Inside the main door, Mr. Baggett clips along the corridor. Perfect timing. I smile at the clerk. "Good day, Mr. Baggett. Can you direct me to Mr. Archer?"

He tilts his head down the passageway toward the workroom. "Number seven's acting up again, Mrs. White. He's hard at it, along with Mr. Franklin."

The news sinks like a stone in my belly. Edmund will be in no mood to discuss lending me some workers. The temperamental machine uncages the beast in him. I twirl the leaf between my forefinger and thumb. Resilience indeed.

"Thank you, Mr. Baggett." I give him a sharp nod then head toward the workroom. Bracing myself for the ear-shattering clank-bangity of the monstrous looms, I shove aside the big door and enter a workroom as frenzied as a beehive that's been hit with a large stick. Men, women, children, all buzz about, focused on their labours. Two women spare me barely a glance as I sidestep them and head down the outer aisle.

Ahead, Edmund stands wiping grease off his hands with a rag. Even after all these years and heartaches, the pull of him quickens my steps. The big machine next to him is alive. Gear shafts spinning. Wheels turning. Thread twisting into intricate patterns. I catch Edmund's gaze, and a smile breaks wide and pleasant on his face. Relief fills me. Maybe asking him to part with two workers won't be a problem in light of his obvious triumph over the cantankerous machine.

Without a word—for really, there is no point in trying to converse amidst this clamour—he sweeps out his hand and directs me back the way I came. Once we are both outside the workroom, he shuts the heavy door, and I turn to him. "Congratulations on vanquishing the dragon."

"For today, at any rate." Though the corridor is shadowy, his blue eyes gleam, the twinkle stealing my breath. "I've not seen much of you this past week. I was beginning to wonder if you'd been done in by the ledgers."

"No." I smile. "I believe I've managed to conquer that beast as thoroughly as you have number seven."

"Perhaps it is time, then, that you move on to learn about the workings of the machinery, or at the very least, what machinery we have."

My hands clench. The enormous contraptions on the working floor intimidate me in ways that steal my breath—but I cannot show weakness to my business partner. "You may be right," I concede, "but for now, I am finalizing plans to renovate the Old Lace Shop."

"Ahh, yes. I'd forgotten your latest project." One of his brows rises slightly, an endearing and exceedingly handsome quirk. "So you've raised enough money? I am ashamed to confess I didn't think you'd be able to do it. Well done. Well done, indeed."

His praise scalds my ears, but even more scorching is the admiration deepening the blue in his eyes. My throat closes. There's no way I can admit to him it is primarily by my own funds that the building will be renewed.

"How is it coming along?" The interest in his voice indicts me further.

"Actually," I drawl, desperately trying to ignore my conscience, "that's why I'm here. I've hired a Mr. McGreary to begin renovations, but he is short several workers due to the Birkin warehouse construction. I should like to borrow two factory men to send over to him for the next eight weeks or so."

Edmund shakes his head. "Sorry, but I cannot spare any. Not now."

I press my lips into a thin line of challenge. As majority owner, I don't have to ask him permission before acquiring the workers on my own. But neither do I wish to become the overbearing tyrant my husband was. Compromise seems the best solution. "What about half days, then? If I use four men instead of two, but each for lesser hours and taken from different duties, the loss at the factory should not be felt as keenly. And I only need them until Christmas."

The vein near his temple pulses. Not a good sign. Why is he being so obstinate?

"Allow me to be plain." He rakes his hand through his hair with a sigh. "I've upped the hours here. Every man, woman, and child is putting in fourteen-hour shifts. Even were you to solicit the help of a few men for after hours, I doubt they'd have the stamina."

Fourteen hours? Women *and* children? I suck in a sharp breath, and the ivy leaf I've been clutching drops from my fingers. "That sounds rather inhuman. Why are you driving them so hard?"

His eyes narrow at my accusing tone. "I received an order from Lord Hampton, one that will finally afford the workers increased wages come the new year. It is an opportunity that can make or break us. *All* of us."

I bite my lip, chewing on the information. An order from a peer is an unexpected boon. Lord Hampton could have gone to any of the other businessmen I'd solicited last week, yet he'd come here. This is no small thing.

But my stomach twists at the thought of the workload the women and children must carry. "I understand, I truly do, yet how can you expect them to toil for so long each day?"

"By instituting one of your ideas. Come." He turns down the passageway and motions for me to follow. "I have something to show you."

I hasten after him, mentally riffling through all the suggestions I've shared with him over the past month. The new filing system, perhaps? Or maybe he's provided the hand-finishers with the extra oil lamps I recommended?

He leads me through a door and down a few stairs to a storage room filled with crates. A double-wide opening on the other wall ushers in the cool autumn air, and my jaw drops. In that space, upturned wooden boxes form a serving table of sorts. On the outside, workers shuffle by, receiving steaming cups of tea from one of the errand boys on our side of the crates. Another boy offers a splash of milk from an old porcelain pitcher. The scent of orange pekoe wafts deliciously on a crisp breeze, and warmth flares in my chest.

Edmund turns to me. "This is all made possible by that error you found in the ledgers. The extra funds you discovered—albeit small—were enough to purchase tea and milk. It's not much to give in return for the hours these people work, but hopefully it helps."

I peer up at him, touched at his show of compassion. "You do care for them."

His brow folds, weighted by sorrow and years and too many unspoken hurts I cannot fathom. "I am not the ogre you make me out to be."

Ogre? No. He is many things, this man of foibles and fallibilities, but he is certainly not the same sort of fiend I lived with for eight years. "I own I have harboured unkind thoughts toward you, but never once have I thought of you as such."

"Not even when I left without saying goodbye?"

"Well." My mouth quirks. "Maybe then."

He reaches for my hand and squeezes. "Dare I hope you have forgiven me?"

His bare palm presses against mine. My first urge is to pull away. To run. To hide. An ingrained behaviour after years of Mr. White's harsh touch.

But a secret part of me bids me stay, and the longer I stand there, holding his hand, the more my anxiety fades. Like the starting up of one of the great machines in the workroom, my pulse stutters at first then takes off. It is a queer feeling, forgotten yet not unwelcome, and I cannot stop the smile that curves my lips.

"Does not our God forgive us even to the point of death?" I squeeze his fingers in response. "I can do no less. Besides, we were different people then. Young. Foolish. Let us leave the past behind."

He stands so close, the warmth of his breath brushes across my cheek, and my heart flutters. The space between us charges with prospect.

"To the future, then?" A husky promise lowers his tone.

"To the future," I murmur, a strange hope rising from the ashes of my heart. For the first time, I dare to believe there might just be a future for us. Is this strange convergence of events—Mr. White dying, me choosing to manage a small manufacturing company—a God-given second chance for the love Edmund and I once shared?

Slowly, he lifts my hand and dips his head. It is insane how much I want to feel the press of his lips against my skin.

"Sorry to interrupt, sir. Urgent message." The clerk's voice violates our sacred space.

Edmund wheels about, dropping my hand, and nods at Mr. Baggett while retrieving the offered note. As he scans the paper, the blue of his eyes deepens to a stormy grey sea, quite the contrast to the paling of his face. Something is very wrong.

"What is it?" The question barely makes it past the sick tightening in my throat.

Without a word, he crushes the note in his fist and stalks out the door.

Chapter Thirteen

Edmund

M ove. Fast. Don't think. Just move.
Strange how my legs function when my heart is dead-still—and it may never beat again if I don't reach home at breakneck speed.

"Wait!"

Bella's frantic cry stabs me in the back, but slowing my pace is out of the question.

I shove open the main door and dash across the factory yard to the gate. Time is my enemy. It will be faster to hire a carriage than waste precious minutes harnessing my horse.

Out on the street, I crane my neck, praying to God for a cab. Sunshine breaks through a cloud, blinding me, and I choke back a curse. How dare the sun shine so brilliantly when my world teeters on the edge of blackness?

Oh, God, get me there in time.

Footsteps pound the cobbles behind me. Honeysuckle wafts over my shoulder, followed by Bella's "Edmund, please." Her hand rests on my sleeve, turning me toward her. Worried brown eyes search mine.

"I know something's wrong. Tell me."

Words snarl into a ball in my throat. I cannot bear to speak aloud what I read in the note.

"I will not be put off." The jut of her jaw concurs.

I swallow, fighting against the irrational fear that naming the crisis somehow guarantees a tragic end. "Flora is missing." The words kick me in the gut, stealing my breath.

Bella's too. She gasps. "Gone? But how?"

"I don't know." My hands curl into fists. I want to punch something. *Do* something. But I am useless standing here in the middle of a dirty street while my daughter might even now be crying or bleeding or both.

The *clip-clop* of a horse rounds the corner—harnessed to a cab. I thrust my hand into the air and wave. "Here!"

Bella peppers me with more questions. Each one settles under my skin, prickly and hot. I have no answers, so I busy my hands with retrieving coins to pay for the ride. It is cruel to ignore her, but necessary.

The jarvey stops the coach in front of me, and I offer up the money. "Bright-horn Cottage. Quickly!"

I turn to the door. Bella is already there.

"What are you doing?"

She yanks the door open. "Helping you look for her."

"No." I shake my head. The more people involved in Flora's life, the greater chance the secret of her will be exposed. "You should go home."

She grabs the handle in one hand and her skirt in the other, tossing me a look as she hoists herself up. "Who else is going to help you? Your old butler couldn't hear a child whimpering even with his ear trumpet, and your house-keeper and the nurse both lost track of Flora to begin with."

A sigh rips out of me as she disappears inside the carriage. It is faster to climb up behind her and shut the door than to argue. Besides, she is right. Another set of eyes scanning the woods surrounding the cottage will be a boon.

I settle next to her, and the cab takes off, not fast enough to my liking, though at this point anything short of flying is a snail's pace.

Bella looks over at me, her eyes impossibly wide and shimmering with compassion. "She can't have gone far."

Of course she's right. How much ground can a seven-year-old hobbling on a clubfoot and a crutch truly cover? Even so, I turn my face and stare unseeing out the window. A small brook runs behind the house. If Flora makes it that far, it won't take much—a misplaced stone, a slant in the path—to knock her off balance. She cannot swim.

It is a terrifying prospect.

Rubbing my temple with two fingers, I close my eyes. "I cannot stop think-ing about her being afraid. Lost. Alone."

"Look at me, Edmund." Bella pulls my hand away and wraps both of hers around my fingers. A bold move, one that draws my attention.

"We will find her." Her gaze holds mine. "With God's help, we will."

The fortitude in her stare catches me off guard, and I study her face. The strong line of her jaw. The determined set of her full lips. This is not the same fragile young woman I once knew. This is a lioness, confident in her faith—and more beautiful than ever.

I don't squeeze her hand in return, but neither do I pull away. "Flora hasn't stopped speaking of you, you know. Not since that day you came to the house.

She calls you the 'pretty lady.' I should have listened to her. Why did I not?"

"What do you mean?" Fine lines pull together on her brow. "Listen to her about what?"

"She wanted to see you again. Threatened she'd run off and find you herself if I didn't bring you to her." I shake my head. What a dolt. I should have seen this coming. "But I didn't take her seriously. If Flora gets hurt, it will be my fault."

"Blaming does no good." Pain thickens her voice, and she clears her throat. A slow, wry smile quirks her mouth. "A lesson I learned the hard way."

Guilt upon guilt presses against my chest, a deep ache, crushing my spirit. I failed this woman every bit as much as I've failed my daughter.

I withdraw my hand from hers and once again face the window. Bella whispers prayers, and I hang on to each word like a lifeline. Her faith-filled murmurings give me something else to think on than the hellish image of my broken little girl floating facedown in the water.

The cab finally stops in front of my home, and I jump out, not wanting to spare the time to assist Bella but offering my hand to her anyway. Once her feet land on the gravel, I flip another coin up to the jarvey—for indeed, the driver has made good time—then stalk toward the cottage.

Mrs. Harnuckle flies out the door, wringing a towel in her hands. She stops short in front of me and bows her head. "Oh, Mr. Archer, it's my fault, sir. Nurse asked me to keep an eye on the girl while she used the necessary, but my bread were burning. I tended the oven when I should've been tending Miss Flora." One by one, tears fall from her cheeks and hit the ground. "I'll pack my things at once."

I rest my hand on her shoulder. "No need. You've learned a hard lesson and blaming does no good." I glance over at Bella then jerk my gaze back to the cook, anxious to be out on the hunt for my girl. "Which way did Flora go?"

Mrs. Harnuckle's red-rimmed eyes lift to mine. "The back door were open, sir, so like as not she hied it off to—" A sob rends her voice to a howl.

Bella grabs my sleeve. "To where? Where might Flora be?"

"The river." I take off at a dead run.

My little girl's name rips from my throat as I charge into the woods, my desperate shouts violating the sanctity of the autumn morn. My wild steps churn up leaves—but there is no evidence of any other wide swath of disturbance on the ground. Did Flora come this way? Ten paces later I slow my mad pace. No. The leaves here are markedly undisturbed, untouched by a crutch or a crippled foot.

I turn off the path and bat my way through brush, not that Flora could've managed such a feat, but it is the shortest route to the water. I must see with my own eyes that my girl is not forever trapped grey and lifeless beneath the flow.

I stumble to a stop on the bank. At this time of year, the river runs shallow and murky. A felled tree troubles the waters to my left, but other than that, no broken little body inhabits the water.

Nearby, footsteps rustle through the leaves, followed by Nurse Goodfinch's warble. "Flora! Flora!"

The woman rounds a bend, and I hail her. "Any sign?"

"Nothing, sir." She twitches her head like a nervous bird. "I've searched up and down the banks at least a half mile each way. She can't have gone farther than that."

"Agreed." A scowl weights my brow. "She can't have come this way, then. Let us—"

"Edmund!" Bella's voice—from the direction of the house.

I bolt, leaving Nurse Goodfinch in my wake. I know in my gut that Bella has found something.

As I break through the wood's edge, my knees weaken and I stumble. Bella stands but ten paces away from me, holding hands with a lopsided, smiling girl. I gather Flora in my arms and lift her high, swinging her around, her shrieks and laughter a salve to my soul.

Then I stop and study her sweet face, looking for any hint of scratches or scrapes. "You're not hurt, are you?"

She giggles. "No, Papa. Silly Papa!"

I crush her against me, relief making my arms and legs jittery, and glance over at Bella. "Where did you find her?"

She shrugs and tips her chin. "Sometimes when the world isn't going your way, a girl just needs to hide. I looked where I would've hidden were I a young girl bent on being alone."

Her logic makes no sense to me. "And where might that be?"

"Under her bed, with her kitty and a handful of stolen biscuits."

I tilt back my head and eye Flora. "Is this true?"

Teeth she's not yet grown into gleam white in her huge grin. She unwinds one of her arms and reaches toward Bella. "You brought the pretty lady, Papa!"

I heave a great sigh. How can I be angry with that? "Yes, Flora. I brought the pretty lady."

Indeed. The consequent smile on Bella's face lights the world.

Clutching Flora tightly with one arm, I retrieve her crutch and set her down. Once she's steady, I kneel in front of her, forcing a stern edge to my voice. "Next time you hide under your bed, you must first let Nurse or Cook know, am I understood?"

Flora's grin wavers, but only momentarily. She nods then peers up at Bella. "Will you stay with us now? Forever and ever?"

Heat burns a trail up my neck. I don't dare look at Bella. Instead, I crook my finger beneath Flora's chin and guide her gaze back to me. "No, Flora, Mrs. White cannot live with us. But I think, perhaps, I can persuade her to stay for lunch. Would you like that?"

My little girl squeals. Oh, how easily she is pleased. Would that we all might know such uninhibited joy at naught but a shared bowl of soup.

I press a kiss against Flora's brow then rise and face Bella. "Do you mind?"

"There's nothing I'd like more. Come, Flora." She offers her hand, and the two of them turn and head toward the cottage.

I stare after them, unable to move. Bella's fingers entwine with Flora's, yet she does not tug the girl along nor slow inordinately. She is a gentle encourager with my girl, leading yet allowing the child to hobble along at her own pace. The sight does strange things to my heart. Flora would flourish with a mother's touch. . .with Bella's touch. *I* would flourish beneath Bella's touch.

But after the dismal failure of my last marriage, am I prepared to take another wife?

November

CHAPTER FOURTEEN

Bella

November is a melancholy month, the gloomy space between summer past and Christmas future. Usually it drapes over me like a burial shroud. This year I laugh in its face.

Even now I can't help but smile to myself as the cab rumbles along Nottingham's streets on my way to visit Hester. Since Flora's disappearance, Edmund allows me to attend the girl each week, and my Friday mornings with her have transformed me. Her lopsided grins and joyful disposition are infectious. As the cab rounds a corner, I pray I will be as merry a catalyst of cheer for Hester. According to the blind ladies stationed in front of the Old Lace Shop, the dear woman's cough has landed her in bed.

The cab rolls to a stop, and I collect the basket near my feet. As I step out, my hand rises toward my nose, but I force it to stop midascent and instead tighten my fingers around the pearl resting over my heart. Dung, filth, and despair permeate the air in this part of town. Betty will be none too happy when I arrive home tonight, reeking of the slum.

I enter the narrow throat of a passage that leads to Stranglebeck Alley. The stink is worse in here, and I clutch the basket to my chest, trying not to breathe. Clearly the men of this neighborhood are not familiar with a chamber pot.

The passageway opens into a grim courtyard that easily rivals a London rookery. Squalor lives here. So do rats. A fat grey rodent snuffles along the drainage gutter, not even bothering to look up at my arrival. All my good intentions to bring light to this dark nook of the city slowly dim. Stench or not, I inhale deeply for courage.

Go with me, God.

Rallying, I rap on the first door to my right, thankful Hester does not lodge farther down the row of ramshackle buildings, for that is the route the rat takes.

"Hester?" I rap again.

"Missus?" Hester's voice leaches through the scarred wood. "Come in, child."

I shove open the door and immediately press my lips tight to keep from moaning aloud. Hester lies on a pile of rags in the small passageway next to a shadowy stairway. The only light filters in from a transom window overhead. For the first time, I count Hester's blindness as a blessing. I cannot imagine waking up to such dismal surroundings each day. There is barely enough room for the other residents to pass her by. How many times has she been stepped on or kicked? My sufferings at the hands of Mr. White in a gilded and heated town house pale in comparison.

Heedless of the dirt that is sure to grind into my gown, I kneel on the cold floor next to her and force a jolly tone to my voice. "It is lovely to see you. How are you today?"

"A bit weak." She moistens her lips and pushes up to sit. The air in her lungs rattles from the effort, and her breath is wheezy. I reach out to help her. I'd thought her cough bad enough, but this weakness is far worse.

"Thanks, dearie. I'll be better tomorrow. I'm sure of it."

Brave woman. We both know the odds are against a speedy recovery—or a recovery at all.

I reach for my basket. "I've brought you a cottage loaf and jam, and I'll not hear one word about you refusing it. It's not charity. It's a gift, fair and square, just like you gave me with that exquisite piece of lace. Now then, shall I spread some jam for you?"

She shakes her head, loosening a grimy strand of grey hair that falls forward on her brow. "Not much of an appetite, I'm afraid. Maybe later. But tell me, how are the other ladies? Martha? Dorie? Alice and Anne?"

A small smile ghosts my lips. How like her to ask after the welfare of others when she is the one sorely in need. "They are missing you very much."

"Tell them—" Hester winces and shifts her position. "Tell them I'll be back in no time."

"Oh, Hester." Tears burn my eyes, and I cannot hide the emotion thickening my voice. "You shall come home with me. This instant."

"There now, missus." Hester's fingers search the air and land on my arm, as if to press warmth and strength into me. "This *is* my home. I know it ain't much, but this here patch o' wood and nail is mine, bought with me own pennies, and I won't be leaving it." Her voice quavers with pride and dignity.

But I'll have none of it. This rat hole of a corner at the intersection of a staircase and a corridor isn't fit for a dog, let alone an elderly woman.

"Well," I murmur. "We'll see about that."

Hester cocks her head, angling her ear toward me. "What's that?"

"I said I should see about stowing this bread and jam until your appetite returns. Where shall I put it?"

Her hand lifts from my arm, and she points across the small vestibule, to the dark corner behind the door. "Should be safe over there, missus."

Rising, I cross the space in two steps and set down the basket near the rest of her belongings—a comb missing several teeth, a small amber bottle with a cork, and two broken buttons atop a folded scrap of rag. I turn to bid her farewell, when something shiny catches my eye. Once again I stoop, and with my fingertip, fish out a small piece of metal and glass that has dropped into a crevice between the baseboard and floor.

A tiny oval frame, no bigger than the pad of my thumb, surrounds a finely cut black silhouette of a man. Or it used to be black, I assume. The colour has faded to an ashen grey against a jaundiced background. It might be Hester's, for it is relatively near her things.

I return to her side and press the keepsake into her palm. "Is this yours, by chance?"

Her fingers rub over the offering, and the wrinkles on her face fold as her lips purse. A single, stray tear leaks down her cheek. "Ye've found it!" she breathes out. "And here I thought I'd lost him."

Hundreds of questions bloom in my fertile mind. A lover from years past? Or maybe her husband? "Who is it, Hester?"

"It's my boy, Clarence." She curls over the miniscule portrait like a prayer and kisses the glass.

"You have a son?" The news hits me hard. Why in the world is the man not here, caring for his ailing mother? But guilt tags the heels of that thought. He might very well be deceased.

"Aye, missus. My Clarence has been in America all these years. Probably a right fine gent by now. It's been so long since I've heard from him. When I moved here from Thorneywood and fell on hard times. . . Well, I ain't had the heart to write and tell him. Couldn't afford to, anyway. No, 'tis better he remember me as baking pies in our old sweet cottage."

Slowly, she slumps to the floor and hugs the small picture all the tighter. It is a holy moment, too scandalously pure for me to witness.

Not wishing to intrude any further, I pat the old woman on the shoulder then rise. "Goodbye, Hester," I whisper.

I take care in opening the door and step outside, intent on two orders of business. First, I must inquire with Edmund about any other buildings that might be owned by the factory but are not currently in use. Housing for Hester and perhaps the other blind women is now as important as finishing the Old

Lace Shop for their employ. Secondly, I will dash home and pen an inquiry to Mr. Barlow, enlisting his help as a law clerk to locate Hester's son. With Christmas fast approaching, what a lovely gift it will be to have Clarence visit the dear old woman—

If she lives that long.

CHAPTER FIFTEEN

Edmund

The numbers on the page blur, and I pinch the bridge of my nose. After an hour of mathematical wrangling, perhaps it is time to rest my eyes.

I shove back my chair and stride over to my coat, where it hangs on a hook by the door, just as a rap rattles the wood. If this is Gramble—again—he'll find himself well acquainted with the Stoney Street curbstone, for that is where I intend to throw him. Scowling, I yank open the door, ready to collar the man.

But it is Bella's sweet face that lifts to mine. So does one of her brows as her gaze skims from my ruffled hair to my loosened collar. "Is this a bad time for me to call?"

All the tension of numbers and Gramble eases at the sound of her voice, and my scowl vanishes. "Just leaving off from paperwork. May I buy you a cup of tea? I hear there's none quite like a stout factory brew."

Her lips quirk. "As co-owner of the factory, I suspect I've already paid for it."

"Humour me." I wink and close the door.

Bella falls into step with me as we descend the stairway, and I glance over at her. "Actually, it's quite convenient you stopped by. I received word this morning that there's to be a machinery exhibition in London—remnants of the great Paris showing. And just in time, the way number seven's been acting up. Perhaps I can find a solution by meeting with some of the machinists."

"That would be helpful. And London in December is so festive."

At the bottom of the stairs, she turns to the right without my prompting. It is a small thing she knows the layout of the factory so well, but one that strangely warms my heart. Catherine, my former wife, would have nothing to do with my work, save for scorning it as a scabrous cavern of noisy manufacture.

Bella peers up at me as I join her side. "I'm not sure why you think it's convenient I stopped by, though. While I am happy you are eager to attend, it seems you could have told me the news at any point in time. Today, tomorrow, next week. Would it really have mattered?"

"Indeed, it does if I am to arrange for rail passage and lodging."

"And that concerns me because. . . ?"

With a touch to the small of her back, I guide her to a stop near one of the windows and turn to her. The lighting here is perfect, for I am keen to probe the depths of her eyes when what I propose settles in. I'm still not completely certain this is a wise thing to do, but since opening the letter detailing the exhibition, the idea has taken root and grown.

"I thought, perhaps, you might like to go along with me. . .as my partner."

"You want me to come along?" She rubs behind her ear, like she does every time she is uncertain.

I nod. "I do."

"But. . .I know nothing about the machines or repairing them."

"What better time and place to learn about them? That is. . ." I suddenly hesitate, doubt wriggling into my mind as I remember she is here, not by choice, but by the greed of her husband. "Would you like to learn about them?"

Her gaze locks onto mine, and her nose scrunches, like a child who's been handed a platter of sugarplums and is unsure if she may pick one up and devour it. Slowly, a smile spreads like a dawning sun. "Indeed, I would. How thoughtful."

"Good. Then it is settled." Though I likely look the part of a besotted schoolboy, I can't help but grin back at her. It will be like old times, taking her about London—and the thought sobers me. What am I doing? Surely I cannot rekindle a flame that was doused years ago. We are different people now. Older. Disillusioned. Scarred by unhappy marriages.

My grin fades. "Now then, what was it you came to see me about?"

Golden flecks in her brown eyes gleam. "Must I always need a reason?"

"You usually have one."

A pretty pink blush spreads over her cheeks. "You know me too well, sir."

Not as well as I'd like to. I clench my jaw, trapping the crazy thought behind my teeth.

"But you're right," Bella continues, her fingers nervously working the edge of her beige leather gloves. "I did come with a purpose in mind. I am wondering if there are any more buildings such as the Old Lace Shop that might be reno-vated? The squalor the blind women live in is appalling. I should like to house them in a dormitory."

My gaze drifts out the window at the ring of old buildings surrounding the shipping yard, though it is a moot endeavor. Every available corner is loaded with all the new supplies for Lord Hampton's Christmas order.

"You are already providing the women with a warm and dry place to work." I shift my gaze back to her. "Are you not?"

"Yes, but they need better housing." Her tone rises, as does the colour on her cheeks. "Hester especially!"

With a sigh, I gather her gloved hands in mine and rub my thumbs over the tops. It is a soothing movement, one I've learned calms Flora when she is distraught. "You have a tender heart, and I wish I could help you. But there are no more buildings to lend you the space you'd like. I'm sorry, but you cannot save the world, you know."

A great glower darkens her face, the dimple on her chin frowning at me as well. "Clearly you have a penchant for sheltering and protecting those others would disparage. Why can you not extend me the same charity?"

"Oh? Are you in want of my protection?" My attempt at humour falls as flat as the press of her lips.

"That's not what I mean, and you know it."

Ahh, but she's a beauty when she's fired up, the jut of her jaw, the flare of her nose. I stifle a wicked grin. "Then what do you mean?"

"I want your support. Your backing. Something other than the irritation that I see in your eyes."

"You're wrong." With one firm tug on her hands, I pull her close. "Look again."

As soon as the words pass my lips, I know I've blundered. A breath away, her face lifts to mine, and I am intoxicated. Without thinking, I release her hands and wrap my arms about her. She fits against my body like a second skin, and a need fires deep in my gut to make her flesh of my flesh. It's wrong. Base. Shameful, even. I should release her. Back away. But I cannot pull my gaze off the fullness of her lips, and I am drawn in. Closer. Breathless. Helpless.

The first taste of her is soft and sweet, but when she clings to me, grabbing handfuls of my coat and drawing me tighter against her, something is unleashed. Desire. Hunger. Memories of a love so pure it arcs across time and drives me to kiss her deeper, harder, longer. A tremor runs through me—or her—hard to tell, for we are one. We were always meant to be one.

My lips travel lower, and I whisper her name against the curve of her neck. But when she moans in response, I stiffen. By all that is holy, what am I doing?

Swallowing hard, I set her from me—and just in time. The clip of hurried footsteps rounds the corner of the passageway and closes in on us. I turn, sheltering Bella from whoever it is that approaches. She'll be mortified if anyone suspects what I've just done.

Clerk Baggett, sweat beading his brow, swipes his arm along his forehead as he trots up to me. "You're wanted on the floor, sir."

All the magic of the stolen kiss dissipates, and I shake my head. "Don't tell me."

Baggett shrugs. "Number seven, sir. And Gramble would like a word with you as well."

Seven *and* Gramble? Both the machine and the man are a burr in my side. I stifle a growl. "Very well." With an apology on my tongue, I turn to Bella, but she's gone.

My gaze darts out the window, and yes, green skirts billow toward the gate. A rock thwunks to my gut. Whatever chance we may have had at repairing the past is now ripped wide apart by my rash behaviour.

Two other figures pass by in front of the glass. Gramble's scarred face grins over at a black beetle of a fellow, who's got his arm slung across Gramble's shoulders. For all the world, the stranger appears to be a parasite. A bloodsucker of the worst sort, especially the way he leans his head toward Gramble and conspires about Lord knows what.

I turn back to Baggett and hitch my thumb over my shoulder. "Who is that fellow out there with Gramble?"

Baggett cranes his neck toward the window. "Why, that's your new man, sir." "What new man?"

"Arrived a day or so ago. Something about your recommendation, or maybe it was Mr. Franklin's. Can't be certain." Baggett angles his head, his eyes narrowing. "Is something wrong, sir?"

I glance back at the duo, unable to shake a queer sense of disquiet, and mutter beneath my breath, "I hope not."

December

CHAPTER SIXTEEN

Bella

Across from me, Edmund stares out the train window, and I stare at him, prepared to avert my gaze at the merest hint of him catching me at my game. But after the past fortnight, I am an adept player.

Grey afternoon light brushes soft over his prominent cheekbones, the strong cut of his jaw, the wide line of his lips. As always, his mouth is where my gaze stops, and a familiar warmth settles low in my belly. That one stolen kiss in a loud and dust-filled factory corridor changed everything, opened wide a hunger I hadn't expected to ever feel again—yet it is one I must forget. Though I am still ignorant in the ways of business, I know without doubt we crossed a forbidden line that day, one we are both trying to scramble back across.

And I am failing. Miserably. Every fiber in me wishes for him to pull me into his arms, crush me against his body, kiss me again until I am breathless. Remind and restore in me what a righteous love should be.

The train jerks to a stop. He rises and ushers me out into the cold air of King's Cross Station. People swarm, smelling of damp wool and soot, some boarding trains, others greeting friends and family. A porter juggling one too many portmanteaus rushes past me, too close. The corner of one of the big bags catches me on the hip, knocking me off balance, and my step falters.

Edmund grabs my sleeve and rights me by entwining my arm with his. The flex of his muscles beneath my touch is rock hard.

"Are you hurt?" he asks.

"I am not, thank you." I don't dare peer up at him. He'll see. He'll know. The heat in my cheeks is a dead giveaway of how his nearness affects me. I am no fit business partner. I am a wanton woman unable to keep my emotions in check.

"Edmund, my boy! Is that you?"

A loud voice honks louder than the din on the train platform, and we both turn to see a great goose of a man advancing, flapping his arms as he waddles toward us, a valise in each hand. He narrowly misses whapping a passing child in the head.

He is an odd-looking fellow, with a wiry brush of a beard. Tufts of dark hair cluster on each side of his head, tipping his hat to a rakish angle. His dark eyes are big, his gaze direct, as if he catalogues every minute detail the world has to offer.

"Uncle Charles, what a surprise!" Edmund releases me and embraces him. "I didn't expect to see you here."

"It is fate! Fortune! An amazing quirk in the time and space continuum. Why, just this morning I posted you a letter, and now here you are." His shoulders jiggle with a great laugh. Everything about this man—Edmund's uncle, apparently—is larger than life, though he is fine boned and without an ounce of fat to spare.

His gaze swings to me, so intent that we may as well be alone on the platform, for I doubt he sees or hears the rest of humanity rushing past us.

"Who is this angel? This fairy? This goddess divine?" He drops his bags and, sweeping off his hat with one hand, flourishes an ornate bow.

I blink, speechless.

Thankfully, Edmund fills the gap. "Uncle, allow me to introduce Mrs. Arabella White." He touches the small of my back and speaks into my ear. "This is my uncle, Mr. Charles Dickens."

Dickens? The writer? Ahh. No wonder the man is unorthodox. One would have to be to create such masterful stories.

"Pleased to meet you, sir." I smile, hiding my annoyance with Edmund for never having told me he is related to this icon of literature. "I am very fond of your Christmas ghost story, as is most of London."

"No, no. The pleasure is entirely mine." He reaches for my fingers and presses a light kiss to the back of my hand; then he straightens and sniffs with a dramatic flair. "Just as the aroma of frankincense lingers blessedly upon a holy priest, so shall I forever carry the sweet fragrance of your acquaintance, my dear."

"Th–thank you," I stutter, unsure what else to say. The man is so masterful with words, I suddenly feel like a tot trying to converse with an Oxford scholar.

"Your letter, Uncle?" Once again, Edmund comes to my rescue. "Why did you wish to contact me?"

"Oh, the despair of it all." Blowing out a huge sigh, Mr. Dickens claps his hat back atop his head and turns to Edmund. "There has been a great spiraling down, a cooling of youthful yearnings to ash and dust. Tell me, my boy, how does one revive the beat of an ardent and amorous heart?"

"I am sure I do not know." Edmund pauses as a train whistle blows. "But whatever has happened sounds rather dreadful."

"It is." Mr. Dickens's face folds into great lines of sorrow. "With my writing and public reading schedule, I am afraid I have neglected my poor sparrow, my dearest Kate. I fear she may be headed for yet another nervous collapse. It is my fervent wish to mend the strain in the fabric of our marriage. That is where you come in."

"Me?" Edmund's brows are twin arches.

"Indeed, my boy. How better to return to Kate's good graces than with a Christmas gift of a fine bit of lace? A fancy. A frippery. Something to intrigue and delight the feminine psyche. Would you not agree, Mrs. White?" His penetrating stare darts to me.

"I—" Completely at a loss, I swallow, hoping the action will produce eloquent words, or any words at all. A simple "Yes" is all I manage.

"Well put, madam." He winks then once again faces Edmund. "So, Nephew, I will need your finest. Your best. Your most excellent ornamentation of gossamer thread and wonder. But just a small swath, mind you. Enough for a new fichu, something to reside proud and royal against my lady wife's swanlike neck. I can only hope it will woo her and restore me to a more noble standing in her eyes. Can you have it to me by Christmas Day?"

I bite my lip. With all the machines tied up in meeting Lord Hampton's order, there is no possible way Edmund can say yes to his uncle. And my heart breaks a little over that. Clearly the man is trying to save his marriage. What would it be like to have a husband who actually cherished his wife?

Unbidden, my gaze is drawn to Edmund's handsome face. Could he ever love me like that?

La! What am I thinking? I gasp from the wayward thought and from what comes out of Edmund's mouth.

"Yes, Uncle. I shall have that piece of lace to you by Christmas. I vow it."

I can't help but gape. How on earth will he pull off such a miracle?

Chapter Seventeen

Edmund

What is it with women and their obsession to spend copious amounts of time preening in front of a mirror before facing the public? Bella does not need powders or creams or whatever concoctions females use to make themselves beautiful. Loveliness radiates from her—so much so that since the kiss, I've purposely kept my distance. It isn't safe to be near her, and every time I cannot avoid it, it takes all my strength to keep from kissing her again. The first time was a mistake. One more and she'll surely run away, which would be to Flora's detriment, for my daughter is smitten by her. . . every bit as much as I am.

This partnership is doomed.

I stroll to the far side of the hotel lobby and stop near the mantel, where I pull out my watch and frown at the glass face. Half past nine. What is keeping her?

"Running late, are you?"

A deep voice booms behind me, and I turn. Then tense. My nemesis stands a pace away, huffing like a bull. Though Richard Birkin can be no more than fifty, his lungs wheeze as if he's eighty. The skin below his eyes wrinkles like walnuts, scrunching in layers from his know-it-all smile. Despite the well-tailored suit that rides the lines of his shoulders to perfection, he is a coarse man, all burlap and sandpaper. I know Birkin to be a shrewd opponent, always looking for an edge upon which to stand and leer down at others. But working in the mills since the age of seven will do that to a man.

"I'm surprised you're here." I tuck away my watch and fold my arms. "Were you too busy this summer with your gold medal in Paris that you did not take in the exhibits?"

"Ahh, so you heard about that, did you?" A chuckle rumbles out of him, riffling the lengthy whiskers of his moustache.

It's a struggle to keep from rolling my eyes. All of Nottingham has heard of his manufacturing award and still does. How much does it cost him to continue to run newspaper articles elaborating upon his achievement?

"Indeed." I force a pleasant tone and step aside, allowing him plenty of room to bypass me. "By all means, don't let me keep you."

"Nothing of the sort. Just waiting for Adams, who I daresay will be ready to go before your new associate is." He advances and elbows me. "It's a folly, you know, this partnering with a female. You won't be winning any awards of your own if you keep her on."

So, word has travelled about town. Though truly, it's a wonder it's taken this long. I lift my chin and stare him down. "Mrs. White is doing her best to learn the business, a valiant effort if you ask me, in light of losing her husband."

Birkin sniffs, his broad nose flaring all the wider. "You'll be sorry, Archer. Women are better ornamentations in the home than in a factory, though she is a feisty one, I'll grant you."

I narrow my eyes. "How would you know that?"

"She came to my office, begging for money"— a scowl pulls down his fleshy brow— "or more like she was sent to my factory to do your dirty work. Did you really think I'd fall for the wiles of a sweet smile in a skirt?"

Bella visited this piranha? I shake my head, dumbfounded. "I have no idea what you're talking about."

"That's right. Play the innocent. It was a good try, but a failed one." He pauses as a man in a grey coat clips past us and heads out the front door, leaving behind the scent of far too much bay rum shaving tonic. Birkin pokes me in the shoulder with a podgy finger. "You'll have to work harder than that to get a spy into my factory."

Unfolding my arms, I clasp my hands behind my back. It's either that or punch the smirk off the man's face. "I assure you, sir, I have better things to do than spy on you."

"Ahh, yes." Something glimmers hard and bright in his dark eyes. "Lord Hampton's order, eh?"

My breath catches, so stunning are his words and vivid in my mind is the jaunt of the new factory worker as he'd sidled along with Gramble...something I needs must check into when I return. Is Birkin's accusation of spying naught but a cover-up for his own activities? Is he responsible for planting eyes and ears at Nottingham Lace? For now, I school my face into a mask of indifference. "How would you know about that?"

"I have my ways." Birkin shrugs. "It is strange, though, why you've chosen to come to London when you should be managing production. A bit brassy of you, if you ask me."

My jaw clenches, rock hard.

"Come, come. Why not be done with this rivalry?" He claps me on the back. "Get rid of your lady partner and join Adams and me. The three of us together can put a stranglehold on prices instead of this profit-hindering competition. My new warehouse is ahead of schedule, and there will be space enough for us all to store and mete out lace at will. The bottom line is supply and demand. Strangle the supply now and then, and demand ups the price, benefiting us all."

"All except our buyers, and ultimately the customers who only wish to improve their lot in life by a little bit of finery. No, Birkin. I've told you before, I'm not interested."

"Turning us down again, eh?" Thomas Adams, a scarecrow of a man, gains Birkin's side. "It's your loss, Archer, especially if you cannot make Lord Hampton's order."

Blast! Adams knows of it too, though not surprising. The two are thick as scabs on a pox victim.

"I suppose we shall see about that, hmm?" I reach for my pocket watch once again and flip open the lid, studying the glass face instead of the two manufacturing scoundrels in front of me.

Adams huffs. "Come, Birkin. There's no helping some people."

They stride out the front door. The gust of cold air blasting in from their departure barely cools the anger running hot through my veins.

Snapping shut my watch, I wheel about and stalk from the lobby, intent on pounding at Bella's door to urge her along—but I stop before reaching the stairs. A woman's light laughter rolls out from an open door not far down the corridor to my left—Bella's laughter. Have I seriously been waiting all this time, the exhibition already started, while she partakes of idle chatter with some acquaintance?

I turn down the passageway then stop before entering the room. From this angle, I have a clear view of Bella's back as she converses with a man who clutches a leather messenger bag. Light from the windows glints off his spectacles, so he's likely not seen me. In reflex, I retreat. Surprise, confusion, and not just a little jealousy battles for the upper hand in my mind. Who is this man she meets with alone, and why is she—

"Thank you, Mr. Barlow. With your legal help, I have no doubt I will be victorious."

Bella's words curl out the door and prod me, along with my own rising fury, to hie it back to the lobby. I knew my impulsive kiss had upset her, for such has the awkwardness been between us since, but is she seriously trying to find some way to oust me from my own business because of it?

CHAPTER EIGHTEEN

Bella

Stares. Whispers. I am a skirt amidst suit coats at this exhibition, drawing more attention than most of the machinery. Some women might relish the power of turning men's heads, but I huddle closer to Edmund's side. He spares me a glance but not a word. He's hardly said a thing since leaving the hotel this morning.

The longer we stroll through the aisles of black-iron machinery, the more my good humour fades. Several times I've turned to Edmund to tell him of my conversation with Mr. Barlow and how hopeful the law clerk is to find Hester's son in America. But Edmund is engrossed in the industrial wonders housed in these three large rooms. Perhaps this is what a normal business outing is like, solely focusing on the new innovations in equipment and tools. This is the world of men, after all.

Yet I suspect something more is at play. Storm clouds brew thick and dark in Edmund's gaze. Something is not right.

When we stop near a loom that is soon to be demonstrated, I turn to him before the noise of the machine begins. "Have I done something to offend you?"

He studies me for a moment instead of one of these infernal machines, and I study him right back. His jaw doesn't clench, so he is not angry. There is no tic near his left eye, ruling out irritation. But that is all I can discern, for his handsome features give nothing away.

"What makes you say that?" he asks.

"You have not said more than two words since we left the hotel."

"This is not a ladies' tea. It is an exhibition. I am here to learn, as should you be."

A flash of heat rises up my neck and burns across my cheeks. He is right. What a childish, self-centered woman I am to think his reticence has anything to do with me. We are here on business, nothing more and nothing less.

I offer Edmund a sheepish smile. "It might help if I knew what I was looking at."

"Here, stand in front of me." With a light touch on my arm, he ushers me close to the rope separating the crowd from the large machine. "The demonstration is about to begin. Perhaps the exhibitor's explanation will help."

On the opposite side of the rope, a paunch-bellied man in a leather apron and sleeve protectors wields a long pointing stick. His booming voice rises above the crowd and the click-clacketing of the other machines currently being presented. The tip of his stick points to various parts on the machinery. I fix my gaze to each different assembly and strain to understand. But as the exhibitor goes into detail on dobby mechanisms, cam shedding, and jacquard cards, he might as well be speaking Portuguese.

The man starts the machine, and while it runs, I peek over my shoulder at Edmund. He is wide-eyed, his gaze following the movements of arms and levers and whirling gears. I am not surprised. He understands everything said, comprehends each detail of the moving parts that weave thousands of threads into a gossamer piece of lace. My admiration for him grows—and confidence in myself shrivels. The men here have every right to look at me askance, for I am an imposter. A little girl who's stepped into her dead husband's shoes and pretends to walk tall while woefully shuffling amongst giants.

The exhibitor shuts down the great machine. The crowd disperses. Edmund advances and engages the machinist with all manner of questions and comments. I try to listen, to learn, yet my rumbling stomach distracts, and I press a hand against it. We've been here all day without a bite to eat. Perhaps we might take a short break for some tea? I turn to Edmund and wait for an opening to ask him.

But his gaze is pinned on the man. "How much?"

"Eight hundred pounds."

I gasp. So much? Such an enormous amount could provide housing for all of Nottingham's blind women, not just the five I hope to help.

Edmund doesn't so much as flinch. "Will you take half up front and the other half come the new year?"

My jaw drops. He cannot be serious. Perhaps this is some industry ploy to determine what sorts of financial boundaries apply in different situations. Maybe it's simply an academic pursuit or a bout of mental mathematics.

The exhibitor narrows his eyes at Edmund, as if by stare alone he can sift and measure the reliability of a potential customer. "I suppose that could be arranged, sir, depending on the amount of your collateral."

Edmund doesn't bat an eye. "Nottingham Lace and Hose is my security."

I stiffen. This is no game.

"Ahh, Mr. Archer, is it? Your wares are well known, sir. As such, I think I can safely say that yes, such a restitution can be arranged." The man shoves out his hand.

I barge in front of Edmund, blocking the handshake. "Pardon me." I smile sweetly at the exhibitor then turn to Edmund. "We need to talk about this."

A frown worries his brow. "There is nothing to discuss."

I lean toward him and lower my voice, speaking for him alone. "As majority owner, I say there is."

The earlier storm clouds I'd seen in his gaze now billow to a dark rage, deepening the colour in his eyes to blue black. I've pushed him too far, but so be it. As Edmund's partner, it is only right he hear me out.

He looks past me to the exhibitor. "I shall return shortly."

"Very well, Mr. Archer. You know where to find me."

Without a word, Edmund turns and stalks off. I gather my hem and follow his long legs. My empty stomach churns all the more. This will not be pleasant.

Edmund stops at a cleared space near a wall, and when he faces me, my throat closes. Fury clenches his jaw, and I flinch—but do not retreat. If this were Mr. White, I'd be inching back, hoping he didn't notice my movement. But this is Edmund. He will not strike me. Or so I hope. I rub the old scar. *God, go before me.*

Holding on to that thought, I lift my chin and soften my voice. "I am sorry to have been so high-handed, but it was the only way I could think of to get you to listen to me before spending such a monumental amount."

A deep sigh rushes out of him, and he plows a hand through his hair. "I do not mean to leave you out, but I am used to making snap decisions on my own. Your former husband never questioned me on purchases as long as I provided justification for my actions. And this *is* justified. You know we need to meet Lord Hampton's order. That machine guarantees we will. The speed is unlike anything I have ever seen and that is with two less people to operate it. Why, we can decrease our payroll by cutting several workers and increase production simultaneously."

"But eight hundred pounds!" I shake my head. "You know there is not enough money in the books to provide for that."

"There will be that and more once we fill the earl's order. It is the way of business to take calculated risks."

If this is the way of business, I don't like it. Not at all. The clatter of machinery and low drone of men's voices pound in my head so that I want to scream.

I stifle a groan and splay my hands. "Can you not simply repair machine number seven? I thought you came here to speak with a machinist about just such a possibility."

"I did, but that was before I knew what kind of innovations have been brought to market, and, well. . ." His Adam's apple bobs, and he averts his gaze.

I step closer and wait.

"This machinery. . .I have not seen the likes of some of it. I was not able to attend the *Exposition Universelle* this past summer. Leaving Flora for that long was out of the question. Had I been able to, I would not currently be battling old seven, for I would have purchased a new machine then and there."

His voice is strained. So are the cords on his neck. Telling me this costs him in ways I don't understand.

I reach out a tentative hand and place it lightly on his sleeve. "I am not your enemy in this, truly I am not. All I ask is that you take the time to consider such a large expense before committing to it."

"There is no time!" His gaze darts back to mine. "With seven breaking, we are falling behind on production."

"Then you shall fix it. I know you shall. There is no one better suited to the job."

His lips twist into a wry smirk. "I am not a miracle worker."

"No, but you know the One who is."

"It takes more than faith to fill an order."

No. He is wrong. Without faith, there is nothing, a lesson I have learned the hard way. I press my fingers into his arm, praying to drive home my words. "I may be uneducated in the ways of business, but there is one thing I know. Either your faith will move mountains, or your doubt will create them."

He sucks in an audible breath, and ever so slowly, the rigid lines on his brow ease. "You are a wise woman, Arabella White."

It is my turn to smirk. "Lest you put me on too high a pedestal, you should know I did not understand one word the exhibitor said about that new machine."

A soft chuckle rumbles in his chest, small, but it feels like a great triumph. Perhaps this little talk has smoothed some of the tension between us.

Edmund looks past my shoulder, and something sparks in his eyes. He pulls from my touch. "Excuse me a moment, would you? I see the fellow who might be able to help me with number seven."

"By all means."

He strides away, and I am left as a solitary female island floating amongst a sea of men. I falter, but only until I lift up a prayer.

God, I trust You to help me learn at least one thing about one of these machines.

Then, throwing back my shoulders, I enter the fray. Nearby, another demonstration begins, and despite questioning looks, I make my way to the front of the crowd. Once again, foreign mechanisms clack into motion, but this time, I focus on only one part, not the whole. Thread travels from a spindle to an arm that reaches to grab another thread then pulls back. Quickly. Repeatedly. And slowly, I begin to see that those threads are now joined and grabbed by a different arm to be fused with another thread. The rest of the process is a magical mystery, but no matter. If nothing else, I have witnessed the spawning grounds of a new piece of lace and understand exactly where in this great monstrosity of a machine the whole process begins.

With a new bounce to my step, I continue on. Nearing the end of an aisle, I am faced with either continuing a circle of this room or passing through an open archway into another room. I hesitate, pondering which way to go, when a raspy bass voice snags my attention. I turn toward the somewhat familiar sound. Advancing my way are two figures conferring together—one of which sports bushy side-whiskers, a creased face, and a wide nose. . .Mr. Richard Birkin. Our one and only meeting flashes back to mind, and I whirl, suddenly very interested in seeing the other room. I dash around the corner and flatten against the wall, in case they decide to come this way as well.

In my hasty move, the swirl of my hem snags on a moving part of a machine. I tug the fabric back. It does not release. On the contrary, I watch in horror as inch by inch the equipment pulls in more and more of my gown.

"Miss! Back away from there," the operator growls.

I try. No good. I am no match for at least two tonnes of iron. Pulled irresistibly forward, I stumble a step closer toward the grinding gears. Panic rises up my throat, tasting like acid.

Uncaring if my skirt rips, I bend and yank with all my might—but the big machine will not let me go.

CHAPTER NINETEEN

Edmund

There is no hope. It will be a long, painful death. I should have cut my losses on seven long ago.

I clap the machinist on the back. "Thanks for your information."

"Sorry I couldn't have given you better news, Mr. Archer. Good day."

Wheeling about, I return to the exhibitor who promised me a fair deal on a new machine. Bella won't like it, but so be it. Neither do I like that she's met with a law clerk behind my back, nor that she's not said one word about it all day. She clearly has her secrets. This will be mine. Besides, I cannot fulfill Lord Hampton's order or Uncle Dickens's request with my hands tied—which they will be if I continue to nurse seven along. Even then, there are no guarantees the old dragon will continue to work.

I arrange to have the new machine installed a week from Friday. Seven will be junked and production will speed along. It's the right thing to do. Expedient and necessary.

So why the drag in my step as I set off to find Bella? I can practically hear her cry of opposition when she finds out I made the purchase despite her mis-givings. Hold on—I cock my head. That cry is not my imagination.

It's Bella.

I take off at a dead run, plowing through suits, pushing my way toward the sound. Fury pumps hotter with each step. God help the man who dares accost her.

Ahead, a few men huddle, and as I draw closer, my blood turns to ice. Bella fights with a machine—and it is winning. She bends, tugging in a frenzy on a skirt that's slowly being mangled between two gears. Much closer and it won't be only fabric that is ripped and pulverized.

God, no!

The two men nearest her stand immobile, doing nothing but slack-jawed staring. Worthless cowards! The exhibitor dashes toward the off switch on the far end of the machine, but judging by the distance, he won't make it before

Bella's flesh is snagged into the gnashing iron teeth.

God, give me strength.

I butt one of the men with my shoulder, knocking him out of the way, then lunge for Bella. Wrapping my arms tight around her, I tackle her. Fabric rips. We crash to the ground, Bella still in my embrace. She is safe. Thank God, she is safe!

"That's why women don't belong here," one of the spineless onlookers drawls.

"Skirts ought to stay in the home, eh?" rumbles the other. "Though can't say I mind looking at those shapely legs."

I ease Bella from me then shoot to my feet and level a malignant glower at the men. "Shove off."

Turning my back to the hecklers, I block Bella from any further untoward gazes, and lift her to her feet. The left side of her skirt is missing, nothing but ragged threads hang from her thigh on down. Indeed, the men were right. Her stockinged leg curves in all the right places.

I've got to get her out of this lion's den.

I shrug out of my suit coat and wrap it around her waist. It's the best I can do for now. Through it all she stands silent, face pale, eyes impossibly large and welling with tears. She doesn't appear to be injured, but all the same I ask, "Are you hurt?"

Fine white teeth bite her lower lip, a failed attempt to stop it from quivering, but thankfully, she shakes her head.

I breathe out relief. "I am happy to hear it."

Behind us, the exhibitor lets loose a barrage of colourful curses. Though I wince to have Bella witness such language, I don't blame him. It will take quite some time to disengage the fabric from the machine—time he could use in attracting new buyers.

Bella peers up at me, and a single, fat tear slides down her cheek. "I am sorry. So, so sorry."

"There, now. All is well. Chin up." I crook my finger and physically lift her chin. With my other hand, I brush away the dampness on her face. I am well practiced at drying Flora's tears, but the feel of Bella's warm skin beneath my touch twinges deep and low in my belly.

I pull back, wary of the desire she never fails to excite, then notice the eyes of passing businessmen. Gleams of interest flare in their gazes. Though I've done my best at covering her exposure, a suit coat only drapes so far.

I offer Bella my arm. "Let's get you back to the hotel, shall we?"

She says nothing, but her fingers rest lightly on my sleeve. I huddle close to the torn side of her gown all the way to the coat check. After retrieving her wrap, I help her into the woolen length of it. "Good thing you wore your long coat today. I cannot notice a thing."

"You are too kind." She blinks up at me, still pale, and that concerns me.

A little levity is in order, but how long it's been since I've tried to coax a woman to smile. Even so, I force my own small smile and nudge her with my arm. "I have never known a woman yet who did not pine for a reason to buy a new gown, and now you have a good excuse."

"Oh, Edmund." Her voice strangles—the opposite effect I was hoping for. "Thank you, for everything."

"No need to thank me. It is providence I came along when I did." Once again, I offer my arm. "Ready to go?"

She nods, and I shepherd her outside. She is close enough that I hear her soft intake of breath when we step through the door—and no wonder. It is a new world we enter. Gone are the blackened streets and gloom of a city coated in filth. Large flakes of white drift down from the heavens, and the snow gathers in a fluffy layer, forgiving the many sins of soot and grime. Twilight adds contrast to the flurries, as does the glow of a nearby streetlamp, recently lit for the coming night. I must admit, it is an enchanting scene, one that makes a man feel reborn simply by virtue of its freshness.

With renewed vigor in my step, I guide Bella over to the curbstone and crane my neck to spy a cab. There are two. Both are taken. I am tempted to frown—until a waft of smoky roasted chestnuts from a nearby street vendor hits my nose. My stomach rumbles, and I glance down at Bella. "Are you hungry?"

She peers up at me. "Famished."

Sixpence later, we both hold a paper cone filled with blackened chestnuts, cracked open to reveal their creamy yellow filling. I nearly burn my tongue on the first one, but the earthy-sweet flavour is worth it.

"Thank you." Bella blinks. A snowflake hangs from one of her long lashes, a perfectly charming sight, and I smile. I've not forgotten her meeting with the law clerk, but somehow the sting of it doesn't irritate quite as much.

"You are very welcome," I mumble between bites.

"I hope you will forgive me for embarrassing you in there." She nods back at the building. "I am discovering there is more to running a business than simply balancing numbers in a ledger."

She rubs behind her ear, a now familiar gesture—yet it turns my blood cold. Did she hit her head when I drove her to the hard floor yet is too ashamed to admit it? Gently, I pull away her hand and lean close, praying to God I will not see any blood. "Are you hurt?"

She turns her face. "I am fine."

Little liar. With the crook of my finger, I guide her chin back to me and tilt her head. "I insist."

She stands tense beneath my probing, and as I brush back some loose hair and my finger rubs her skin, my muscles begin to clench as well. The curved welt of flesh beneath my touch is no recent injury. It is a scar—one her nervous habit has worn nearly smooth.

Horrified, I drop my hand. "How did that happen?"

A timorous chuckle chirrups in her throat. "Oh, you know. Clumsy me."

No. Not for a minute do I believe she caused such a wound, especially not with the way she averts her eyes. Someone harmed her. Someone she's protecting. . .or is it, perhaps, self-preservation? A way to avoid confronting past hurts?

"Bella." I soften my tone and once again tip her face toward mine. "You cannot heal from that which you will not acknowledge. Who did this to you?"

Tears well in her eyes but do not fall, and emotions rampage inside me at the sight. Would that I could kiss away all her anguish, to flatten whoever dared mar her tender flesh. . .to promise to protect her from ever getting hurt again.

But I stand mute on the slushy street corner, waiting for her to finally open wide a door to her past that she need no longer hide behind.

She clutches her cone of chestnuts so tightly, the paper crinkles. Her voice is crackly as well. "It was. . .it was Mr. White. He—his temper—" She sucks in a breath. "It was a relief when he died."

My heart thuds violently against my ribs. The cad! Though I've had my suspicions all along, this confirms it. The man was a monster. A lucifer. And so was her father for giving her over to such a brute. I clench my teeth, trapping a howl—but when Bella's eyes widen at my reaction, repentance punches me in the gut. She's seen enough rage in her life.

I swallow the burning ember in my throat and rub my knuckle along the swell of her cheek. "I am sorry, *so* sorry, for what you must have endured."

She leans into my touch. "It is over now. Done. I do not dwell on it. Neither should you."

Sweet, brave woman! Every muscle in me yearns to reach out and pull her into my arms, but instinct warns that's a danger—that this desire in me is a danger—for her and for me. No, the best way to protect her is to make the business succeed, give her the means to support herself, and hopefully begin to erase the stain left behind by Mr. White.

I drop my hand and shove the last chestnut into my mouth, then crumple up the paper and toss it into the bin before I face her again. "Well then, I am glad you were not hurt from the machine or my rude rescue. Flora would be devastated were you not to pay her a visit on Friday."

"She is a dear girl." Bella's first smile since the skirt-tearing incident flashes as innocent as the falling snow. In the soft glow of the streetlamp, she is a picture with her now rosy cheeks and a halo of white coating her bonnet.

A memory resurrects, one I thought I'd long since buried. Nine years ago, on a snowy evening just like this, we stood on a street corner, gazing at one another, our stomachs heavy with a holiday dinner and our hearts just as full with love. How young we were. Such dreamers. What would've happened had I grabbed hold of that dream instead of caving beneath the weight of her father's?

Banishing the question, I glance down the street for a hackney. Another one appears—yet again it is already hired.

Bella shivers. No wonder. Cold air is likely creeping up beneath her cloak to her exposed leg. I wrap my arm about her shoulder and pull her close. It's not a socially appropriate position, and if Birkin or Adams comes out and sees us thus, there will be wagging tongues to defend against, but I will not have her taking a chill.

She raises a brow at me. "I am not a fragile flower that you must shelter me so."

"Perhaps I am the one who seeks a wind break." I smirk while keeping my eye on the street, but I know I must give us both something else to think about other than the feel of our bodies pressed so close together. "How is the Old Lace Shop coming along?" I venture. "You never told me how you resolved your lack of men for renovating the building."

"Thankfully, I did not have to. The Birkin warehouse is ahead of schedule, and Mr. McGreary was able to use some of those workers. In fact, things are going so well that all shall be set to rights for the Christmas dinner I intend to hold—oh! I have been so preoccupied, I nearly forgot to invite you." She gazes up at me. "You will come, will you not? You and Flora?"

She can have no idea her question is a grenade, loaded and ready to blow. I tense and look away from the hope on her face, pretending to continue my search for a cab. "You are hosting a dinner at the Old Lace Shop?"

"Yes. The five ladies who will work there have all agreed to attend, which is quite a feat since they have refused my previous overtures. Well, at least I hope and pray Hester will be well enough to attend."

She falls silent, and one by one my muscles loosen. Sweet heavens, that had been a close call.

But then she continues. "I cannot wait for you to see it! In fact, Flora and I have already begun making decorations for the most festive Christmas dinner ever."

Refusing to look at her, I blow out a long breath. "I am sorry, but you know it is impossible for Flora and me to be there."

She pulls away from my side and stands square in front of me, lifting her face to mine. "Surely at Christmas you can allow one small visit."

I shake my head. "It is too risky."

"Were you not just telling me earlier today that one must take calculated risks?"

"That is in business. I will not jeopardize Flora's life."

"But the ladies are blind." She throws out her arms. "They will not see her impediments, and they will love her for who she is on the inside."

"That may be, but it will not prevent other eyes from seeing her. I am her only protection, and I will not fail her. Flora will not be put into an asylum."

"Of course not, not with you as her father. And you are wrong, you know. You are not her only protection. Perhaps it is time you hand that job over to God, hmm? After all, you cannot keep Flora hidden forever."

I turn from her, desperately seeking a cab to escape continuing this conversation. Bella is right, and the knowledge of it hits me like a hammer to the head. Yet I cannot blame her for speaking aloud the heinous words that I've been trying to ignore these past seven years. . .I cannot keep Flora hidden forever.

And that's what worries me.

CHAPTER TWENTY

Bella

A nagging suspicion that I am destined to fail at business follows me home from London. So does the snow. All of Nottingham lies tucked beneath a mantle of white, which is beautiful, but not quite as breathtaking as the view from the mullioned front window at Edmund's cottage.

Sitting with Flora, we make decorations for Christmas dinner, which is only two weeks away. Thus far, Flora and I have constructed orange pomander balls, ivy ribbons, and lace ornaments during my visits, which are now more frequent since Edmund's time is overstretched at the factory. Today, we work on a fruit-and-nut garland, and I hold out my hand, waiting for the girl to pass me another raisin.

She crams five into her mouth before offering me one. Her nurse will surely not be happy with me for allowing Flora so many treats. But when she murmurs a happy "Mmm" and lifts her face to the ceiling, supremely content, the thought of Nurse's frown doesn't matter. Should not such small ecstasies be allowed during the holiday season? Or for this overly sheltered little girl, any time at all?

I stab the needle into the gummy dried fruit, pull the thread through, and tie it off. "There now." I set down the needle. "Would you like to—"

"Yes, sing it!" Flora bounces on her seat, her brown ringlets bobbing against her collar. A lopsided smile spreads wide and toothy. "Sing again!"

Though singing was not what I'd been about to suggest, I cannot help but grin along with her. She is easily amused with my poor rhymes and asks for them frequently. I am helpless to deny such a passionate request, and so I begin: "Come holly, and ivy, and friends, and good cheer."

Flora sways in time with the meter.

"For Christmas is coming, the best time of year!"

"Yay!" She claps her hands and laughs, the warmth of which thaws the thin cracks in my soul. How I wish I could bottle up the child's laughter and carry it around with me, opening it now and then for a draught of joy when needed.

"Shall we have a look at our garland?" Bit by bit, I hold up parts of the long string, inspecting the line for any misplaced gaps between nuts and fruit.

"Pretty," Flora breathes out, hushed and hallowed—and the reverence of it shames me. Would that I might be as awestruck in worship when gazing upon the beauty of the Lord. Oh, how much this uninhibited child inspires me simply with her zest for life. It is cruel to keep her from inspiring others. Why does Edmund not see that?

"How festive Christmas dinner will be with the decorations we have made, and all because of you." I tap Flora on the nose. "Now, will you help me gather this long snake and put it into the basket?"

"Pretty snake, pretty snake," she singsongs while we tuck away the length of the garland.

We are just about finished when Nurse sweeps through the door then hesitates when barely a few steps inside the room. The lines on her face soften and a small "oh" coos out of her mouth. "If only Mrs. Archer had shown half as much care," she breathes.

My ears perk. This could be my chance to discover more about Edmund's previous wife. Lord knows I shall never hear about her from him, for no matter how awful his marriage had been, he is far too gallant to dredge up ugliness.

With Flora occupied, I meet the nurse's gaze. "You knew Mrs. Archer?"

"Aye." A faraway light fills her eyes as she nods. "I was hired shortly after little Flora arrived in this world. Such a beautiful girl—despite what her mother said." Nurse's brows draw into an angry line. "Thank God Mr. Archer didn't listen to her. Imagine! Sending off your own babe to an asylum. The woman could no more stop badgering him about that than she could leave off telling him how to run his business. She were such a scold. Such a—oh!" Nurse's face blanches to the colour of a freshly boiled sheet. "Forgive me, missus. It's not my place to. . ."

Her head hangs. And no wonder. One word from me about her passionate slip and Edmund will send her packing.

Hoping to restore the woman's dignity, I avert my gaze. "Apology accepted. Your words will go no further than my ears."

"Thank you, missus." Nurse clears her throat, and the spunk returns to her voice. "Come, Flora. It is time for your dinner."

Without even looking at the woman, Flora shakes her head. "Not hungry."

Oh, dear. I refuse to look at the nurse as well. The colour warming my cheeks is surely a giveaway of my guilt for ruining Flora's appetite. Perhaps I should've gone with a pine centerpiece today and done the garland on my own—yet I cannot help but be thankful the error has provided me with a better understanding of Edmund's past.

Nurse's shoes clip against the floor. "Come, child. Cook's made your favorites, pork pie and a jam roly-poly."

Flora tucks her head, curling into the smallest possible ball on her chair—and it's all my fault.

Gathering my skirt, I kneel and ply Flora's hands from her face. "Be a good girl, and do as your nurse asks, hmm?"

Flora's brows pull into a defiant line, a sure sign I've overstayed my visit. The four tolling chimes on the mantel clock agree.

"I don't want to eat." Flora pushes out her lower lip. "I want to stay here with you."

"But I am leaving now, my sweet. I shall return, I promise."

She lurches forward, wrapping her arms tight around me and pressing her cheek to my breast. "I wish you could stay here forever and ever."

I swallow back emotion, the heart I once thought dead and buried from Mr. White's abuse now impossibly full. The child clinging to me is life and love and heaven-sent. I press a kiss to the crown of her head. "I wish it too, love."

Flora pops up, her skull narrowly missing cracking against my chin, and flutters on her chair. "Tell Papa! He'll make it so."

Nurse frowns.

I laugh. "It is not that easy, darling."

"But Papa loves you!"

"Flora!" Nurse barks the child's name and marches to Flora's side. "You will come with me this instant." She pulls the girl to her feet, balancing a flailing Flora as she grabs the crutch leaned up against the table.

I can only stare, stunned by Flora's childish announcement. My pulse thrums in my ears. Though her words are merely the nonsense of a young girl, a strange desperation expands in my chest until I can hardly breathe. I wish it to be true.

I wish Edmund *did* love me.

"Beg your pardon, Mrs. White," Nurse calls over her shoulder while struggling to keep hold of the wriggling child. "Flora's a bit unpredictable but will be right as rain by your next visit. Cook's put a basket of dinner for Mr. Archer by the door, if you wouldn't mind delivering it?"

"I will be happy to. Good day, and to you as well, Flora."

I doubt she hears me above her sobbing. She and the nurse disappear out the door, and as I gather my things and Edmund's basket, I try to collect my crazed emotions as well. What a silly-heart I've become. Despite a well-placed kiss in a factory corridor, I am Edmund's business partner—and it is best I remember that.

Outside, the carriage I hired earlier awaits. The ruddy-skinned jarvey lends me a hand, and as we set off for town, I focus on the passing snowy wonderland instead of my jumbled thoughts. Tree shadows stretch long in the waning daylight, and the deepening blue light of the coming evening is soothing. By the time we near the factory, I am once again composed—until the carriage stops unexpectedly. The driver leaves his seat and paces to the front of the horse. What in the world?

I venture out to where the man crouches and inspects the horse's hoof. "Is there a problem?"

"I hate to say it, but aye, miss." He sets down the hoof and rises, facing me. "It appears Nelly here threw a shoe. Beg your pardon, I truly do, but I can't take you any farther."

"I see. Well, I am only a few blocks from—"

Wicked laughter and taunting voices erupt behind us. We both turn. Just off the side of the road, in a narrow gap between buildings, boys gather like a murder of ravens. Some throw balls of dirty snow laced with gravel. Others hurl awful obscenities. A few heft bricks.

"Take that, ye scoff-faced devil!"

"Freak of nature. You don't belong on the streets."

"Better you weren't born, a great snail-back like you!"

"Wither arm. Blither man. Crawl back in yer hidey hole!"

The object of their scorn moans. Between breaches in the boys' semicircle, a lump of rags rises, trying to stagger off. He is a hunchbacked man with one arm and leg shorter than the other. But his movement only froths the attackers into more of a frenzy. A brick catches him on the brow, and his head jerks aside.

I clutch my hands to my belly, my heart sinking. Ugly memories rush up like bile, and suddenly I am once more the one cowering before my husband's raised hand.

Sucking in a breath, I turn away from the memory and grab the driver's arm. "Do something. Please. Stop them!"

"Ahh, now, miss." He chuckles. "Just boys havin' a bit o' fun. If ol' gnarly Ned doesn't want so much attention, he shouldn't have come out so early. 'Tisn't full dark yet. It's a hard lesson, but one I warrant he'll remember from now on."

Horrified at his callousness, I retreat and grab the two baskets from the cab. Perhaps Edmund is right in keeping Flora well hidden. Too easily can I envision those same boys torturing her, and rage burns a hot trail up to my scalp. Though they outnumber me, I cannot abide such a great injustice. I grip the handles so tight my hands shake, and I whirl from the carriage. If I rush the boys and swing baskets at their heads, it will pull their attention off the defenseless cripple. And once I have gained their notice. . .

Well, I'm not really sure what I'll do then.

CHAPTER TWENTY-ONE

Edmund

After thirty minutes, I've broken four pen nibs and bitten one of my nails to the quick, but no answer rises from the columns of numbers. I wad up the paper on my desk and throw it into the basket. Meeting Lord Hampton's order will be tighter than I like, the last panels for his windows coming off the loom at midnight on the day before Christmas Eve, and that's with the new machine arriving in three days. . .or is it two? I press the heel of my hand against my nose and heave a sigh. Mrs. Harnuckle may be right. Perhaps I am mad with sleep deprivation. Since my return from London, it is all I can do to keep the factory running smoothly fourteen hours a day, with an additional three hours seeing to the proper handling of all that's been produced. Given the extra load, I've had to open the old warehouse to use as storage.

Leaning aside, I pull out the top drawer and retrieve the invoice for the new machine, dated with a delivery of December 14. Two days, then. The tightness in my temples loosens. Sweet mercy, why had I not thought to read this sooner? The arrival of the new loom a day earlier than I remembered means the order will be filled faster than I reckoned. Good news, that. And bad. I've yet to tell Bella of the purchase. The time's never been right, but I've not the luxury of waiting anymore. I shall tell her when next we meet.

I scrub a hand over my face, hoping the action will wipe away some of my weariness, then jump when a rap on my office door startles me.

In peeks Baggett. "Lord Hampton here to see—"

Lord Hampton himself pushes past Baggett and charges into my office. "Niceties are for women."

His cheeks are nipped red from being outside—or is that anger? Judging by the way Baggett vanishes in a flash, I'm guessing the latter.

"My lord, this is a surprise." I rise from my chair. "Please, take a seat. May I offer you—"

"No need, I shall not be staying long." The colour on his face deepens to a murderous shade, and he cuts the air with his hand. "I thought we had a deal, sir."

"We do," I drawl, desperate to figure out what the devil has raised his doubts. Nothing comes to mind.

He advances to my desk and slams his fists on the tabletop, rattling the inkwell. "Listen here, Archer, if you are not going to meet my order in time for Christmas, then be a man and tell me now."

Confusion vies with the fatigue fogging my brain, and I shake my head. "What makes you think I will not?"

Lord Hampton raises his chin and stares down the length of his nose. "I have word that you are down a machine."

"Whose word?"

"Not that it signifies, but my valet's brother is some sort of kin to Mr. Birkin, your competitor. Though he is but a servant, I trust Davis with my life." Hampton straightens and folds his arms like a shield in front of his chest. "There, I have been more than forthright with you. I expect the same courtesy in return."

Heat floods me. *Birkin!* I might've known.

Turning from Hampton, I rake my fingers through my hair and stare out through the production-floor window, my gaze darting from one labourer to the next. Which worker is Birkin's rat? As quickly as my eyes land on the newest worker, I discard the idea. In all the questioning I'd done upon my return from London, my distrust turned out to be naught but miscommunication. For all the man's suspicious appearances, he had been legitimately recommended by Franklin. But if the spy isn't him, then who?

"As I suspected, then," Hampton growls behind me.

I whip back, fueled by a keening rage that Lord Hampton's trust in me has been broken. This time Birkin went too far. "The truth is, my lord, that yes, one of my machines is not operating at optimum performance."

Hampton's upper lip curls. "Then why the blazing fires did you not tell me sooner! I could have—"

I shoot up my hand, blocking further retort. "I assure you I have kept a strict eye on production, and had I any doubts, I would have come to you immediately. The situation with the machine in question is not only soon to be rectified but improved upon. In a mere two days, a new loom is arriving, one that works at twice the speed." I snatch the invoice and hold it out. "Would you care to see the proof?"

Hampton's blue eyes drift to the paper then back to me. "Are you saying my concerns are unfounded?"

The question is a loaded pistol pointed straight at my head. If I say the man was in the wrong, he will be offended. Yet affirming his concerns as valid will only heighten his doubt. There is no safe ground on which to stand.

So I widen my stance and drop the paper onto my desk, praying to God for the right amount of candor and humility. "I admit there was an element of truth to your trepidation, but it was not the full truth. You did right in coming here; yet as you see, there is naught to be agitated about. Barring an act of God, there is nothing that will keep me from meeting your order."

"Well," he gruffs. It's more of a coughing sound than a word, but the lines on his face visibly soften. "Very good, then," he mumbles. "Carry on."

Lord Hampton bobs his head in a curt nod then pivots.

But before he can exit, I step to the front of my desk. "Pardon me, my lord, but I have a small request."

He turns back, one brow arched. "Which is?"

"I would appreciate if you would keep to yourself the information about my new machine. I have not yet told my workers of the arrival, and several will not be happy about it, for they will lose their jobs."

His brow sinks to a dip. "Why not tell them now?"

"Remember the Bankside riot?" It's a moot question, for he must. Everyone in a twenty-mile radius heard of it. It's a devious query, yet I ask him anyway, hoping the question brings to mind bloody images.

"An ugly affair," he growls, his big head bobbing.

"Indeed. The mistake made by Bankside was in allowing those he was going to let go to continue working after he told them. Those men spread their unrest and all manner of lies to the others. Bankside did not stand a chance." I advance a step, meeting Hampton's gaze. "It will be a blow to the two I must let go, for they need the money, and so I intend to keep them on as long as possible. But the morning that machine arrives, they will be barred from the factory. Once production increases, *if* all goes well, I hope to hire them back within a few months' time."

Hampton rears back his head. "You are an astute businessman, Archer. Forgive me for ever doubting you."

"I take no offense, my lord. As you well know, business is an exacting master and not for the faint of heart. You were right to question."

"Good man." He nods. "And good day."

Lord Hampton breezes out of my office, leaving behind a waft of bergamot. I blow out a long, low breath. That was a close call.

Mind whirring, I stride back to the production-floor window to make sure seven is still running. Gramble stands to the side of it, arms folded and head bent as if he's monitoring the swing arm. I know better, the slackard. Is he Birkin's spy? I choke on the thought and cough aloud. No. Gramble is many things—lazy, dissolute, all bluster and blowsy—but I do not think him savvy enough to pull off such espionage, nor do I believe him or his family adequately upstanding to be related to Lord Hampton's valet. Besides which, Gramble wouldn't want his job to end, which is what would happen if Hampton pulled his order. No, it must be someone else.

Once again my thoughts turn toward the new man, hired so recently by Franklin. Was Franklin thorough in checking the man's references? I knead a muscle at the back of my neck, entertaining the possibility—but what am I thinking? Of course Franklin was thorough. I am wasting time with such doubts.

I turn from the window and stalk out the door, keen on locating my foreman. He's not got the time to spare either, but between the two of us, perhaps we can uncover the culprit.

Before any more of my trade secrets are laid bare.

CHAPTER TWENTY-TWO

Bella

Thank God for constables, and I say as much to the officer in the long black coat who escorts me to the factory gates. Had he not come along and chased off the boys before I rushed at them like a ruffled rooster, who knows what would've happened?

"Here ye be, miss. Good day to ye." He tips his hat and strolls away, the baton attached to his belt swinging with his long strides.

I enter the yard and head for the main building, scurrying past one of the errand boys who lights the outdoor lanterns, staving off the gathering darkness. Though I try to dismiss my unease, the violence I witnessed back on the street still troubles me. How I wish I could help that hunchbacked soul dressed in rags and cursed to venture into public only when covered by the cloak of night.

"You cannot save the world, you know."

Edmund's admonition barrels back from weeks ago, and I grip the railing as I ascend to his office. He is right. I am not God. So why do I continually try to be? Shame flashes heat up my neck.

Oh, Lord, forgive me for dashing headlong into things, trying to right what is rightfully Yours to govern. Bless that crippled man with Your protection, for You are a far better guardian than I could ever hope to be.

A new lightness quickens my steps. I don't know for sure the old fellow will never again meet with such cruel taunting, but I do know that God is good and I may safely trust in His provision, for has He not saved me out of affliction time and time again?

I set down my basket containing the garland and rap on the door to Edmund's office. Just like the first week—which seems a lifetime ago now—there is no answer.

I knock once more. "Edmund?"

Nothing.

I purse my lips. Traipsing through the whole of the factory in search of him does not appeal, yet he surely must be hungry and in need of the dinner I've brought. Perhaps the foreman, Mr. Franklin, knows of his whereabouts, or— La! Silly me. More than likely Edmund is wrestling with machine number seven, and there's no better way to find out than to peer over the entire production floor from the window in his office.

I reach for the knob and open the door, keeping it wide so that a swath of light from the corridor shines inside. I cross to the big glass window and peer out at a winter wonderland. Thread dust hovers in the air, made all the more magical by the light of the glass-globed lamps.

My gaze shoots to seven first. The hulk sits idle, but Edmund is not elbow deep into it. All over the great floor workers scurry about, but I turn my face toward a huddle near the door—the only ones who are not moving—and am rewarded. Edmund converses with Mr. Franklin. The scarfaced Mr. Gramble is anchored near their elbows. This won't be as difficult as I thought.

On my way out of the office, I swing Edmund's dinner basket atop his desk. There is no need to lug it with me. A paper catches a breeze from the basket's movement and flutters to the floor. I snatch the thing up, intending to put it back, when a large sum printed at the bottom of the page, along with the words *Half Due upon Arrival*, catches my attention.

Lifting the invoice closer, I frown while I read. Understanding creeps into the dark corners of my heart where fury hides, rousing the beast, and a great ugly glower weights my brow. This is not to be borne!

I clutch the paper and fly from the office. The factory walls blur as I steam ahead and charge through the production-room door. Edmund turns toward my arrival, but my throat is so tight all I can do is growl, the sound of which is lost in the noise of the clackety machines. How dare he gaze so innocently at me when all along he knows what he's done?

He angles his head, his blue eyes studying me. "What is wrong?"

"This!" I thrust the invoice up to his face. The pounding of my heart rises. So does my voice. "You went behind my back and bought the machine! How could you?"

Before I draw another breath, he grabs hold of the upper part of my arm and hustles me off the production floor and into the bowels of a corridor. He doesn't stop until we are well beyond the door; then he shoves his face barely an inch from mine. "You little fool. Your lack of discretion could be our ruin."

"If ruin comes, it is not by my hand!" I wrench from his grasp, shaking with fury. "You are the one who moved ahead on a purchase without consulting your majority partner. I daresay Mr. White would have had your head on a platter, as should I."

His eyes deepen to blue black, and the line of his jaw hardens. He is deathly quiet. Though everything inside me screams to flinch, to run away, to hide as I did whenever Mr. White looked at me so, I plant my feet and lift my chin. I am in the right, and here will I stand.

Edmund closes his eyes and, ever so slowly, inhales deeply before blowing it out, long and low. Several times. When he next opens his eyes, I hardly recognize the man staring out. Weariness lives behind the blue. The kind that's tired of life. The kind I know so well.

"You are right," he murmurs then clears his throat. "I should have spoken to you first. To be fair, I have meant to discuss the purchase with you all along, but I have been so consumed with meeting the Christmas deadline for Lord Hampton there has not been a good time."

His excuse rings true. I see it in the lines crisscrossing his face. I lower my hand and take a step back. "You have been rather preoccupied."

"Obsessed, more like it, though for good reason." A sheepish smile lifts his lips, and the fatigue in his gaze eases. "Even so, can you forgive me?"

The tilt of his head. The veracity in his tone. A schoolboy caught wagering at cards couldn't look more contrite. The rock-hard fury in my heart softens. I reach for my reticule and pull out the coin entrusted to me by Mr. Barlow, finally knowing that this is the right place and time to give it away. I hold it out on my palm.

Curious, Edmund retrieves the bit of gold and holds it at eye level. "What is this?"

"A second-chance coin. When I first considered this venture, my law clerk warned me against it, but seeing my determination, he thought I might need to give a second chance to those around me, especially my new business partner. Turns out he was right." I step closer to Edmund, breathe in his familiar, manly scent, and the rest of my anger melts away. "I forgive you, but please, let there be no more secrets between us."

He clutches the coin and lowers his hand, then peers down at me. "If that is the case, then there are a few more things we should discuss."

My throat tightens, and I swallow down a rising fear. "Such as?"

"Let us start with your law clerk."

My law clerk? Though I know it's unladylike, my nose squinches, for I am at a loss as to what he could possibly mean by this turn of conversation. I shake my head. "I do not understand."

"When we were in London, I saw you speaking with the man before we attended the exhibition."

"Oh, yes. I completely forgot to tell you about that."

His brows lower into a menacing line. "Is it so easy to forget a planned takeover?"

"Takeover? You mean you thought. . ." I shake my head. "Why, I could not manage this factory on my own! I am still learning how one of those confounded machines in there works." I flutter my fingers toward the production-room door. "My meeting with Mr. Barlow had nothing to do with you or the business. I had asked him to find Hester's son, and he told me of a breakthrough in locating the man. That is all."

"Hester?"

"One of the blind women."

"Ahh. . ." Understanding flashes in his eyes. "The one who is ill, yes?"

"Indeed. Though thankfully, she is on the mend."

"I am happy to hear it, and even more happy to hear you are not thinking of buying me out." He winks.

My heart skips a beat in response, and warmth floods through me. I cannot help but grin up at him. "You will not have to worry about that. Ever. I am content to be a mostly silent partner."

He steps close, hardly a breath away, so near the heat of him flushes my cheeks.

"There is no one I would like better to partner with." His voice is husky, laden with promises and desire.

Unbidden, I lean toward him. Will he kiss me again? Every nerve in my body yearns for it. The slightest movement on my part, and I could be in his arms, could get lost in his embrace.

Gracious! What am I thinking?

I suck in a breath and pull back, resisting the urge to fan my heated face. "And the other thing we should discuss?"

"The other. . . ?" He falters for a moment, then glances over his shoulder before answering in a low voice, "From now on, anything business related must be discussed inside my office with the door shut. I have reason to believe Birkin has planted a spy amongst the workers—and he will try everything in his power to keep us from meeting Lord Hampton's order."

Chapter Twenty-Three

Bella

December air stings my cheeks as I step outside the main factory door. Night has fallen in earnest. Large white flakes drop from the heavens, one landing wet on the tip of my nose. I swipe it away with a shudder, yet neither the dark, the chill, nor the snow is to be blamed. Something else is at play. Something indefinable. Elusive. Though I try, I cannot name the unease creeping up my back.

As I scurry toward the gate, I scan the yard. The loading dock stands idle, the last dray of the day having been discharged at least an hour ago. The stillness of it feels like a death, but an empty dock certainly poses no threat. Farther down the yard, the old warehouse sits black against black, its silhouette as forlorn as a widow long forgotten. Not one of the lanterns hung at intervals around the yard stretches to that neglected corner.

All manner of dark shapes and shadows are rife in the silent space, yet no danger resides here. Until morning calls in twelve hours, the hub of activity lies inside the factory. I chide myself for being a skittish filly. Edmund's talk of subterfuge and spies must've crawled into my subconscious and taken up residence in the gothic part of my imagination.

I reach for the latch on the gate, and my hand pauses on the cold metal. I stare at my coat sleeve, unable to shake the feeling that something is behind me. An insane battle wages in my head—rush pell-mell out of here or spin about and face the unknown monster at my back? I stand immobile, giving in to the niggling unrest that caused me to hesitate in the first place.

And that's when it dawns on me. My arm is empty. No basket handle loops over the green wool of my coat. All this caginess for wont of a forgotten basket filled with holiday garland? What a ninny!

I turn, intent on retracing my steps, when a streak of black blurs at the corner of my eye. I snap my gaze toward it and squint. A man darts along the line of buildings, keeping close to the walls, headed toward the old warehouse. Edmund doesn't use that space anymore, so there's no reason for the fellow to go there, especially with such haste. . .unless he's up to no good.

Unless he is a spy.

Keeping my distance, I follow on quiet feet, praying to God my skirts won't rustle overloud.

Too late.

The man wheels about, and I flatten against the wall, hoping the long gutter reaching from roof to ground is enough to block the sight of me from where he stands. It's a small hope, but one I cling to with white knuckles. I strain my ears, prepared to flee at the first sound of footsteps crushing gravel.

All that fills the air is the muted click-clacketing of the looms, a team of horses' hooves clopping on the cobbles outside the factory gates, and the erratic pounding of my heart.

I inch closer to a small crack between gutter and wall. The man still stands looking in my direction, as fixed as a roebuck scenting a hunter. I hold my breath.

Apparently satisfied, he retreats a step before turning away, and that is his mistake. The glow of the lantern on the wall nearest him catches on the ridge of a long scar snaking over his face.

Mr. Gramble. Of course. I've harboured doubts about the man since the day we first met, and he was on hand when I foolishly confronted Edmund about the new machine. Underhanded scoundrel!

He continues his stealthy trek. So do I. Keeping a safe distance, I trail him, fully expecting him to dart into the empty warehouse. What better place for a covert rendezvous with one of Mr. Birkin's collaborators?

I stop and watch—but Mr. Gramble bypasses the dark building and slips around the corner of it. Should I follow into such a black abyss or return for Edmund? Either way, other than an uncharitable disposition toward the man, I have no proof Mr. Gramble is up to no good. Perhaps he simply seeks privacy to relieve himself.

Undecided what to do, I remain, watching, wondering if he will soon reappear—when footsteps and a low voice travel out from a darkened alcove twenty or so paces to my left.

"Birkin's, the biggest house on the hill. You know it?"

"Aye."

"Then repeat it, boy, so I know you've got it right."

"I'm to go to Mr. Birkin's rear door, ask for the valet, and tell him of a new machine that's to arrive by—"

Hearing more than enough to condemn, I whirl, fury pulsing through my veins. Whoever the spy is, it's not Mr. Gramble.

I snatch the nearest lantern off a hook and storm toward the sound. All I need is one peek on my way past the darkened recess, and I shall fly to the safety of Edmund and let him handle the situation.

A boy-sized shape tears out and plows into me, knocking me akilter. I teeter precariously while the boy skitters off, desperately trying to retain my balance while holding tight to the lantern lest it fall. I barely catch myself and my breath when out steps a man.

"Mrs. White?"

The light in my hand casts macabre shadows upward on the foreman's face, ghoulish and altogether unnerving—and once more I stagger. Mr. Franklin, one of Edmund's most trusted men, is the traitor selling secrets to our competition?

He frowns. "What are you doing out here?"

I inch away, hoping to engage him long enough to gain sufficient space that I may outrun him. "Though it is none of your business, I am looking for a glove that I may have dropped out here earlier today. You have not seen it, have you?"

His gaze darts to my hands, and the lines on his face carve deeper.

My tan kidskins—both of them—are a dead giveaway.

I bolt.

Not soon enough. Fingers dig into my upper arm and yank me backward, hurtling me around. I yelp, but before I can call out, I am relieved of my lantern and the ability to scream. Mr. Franklin's forearm wraps tight around my neck, pinching off my air supply and pinning me tight against his chest, despite my wriggling.

I claw at his sleeve, desperate to breathe. My feet drag over the frozen gravel. I writhe and wrench, but the man is as much iron and steel as the machines he oversees. My lungs burn. My vision fades. And just when I am ready to give in to the foggy void that beckons me to surrender, I am shoved to a cold, hard floor.

Gagging and choking, I roll to all fours, my chest and gut convulsing with the sudden intake of air. Once again I am yanked from behind, this time upward, to my feet, and my arms are pinioned behind me. Rope cuts into my wrists. I'd cry out, but I'm too busy trying to regain my breath.

"Move." Mr. Franklin prods me toward the rickety stairway leading up into thick darkness. Lantern light spills over bundles of cotton stacked in neat rows. It doesn't make sense. Any of this. The warehouse that should be empty. The man who should be loyal. Why was I foolish enough to get myself into this predicament?

The first steps are solid, but the rest are in varying stages of rot. There is no railing, and I stumble. Falling off either side means a broken neck. But the jabs to the small of my back compel me to keep climbing.

"You cannot do this!" The words are hoarse, as burning and ruined as my throat. "When Mr. Archer hears what you've done—"

"I'll be long gone before Archer hears anything." A devilish chuckle raises the hairs on the nape of my neck. What exactly does he intend to do with me?

Three stairs from the top, wood splinters, and my shoe goes right through the step. I pitch forward, the urge overwhelmingly strong to flail my arms. Yet I cannot. There is nothing I can do but plummet sideways, until I am jerked upward and thrown to the landing. My chin scuffs along the wooden floor. Pain explodes in my face. And once more I am broken and bleeding at the feet of a man. Will this cruel cycle never end?

Mr. Franklin hauls me up and shoves me through a door into blackness. I know all too well what sins are committed in the dark. I stumble forward and pray.

God, help me.

Will He hear me this time?

I clench every muscle, waiting for the inevitable hot breath against my cheek—when a door slams. The light recedes. I am left alone, trembling, but untouched. My chin drops to my chest.

Thank You, God.

The second my whispered words pass my lips, wood cracks.

I jerk my head up.

Mr. Franklin curses.

A sickening thud hits the warehouse floor below me. Glass shatters.

Then all is quiet.

I rush to the door and holler against the wood. "Mr. Franklin?"

No answer.

"Mr. Franklin!"

I strain to listen for a moan or a groan, for surely he's fallen through the rotted stairs. Again, only silence. I slump against the door, weary, broken, defeated. What will Edmund say when he finds me locked up, incapable of protecting myself let alone the secrets of the trade. I should have gone to him first. What a stupid, *stupid* girl! With a shaky hand, I reach for my mother's necklace. My fingers touch nothing but the feverish skin at my collarbone.

No!

I claw at my bodice, hoping frantically to feel the chain, which was likely broken in the scuffle. *Please let it be tangled in my fichu. Please let it be snagged on a button. Please let it. . .*

My hopes fade. My hands drop. It's gone. Lost. Everything is lost! A sob starts to rise, animalistic, primal—but dies before it passes my lips. I stiffen then press my ear to the wood, praying I am wrong in what I think I might hear. But the longer I listen, the more terror steals my breath.

Small crackles. A sharp pop. An increasing unholy whoosh.

Fire.

CHAPTER TWENTY-FOUR

Edmund

What a day. I shove away the uneaten basket of food on my desk, plant my elbows on the hard surface, and drop my head into my hands. For one blessed moment, I breathe. Just breathe. Lord, but I am exhausted. Weary of the long hours, the fight to meet Hampton's order, trying unsuccessfully to balance my time between work and caring for Flora.

But most of all, I am tired of fighting my attraction to Bella. Once again, we'd come far too close to an embrace, a kiss, a promise. Things unseemly for business partners.

My cheeks puff with a sharp breath, and I lean back in the chair. On a whim, I fish the coin from my pocket and hold it up to the lamplight. The edges are jagged. The embossed lines on one side are nearly worn smooth. I rub my thumb over the lettering, the coin warming beneath my skin. How many people before me have held this bit of metal in their hand? Of what crimes have they needed forgiveness? Were they desperate? Grateful? Sinners or saints? Valid questions, all, but not nearly as significant as those rising in me like a prayer. I lift my eyes to the ceiling.

Is this a sign, Lord? Are You giving me a second chance with the woman I can no longer deny that I love?

The banging and clanking of machinery is my only answer. Even were God to send down a lightning bolt with a big *yes* skewered to the end of it, it is impossible for me to pursue her. She is my associate. The majority partner. And there is nothing I can do to make it otherwise. I am not a miracle worker.

"But you know the One who is."

Startled, I freeze as Bella's words from the exposition return in full force. *"Either your faith will move mountains, or your doubt will create them."*

I rub my thumb over the surface of the second-chance coin then set it on the edge of the desk, staring at the thing. Is that my problem? Am I creating a mountain between us because I refuse to trust God to make a way for us?

Before I can follow that thread of thought further, the door bursts open.

Gramble charges in, tugging an errand boy by the ear along with him. I shoot to my feet. The man's audacity to barge into my sanctuary unannounced is stunning.

"What is the meaning of this?" I bellow.

Gramble pushes the boy forward. "Tell him."

The errand boy—Jack, if I remember correctly—shrugs. "I were just doin' me job, Mr. Archer. That's all."

My gaze darts to Gramble. Despite Jack's innocent explanation, the smug line of the man's mouth doesn't falter.

"Why have you pulled this boy away from his duties?" I rumble.

Gramble stares me down. "I caught him outside, running off to—"

"Outside?" I snort. Does the oaf not realize he's just condemned himself? "What the blazes were you doing outside when you should have been on the production floor managing seven?"

He doesn't bat an eye. "A man needs a moment to himself now and then."

Right. Like I believe such a tale. I face young Jack. "Did Mr. Gramble find you near the privy?"

"No, sir. I were over by the old warehouse."

I narrow my eyes at Gramble. The boldness of him, using an errand boy as some sort of makeshift scapegoat to cover for his own slothful ways. My hands curl into fists. "You were smoking, were you not? You took time away from your station, endangering the filling of our largest order ever, all for the sake of a pipe. I ought to—"

"Aye!" Gramble throws his hands into the air. "I admit it. After working ten hours straight, I needed a bowl o' tobacco. But had I not slinked off when I did, I'd not have snagged this boy on his way to Birkin's, about to rat off with information about the new machine. That's right, I said Birkin's!"

Heat flashes through me. Of all the suspects I've accused in my head for being a traitor, never once did I imagine one of the errand boys. I clench my jaw and glower at the little scoundrel. "Is this true, boy?"

Jack's eyes widen, the whites stark against his face. Good. May the young rogue know fear for his treacherous ways.

His Adam's apple bobs like a cork on the water. "All I knows is I'm paid to run errands, sir. When Mr. Franklin tells me to go, I go. I learned long ago not to cross him."

Hmm. The words slide easily enough from his tongue. Is he telling the truth, or is he an accomplished street brat used to handing out candied lies?

I angle my head and study him. "And where exactly did Mr. Franklin tell you to go tonight?"

"I were to go to the big house on the hill, Mr. Birkin's, and call at the back door for his valet. I were to tell the man"—his eyes slide up to a corner of the ceiling, as if he's retrieving a message verbatim—"seven's being pulled. New machine Friday. Stop the delivery."

My gut knots. Heat flashes through me. "Franklin told you this?" My voice booms and the boy winces, but it is not to be helped. "Are you absolutely certain?"

"Aye, sir." Jack nods.

I wheel about and stalk to the window, quaking with rage. My gaze darts to Franklin's usual station, a raised platform halfway across the production floor. It is empty. A boon, that. Were he there, I'd have surely leapt through the glass without a second thought.

How could he do such a thing? Franklin's been my right-hand man these past nine years. Trusted. Favored. More a partner than Mr. White had ever been and—

I suck in a breath, though I shouldn't be surprised. No doubt Franklin had expected to rise in station and become my copartner at the demise of Mr. White, only to be passed over and by a woman.

I turn back to Jack. "Where is Mr. Franklin now?"

"Dunno, sir." The boy blinks. "I left him by the old warehouse when I run off."

"Very well, boy. Get back to work, but do not think of going to Birkin's, now or ever. And if I hear that you do, you are out of a job. Understood?"

Jack nods, and I grab my coat, intent on throwing Franklin out into the street—and if a carriage happens to be barreling along, all the better.

"Oh, Mr. Archer? One more thing, sir." Jack stops on the threshold and hangs his head. "I'm very sorry," he mumbles.

I shove my arms into my coat. I haven't time for this, but clearly the boy's conscience troubles him. "About what, boy?"

"It weren't kind o' me to smash into the lady full on."

"What lady?"

"Mrs. White."

Everything crashes to a halt. My heartbeat. My breath. Bella? No! Am I wrong about Franklin's motives? Is she somehow tied in with him?

The coin glints from my desk, accusing me for even thinking such a thing. Yet the need to know burns like an ember in my chest. In two long strides,

I close the distance between Jack and me and crouch, face-to-face. "Think very carefully, boy. Was Mrs. White with Mr. Franklin when he gave you the information?"

"No, sir." His gaze doesn't waver. "She were just nearby, walking with a lantern. Only. . ."

The mantel clock strikes six bells, each metallic dong overloud as I wait for the boy to speak. Jack's mouth twists with some kind of ugly secret.

"Only what?" I prod.

"Well, I can't be sure, sir, bein' I run off, but I don't think Mr. Franklin were too kind to the lady."

Behind me, Gramble's feet shuffle and a single pearl tethered to a silver necklace lowers in front of my face. "Found this out in the yard, sir. I'm inclined to believe the boy. I know what Franklin is capable of, bein' on the receivin' end o' his fist more times than naught."

I snatch the necklace from Gramble's grip and crush it to my chest, a deadly rhythm throbbing in my temples.

Jack scuffs the floor with his toe. "Dunno what Mr. Franklin said to her, Mr. Archer, but I do know the tone o' voice he were usin', all growly and mean. I know what comes after it too, and I don't think the lady will like it."

White-hot rage stiffens my spine. I cannot undo the past and protect her from the fist of Mr. White, but if Franklin has so much as left a bruise on her, then God help him. I rise and cast a dark look over my shoulder. "Gramble, with me."

Without waiting for an answer, I shove past the boy and bolt from the room. I down the stairs two at a time, each step hammering a mantra inside my skull.

Find Bella. Find Franklin.

What I'll do to the man afterward depends upon the state in which I find Bella.

Only Franklin and I hold keys to the old warehouse. Why he was prowling about there at this time of night is anyone's guess, but hopefully the blackguard is still there and Bella is safe. I yank open the door to the yard.

And my world explodes.

"Fire!" Gramble yells at my back.

I take off at a dead run.

Smoke billows out the top half of the open warehouse door. No matter. I charge inside. "Franklin!" I roar. "Bella!"

The worst of the flames are to my right. Heat singes that side of my body. I swivel my head like a madman, frantically searching the hellish light for Bella or Franklin.

"Bella!"

Sparks spread. I see no sign of her. Fear and smoke drive the breath from my lungs.

"Bella!" I try again and again.

Nothing.

Do I go on? Perhaps neither are here. Perhaps Franklin has spirited her away. Perhaps the boy got it all wrong to begin with. Coughing, I turn back toward the door, desperate for cold air, only to hesitate again. What if I am wrong? What if Bella is here? Fear and need pull me in opposite directions. I no longer know who or what to trust…except for the One I should have trusted from the beginning.

Which way, God?

CHAPTER TWENTY-FIVE

Bella

All is black. The air. My lungs. Hope. The floor is white hot, but I press my cheek to it anyway. I'd trade anything for a cool draught of winter wind. How careless that I've never once thanked God for the simple act of breathing. How many other mundane blessings have I missed savoring in my lifetime? And now it is too late.

Oh, God, forgive me.

A fitting prayer for my last.

There's no point in closing my eyes. The room is dark, save for the dull flicker of reddish orange in the space between door and threshold. It's coming for me, that scorching heat. I try to care, but I can't make myself. Smoke clogs my nostrils, my throat, my will.

"Bella!"

My name crackles. Is this what happens the moment before death? You hear your name and then fly away? I'd spread my arms wide and soar from here were it not for the bindings cutting into my wrists.

"God?" I whisper.

"Bella!"

Hmm. My name comes from below. In a man's voice. Sharp. Frantic. Edmund.

A smile cracks along my lips. What a happy dream. A blissful memory. One I will embrace as I leave this world. There is no other sound on this earth I would rather take with me.

"Bella!"

Edmund's deep bellow cuts through my stupor. This is no dream. I roll to the door and shove my face close to the gap. "Edmund!"

It is little more than a croak, one the fire drowns out with its demonic snapping and popping.

Bracing myself for the sweltering pain that will surely consume my chest, I suck in a huge breath—then blow out a final cry along with the last of my strength. "Help me!"

It is the best I can manage.

But is it enough?

I close my eyes. There is nothing more to do other than lie here and wait for my savior. Either Edmund has heard and will deliver me from the flames, or Jesus will lift me in His everlasting arms—and with that realization, peace and light waft over me like a warm breeze.

Wait a minute. . . .

I blink. True light, albeit devilish, glows in the doorway—the *open* doorway. A dark figure crouches then pulls me upward. Solid muscle and flesh cradles me against a rock-hard chest and spirits me away. Enough of my wits remain that I know it is not the Son of God come to call. We judder down the broken stairs, sometimes teetering sideways, until finally I am carried out into a chaos I can barely comprehend.

Men shout. Scramble over one another. Curse. Arcs of water spurt against the old warehouse, doing nothing to lessen the hellish glow lighting the macabre scene. When the first fresh draught of air scrapes down my throat and fills my lungs, I convulse. Hot pain pulses in my chest. This is salvation?

Coughing, I turn my face against Edmund's waistcoat and shut out the horrific sight, but not my hacking. His arms tighten around me.

"Gramble, here!" Edmund barks and sets me down.

Cold seeps through my skirts, and I tilt sideways. With my hands yet bound, there is no way to right myself. Even were I freed, I'd tumble anyway. Uncontrollable coughing shudders through me, so sharply my ribs may crack.

But I don't hit the ground. Edmund's strong arms support me.

Boot steps stop next to where Edmund crouches. Mr. Gramble's. Edmund holds up his hand. "Give me your knife."

A moment later, the ropes on my wrists fall away. In reflex, I slap my hands to my mouth and double over, riding the crest of a powerful coughing wave.

And through it all, Edmund is there, patting me on the back, keeping my world upright, murmuring encouragement into my ear. "That's it. Get it all out. You're going to be fine."

Yes, by God's good grace and Edmund's act of bravery. . .but what of Mr. Franklin? Is he even now lying in a charred heap, or had Edmund gotten him out first?

"Mr. Fr—" I gasp for air and fight against another bout of hacking. "Mr. Franklin."

Edmund's arms tighten to steel. "What of him?"

"He's—" I hack once more then slowly inhale a soothing breath. "He was in there. Below the stairs. Did you get him?"

Edmund peers at me, the whites of his eyes stark against his soot-smeared face. "Are you certain?"

Am I? I fight to remember. The crack of the stairs. Mr. Franklin's profanities. The *whump* of his body hitting the floor along with the shattering of the lantern.

I nod.

"Blast it!" Edmund's voice rages as hot as the fire.

He shoots to his feet.

And is gone.

I roll to all fours and push up onto wobbly legs. I want to holler at him to stop. To order someone else to search the inferno for Mr. Franklin's broken body. But Edmund sprints, his long legs running headlong toward a fire growing larger with each passing moment. All I can do is stare, straining to breathe. By now Mr. Franklin might already be dead. Edmund could be risking his life for a man beyond saving.

I sink to my knees. What have I done?

Chains of men continue to pass buckets. Their toil and sweat, while valiant, accomplishes nothing but spits and sizzles where the water hits. Flames taunt the night sky with their brilliance.

"Over here! Now!"

I jerk my gaze toward the yelling. Fire leaps across the gap between buildings, spreading like a malignant cancer to the main structure. The men move as one to combat that side of the complex instead of the old warehouse where Edmund has disappeared—maybe forever.

Tears roll hot down my cheeks, and I clench great handfuls of my skirt.

God, please. Don't take him. Not now. Not yet. Flora needs him. I need him!

Once again I stagger upright. I will grab one of the men away from the line. Plead, scream, anything to get someone to bring Edmund out of the fire. Three paces later, I stop and cup my hand over my brow, squinting into the impossible brightness of the old warehouse.

A dark shape emerges, man sized, with a body slung over one shoulder. Edmund! He lurches away from the building just as the walls collapse inward. Sparks burst wild against the night, flying high, shooting outward, but I don't care. I run toward the blaze on shaky legs to where Edmund slings the body he carries onto the ground. Mr. Franklin moans. He is alive, for now.

Edmund swipes his forearm across his eyes. He is blackened and blistered, his hair singed and skin streaked. And he is the most beautiful sight I've ever seen.

"Gramble!" he shouts.

"Edmund!" I cry and launch toward him.

He turns his head at my approach and his arms open wide, catching me. Great sobs rip from my throat.

"Shh," he whispers into my ear. "You are safe, as am I."

I cling to him as he orders Mr. Gramble to haul Mr. Franklin to a doctor. Edmund's heart beats strong against my ear, and for one blissful moment, I pretend the heat I feel from the raging fire is nothing but the sun shining down on us. But when I pull away, the nightmare rears its ugly head.

Hand in hand, Edmund and I stand together along with the workers, staring as Nottingham Lace and Hose burns out of control.

CHAPTER TWENTY-SIX

Bella

Sullen morning light creeps in through my bedroom window. I sit at my desk, trying hard not to think how the wispy flakes floating outside look like falling ashes, but it's not working. Since the fire two days ago, whether my eyes are open or closed, all I see is destruction. My hand reaches to rub my mother's pearl necklace, only to meet bare skin. It, like so much else, is irretrievably gone. Lost because of my rash and prideful decision to come to Nottingham. Never again will I run ahead of God's will instead of seeking it in the first place. Oh, the vanity of wishing to become my own woman!

I pick up my pen. It is a small penance, this flourishing of ink on paper, but I pray it will somehow mend and heal the ugly wounds I've caused. It is cowardice to write to Edmund instead of saying goodbye face-to-face, but that is the least of my sins. Had I not confronted Franklin on my own, his factory would still be standing. Catherine may have disparaged his business, yet I am the one who ruined it. I begin to write:

> *Dear Edmund,*
> *It appears it is my turn to leave you behind, though I suspect you shall not be disheartened to see me go. Today, I travel to London.*

I draw back my hand before the trembling in my fingers causes an indelible blob to drip from the nib. It is so final, this parting. A death. Like a handful of dirt thrown atop a casket in the ground. I don't want to leave Edmund. His strength, his encouragement, his no-nonsense way of managing the world have all influenced me in the time I've been here. I shall sorely miss his steadying presence. Without him, I am adrift on a lonely sea. But after all that has happened, why would he wish to see me ever again?

Sucking in a shaky breath, I blot my pen and start again:

> *Words cannot express my sorrow at the mess I've created.*

Had it not been for my blundering indiscretion, the factory would still be standing. For that, I am truly sorry.

And I am. More than I can express. Sorry for the trouble I've wreaked in Edmund's life. Sorry for ever thinking I could be an independent woman, reliant on my own weak self. I should've known. How many times had Mr. White pointed out my shortcomings? Why did I not believe him?

I dip the pen once more and continue:

For what it's worth, I am enclosing the signed paperwork naming you as the sole owner of Nottingham Lace and Hose. It is a dreadful case of too little, too late, I'm afraid, yet I hope in some small way the banknote I've attached will help you to rebuild and start again.

Please give Flora my regards. She is a darling girl. The world is a brighter place because of her, and I count myself fortunate to have spent so much time in her presence.

I wish her and you well, for now and for always.

Sincerely,
Arabella White

The world turns watery, and I blink rapidly to keep tears from falling and marring the page. Never again will I see Flora's ready smile or the way she bobs her head when she's excited. My stomach twists. How I will miss her.

I press my knuckle to the corner of my eye and dab away the moisture. It is best I remove myself before doing any more damage to Edmund and his daughter. I know it in my head. . .but my heart rebels.

Ignoring the burning in my chest, I reach for the pounce pot, and my gaze lands on the folded piece of Hester's lace laid nearby. I'd nearly forgotten.

Once again, I reach for the pen:

P.S. Though I can do nothing to rectify the loss of Lord Hampton's order or all the stock that was destroyed, please send this lace-work to your uncle Dickens with my wishes for him and his wife to enjoy a very merry Christmas.

A knock on the door ends my correspondence. Betty peeks her head inside. "The solicitor has arrived, mum."

"Thank you." I push back my chair and rise. "Are you ready to travel?"

"Yes, and the cab is waiting out front."

"I shall meet you out there, then."

Quickly, I collect Edmund's letter and the lace, tucking both inside a large envelope with the banknote and ownership document. It weighs heavy in my hand and heavier on my spirit. Of all the things I'd imagined when coming here, I never thought it would end this way.

But there is no time to hold hands with regret now. I snatch up one more envelope then hurry downstairs to the sitting room.

A man in a somber suit coat turns at my entrance. Of course Mr. Smyth would be wearing black. Most solicitors do. Still, the colour grates against my senses.

He dips his head. "Good morning, Mrs. White."

"Good morning to you, sir. Thank you for coming." I force what I hope is a small smile, though more likely than not, it is a grimace. All my smiles lie in an ashen heap over on Stoney Street.

I cross the carpet and stop in front of him. Standing this close, I am but a mouse compared to his height. I try not to fidget with the envelopes as I peer up at him. "I appreciate you managing the last of my business here in Nottingham on such short notice."

"Your wishes shall be carried out as if you were here, madam."

"Very well." I hand him the smaller of the envelopes. "Deliver this to Mr. McGreary. Also, be sure to see that the Christmas goose is cooked and brought 'round to the Old Lace Shop by three o'clock sharp on Christmas Day."

He tucks the missive into a pocket inside his coat. "I've already checked with the butcher and the baker. All is in order for a hearty feast, and I shall escort the ladies into the building myself."

At the mention of the ladies, I turn away, biting my lip lest I whimper. I will not be here to witness their merrymaking. I will not share a meal with them on this sacred holiday. My own foolish promise made at the altar of a chest of widow's weeds on a sunny September day comes back to haunt me.

This year I will celebrate Christmas with holly and laughter and a large stuffed goose.

Except I won't be. I will sit alone in an empty London town house, dining with none but ghosts of the past under the glower of my dead husband's memory.

"Mrs. White?"

Inhaling for courage, I turn back and offer over Edmund's letter. "This is for Mr. Archer. It is imperative you put the envelope into his hand, none other. Do you understand?"

The solicitor gives me a sharp nod. "I shall have it to him tomorrow."

"As for the rest of this"—I flutter my fingers around the room—"I trust you'll see to the packing of my belongings and have them delivered to number twelve Portman Square, London."

"Even now my men are standing by, ready to work." With a tip of his head, he indicates a huddle of three men just outside the front window. "Safe travels to you, Mrs. White."

I bid him goodbye and clip out to the foyer, anxious to be on my way. As I don my hat and coat, the white-faced woman looking back at me from the mirror gives me a shiver. Gone is the wide-eyed hope and expectation that accompanied me to this house. I leave here with shame. It is an ugly truth, one that will not be stabbed away even with the forceful jab of my hatpin.

Each step to the cab feels like I'm treading through treacle. Betty scoots over as I settle next to her on the carriage seat. The jarvey urges the horses to walk on, and I stare out the window to avoid conversation with my maid. Only when the cab turns onto Stoney Street do I realize my mistake.

We roll past the Old Lace Shop, and my heart constricts. Five black lumps sit next to a cleaned brick building with new glass-plate windows. I memorize the lines on the faces of each dear woman, and as I linger on Hester's unseeing gaze, my own chin rises a bit. What an inspiration she is, meeting every hardship with a fierce faith in an unfailing God.

But half a block after resolving to be more like Hester, we pass by the rubble of the factory, and my resolve crumbles. Charred timbers poke up like blackened skeletons rising from a grave. Portions of brick walls stand scorched and jagged. The once thriving hub of business lies dead and silent. A funny sort of gurgle strangles me.

Betty reaches for my hand yet says nothing. Just as well.

There is nothing to say.

CHAPTER TWENTY-SEVEN

Edmund

What should've been a victorious moment is as dark and sooty as the train station loading dock. I barely register the acrid stink of creosote as I stare up at the large wooden crates strapped to the flat car. NOTTINGHAM LACE AND HOSE is stenciled on their sides, and I glower at the black letters. It was a waste of time that the new machine had been broken down and boxed up. A waste of sweat and grunts from the men who loaded them. Yet the biggest waste of all are the minutes I stand here lamenting all the what-might-have-beens and should-have-nots.

But I have nothing else to do.

My glower deepens as I pull out my pocket watch and glance at the hour. It's merely a formality, yet a habit I can't seem to break. What does it matter if it's nine in the morning or nine at night? I have no workers to manage or machines to wrangle. No factory to consume me. For the past two days I've drifted about like an unmoored ghost with nowhere to land. The only thing I've accomplished is fixing the clasp on Bella's necklace, waiting even now in my pocket to be returned to her. But how will I face her? If the fire has ruined me so thoroughly, how much more her?

"Mr. Edmund Archer?"

Shoving away my watch, I turn and face a man in a black long coat. He is tall. Quite so. At least a handspan more than me. His deep-set eyes are so dark they appear empty, endless, cold. Add a cowl over the fellow's head and he'd make a very fine grim reaper.

"I am he. Why do you ask?"

"I am Mr. Smyth, solicitor for Mrs. White. She asked me to deliver these papers to you. Since they are of a timely nature and you were not at home, I took the liberty of asking your butler for your whereabouts, which brings me here." He holds out a large envelope sealed with twine.

Strange, that. I stare at his offering. Why would Bella hire a man for such a menial task when she could've done it herself? Unless—*oh, God, no.* Has she succumbed to some sort of illness after the trauma of the fire? I should have checked on her, or at the very least, sent an inquiry 'round to her residence.

I jerk my gaze up to the man's face. "Is Mrs. White ill?"

Mr. Smyth shakes his head. "No, leastwise not that I know of. When she departed yesterday, she appeared to be in the best of health. Now, if you wouldn't mind, I am to see that you are familiar with the contents before I leave you."

Absently, I pull the envelope from the man's fingers. Departed? Where would she go? I unwrap the twine and pull out a piece of folded lace—exquisite lace. The sort that would sell at a premium. What the deuce?

I glance up at Mr. Smyth. "What am I to do with this?"

"Keep at it." He nods toward the envelope.

Once again, I reach in. This time I pull out a banknote, and when I read the amount, I suck in a sharp breath. Lace and money? It makes no sense. How did Bella come by such riches?

I'm about to ask Mr. Smyth when he urges me to continue.

There are two more sheets of paper inside. My knees nearly buckle when I read the heading of the first. Sole proprietorship with Bella's neat signature gracing the bottom. I am the owner in full of Nottingham Lace and Hose. My dream come true—but two days too late. In reality, I am the owner of a heap of ashes. . .yet with such a sum written on the banknote, the first spark of a new hope begins to kindle. Could I rebuild? Dare I?

My mind whirs with questions and calculations. What to do first. Where, when, and how. The workers will be ecstatic. Gramble, especially. But is there any possible way I can make things right with Lord Hampton? Not in time for Christmas, but maybe next—

"Not that I mean to prod, Mr. Archer, but I have another engagement." Mr. Smyth taps the envelope. "If you wouldn't mind?"

Reining in my wild thoughts, I empty the envelope and unfold a paper smelling of rose water. Bella's handwriting covers one side. As I read, the embers of the hope I entertained so briefly die a quick death. She's gone. Well and truly. Left me behind along with every penny she must've inherited from Mr. White. I close my eyes, fighting back a sob.

Oh, Bella.

How will Flora live without her? How will I? Bella brought such life and light into our dark little world. Giving to others. Rearranging my business and my priorities. Determined and compassionate and endlessly serving. Flora is a different girl for having shared time with her. I am a different man.

My shoulders slump as I slowly realize the biggest difference of all. . .how changed Bella's life will be in London without her inheritance.

No. I will not have it.

I shove the papers and lace back into the envelope and snap my gaze up to Mr. Smyth's. "What is Mrs. White's forwarding address?"

He frowns. "I should think that if she'd wished to divulge such information, she'd have said as much in her letter."

"Yet you know where she is, do you not?"

"Naturally."

"Please." On impulse, I grip his arm. "I give you my word of honour, sir, that I mean her every possible best intention."

Mr. Smyth's gaze shoots from my grasp to my eyes. It's an unnerving stare, one that lasts an eternity, until finally he sighs and pulls from my grasp. "Well, I suppose it is a matter of public record. Number twelve Portman Square. Wait! Where are you—"

His voice fades as I dash down the stairs of the dock and tear around to the front of the train station. I should've guessed she'd have gone to the home she shared with Mr. White. She's likely already acquainted with the new owners and has some sort of rapport with them. Perhaps they've hired her on as a maid or at least given her shelter until she can find employment.

I buy a ticket for the next available departure to London, which—God be praised—is in little more than a quarter of an hour. For the next three hours as I rumble across the country to King's Cross Station, I memorize every last word of Bella's sweet letter. How broken she must feel. How scared and vulnerable. If it takes the rest of my life, I vow I will erase every tear and fear she's suffered.

Portman Square, while not the most elite neighborhood, is nonetheless fabulously upstanding. I garner a cross look or two as I make my way to number twelve. No wonder. I left the cottage without shaving this morning in my haste to turn away the new machine before it was unloaded. Fresh wrinkles crease my coat from the train trip as well.

But none of that matters as I trot down the steps to the servants' entrance and pound on the door.

Moments later, a mobcapped woman wearing a flour-dusted apron and a glower answers, ushering me in with a wave of her hand. "Come in! Come in. And about time too. I expected you a half an hour ago."

I slip past her, catching a waft of yeast and sugared sorghum, and enter a rather wide and long passageway that ends at a staircase. A door on one side opens to a kitchen, and farther down there are several other rooms.

The woman—who I assume is the cook—shuts the door, and when she turns to me, her hawkeyed stare swoops to my hands. "But what's this? Where's my crate o' apples?" Her eyes narrow, and scarlet patches of anger bloom on her cheeks. "Flit! Don't tell me you be bringing me an invoice before the goods. This be the last time I order from Nagle's, and you can say as much to yer snipin' owner. How am I to make dumplings in time for—"

I shoot up my hand, warding her off. It's either that or turn tail and run. "Sorry to interrupt, madam, but I am not a delivery man, nor do I know anything about apples or Nagle's. I am come to call for a Mrs. Arabella White. Is she here?"

"The missus?" She cocks her head and studies me once again, this time taking note of more than just what I carry as her gaze sweeps from my beaver hat to my leather shoes. She hitches her thumb over her shoulder, toward the door. "You know that be the service entrance?"

At a loss, I rub the back of my neck. Is the woman daft? "I do, yet you have not answered my question. May I speak with Mrs. White?"

"Wait here," she grumbles, along with a whole host of complaints she mumbles while hiking up the stairs.

I take to pacing a route in front of those stairs. What I am about to do will change Bella's life. My life. Flora's. Am I ready for this? Are any of us?

But as Bella's light step taps down the stone stairway and I once again behold her sweet face, any doubts I might've harboured sail far and away. She is a vision in her yellow gown with her brown hair coiled in ringlets atop her head.

"Edmund?" She stops in front of me, endearing little creases marring her brow. "What are you doing here?"

The cook lumbers down the stairs next, and I wait for her to pass and disappear into the kitchen. "I came to talk to you."

"But what are you doing here?" Bella flourishes her fingers in the air. "Why come to the back door?"

Again with the back door? Suspicion sparks in my brain and is fanned to fiery life by the spark of confusion in Bella's eyes.

She cocks her head. "Are you under the impression I am in service to this house?"

"I—I... Did you not come to London for employment?"

"No. This is mine." She flings out her arms. "Mr. White left everything to me, for there was no one else. This is my home." A shadow of melancholy darkens her voice.

Knocked off balance, I retreat a step, and my back hits the wall. "Do you mean to say you are not destitute?"

A bitter laugh nearly chokes her. "I grant my funds are considerably lower since, well. . ." Her head dips. "You were right. As was Mr. Barlow. I should have signed the factory over to you in the first place."

The sorrow in her voice stabs me in the heart, and I fish around in my pocket to retrieve a coin. A farthing is a poor replacement for the second-chance coin she'd given me. Hopefully it will suffice. But then my fingers brush against the coolness of a silver chain, and instead I pull out Bella's necklace and hold it aloft.

Staring at the pearl, she reaches for it, her chin trembling. "What? Where?" she sputters as she grasps the keepsake. "*How* did you find this?"

"Gramble found it. I regret to tell you the second-chance coin was lost in the fire, but I am hoping this will do in its place. Because, more than anything, I want us to have a second chance to be partners. . .*life* partners."

Her lips part, and she blinks. I don't blame her. I can hardly believe I will dare to marry again. But will she consider such a commitment, especially after a ruined marriage to an ogre thrice her age?

"Bella—" My voice breaks, and I clear my throat, hoping, praying, desperate. "I know things were not easy between you and Mr. White, but I am not a bully who will bend you to my will. I am a man who is wholly and helplessly in love." I sink to one knee, holding on to her hand like a lifeline. "Will you marry me?"

Emotions flash across her face. Shock. Disbelief. And for a heart-stopping moment, her gaze darts about as if she looks for an escape route.

My gut clenches, and defeat nearly smothers me. I was wrong. Bella not only doesn't need me, she does not want me. What an idiot. I clench the envelope I've carried all this way so tightly that it shakes. That's what the payoff was about. A way for her to say goodbye and be done with me forever. No wonder she didn't deliver the message in person.

I rise and turn so quickly, she gasps. And why not? She likely has no words to say to such an unexpected and unwelcome proposal.

"Wait!" Her footsteps catch up to mine at the door. "Where are you going? You have not yet heard my answer."

A bitter laugh rumbles in my chest. "I have all the answer I need. Goodbye, Mrs. White."

Before I can open the door, her hands slide around from behind and embrace me, pressing her body close to mine. The warmth of her cheek burns hot against my shoulder blade. "Yes," she breathes.

I stiffen, hardly able to believe my ears.

Slowly, I turn.

Bella lifts her face to mine. Tears shimmer bright in her eyes. So does a love so pure, it aches in my soul.

"I accept, my love." She smiles, a gleam twinkling in her eyes. "And rest assured, this is a partnership I will *never* sign away."

CHAPTER TWENTY-EIGHT

Bella

Of all the merry sights on Christmas Day, there is none quite so gay as the smile of a friend—five, to be exact. Oohs and aahs fill the Old Lace Shop—and my heart—as the blind women wander about the grand space, their arms outstretched and their faces alight with wonder. This is where they belong, far from the grip of cold and hunger, and I say as much as I usher them to the large table spread with a holiday feast.

And what a table it is. Bowls of filberts. Dishes of buttered Spanish onions. Baskets of bread shaped into stars and angel wings. At center, there is a pyramid of apples, pears, and grapes, adding colour and a sweet, fruity aroma—one that mixes well with the twangy scent from the pine swags draped across the ceiling. On the walls, the orange pomanders Flora and I made hang at intervals from the fruit-and-nut garland. Granted, the decor is rather homely compared to the richness of a London town house bedecked for a Yuletide dinner, but I wouldn't trade places for all the queen's jewels.

Church bells toll the hour, and I count each chime. Three o'clock. It's a struggle to keep from bouncing on my toes, so I settle for fingering my mother's pearl necklace instead. I've never felt so at peace, so alive, so grateful to God for the blessings He's bestowed. The crowning touch will soon arrive—a roasted goose, all buttery and sizzling. I cannot wait to share this meal with the women I've come to love—and the man I love even more.

Outside, jingle bells festooning a horse tinkle like laughter. I rush to the window, where afternoon sunshine beams down on an approaching coach. This time I do bounce. Such joy is simply not meant to be contained. Because this year I *am* celebrating Christmas with holly and laughter and a large stuffed goose.

"Ladies." I whirl from the glass and clap my hands. Five faces turn my way. "I have a grand surprise I've been waiting to share with you. Today, we not only celebrate the birth of our blessed Lord, but also my upcoming marriage. I am to be wed in the new year, and I wanted you to be the first to know."

Cheers and blessings ring out. My, how drastically things can change in little more than a week. Had I not seen firsthand how beauty can rise from ashes, I'd never have believed it.

But this is no time to wax philosophic. The love of my life waits outside. I dash to the door, yet before I yank it open, I rein in the women with another clap. "And now, my dear friends, I should very much like to introduce you to. . ."

The words slip off my tongue as I stare into the green eyes of a stranger.

It is a man in a red woolen muffler. A frosty moustache clings to his upper lip, or maybe it's a shadow, so thin is the line. The December air has nipped his cheeks and nose to a hearty ruddiness, all splotchy and mottled, as if he's travelled quite a distance this day. There is something vaguely familiar about the dimple on his chin, but though I try, I cannot place him.

"Merry Christmas, madam." He dips his head. "Are you Mrs. White?"

"I am."

"Thank God!" He blows out a puff of air that mists into a tiny white cloud. "I've had quite the time tracking you from London to Nottingham. A Mr. Barlow of Smudge and Gruber contacted me. I believe you are familiar with him?"

"Yes." I scramble to figure out how and why this man is related to my lawyer and his clerk. "Mr. Barlow is—"

"Clarence?" Behind me, Hester's voice fairly shrieks. "Is that you, my boy?"

"Mother." The man angles past me and rushes into the room, where Hester is already halfway to the door. He gathers the old woman into his arms and swings her around. Both laugh, though Hester's gaiety warbles with happy tears.

The big man gently sets her down yet does not release his hold of her. He gazes into her blind eyes, and the adoration on his face squeezes my chest.

"Oh, Mother, I thought I'd lost you. That you were. . ." He presses his lips tight, visibly trying to regain his composure. It is an intimate moment, one I should turn away from, yet the display of love is so compelling, I cannot.

Though his mother cannot see his response, she clearly hears the emotion in his voice. Hester reaches up and lovingly places her hand on her son's cheek, as if he is the most precious of all God's creations. "Don't fret about me, boy. Yer old mother comes from hardy stock. But whatever are ye doin' here?"

Clarence covers her hand with his and leans into her touch, nuzzling against it. "I've come to take you home, Mother. My home. And a grand home it is. I've made quite a name for myself in America." Grief etches lines deep on his brow, and the moustache on his lip quivers. "Had I known you were yet alive, I'd have come sooner."

"Oh, Clarence, I din't want to be a millstone 'round your neck."

"You're not a millstone, Mother. You are a gem. A brilliant, shining gem." He crushes her to his chest and plants a kiss atop her head.

I suck in a shaky breath, as do the other women, for such is the holiness of the moment. A Son was given on Christmas Day, and now one is returned. I lift my gaze to the rafters.

How kind You are, God.

I cannot help but smile, and though I hate to interrupt the magical scene, the goose and Edmund will soon be here. I nod to Clarence and sweep out my hand. "Please, won't you join your mother and us for dinner? There is always room for more here at the Old Lace Shop."

Clarence pulls away from Hester and doffs his hat, flourishing it toward me with a bow. "Thank you. I shall."

Pounding rattles the door, and my grin grows. Edmund! At last. And it sounds as if he's as eager to see me as I am to finally be at his side.

I swing the door wide and a small body plows into me. An arm wraps around my waist. The other clings to a crutch. Girlish giggles muffle into my skirt.

Flora? What on earth?

My jaw drops, and I stare past the girl to where Edmund strides away from paying the jarvey. When his gaze meets mine, my breath catches. I will never tire of the barefaced adoration blazing in those blue-grey eyes.

He stops in front of me, sandwiching Flora between us, and I breathe in his manly scent of horses, wintry air, and promise.

"If you do not close your mouth, my love, I fear I shall have to kiss those pretty lips shut. . .which shouldn't be a problem." He taps me on the nose and pulls out a sprig of mistletoe. The smouldering gleam in his eyes lights a fire inside me that burns clear up to my cheeks.

"Now then, are you going to invite us in, or am I to use this weapon"—he waggles the mistletoe—"right here in front of God and country?"

"I—I. . ." How is it that by one sultry look, he can drive the words clear out of my head? I clear my throat and try again. "Yes! Come in. The ladies are eager to meet you."

I peel from Flora's grip and stoop to the girl's level. "There are many new friends for you inside. Go see for yourself."

"Hooray!" Her lopsided smile is a Christmas gift in and of itself.

I rise and step aside, allowing both Flora and Edmund to enter, then announce, "One and all, please welcome my intended, Mr. Edmund Archer, and his sweet daughter, Flora. I know you will love them every bit as much as I do."

Flora hobbles as fast as she is able toward the women—who await her with open arms. And how could they not? Her sweet laughter could make a pinch-faced money lender giggle like a schoolboy.

Edmund pulls off his hat just as the back door bangs open.

"Coming through! Piping hot." A delivery man in a grey coat and grease-stained apron barrels into the room, carrying a silver-domed platter. He sets the tray down at the end of the table, and when he removes the lid, a rich, meaty scent fills the air. The goose is browned to perfection.

"Come, Miss Flora!" Martha pats the empty place on the bench beside her. "You shall sit right here by me. This roast goose won't get eaten by itself, you know."

Flora glances over her shoulder. "Papa?"

Edmund laughs. "You heard the lady, Flora. She needs your help."

Flora fairly flies to Martha's side, clattering her crutch to the floor and whumping her little bottom onto the seat.

I peer up at Edmund and lower my voice, speaking for him alone. "I did not know you were bringing Flora. I thought you meant to keep her from the public?"

"I did. . .until you came along." He pulls me to his side with one arm and gazes down at me. "You made me see that despite Flora's impediments, she can be loved for who she is on the inside, even by a stranger, and she's blossomed because of it. Because of *you*. All these years I have denied her that sort of fellowship, but no more."

The ugly memory of the hunchbacked man taunted by the boys on the street flashes in my mind, and I frown up at Edmund. "Yet you were right to protect her. The world is a cruel place, especially for those who are different."

He nods. "We are all different. We all bear one cross or another. And because of it, do we not each face our own particular cruelties?"

In reflex, I press my hand to my stomach. How many times have I cursed my barren womb that refuses to hold life? "Yes, I suppose we do," I murmur, and once again doubt rises up my throat like soured Christmas punch. Though Edmund has said otherwise, will he not be sorry to marry a woman who can give him no son? "But are you certain about Flora, about me?"

He lays his finger on my lips, pressing them shut. "I have never been more certain of anything in my life. The truth is, love, that we serve a God who transcends everything and is far more capable of protecting Flora than I—and One who is also able to bless us with new life if He so wills it. After all, faith moves mountains, right? So let us leave Flora and any future children in His very capable hands." Bending, he brushes a kiss to my temple. "And I vow that as long as I draw breath, I will love you both so well, the cruelties of this world shall fade in comparison."

I nestle my cheek against his shoulder. I can want for nothing more. "I do not deserve you."

"No, love, you deserve far better. Now, as your lady friend said, that goose will not get eaten by itself. Shall we—"

Another knock cuts him off. Edmund lifts a brow at me. "Expecting more guests?"

"None that I know of." I turn to the door, as does Edmund, and this time when I open it, I am not the only one whose jaw drops.

"Mr. Birkin?" I gasp.

"Merry Christmas to you, Mrs. White." He dips his head. "Archer. Might I come in? I shan't take more than a minute."

"Of course." I step aside.

A quiet growl rumbles in Edmund's throat, and he ushers me behind him with a protective touch.

Birkin merely chuckles. "Stand down, man. I've not come to maul you or your associate on Christmas Day."

Behind us, the women's voices hush. Edmund folds his arms while widening his stance. "Then why are you here?"

Mr. Birkin reaches inside his coat pocket and produces a single silver key. "For you."

Slowly, Edmund unfolds his arms and retrieves the offering, turning it over in his hand. "What is this for?"

"Now that Franklin is awake and able to talk, he told me it was you who saved him from the blaze." Mr. Birkin's gaze drifts to me. "And you, madam, who discovered him passing on confidential information. Yet even in the knowing, you saved his life. The both of you."

Edmund grunts. "Life is precious, even that of a traitor."

"Well said." Mr. Birkin claps him on the back. "Look, Archer, I know we've had our differences, and likely will continue to in the future, but in the meantime, until you're back up and running, my new warehouse stands empty. That's what the key is for. Use it. Rent-free. Set up shop there temporarily until Nottingham Lace and Hose is rebuilt."

My fingers fly to my chest. Surely, he cannot be serious.

Edmund must think the same, for he holds out the key. "I cannot accept this. You are my competition."

Birkin merely shoves his hands into his pockets and pushes out his lower lip. "Actually, at the moment, I am your associate. When Lord Hampton learned of the fire, he came to me. Apparently, his wife and her sister are set upon a particular pattern of yours for the estate and will not be moved, even though the deadline for it has come and gone. I have the machinery to meet the order. You have the knowledge of the pattern. If we work together, split the profits fifty-fifty, we both stand to make quite a sum. Not as much as you would've made on your own, but that's rather a moot point now, I suppose. So what do you say?"

I bite my lip. Edmund is a proud man. It's been a slow adjustment for him to take me on as a partner. But this? His competitor? An avowed enemy? I doubt very much he'll warm to this opportunity.

And as I suspect, he shakes his head. "I hardly know what to say."

"Well, I do." I shove past him and pump Mr. Birkin's hand. "I say yes, and God bless us, everyone!"

"God bless us, everyone!" Laughter and cheers ring out behind me.

But the most endearing sound of all is Edmund's warm chuckle. Strong hands grip my shoulders and gently pull me around. My pulse races at the light of love in Edmund's gaze.

"And may God bless you especially, my love," he murmurs. "At Christmas and all the year through."

EPILOGUE

Later That Evening

Twilight fell heavy and hard and altogether too quickly for little Billy Tom-kins. He hadn't wanted to come today. Not on Christmas. Not when he had a more important matter to attend. He'd tried his best to skulk through back lanes and narrow alleys, even hid his precious cargo and doubled back just to be on the safe side, but his employer—Scruggs—had collared him all the same—and nobody said no to Moffit Scruggs.

Nobody.

"Get a leg on, Tomkins! Yer the last one!"

Billy scowled. Scruggs couldn't be more right. The bigger boys had already hunted out the best bits from the factory ruins. All he'd found were two clay inkpots and the bone stem of a pipe. He'd earn a cuff on the head for that.

He upped his pace, sifting through ash and rubble in the blue-black light of the coming evening. Soon it would be too dark to see. His knuckles scraped on a jagged piece of metal, and he jerked his hand to his mouth, sucking away the saltiness and pain.

"Tomkins! Just cuz that high-and-mighty Archer ain't here to kick us out don't mean ye gots to take all night."

He kicked at a charred piece of brick. Stupid Scruggs. Always badgering and bellowing. Twisting his lips, Billy glanced across the yard to the hulking shape near the gate then huffed out a defeated breath. A cuff on the head it was, then. But at least after that, he could be on his way, and a good thing too. He desperately needed to be. He'd heard that miracles happen on Christmas, and there were precious few hours left of it.

Shoving his hand into his pocket, he pulled out the inkpots and pipe stem and trudged toward Scruggs, but before he reached him, he stopped.

Blinked.

Stooped.

And marveled as he fished out a golden coin from beneath a charred timber. Glory! How had the others missed this treasure?

"What ye got there?" Heavy footsteps pounded behind him.

Swallowing down want and need, Billy eased the coin up his sleeve. Such a prize could buy his miracle. Slowly, he turned to face the man—then retreated a step.

Gads! But Scruggs was a timeless old troll—the sort who might've crawled out of a cave eons ago and would one day return to the damp and darkness of it. He smelled musty. Mouldy. An odour of perpetual rot hovered about his scrappy frame, his shabby cloak, the yellowed teeth that clung to his mottled gums when he smiled—which he did now. Billy shivered. He'd take a scowl from ol' Scruggs any day of the week and twice on Sunday to avoid that leering grin.

Beneath the wilted brim of a patch-haired beaver hat, Scruggs's dark eyes studied him. "What 'ave ye got for me, then?" He shoved out his palm. Bony white fingers poked through the three ripped ends of his tattered gloves. "Let's 'ave it."

Fear festered deep inside Billy's belly. Scruggs wouldn't like the paltry finds he had to offer. If the man pressed him and discovered the coin, Billy would be in the worst kind of trouble—and he didn't have time for that, not with night falling. Should he just go ahead and give the snipin' codger the coin or try to keep it hidden?

Scruggs struck so fast, Billy's head jerked aside. Pain exploded in his skull. And though his mother—God rest her—had taught him otherwise, a curse flew past his lips.

"Ain't got all night, boy!" Scruggs hissed.

Keeping the coin carefully tucked in his sleeve, Billy thrust the inkpots and pipe stem toward the man. He'd be hanged if he gave such a wicked cully his hard-won fortune. "Here's all I got. Ain't nothin' else left."

Scruggs snatched the items from his hand, his upper lip curling as he stared at the salvaged bits.

Billy retreated another step, his ears still ringing from the last blow—then froze when the weak cry of a babe travelled on the air from outside the gates. His gaze shot to the sound. Dash it! Time was more than running out.

"Worthless little street rat!" In one long step, Scruggs grabbed him by the collar and hoisted him so high, his feet dangled. "Makin' ol' Moffit wait in the cold for nothin.' I oughta slit yer throat 'ere and now fer such disrespect."

Billy thrashed, desperate for air. If Scruggs made good on his threat, his wouldn't be the only life taken. There was nothing for it, then. He *had* to give Scruggs the coin.

"I—I—" he tried to explain, but Scruggs shook him so hard, it was impossible to speak, to breathe, to anything.

With a shove, Billy flew backward. His head slammed onto the ground. So did his body. Tears stung, and instinctively he curled into a ball, tucking his throat out of reach. Was this it? Would the cold edge of a knife be the last thing he felt?

But no sharp steel sliced. Not even any boot kicked. Billy dared to open one eyelid, only to see the back end of Moffit Scruggs swooping out the front gate, his tatty old cloak hem unfurling behind him like great black bat wings.

Billy staggered to his feet. Mother was right. Miracles truly did happen on Christmas! Loosening his collar, he picked his way out of the factory ruins and, once out on the street, dashed to a nearby heap of recovered bricks. After a wild glance about to make sure Scruggs was well and truly gone, Billy dropped to his knees and pulled down the makeshift wall he'd thrown together earlier. The more bricks he removed, the louder the baby's cry became, until finally, he edged out a small basket.

And his sister ripped loose a frightful wail.

Fast as a pickpocket, Billy flung away the rags he'd piled on top of her and shoved his face close to Mimi's. "Shh. Brother's here. I'll set things right, I will. Yer belly's soon to be filled."

Mimi shot out her little hand and grabbed a handful of his hair, yanking hard.

"Kipes!" He jerked back and rubbed the sore spot, yet he couldn't keep from smiling. She was a fighter, she was. Just like him. But just as quickly, his smile faded.

If only Mother had been a stronger fighter herself.

Mimi's face reddened, a sure sign a lusty squall was about to break. Billy tucked the rags about her and snatched up her basket, swinging it as he whipped around. The sudden movement quieted his sister—but it wouldn't for long.

He set off at a good clip. As he passed the Old Lace Shop, the golden glow in the windows and merry laughter from inside turned his head. A cluster of smiling old women bent their heads together near a table laden with the remnants of a Christmas feast. A girl—roughly his age—sat on the lap of another white-haired lady, cracking nuts. Off in a corner, a tall man and a pretty lady gazed into each other's eyes beneath a sprig of mistletoe. Gaff! But they looked a kind sort. The way she smiled at the man. How he slowly brushed his fingers along her cheek, almost as if he were afraid he might break her. He pulled the lady into his arms and kissed her a good one right on the lips.

Smirking, Billy turned from the sight and upped his pace. That's what Mimi deserved. Not the kissing part, but the gentleness of it all. Tender folk to care for her. A warm home. Lots of love and plenty of food. Slab-nabbity! But she would have it!

Cold seeped through the threadbare fabric of his coat as he rushed along. Slushy snow dampened his socks, seeping in from the holes in his shoes. He shivered, but through it all, he set his jaw and trudged onward, past the lace market, through the winding streets of Hoxley Green, and finally up to Broxtowe.

Hours later, he stopped in front of a church. The stained glass was dark by now; any worshippers that had been inside had long since left. Had midnight already come and gone? Was he too late? Panic tasted sour at the back of his throat. No! Not when he was so close. It wasn't right. It wasn't fair.

Pivoting, he skirted the church's stone walls and slipped around to the side yard. A tiny vicarage sat toward the back of the lot. One candle flickered in the window, lessening some of his unease. Perhaps the vicar was still awake.

Oh, God, make it so. For Mimi.

On quiet feet, Billy crept to the front door and set down his sister's basket; then he retrieved the coin and laid it on top of the rags. Surely with such a fortune accompanying her, Mimi would be welcomed. He brushed a parting kiss against his sister's brow, her skin soft and warm.

The baby's eyes shot open as he pulled away. Her mouth opened into a big O.

And that was it. No more time.

Billy scrambled away, taking cover behind the shadow of an upturned wheelbarrow just as his sister let out a frightful cry.

The front door of the vicarage opened.

"What's this?" Vicar Joseph Grammelby's voice, honed by countless Sundays of exhortations, pealed out into the night.

Billy bit his lip, hoping and praying he'd not be spotted. He'd be trundled off to an orphanage for sure, or worse, the workhouse. Kipes! More like the dead-house, if you asked him. Why, he'd rather move in with Moffit Scruggs than go to that carpin' place.

Thankfully, his sister's next cry drew the vicar's gaze. Stooping, the man gathered Mimi into his arms, shushing her with steady murmurings while patting her back.

Even so, Billy didn't dare breathe. Not yet. Not until Mimi was safe inside the vicarage.

When she quieted, once again Vicar Grammelby scanned the darkness.

"Who brings this child?"

Billy squeezed his eyes shut.

Please, God. A Christmas miracle for Mimi? Just like Mother said before she died? Can You do that even if I got my sister here a little late?

He listened hard for an answer, but how would he know what God sounded like? He'd never heard from Him before.

"*Secundus casus.*"

Billy stiffened. God spoke a different language? How was he to understand that?

"Second chance."

His eyes shot open. That baritone voice came from the open door of the vicarage, not from heaven.

Sure enough, Vicar Grammelby secured Mimi against his shoulder with one hand, and with the other, held the coin up to his eyes. Did the piece of gold have writing on it? Billy frowned. He'd not taken the time to notice.

The vicar's arm dropped, and he lifted his face to the sky. "Truly, God? Can it be? After so many little ones lost to us?" His voice broke, and for a moment his head dipped; then stronger and purer his words rang. "Christmas or not, Lord, Your grace knows no bounds."

He turned then, taking Mimi with him into the vicarage. "Wife? Mary! Come see what miracle God has wrought."

The door shut.

The night stilled.

Billy smiled. Satisfied, he crept from his hiding spot. God had done it! He truly had, even if it was past midnight. Mimi would have a good home with Vicar Grammelby and his wife. He was sure of it.

Leaving the church behind, he cut onto Boxford Lane and shoved his hands into his pockets. Perhaps tomorrow he'd stop by the Old Lace Shop and see if that kind-looking lady and man would hire him on.

Who knew? Maybe miracles didn't happen only on Christmas.

HISTORICAL NOTES

Richard Birkin & Thomas Adams
Birkin and Adams are the real movers and shakers of the Victorian lace industry. They were the risk-taking innovators who caused the trade to flourish. By casting aside tradition, they dared to transfer lacemaking from residences to factories and warehouses.

The Lace Market in Nottingham
The Industrial Revolution put an end to cottage industries where lace was made in homes by hand. Steam engines made it possible to power machinery that increased production dramatically. By 1870, nearly all types of handmade lace had machine-made copies available at a cheaper price—and there was no greater emporium of lace and hosiery manufacturers than in Nottingham.

Blind Ladies of Nottingham
Lacemaking is an exacting craft that requires hours spent working tiny threads into delicate patterns. Women often went blind perhaps because of the strain on the eyes while working in very dim lighting or, more likely, from repeated and chronic eye infections due to the irritation from the cotton fluff in the air. I took artistic license with the number of blind women in Nottingham, for there are no hard-and-fast statistics from that era.

Death Ornaments
Mourning the death of a loved one, especially in Victorian times, was an elaborate affair that often lasted for at least a year, and in the case of Queen Victoria, for her whole life. One of the ways in which the deceased were remembered by the living was to have their hair woven into ornaments such as brooches, framed artwork, earrings, or even elaborate centerpieces kept under glass.

Mistletoe
Victorians used mistletoe for the same reason we use it today: to steal a kiss from someone passing under it. But the tradition of kissing beneath the mistletoe goes way back to ancient Greece, when they used the ornament during the festival of Saturnalia and in marriage ceremonies because of the

plant's association with fertility.

Orange Pomander Balls

Pomanders—or "scent balls"—date back to medieval times, when sanitation was lacking and odours were rampant. It was believed that the pleasant scent of a pomander could actually fight disease. Victorians not only used them for decoration and fragrance at Christmas but also commonly hung them in their wardrobes to make their clothes smell nice. You can make your own by poking whole cloves into an orange.

DEDICATION

To Chawna Schroeder
*A godly young woman in all her ways,
especially the way she puts the fear of God into me
with each and every critique. . .*
I couldn't do this without you, my friend.
And as always
to the One who gives us all a second chance,
Jesus.

ACKNOWLEDGMENTS

A hearty thank-you to a few teams that made *The Old Lace Shop* possible. . .

My team of intrepid and lovely critique buddies who so faithfully take time out of their busy schedules to help make my writing shine: Julie Klassen, Kelly Klepfer, Lisa Ludwig, Ane Mulligan, Shannon McNear, Chawna Schroeder, Patti Hall Smith, MaryLu Tyndall, and Linda Yezak.

My brilliant and awesome publishing team at Barbour: Annie Tipton, Liesl Davenport, Shalyn Sattler, Faith Nordine, Bill Westfall, Nola Haney, and editor Becky Fish.

My teammate of thirty-five years and my real-life hero: Mark Griep.

And as always, my dedicated team of wonderful readers who make this writing gig all worthwhile!

More than likely I've inadvertently left off someone important to mention, so if that's you, consider yourself heartily thanked because to one and all, I am grateful.

And hey! Guess what? I love to hear from readers. Follow my adventures and share yours with me at www.michellegriep.com.

About the Author

Michelle Griep has been writing since she first discovered blank wall space and Crayolas. She is the Christy Award–winning author of historical romances: *The Noble Guardian*, *The Captured Bride*, *The Innkeeper's Daughter*, *The Captive Heart*, *Brentwood's Ward*, *A Heart Deceived*, and *Gallimore*, but also leaped the historical fence into the realm of contemporary with the zany romantic mystery *Out of the Frying Pan*. If you'd like to keep up with her escapades, find her at www.michellegriep.com or stalk her on Facebook, Twitter, and Pinterest.

And guess what? She loves to hear from readers! Feel free to drop her a note at michellegriep@gmail.com.